3, *Sakina Manzil*
and Other Plays

Ramu Ramanathan

Edited by
Lakshmi Chandra

The English and Foreign Languages University

Orient BlackSwan

ORIENT BLACKSWAN PRIVATE LIMITED

Registered Office
3-6-752 Himayatnagar, Hyderabad 500 029 (A.P.), India
e-mail: centraloffice@orientblackswan.com

Other Offices
Bangalore, Bhopal, Bhubaneshwar, Chandigarh, Chennai, Ernakulam, Guwahati, Hyderabad, Jaipur, Kolkata, Lucknow, Mumbai, New Delhi, Noida, Patna

Co-published with The English and Foreign Languages University
Hyderabad 500 007

First published by Orient Blackswan Private Limited 2012

ISBN 978 81 250 4511 3

Typeset in Classical Garamond 10/12.3 *by*
Trinity Designers & Typesetters, Chennai 600 041

Printed and bound at
The English and Foreign Languages University Press
Hyderabad 500 007

Published by
Orient Blackswan Private Limited
3-6-752 Himayatnagar, Hyderabad 500 029
e-mail: hyderabad@orientblackswan.com

Acknowledgement

My first memory of theatre (at age five) is bawling loudly and subsequently being thrown out of a Shombhu Mitra play in Kolkata. Later, I watched plays of all avatars and genres. From Dada Kondke to Gaddar. From Chandralekha to Satish Alekar.

I still watch plays. Nothing gives me greater joy than being caught by surprise by a piece of theatre which unfolds in the middle of nowhere.

The eight plays in this publication are my response to what I've seen – and understood.

I am fortunate to have met and worked with some amazing talent (producers, directors, actors, production-wallahs and audiences) in the past 25 years.

Mithibai College (for Beckett and Bangwadi – in the same breath); Akash Khurana (for directing *I am I*); Shiv Subrahmanyam (for permitting me to light his production of Athol Fugard's *The Blood Knot*); T M P Negundagi (for introducing me to Adoor, Basheer and theatre positive); Sanjna Kapoor for tolerating me and the play-readings and PT Notes for more than ten years; Mohan Agashe for introducing me to theatrewallahs in Pune's wadas and feeding me sauerkraut in Berlin when I was very hungry; Naushil Mehta for being a vadeel and reading a play in chaste Gujarati to me every time I read one to him; Sunil Shanbag for permitting me to attend his rehearsals in Chetana College and later for three rock-solid collaborations; G P Deshpande and Ram Bapat for making me feel intellectually stupid every time I spent time with them; Ashutosh Bharadwaj for watching every single play of mine and calling me next morning to say, I could have written a better play; and Chander Patil for narrating the best stories about what transpires backstage from Shivaji Mandir to Vishnudas Bhave.

There are others. Some on this planet, some who have moved on.

Thank you so much all of you.

I am indebted to Prof Lakshmi Chandra for believing in these plays, ten years ago. Likewise I must thank Padmaja Anant of Orient Blackswan for being patient (with me) and painstaking (with the proofs). Also I must thank Sudhanva Deshpande and Jaya Bhattacharji Rose for explaining the rights of a playwright, publication laws and legalese.

I doff my hat to Atul Dodiya, whose work I greatly admire, and am honoured and humbled that his painting *Rider* adorns the covers of this collection.

I hope many more plays will be penned, published and performed.

Theatre zindabad.

Ramu Ramanathan

Contents

Dedicated to
KINNARI
(for simply being there –
and putting money in the kitty when it mattered the most)

Introduction

Shanta Gokhale in her chapter 'The Dramatists' in *Illustrated History of Indian Literature in English* says that Krishna Mohan Banerjea's *The Persecuted, or Dramatic Scenes Illustrative of the Present State of Hindoo Society in Calcutta* was the first play written by an Indian in English in 1837. This was more a dramatised debate rather than a play to be seen on stage. After this we had Sri Aurobindo writing between 1890 and 1920, his most important plays being *Perseus The Deliverer* and *Savitri*; Harindranath Chattopadhyaya wrote between 1918 and 1950 (*Chokha Mela* and *Eknath*); A S Panchapakesa Aiyer wrote between 1913 and 1942 (*The Slave of Ideas* and *Sita's Choice*); and T P Kailasam wrote between 1930 and 1945 (his most famous plays being *The Burden* and *Karna*). Most of these playwrights meant their plays to be read and not performed, the essence of closet drama.

It is now almost two hundred years since Indians started writing plays in English. It was only after the 1950s that performance-oriented drama began to appear. The watershed in Indian theatre in English came after Independence. S Krishna Bhatta in his book *Indian English Drama: A Critical Study*, published in 1987, lists more than 200 plays written in or after the 1950s. However, most of them were not performed or published. With the arrival of Asif Currimbhoy things began to change in the Indian English drama scene. He was one of the first Indian playwrights to produce plays that could be performed. Many playwrights writing at this time, in the 1960s, met with more success than the earlier ones, primarily because they were writing plays to be acted. Some of these playwrights were Nissim Ezekiel (*Nalini* and *Sleepwalkers*); Gieve Patel (*Princes* and *Savaksa*) and

Pratap Sharma (*A Touch of Brightness* and *The Professor Has A Warcry*).

It was at the end of this decade, in 1968, that the Theatre Group, Bombay, announced the Sultan Padamsee Award for Indian plays in English. This award was won by Gurcharan Das's *Larins Sahib* and his group produced and staged it in Bombay in 1969. Gieve Patel's *Princes* and Dina Mehta's *Myth-makers* also competed for this award.

Cyrus Mistry's *Doongaji House* won the second Sultan Padamsee award, in 1978. This play dealt with the declining fortunes of a Parsi family living in the Parsi heartland – Bombay. His latest play, *The Legacy of Rage,* deals with the Christian community and is located in Bombay.

Dina Mehta's play *Brides Are Not For Burning* won an international award from the BBC in 1979. In the play she took up the social problems of dowry and highlighted the harassment that brides who don't bring in enough dowry have to face. Her later play, *Getting Away With Murder* (1989), was also shortlisted by the BBC for the World Playwriting competition. It was on the shortlist of seven specially commended radio plays out of 902 entries. Her latest play, *Sister Like You* (1996), a play on domestic violence, was also shortlisted for the British Council New International Playwriting awards. Also shortlisted for the same award was another Indian playwright writing in English, Poile Sengupta, for her play *Keats Was A Tuber* (1996). Her first full-length play, *Mangalam,* was written in 1993.

In the 1980s and 90s, Indian plays written in English came into their own. The others leading this movement were Mahesh Dattani and Manjula Padmanabhan. I believe it is from the 1980s that Indians started using English as their own language, not hesitating to intersperse it with the local language where required. They were and are very comfortable with the English language and are no longer tied down to English as the BBC uses it, or its Received Pronunciation.

Yet, in the world of Indian Writing in English, the genre of drama still has the status of stepchild. There are many dramatists in India who are writing, directing and producing plays, but most are unaware of the work the others are doing. Few publishers like to risk publishing collections of contemporary dramatists. Drama can be both immortal (living through performances) and tragically short-lived. After all, once a play has been performed, it's over. It lingers in the memory of that particular audience. And then, it vanishes from the stage, ephemeral as it is. A few playwrights – Asif Currimbhoy, Gurcharan Das, Manjula Padmanabhan, Mahesh Dattani and Poile Sengupta – have managed to get their plays published. But many other talented playwrights have been forgotten. When I set out to compile this collection, this was one of my aims: to record the work of a contemporary playwright so students, thinkers and the general public have an opportunity to see the world through the eyes of a playwright living in their midst.

My introduction to Ramu Ramanathan was from my visits to Mumbai. I've always made it a point to see a few plays whenever I visited Mumbai. On one such visit, a friend who knew of my interest in drama, called me and said, 'There is this play about Gandhi and his secretary – it's supposed to be quite good. Would you like to see it?' I readily agreed. And what I saw was *Mahadevbhai*, one of the most powerful dramas that I have ever seen. And that was my introduction to *Mahadevbhai* and to Ramu Ramanathan. I have seen this play three times, and each time it got a standing ovation from the audience! I have been fortunate enough to see a few more of his productions. I felt that his plays needed to be published to find a wider audience: and that is how this book came into being.

Ramakrishnan Ramanathan, or Ramu Ramanathan as he is popularly known, belongs to the current breed of writer-directors writing Indian plays in English. Born in Calcutta (as it was then called) Ramu Ramanathan grew up in Bombay, where he started schooling in the early seventies. In an interview with Dr Radha Ramaswamy, Ramanathan describes himself: 'I'm the ultimate national integrationist.' His father is a Palakkad Brahmin, his mother is a Punjabi and he is married to Kinnari, a Nagar from Bhavnagar and their home is Mumbai!

Ramanathan started his journey as a playwright, in college, in 1987, with the award-winning one-act play, *I Am I* (performed by a group of college friends with a lot of talent, who steered clear of theatre!), *What It Is* and *Gagan Mahal*. He has, to date, penned about fifteen plays. One of his outstanding plays *Cotton 56, Polyester 84*, was performed first in Hindi at the Prithvi Theatre Festival in 2006. It won him the META (Mahindra Excellence in Theatre Award) for the best original script in 2007. A well-researched docu-drama, it is about the city of Mumbai where cotton mills are being replaced by malls.

He has also done theatrical adaptations and directed the following: Edoardo Erba's Italian drama *A Play about a Painter*; Adya Rangacharya's Kannada play *Sanjivani*; Thuppatan's Malayalam play *The Train To Argentina*; Herman Hesse's *Steppenwolf*; Marguerite Duras' *L'Amante Anglaise*; Nirmal Verma's *Ded Inch Upar*; Vaclav Havel's *Audience* and *Mistake*; Jean Genet's *Deathwatch*; and Samuel Beckett's *Krapp's Last Tape*.

Ramanathan briefly experimented with writing for the radio. He wrote an eight-episode serial based on P G Wodehouse's *Small Bachelor* called *Funny People, Lovely Lives*. He also wrote a series of 15-minute skits titled *By the Way*. Both these projects were undertaken for All India Radio in 1995. His play *Collaborators* (which is part of this collection) was the Regional Award Winner of the BBC International Playwriting Competition in 2003.

In *MumbaiTheatreGuide.com* (in 2003), in an interview with Deepa Punjani, Ramu says:

> Theatre has never been a career for me. I've never done a play for the money. I do plays in order to share an idea, a thought. I believe in good taste, decent humour, intelligence and above all, progressive values. And in today's times wherein everything has a price tag, it becomes difficult to sustain such hopeless ideals.

> I have been fortunate to work with individuals who have a benevolent attitude towards theatre. They think I'm a modern-day Don Quixote who is dreaming an impossible dream. My wife is pleased I've just one bad habit, viz., theatre.

For Ramanathan, theatre is a passion. He has not only written plays, but he has also written about playwriting – 'Playwriting in a Wasteland' – a paper written for a seminar hosted by the Sangeet Natak Akademi in 2003. In this article he tackles issues that dramatists face and writes very lucidly about the Wasteland of Abundance; the Wasteland of the Ancient Past; the Wasteland of Roots; the Wasteland of Translation; the Wasteland called Indian English Theatre; the Wasteland of Rehearsals; the Wasteland of Metaphor; the Wasteland of Politics; the Wasteland of Words in an Actor's Mouth; and The Wasteland of Naturalism and Language. He writes of the vast number of dramatists, writing in a variety of languages including English – there are 1500 performances in a month in Mumbai! He also takes up the related issue of translation. Posing questions like 'How theatrical are the translations?', 'How many translators are practising dramatists?' he focuses on the need for authentic translation preferably by dramatists themselves. He writes of the rehearsal process, which incorporates the four elements Richard Schechner wrote about in his performance theory, the four elements which are essential for theatre – the text, the director, the actors and the audience. Ramanathan feels that the death of the repertory, the practice of getting a team of actors to stage plays together, is coming in the way of good theatrical performances. The freelance system leads to typecasting of actors, based on what they did well last time and not on the range of their abilities.

Ramanathan has conducted workshops for students of colleges in Mumbai and Pune. These workshops have resulted in an awareness of the importance of theatre in our daily lives and produced plays like *Me Grandad 'Ad An Elephant*, and *Yaar, What's the Capital of Manipur?* which focus on the story of our youth and, of course, on politics. *Yaar, What's the Capital of*

Manipur?, a youthful musical play written in 2002, is about the problems a Manipuri student faces when he goes to college in a place far away from home such as Mumbai.

Ramanathan has written weekly art and theatre columns in *The Hindustan Times* from 2007 to 2008; and also for *The Indian Express, Independent* and Magna Publications. He was Editor of *PT Notes*, Prithvi Theatre's monthly theatre magazine, from 1998 to 2008. He was Editor of *Theatre4u*, a daily bulletin which covered the two-week Prithvi Theatre Festival, Theatre of India, in 1997.

He has conceptualized and coordinated some very diverse activities:

- a one-day seminar on Indian English Theatre in 2004;
- a six-week play-writing workshop for 35 participants along with Katha Publishing and SNDT University in 2003;
- a multi-discipline ten-day workshop for 200 students as part of the Kamala Raheja Workshop series in 2002–2003;
- the Prithvi Theatre Lecture Series;
- *Theatre Positive* – a series of play-readings where unperformed, unpublished scripts were read on the first Monday of every month from 1997 to 2003;
- a few play-reading groups which read and discuss plays by dramatists like Henrik Ibsen, Anton Chekov, Bertolt Brecht, Moliere and Joe Orton;
- a one-day seminar – *What After All Is Modernism* – along with a three-day play-reading festival;
- performances of stage-plays and discussions and lecture-demonstrations of the performing arts in a café called *The Venue* in Santacruz, Mumbai
- an alternative open air amphitheatre – *Amphitheatre YWCA* in Andheri, Mumbai – which staged plays on the weekends;
- a workshop with Katha Publications, which resulted in the production of a popular play *Time to Tell a Tale* based on seven Katha short stories, and

- a three-day play-reading festival of Indian English Plays – *And Then There Is English Theatre* – in 1997.

Ramu has also had exposure to theatre in Europe. He visited Berlin as Resident Observer at the Grips Theatre, in 2000. He also visited Brussels for the International Bozar Festival in 2006. This was also the time when his play *3, Sakina Manzil*, was being translated into Dutch by Rudi Meulamanns. Also in 2006, he was at the Frankfurt Book Fair for a press conference and discussions on *3, Sakina Manzil* and *Mahadevbhai*. In 2007, he was Resident Observer at Kunstenarts Festival in Brussels. Besides this he spent time in Berlin and traced the Grips theatre movement with the help of its founder Volker Ludwig (in Germany) and Mohan Agashe (in India).

Most of the plays in this collection could be classified as docu-dramas – plays which have their base in facts. This involves a lot of research into the events and why they happened; Ramanathan's research is painstaking. As he said about his feeling before writing *Jazz*, 'That is also the beginning of that old feeling I know nothing. This is the same feeling which had surfaced during *Mahadevbhai, 3, Sakina Manzil, Three Ladies of Ibsen, Cotton 56, Polyester 84*.' Because he genuinely feels he knows nothing, he takes the time and trouble to find out all he can about anything that he wants to write. And he is worried by his thoughts which say, 'Should I reclaim the past? Or should the past resonate in the now?' This is why we see the blending of time present and past in his plays.

Along with this movement in time, Ramu has specialised in blending humour with pathos in all his plays. This treatment of serious themes appeals to everyone because there is humour to keep the audience entertained while educating them about issues that they may not even be aware of.

Ramanathan also has a tremendous ear for music. The songs he writes as well as the old ones he uses, emphasise the themes beautifully. This is specifically demonstrated in plays such as *Mahadevbhai* and *Jazz*.

Shanti, Shanti, It's a War bagged the Best Play Award at The

Hindu's All India Playwright's Competition in 1993. It was written in 1993 and was produced by The Madras Players. It was his first full-length play. It takes off from the inter-college dramas, which contain a series of gags one after another. Ramanathan says he was affected by five incidents which served as the trigger-point for this play These are:

1. swelling crowds at Chaityabhoomi in Shivaji Park in Mumbai;
2. the neighbourhood kirana shop changing its name – from a family name to a multinational one;
3. the demolition of the Babri Masjid;
4. a dropped catch by Azharuddin in a World Cup game; and
5. the fact that 90% of our people were unaware of these four incidents.

He chose the Mahabharata as a backdrop because it lends itself to a lot of possibilities.

The Boy Who Stopped Smiling (1998) is a children's play in the Grips theatre style (khushnama document). As Ramu has explained in an interview the Grips originated in Germany and is an offshoot of the Youth Movement, which swept the world in the seventies. Grips is based on the ideology of opposition, and the importance of questioning grown-ups, elders and the status quo. Grips plays were not 'traditional' children's plays with fairy tales and dream-worlds. They tackled real issues and social problems, in an extremely imaginative and entertaining manner. In this play Ramu stresses on the importance of asking the question 'Why?', which Mallika does with great élan. With all its insistence on rote learning our educational system misses out on this essential ingredient of childhood, of learning more about the world around us. What comes through is (in Ramanathan's words), 'the loneliness of Malhar (the boy who stopped smiling), and his bafflement at being misunderstood. It's very tragic. In fact it is pathetic.' Ramu directed the play; it was produced by Sanjna Kapoor for Little Prithvi Players who staged it 150 times all over the country.

Then came *Curfew*, written immediately after the 1992–1993

riots in Mumbai, but staged only in 1999. It's about a pair of twin brothers who can get nothing done because of repeated, unexpected curfews, and a curfew is, to quote from the play, 'the most globalised, privatised, multi-internationalised thing in the world.' This play is a mixture of Hindu mythology pitted against the present pop culture. There is also a peepal tree which tells stories. And even Yama, the God of Death, had to succumb to death and the curfew! Ramu calls it 'a fun play with fabulous songs', but I see in it, through the humour, ironic comments on our times.

Mahadevbhai (1892–1942), written in 2002, was published along with *Collaborators*, by the Sahitya Akademi. Though this play is about Mahatma Gandhi's secretary Mahadevbhai, it covers the whole gamut of emotions seen during India's freedom struggle and I, personally, think the most poignant lines of the play, for us today are, 'It was at Godhra that Gandhiji spoke about Hindu–Muslim unity. He said: "I've only one object in view and it is a clear one, namely that God should purify the hearts of Hindus and Muslims and the two communities should be free from suspicion and fear of one another."' Ramu wrote this play he says, 'as a response to the politics of our times.' This play too, travels seamlessly back and forth from past to present, with around 32 characters portrayed by a single actor! It can move you to tears and make you smile almost at the same time. It is a masterpiece of a combination of style and structure using symbolism along with realism. It has now been performed over 200 times all over India and Europe.

The play *Collaborators,* written in 2003, won the Regional Award in the BBC International Radio Playwriting competition held in 2003; it was further developed into a stage production and premiered in Mumbai in August 2004. Ramanathan was then invited to the National Theatre Festival in 2004. In this play, Ramu plays on the word 'collaborators' with its multiple meanings, travels between past and present, and poses grave problems amidst very ordinary situations like the middle-class English-speaking characters playing bridge while real politics unfolds in the hinterland of eastern Uttar Pradesh. There are only four characters in the play, but it is the character Kranti who is its focus. Notice the name and its meaning. This is a play in the anti-realist tradition, as Ramanathan himself said – a play with a beginning, a middle and another beginning!

The play *3, Sakina Manzil* set in 1944, deals with the Bombay Harbour blast which destroyed homes, but sent down a shower of gold bars through the air. The play has been translated and performed in Dutch. Written in 2004 it deals with a couple who are young when they meet and fall in love. They go their separate ways and are old when they meet again, and are representatives of thousands of Bombayites who lived through 1944 to 2004. This play too moves back and forth in time effortlessly.

Shakespeare and She written in 2008, is about the friendship between two women. In this play, sixteenth century London seems to be equal to twenty-first century Mumbai, the similarities being, and I quote from the play, 'The clamour, the clutter. The endless jostling. Busy bustis and make-shift tradeshops. The stench and the shit. No open spaces. Immigrants and traders and their labourers, arriving, everyday. Infectious maladies. Mosquito bites, TB, pneumonia, encephalitis, maladies, infections, exhaustion.' The characters of Shakespeare (Sheikh Saab in the play) are seen wandering around Mumbai. For example, Shylock is at Masjid Bunder station, Romeo and Juliet are at a shopping mall and Cleopatra is at Vasai Koli village. In this play you get to know Mumbai and Shakespeare's characters and favourite Shakespeare phrases: A great technique using intertextuality at its best! Students from the IDC at IIT, Mumbai and Kamala Raheja Vidhyanidhi Institute of Architecture collaborated on this play. The thousands of photographs by hundreds of students which were shot on the streets of Mumbai became the starting point for *Shakespeare and She*.

Also written in 2008, *Jazz* (played in Amsterdam too) offers a delightful take on Bollywood. Writing on the idea for this play Ramu says that the best things in life happen by chance and that is how the idea for this play was born. He happens to meet

Denzil Smith, they exchanged 101 sms during the day, set up a meeting with Naresh Fernandes (this play is dedicated to Smith and Fernandes) who loves to talk of the influence of jazz on Bollywood and that was the beginning of *Jazz*. It is about the life of an old musician after all the glitz and glamour has faded away. In his interview with this editor Ramanathan explains how many of these plays came into being (see page 368).

While reading this collection, remember that reading plays is not the same as reading collections of any other genre, be it poetry, prose or fiction. Plays are hardly ever written to be read. They have been written to be seen, to be performed. Therefore, before you start reading each play, try and visualise the settings and the characters; also try and hear the sounds – the music and the tones and language that the characters use. Aristotle has given us the six elements of drama – mythos (plot), ethos (atmosphere and background), dianoia (theme), lexis (language), opsis (settings) and melos (music and other sounds). The last three are the important elements that constitute theatre and are peculiar to this genre.

I hope that you will enjoy reading these plays as much as I enjoyed putting them together. Ramu Ramanathan shows us how theatre in English written by Indians is alive and vibrant and he opens up possibilities for younger dramatists writing today.

> [*Cotton 56, Polyester 84*] like Ramu's other plays cannot be underestimated or worse, ignored. His is a voice that our contemporary, modern theatre is in dire need of. Here is clearly a playwright with a good conscience that rightly speaks against the abuse of political power and the unabashed forces of capitalism. In times to come Ramu Ramanathan's name will not be lost in the annals of Indian theatre history. He must be watched out for. (http://www.mumbaitheatreguide.com/dramas/reviews/c56p84.)

Lakshmi Chandra

Shanti, Shanti, It's a War

Dedicated to YAMUNA
(for laughing at all my PJs)

Director: Yamuna

Production Manager: Ravi Baskaran

Production Co-ordinator: Gopi Nair

Research: Vasanti Shankaranarayanan

Cast: Vasanti Shankaranarayanan, Nilu, Unni, Sanjay Bokaria, Aylwin David, Mohd Yusuf, Ashwini Narayanan, Bobby Macedo, Daniel Goodman, Sumeet Bhatia, Srinath, Anita Ratnam, Samyuktha Ramakrishna, Shareen, Shakila, Santanam Swaminadhan, Bhavani Nagarathnam, Selva Pandian

Sets Design: Mithran Devanesan

Set Supervisor: Binny Richard

Carpenter: Raghavan

Lights Designed by: Mithran Devanesen

Lights executed by: Gopi Nair, Suhas Ahuja

Sound: Ravi Baskaran, Bobby Baskaran

Green Room: Bhavani Jankiram, Nanda Devanesen

Make Up: Anuradha Rao, Vishalam Ekambaram

This play is a tribute to the freewheeling lok natya tradition in Maharashtra. It is a rock musical spoof of the Mahabharata. Like a good farce, the setting should have space for the actors to pace. The more agile the actors, greater should be the space to showcase. Theres should be a lot of movement on the satage:entries and exits, posturing. However, for the most part the staging and costumes should be droll and ungimmicky.

Actors should endeavour for impeccable drop-dead timing; and not roar out the lines. Speaking in normal tones would suffice. Comic nuances are acceptable.

ACT I

A Chorus of actors and actresses. See how they sing, see how they prance, see how they run through the auditorium

The Chorus: Twikky wikky wikky wee
Wikky bikky twikky tee.
Spikky bikky bee
The curtain is gone
Your tickets are torn.
Our play is the thing
It will raise a stink.

Jikky wikky bikky see.
Chikky bikky wikky bee.
Twitchy witchy wee.
This play is not wrong
Neither serious, nor is it long
But that's for you to decide
Come inside, come inside.

Witchy kitchy twitchy wee.
Spikky wikky mikky bee.
Chippy wippy ookie
Welcome, welcome, dear friends
To our show that will set a trend
You may laugh, you may cry
You won't forget us, even if you try.
Ding-a-long
Sing-a-long
Our play is here to stay.
Hip-Hip-Hurrah. Hip-Hip-Hurrah.
Ticky tockky pluckky nee.
Plokkity pikkety bumplety dee.
We hope no one's got his ticket free.....

Look, look at the Chorus. They have reached the stage. See how they bow, see how they applaud. But who's that on the stage? He's the producer. And those two? They are his Right-hand and Left-hand men. Why is the Producer so petulant with rage? And why is he pacing so feverishly? ... Wait-wait, we shall find out.

Producer: Cut !!!

Oh, what a spoilsport of a Producer. Look, at the Chorus. They are shocked, in a state of suspended disbelief. Cho chad.

Producer: Cut! *(To Right-hand and Left-handmen)* This is not what I wanted. I wanted a play.

Right-hand Man (rushes to Producer): But sir, this is the best.

Left-hand Man: Better than all the rest.

Producer: Look, let's get this clear. I wanted a play with a *paramparik katha* which is all about our 'rich and glorious cultural heritage'. Our dances, our songs, our folklores. Instead, what do you get me ... a bunch of imported clowns from *bhadralok.*

Right-hand Man: But sir, this is the absolute latest from Broadway.

Producer (snorts): Why should I do the absolute latest from Broadway? Does Broadway do anything our way? They don't.

Left-hand Man: But sir ...

Producer: To Sir, or Not To Sir that is not the question. I want a *shudh* 100% *deshi-nataka*, and get that in your sar!

Right-hand Man: Where are we going to get a play, now?

Producer: What do you mean, where are we going to get a play? All over the wide world, people are doing plays, they are seeing plays – and not all of these plays are Broadway. Now if these people can do their own plays, why can't we?

Left-hand Man: Sir, be reasonable. How can we get a play at such short notice. We don't have any writers.

Producer: Why, where are the writers?

Right-hand Man: Sir, it's a pens-down. All of them have ceased writing ... Tendulkar, Alekar, Elkunchwar ...

Left-hand Man: Yes boss, *dhaandha noh usool che.* Why write when no one reads. Today, an artiste is a genuine artiste only when he suffers from T-V!

And then there is music. That is, Rock Muzik. The trio look up, and the Chorus comes to life. See how they dance, see how they prance, and see how they chant in a Rig Vedic monotone 'We-

want-writer' ... 'We-want-play' ... until Producer hollers 'pack-up'. All-round joy, and chorus exits – with a flourish, even as the Writer enters.

The Writer is dishevelled, bohemian, and shuffling a pack of cards. He wears a huge T-shirt that says 'I'm the WRITHING on the Wall.'

A quick meaningful look passes between the Producer and his two cronies.

Writer (whistling tunelessly): O Yaaras, would you be interested in a game of cards, perchance.

Right-hand Man (whispers): Sir, this is your chance!

Left-hand Man: To be precise, our chance. A golden opportunity to have a play – for his Moha is already in your trance.

Producer: A game of cards. *Haan-haan kyon nahin?* What are the stakes?

Writer: Arrey miya, yeh toh patta ki jagah satta ho gaya.

Producer: Dekh bhai, that's the way we play this game.

Writer: Hmmm. OK. What do you have to offer?

Producer: Ha-ha. These two *(Right-hand and Left-hand Men step up)* If you win, you can have these two as your slaves for the next 365 days.

Writer: Slaves! Are you serious ...

Producer: To do anything you wish.

Writer: That's great. But what if I lose?

Producer: Then you'll have to write a play for me.

Writer: A play ... what in the name of Shakespeare is a play?

Producer: You don't know what is a play ... we're doomed.

Right-hand Man (hurriedly): Oh nothing much. Just something arty-pharty in two acts. You know the formula: A solid beginning. An emotional middle. And a *dhamakedar* end.

Left-hand Man: As you can see, it's quite simple. A story, any *ghisa-pita kahani*. Preferably with dialogues.

Writer: Is that all? *(Shuffles cards)* Alright it's a deal. Let's play.

Producer: Wait, before we begin, let me inform you, in case you haven't realised that my Uncleji will play the game for me.

Writer: Your Uncle, but ...

Left-hand Man: It's a part of the Agreement.

Writer: What Agreement?

Right-hand Man (brandishes a legal document): In the small print. For your eyes only, heh-heh-heh.

Writer: What is the meaning of this ...?

Left-hand Man: A deal is a deal.

Writer: Big deal.

The Producer whistles aloud for Uncleji. Almost immediately, there is eerie music, superseded by an evil cackle. Uncle enters on a tricycle.

Producer: Namaskarams, I salute thee, Uncleji.

Uncle: Asheerwadam bhanje. Now let's get down to real business. I've to rush back to the *Adda*. Arrey, if today I crack a *chakdi*, then apna naam will be in the Guinness Book of Underworld Records, for the maximum number of *chakdis* on earth. *Matka-adda-amar-rahe. (A beat)* OK, so who is my opponent?

Writer: I am.

Uncle: Hi, nice knowing you and all that. I hope you know the rules. Heads I win. Tails you lose.

To which the Writer reacts. Uncle takes a pack of cards, and does a couple of quick tricks. Gradually, we go back into medieval times – lights, music and atmosphere. The game of cards is played exaggeratedly, with the Producer and his two cronies watching with bated breath. And then the Writer loses.

Uncle: Ho-ho, won again.

Producer (very pleased): Was there ever any doubt, Uncleji? What's your record now?

Uncle: One million and one, to one.

Producer: You lost? When did you lose? Was it the time you got Five Aces?

Uncle: No, it was the time I played with P C Sorcar.

Writer: What about me? What am I to do?

Producer: Ha-ha, he is asking what he has to do.

Uncle: What does he have to do?

Producer: He has to write a play.

Writer (groans): What have I done to deserve this?

Uncle: And what does he mean by that?

Right-hand Man (menacingly): Sir, if he doesn't agree to write now should we finish him off.

Left-hand Man: Which way, the easy way or the tough way?

Writer: What's the easy way?

Right-hand Man: Oh, the easy way is, when sir, lovely sir, is happy. And so you'll be put in a vessel of concentrated nitric acid, and slowly roasted for a week, whilst every hair on your body is plucked by a King Cobra, by which time the Thousand-and-One bloodsucking white ants would have sucked your blood.

Writer: This is the easy way! *(Gulps)* What then is the tough way?

Left-hand Man: Twenty-four hours of Sansad Samachar day-in and night-out till death do you apart.

Writer (screaming, and on his knees): Nooooo! Give me a chance, my good folks. An opportunity to be useful. O pray, let me write this play!

Producer: Only one chance. No more chances. Chalo, Uncleji. Chalo Chalo. Chalo Mathura. Chalo Kashi. If that's not possible let's at least go to Vashi.

Producer climbs onto the tricycle with Uncle. They exit. Oh, but look at Right-hand and Left-hand Men, they have closed in on the Writer. With a touch of meta-theatricality

Writer: Is this the end? I'm completely doomed. What do I do? In these times of distress, should I commit self-suicide.

Right-hand Man: Do you really want to commit suicide? In that case, I recommend a vacation to Baghdad.

Writer: Don't you realise the seriousness of the situation. I can't write. I'm not a writer.

Left-hand Man: Ah, a writer's block.

Writer: Nothing of the sort. I've never done it before, that's all.

Right-hand Man: I see, then why don't you contact your fairy godmother.

Writer: Do I have one?

Left-hand Man: Look, every good writer has a fairy godmother. If you're a good writer, you'll most certainly possess one.

Writer: Hmmm, and how do I get in touch with my fairy godmother?

Right-hand Man: I guess, you call out to her.

Writer: Just like that?

Left-hand Man: I don't know … check the Telephone Directory. If she is listed, you can call her.

Writer: Hey that's great, on a telephone …

Right-hand Man: Yes. Through the mind. Shut your eyes, concentrate, and dial her number.

Writer (doubtfully): OK ... but ...

Right-hand and Left-hand Man exit.

Music seeps through the air. The Writer, shuts eyes, concentrates, and prepares to telephone his fairy godmother.

Writer (aloud): Hey, why don't we play another round of cards; after this, just you versus me ... and scrap this deal. Mast idea, what? *(Pause. He opens eyes, looks around)* Ooops, nobody around. All gone ... I'm already feeling quite silly about this writing business, in any case; but then I guess I've nothing to lose *(clears throat)*. Hello, fairy godmother, can you hear me? *(Silence)* Checking-checking. Hello-Hello. Testing ... hey, fairy godmother can you hear me? Are you out there? This is an emergency ...

Sudden burst of static. Then a booming feminine voice.

'This is a Recorded Message from your fairy godmother. I am going out, but should be back soon, if you have any message for me, please leave it after the Third Beep. Thank you. And the next time, call me only after you have completely shut your eyes.' Beep-Beep-Beep.

Writer (pinches himself): Ayeee.... did you hear that ...? She, my Fairy-Godmother, said she will get in touch with me. Is this really – Reality?

Another burst of static. The voice continues.

'Dahling, the message please. I don't have all the time and money in the universe for you. Give me the message, short and sweet. Over and out.'

Writer (abruptly): It ... it's me, and I'm in big trouble. My problem is, I've been commissioned to write a play for which I desperately need help. A story, a plot, preferably a ghost-writer who can write the entire thing for me.

A burst of dazzling light. Look, look it's the Fairy Godmother (FG) riding a skate-board, in a brilliant white gown.

FG: Hi.

Writer (long whistle): Sweetheart, but who are you?

FG: Your Fairy Godmother, silly!

Writer: Ah, you look so beautiful.

FG: Merci, merci beaucoup. Now what's your problem.?

Writer (still stunned): I don't remember ... maybe I want to marry you.

FG (giggles): Well, if I'm not mistaken, I think your problem is of a slightly variant nature.

Writer: Maybe it was. Right now it isn't. Incidentally, do you believe in love at first sight?

FG: Of course I do, silly. But not as a rule. Moreover, this is a business appointment. I've come here specifically to help you write a play.

Writer: You mean we don't even whisper sweet nothings to each other. OK as a concession, let me at least buy you an ice cream.

FG: Sweetie-pie, your problem please ... before it becomes mine.

Writer (decently): OK, as you already know, I've to write a play.

FG: OK. So?

Writer: I've never written one earlier.

FG: Is that all? Then hear this – basically there's really not much to a play, all you need are two theatrical interests. One, a man-woman interest ...

Writer: Sex!

FG: Exactly, and two, a man-history relationship.

Writer: Drama!

FG: Bingo, and so a good play should have both these relationships. Simple. End of message. Curtains.

Writer: Are you serious? I mean you're still beautiful, in fact very beautiful. But I don't think that this much is a play.

FG: Of course it is, dahling. Use your imagination. Apply your mind, and think. Creativity is hotting up. Although personally, I believe all that has to be said has already been said. Stories that are being repeated, music which is imitated. Why, because every situation has been juiced of its final finale. Today even a cliche is a cliche no more ...

Writer: Under such circumstances, what do I do? O beauteous one, prettier and more ravishing than the best of women who lived on this earth. Cleopatra the long-nosed, Helen of Troy, Madhubala from Bollywood, Draupadi ...

FG: Ah, Draupadi. Why don't you re write Draupadi?

Writer: You mean Draupadi as in the *Mahabharata* ... ?

FG: Yes, that's exactly what I mean. Draupadi as in Panchali of the *Paanch Pandav* fame.

Writer: But how ... why ... ?

FG (over-reacts): Why not?

Writer: Although I don't know why I said why ... I think you should re-consider marrying me. Maybe even our horoscopes match. Moreover I'll make a good husband. I can cook, I can clean the house, I can wash the clothes, make love ...

FG: Look mister, whoever you are. You asked me to help you, and give you an inspiration. I've done that. What you now do with this advice, is your personal problem. I'm busy, and I've other schedules to keep. The very best of best luck to you, and now I must be leaving.

Writer: Then is this it? What if I need some more help from you?

FG: What kind of help?

Writer: Where will I get hold of Draupadi in these times?

FG: I don't know ... may be you should look into the *Mahabharata.*

Writer: Er, can I come with you? We could look for Draupadi together. And we could even marry, you know ...

FG: N-O, No!!!

A sudden flash of light. The Fairy Godmother exits. The Writer is all alone, despondent and crestfallen. Just then, he hears strange noises in the air. Conches, gongs etc.

Look who is entering! They are four men. Bheem, Arjuna (with an AK-47), Nakula and Sahadeva (dandy looking, attired in black leather, Ray Bans, gelled hair, ear-rings etc). Bringing up the rear is, Draupadi, looking elegant in an archetypal period costume.

Why are they huffing and puffing? That's because they are climbing a steep mountain. Where is Yudhishthira? He is not to be seen. Where is the Writer? He is hiding.

Bheem: Phew, what mountain is this ... the Everest? It seems to go on and on forever ... can you see Dharmaraja?

Nakula (craning his neck): No, I can't. But he went that way.

Sahadeva: With that dog of his.

Nakula: Are you sure it's a dog? I have a feeling it is a God in disguise.

Sahadeva: A God in disguise?

Nakula: Yes, yes didn't you notice, in the nights whilst we camped, when the rest of us used to listen to FM, that dog was reading 'Five Dialectical Approaches to Hinduism in Modern Times.'

Bheem (in agony): Have a look at your compass, yaar ... are we going in the right direction ... ooof, what I as President of the Arnold Schwarzenegger Trust cannot understand is, that if we have to ultimately go to Narak, why aren't we climbing a smaller hill. I mean, if this is only about symbolically doing something, we could even climb the Malabar Hill or Pali Hill and go to Narak. In principle, we would have climbed a hill, and Dharmaraja would also be pleased ... Ow, these mosquitoes. Christ in Heaven, I wish I had got some insecticide with me ... *Arjuna*, do something.

Arjuna: Whatever you say.

Bheem: Bhaisaheb. *(He lets go an evil cackle, and prepares his AK-47, and shoots at the mosquitoes)* Rat-a-tat-a-tat!!! *(Ceases shooting. Looks around dumbly. Everyone has dived for shelter).*

Nakula (still cowering): Arjuna, you missed that one, over there.

Arjuna (gaping stupidly): I know. In fact, I think he is a reincarnation of Eklavya.

Sahadeva: How did you know?

Arjuna: His thumb is missing.

Bheem (aside): Ha-ha, not even an *angootha chaap!*

Nakula: What do you mean, his thumb is missing?

Sahadeva: I have never heard of mosquitoes having thumbs.

Arjuna: Stop being naive, Nakula and Sahadeva. If a man can have an artificial heart transplant, surely a mosquito can have a thumb.

Bheem: And so, this mosquito is Eklavya. How can you tell?

Arjuna: Can't you see his sponsorship logo.

Nakula and Sahadeva: Why, it's Thums Up!

Bheem: Aaaah .... will you stop chattering, and help me up. Ow, my arthiritis; ouch, my spondylitis. Why, even my back hurts ... How much further is our destination 'Miles to go and promises to keep before we go to Swarag from Narak.' As it is of all the wretched things, I'm supposed to be the last guy to fall of this hill. Total bad luck. In fact, I told VV ... you know Ved Vyasa

... yaar-biddu let me fall off first, I'm not that fit and tough any more but he said he couldn't change the script. Said Ganapati would sue him. I asked him what Ganapati has to do with this. He said 'Everything. You see, Ganapati is the unofficial publisher of all creative works' ... Hey, Nakula and Sahadeva, carry me. What you standing around and gaping at me ... Ow-ow-ow, all that weight-lifting and exercising has finished me. It's all because of Shri Balramji I tell you. Plus all those steroids and performance enhancing drugs. Now look at me. No muscles. .... *(Bheem is hoisted by Nakula and Sahadev)*. Phew, much better, much much better. Onward march. Dharmaraja, here we come. Yamraja, here we come.

Nakula and Sahadeva: Jai Arnold Schwarzenegger!

(A chant to the tune of Jai Mata Di)

Jor Se Bole – Jai Schwarzenegger

Pyar Se Bolo – Jai Schwarzenegger

Prem Se Bolo – Jai Schwarzenegger

Phakr Se Boli – Jai Schwarzenegger

Garv Se Bolo – Jai Schwarzenegger

And in this way, the four Pandavs exit. Huffing and puffing their way up the steep hill. Oh, but look at Draupadi. How pretty she looks, how lonely she seems. Why isn't she following the Pandavs?

By now, the Writer has emerged from his hiding place. He clears his throat ...

Draupadi (screams): Who you?

Writer (in soft undertone): Hey relax. I'm not going to do you any harm.

Draupadi: But – Who you?

Writer: Ah, great men all over the world haven't been able to answer that question, when asked 'who you' ... For instance, am I a man? Or Am I a ghost? Am I a living spirit, or am I an extra-terrestrial visiting this planet? I don't know, and so like all the great men, I ask myself 'Who Am I?'

Draupadi: An incessant bore.

Writer: Ha-ha, and who're you?

Draupadi: Draupadi – the daughter of Emperor Dhrupad; sister-of-Dhrishtadyumna; wife-of-the Paanch Pandavs.

Writer: What are you saying ...? Are you *Draupadi*, I mean the real Draupadi.

Draupadi: Here's my visiting card; if you seek further information, you can have this. *(She hands Writer a pen drive.)*

Writer: What's this ...

Draupadi: A pen drive.

Writer: What's an ancient woman like you, doing with a pen drive like this.

Draupadi (giggling): Oh, I'm heavily into computers, you know. And so, one day I got Mama Vidura to make a file for me, based on a programme I conceived ... If you have a Mac around here, I can show you how this thing works.

Writer: You know how to operate a Mac?

Draupadi: Of course I do. In my spare time, during our thirteen years of exile I even did an NIIT computer course.

Writer: O Yaara, this much too much.

Draupadi (conspiratorial whisper): Yes, yes. But don't tell anyone. I had to do it. You know with the kind of husbands I have, and I had five of them, one can never tell. Agreed they are virtuous, brave and good-looking. But yaar, they never got home any money. And these days without money, you can't do a thing. Oh, once in a way Krishna helped us out. But surely, how long was I going to be dependent on a God. So I thought 'might as well do a computer course.' That way, at least I've a job prospect. Wot, good idea, no?

Writer: What else have you done?

Draupadi: Oh nothing much, except for cooking classes ... in fact, I even made some good money, until ...

Writer: Until what ...

Draupadi: Until my husbands came to know of it, and before I knew it, they took all of my profits, and started to invest in Bows & Arrows.

Writer: What did you do?

Draupadi: Oh, what could I do? *Sab karm ka bhog hain.* And surely, I cannot change fate, can I? It's a curse on our family that 'might is right'. But now, I'm sick of it. Why is it, that every time there is some quiet, we should forfeit it. Why is it that every time there are good times, the bad times loom in the horizon. In fact, even when my husbands were in power, instead of governing properly they would debate if their kingdom was the best in the world? Would history remember them favourably or not? Should they launch a couple of chotta-motta wars to remain in the news? Oh, it was infuriating – instead of providing hygienic gutters and AIDS-free blood banks, their priorities were on invading neighbouring kinds. Even Dharmaraja could not not make a difference. *(Gasps for breath)* As for the rest of them – there was no hope. You don't believe me, but have you seen them, my other four husbands, Megalomanic, pompous, egocentric and self-centred. They fought a war which they knew they would lose, even if they won it ... then pray, why did they do it? They did it, because their *Bharatiya Maryada* told them to. And look what happened – so many millions dead, Bheeshma, Dronacharya, Abhimanyu, my five sons. All of them dead. Hopelessly beyond redem ... And yet, in spite of all that has happened, mankind remains unconcerned. The horrors and atrocities that terrified us only yesterday, they become acceptable tomorrow. The Mahabharata repeats itself again and again like a bad dream.

Writer: I fully sympathise with you. But what are you going to do now?

Draupadi: To begin with, I'm not going to follow them up that hill.

Writer: You're not ... what ...?

Draupadi: I'm not going up that hill. I still have a lot of life left in me. I intend to stay back and do something worthwhile. For the poor and underprivileged sections of our society. I may even join Anna Hazare.

Voices heard offstage

Writer: Oh, they are coming back ...

Draupadi: Who's coming back, my husbands?

Writer: No, not your husbands. My Producer.

Draupadi: Your what ...

Writer: My Producer. *(Desperately and urgently)* Will you help me Draupadiji? Only you can help me now. Please.

Draupadi: Help you do what.

Writer: I'm sorry, I forgot to tell you, I'm a writer by default, and ...

Draupadi: A writer, you mean something like Vyasa.

Writer: Actually I'm more in the mould of a Kalidasa.

Draupadi: Oh, a playwright. An extinct species.

Writer: Not really ... because I may be writing a play. And so when I got in touch with my Fairy Godmother for a concept – incidentally, she is a mind-blowing piece of gorgeousness – she told me to write a play on Draupadi.

Draupadi: On me.

Writer: Yes, and now that you're here in person, will you help me, please Draupadi. *(Writer falls at her feet)*

Draupadi: Why not, seems like a great idea?

Writer: Good, then let me introduce you to my Producer.

Draupadi: Wait wait wait. Just a minute, not so fast, my dear. To start with let's get my terms clear. Firstly, what is my signing amount? Also, how many shifts will I have to give. Further, no indecent exposure. And above all, will Rajinikanth do a movie with me ...?

Writer: Draupadiji, you can put forth all your questions to the Producer, in person.

Draupadi: But where is he?

A cacophonous roll of great music. Almost immediately Right-hand and Left-hand Men enter. They are followed by the Producer. Draupadi sees them, and screams. Freeze tableau.

Draupadi (shrieks): Duryodhana!

Writer: Duryodhana?

Draupadi (to Right-hand and Left-hand Men): Karna. Dushasana.

Writer: Yaara – what the hell is happening.

Draupadi (melodramatically): Et tu, Brutus. Then Caesar falls ... *(A beat)* Ooops, sorry, wrong play.

Writer: What's happening? Will somebody tell me?

Draupadi: The Kauravs of the world have reunited.

Writer: How can that be?

Draupadi: Look, if I can be Draupadi, then surely these guys can be the Kaurav trio.

Writer: But they are supposed to be dead.

Draupadi: Oh come on, this is art for art's sake. Anything can happen.

Duryodhana (alias Producer): Since that's the way, we're playing it. Let's keep the spirit of the game. *(Doing a Darth Vader impersonation, breathing heavily etc)*. Ha, Draupadi. So we meet again.

Karna (alias Right-hand Man) (slapping his thighs): And this time, we meet man to man. No Bheem, No Arjuna. No Gods. No Rakshasas.

Dushasana (alias Left-hand Man) (worried): Are you sure? Things could still go *ulta-pulta*, you know?

Duryodhana: Don't worry bachchu. This time, everything has been planned to a perfection.

He gives an all-knowing wink, and feverishly communicates through a code language.

Writer: Excusez moi, if you have concluded your private celebrations, can you tell me what I've to do next.

Duryodhana: Ah you, you may leave.

Writer: Come Draupadiji, let's leave.

Duryodhana: Hold it mister, what do you think you're doing? Who gave you the bright idea that she is your property?

Writer: Sir, I don't know who you are, or what you are. But this lady here, she is my friend, and her safety is my prerogative ... which is why I request you to let us leave in peace.

Draupadi: Exactly.

Karna (enraged): Why, of all the bloody low-minded cheapest tricks in the book! You atheist! You socialist! You vegetarian!

Duryodhana: Restrain yourself. Show more restraint.

Karna: Duryodhana, give me a chance, and I'll smash his face so hard, that, from a writer he will become a word processor.

Duryodhana: Relax Karna, we have other ways, don't we, eh?

(A sly wink)

Dushasana: What other ways, Bhaiye?

Duryodhana: A pack of cards please, and Draupadi is ours with ease.

Karna and Dushasana (shuffling a pack of cards): A packet of cards please, and Draupadi is ours with ease.

Writer (hypnotised): Hi guys, would you be interested in a game of cards, perchance.

Karna (whispers): Duryodhana, this is your chance.

Dushasana (mutters): To be precise, he is already in a trance.

Duryodhana: A game of cards. Yes, yes, why not. What are the stakes?

Writer: You mean you want to bet?

Duryodhana: That's exactly what I mean.

Writer: Oooh Yaara, this is Las Vegas all over again. Tell me, what do you have to bet?

Duryodhana: Draupadi's freedom, and the services of the two greatest warriors of our times Karna and Dushasana, for the next 365 days.

Writer: What … and what if I lose?

Duryodhana: Draupadi *(slurps)* will be mine!

Karna: And mine.

Dushasana: Ours, to be precise.

Draupadi (screams): Nooooooooo!

Duryodhana: But wait, before we begin, let me inform you, in case you haven't realised it, that my Uncleji will play the game for me.

Writer: Your Uncleji, that creep, but …

Karna: It's a part of the Agreement.

Writer: What Agreement?

Dushasana (brandishes a legal document): In the small print. For our eyes only, heh-heh-heh.

Writer groans. Draupadi moans. Duryodhana whistles aloud for Uncleji. Almost immediately there is eerie music, superseded by an evil cackle. Uncle enters on a tricycle.

Duryodhana: Namaskarams, I salute thee, Uncleji.

Uncle: Asheerwadams Bhanje. Now let's get down to the real business. I've to rush to the Derby.

Karna: Oh, now you have started gambling on horses.

Uncle: Karna, Karna, when will you ever learn. The best of gamblers don't bet on Derby day. We only go there to ogle at the women – whilst the amateurs bet.

Writer (still shuffling a pack of cards): Can we get on with the game please?

Uncle: Oh you, you're still here. Pretty little sucker for losing, aren't you?

To which, the Writer reacts. Uncle takes a pack of cards, and does a couple of quick tricks. Gradually, lights, music and atmosphere change to that of medieval times. As before, the game of cards is played exaggeratedly, with the Producer and his two cronies watching with bated breath. And then the Writer loses.

Uncle (yawns): Ho-ho, won again.

Draupadi (screams): Nooooooo! Not again. Please, not again. Once more a woman has been sacrificed to the vagaries of a game ... ah, when will this stop?

But Draupadi, is already being led away by Karna and Dushasana. The Writer seems a forlorn figure, whilst Duryodhana and Uncle strike a victorious pose. Freeze tableau.

Blackout. Soon after, the earlier chants of 'Jai Schwarzenegger' are heard. Fade in. The Four Pandavs are back. And Bheem is still hoisted on Nakula's and Sahadeva's shoulders.

Arjuna (in front, looking through a pair of binoculars): I still can't see Draupadi. Strange as it may sound, I just can't see her. Although – far away – in the distance, I can see the eye of a parrot. *(Takes-off AK-47 and shoots Rat-A-Tat-A-Tat ....)*

Bheem: Arjune, Arjune calm down. How many times have I told you that every parrot, and every eye is not a target. How many times must you be reminded?

Arjuna: I'm sorry Bhaisaheb ... I suddenly seem to get carried away.

Bheem: It just won't do Arjune, it just won't do. Think of what the world will make of you, if you go on like this.

Arjuna: But I said, I'm sorry.

Bheem: Nothing doing. I want you to do 500 baithaks, after which I want you to write. 'I'll not shoot a parrot in the eye' 1,001 times.

Arjuna: Jo hukum, Bhaisaheb. *(He starts baithaks)*

Nakula: But where is Draupadi?

Sahadeva: May be she's gone back to her *maike* ... you know.

Nakula: Chee-chee, in that case she would have informed, at least one of us.

Sahadeva: I hope nothing terrible has happened to her.

Bheem: Sahadeva, O Sahadeva, when will you ever learn? In your life, you have fought a war, not just any war, but the great grandmom of all wars. For which we killed our relatives and friends. Further, for the last few centuries we've been climbing this hill, and all you have to say is I-hope-nothing-terrible-has-happened-to-her?

Nakula: I remember, I last saw her here.

Sahadeva: Alone and bestride ...

Bheem: There has also been a bit of struggle here ... see, on the floor, her bangle pieces.

Nakula: Maybe she's been kidnapped. O how many times had I told her 'Panchali do what you want, but don't overstep the *Lakshman Rekha.*'

Sahadeva: Nakula, don't confuse the issue. This is the *Mahabharata*. Not the *Ramayana*.

Nakula: What do we do now? Oh ... What do we ever do?

Sahadeva: O come on, stop being senti, yaar.

Bheem (clears throat): Gentlemen, without much ado, let's get down to business.

Nakula: Business?

Bheem: Yes, the business of retrieving Draupadi.

Sahadev But how?

Bheem (wildly): I don't know. Eh, Arjune, do you have any ideas?

Arjuna: Duh!

Nakula and Sahadeva: Good try, Arjune. Good try.

Bheem: At such a time, I wish Dharmaraja was with us. He always used to take these decisions. Agreed, most of the decisions were wrong decisions, but at least they were decisions.

Nakula: But Dharmaraja is absconding in *swargalok*.

Sahadeva: Out of sight, and out of mind.

Bheem: Hear, hear. This is my decision. Now, we have been climbing this wretched hill for all these centuries. Have we achieved anything? No. And at the end of it. What are we going to achieve. A trip to Narak.

Arjuna: Narak? How do you know Bhaisaheb?

Bheem: Ah, I read about it in Rajagopalachari's abridged version of the *Mahabharata*.

Arjuna: Oh, does he mention in his book, who is the greatest target-shooter in this part of the world?

Nakula and Sahadeva: Ram. Limba Ram!

Bheem: Order, order ... yes, thank you. And so I've decided that instead of pursuing our futile climb of this hill. We shall culminate our climb, here and now.

Nakula (gasps): What?

Bheem: Yes, and hereby go our individual-separate ways, living our respective lives. Because all said and done, we must keep with the times, and today the times state that the joint family is out of fashion. In fact you can even quote me on this: 'When in Doubt, consult Time.' Not as good a quote as Krishna, or Dharmaraja, but then I'm only a beginner in this quoting-loathing.

Arjuna: And Draupadi?

Sahadeva: Exactly, what about Draupadi?

Bheem: Not to worry, I've made some arrangements for that too.

Nakula: What arrangements?

Bheem: Arjune, give me a one-gun salute.

Promptly, Arjuna turns his AK-47 skywards, and let's go Rat-A-Tat-A-Tat ...

Meanwhile Bheem unfurls, a huge poster/banner with Draupadi's photograph on it.

Hayan Pailas Ka?

Mrs Draupadi Pandav

Vaya – Daha Hazaar Varsh

Savli Surat – Gare Kase

Fade out.

Fade in. Duryodhana, Karna and Dushasana enter with a flourish.

Duryodhana: Has Draupadi been dressed up? Sufficiently

informed and all, no. Look, I want no last-minute nakhras.

Dushasana: Not to worry, Bhaiye – everything is tip-top.

Duryodhana: Have you spoken to the astrologers? Is the time sufficiently auspicious? Are the stars in their proper place?

Karna: All is well. *Shani-pradosh* will elapse any moment now. And then, your *shukl paksh* period starts.

Duryodhana: Goody-goody. How I wish we could have invited more people on this occasion. A few chamchas, the usual hangers-on. For nostalgia's sake we should have at least asked Pops and Drona and even Bheeshma Pitamah ....

Dushasana: O Bheeshma Pitamah can't come. He is very busy these days. Delivering some lecture-series on 'Life Is Not A Bed Of Arrows'.

Karna: Just the right sort of vocation for the old geriatric. Remember how he spoke for days on end, resembling a porcupine with arrows. Simply refused to die. And we all had to go and listen to the bugger – yak-yak. It wasn't even fun. Personally – I prefer Murari Babu to him.

Duryodhana: Yaar Karna – relax maan. Be cool. The old man was OK. It's just that the two of you had ego problems.

Karna: And why not. After all, like everyone else he was partial to Arjuna – even though, I always tried to be decent with him. Remember – when he was dying, he refused boiled-purified water from me – but when Arjuna, gave him the Ganga Jal straight-out of the bloody ground, he drank it and said – hip hip hurray to Arjuna, for having discovered the water cooler.

Duryodhana: One must overlook such things – because basically *banda theek tha*. *Yaad hai*, last time round, when we beckoned Draupadi to the court, he didn't utter a single syllable. Correct or no? If he had, then *sab kiye pe paani ho jaata*.

Dushasana: ... Bhaiye – about this Draupadi ...

Duryodhana: Yeah – what ... ?

Dushasana: I genuinely think it's not such a great idea to mess about with Draupadi. She is bad news, you know ...

Karna: What *bakvaas*. Ah, Duryodhana, you better begin,

right away. It's the time for the Muhurat – the Full Moon is in conjunction with the third ring of Saturn, beneath the shadow of Alpha Centauri – your *shubh* period begins *now*!

Duryodhana: OK. *(claps hands)* Silence! Ladies and Gentlemen. You are gathered here to know why Swarag, Narak and I are here.

Now listen to this carefully, I say to you today... *(a la Martin Luther King)* that in spite of the difficulties and frustrations of the moment, I still have a dream.

I have a dream that one day, Draupadi will be brought in front of me, and I'd humiliate her. If you remember, the last time I tried to do it, that son-of-a-holy-cowherd Krishna intervened. This time, there is no Krishna. This time there is Draupadi, and ha-ha she is all mine ....

Karna: And mine.

Dushasana: Ours, to be precise.

Duryodhana: Then what are we waiting for ... bring Draupadi that maidservant to my court. In open durbar we will humiliate her.

Karna: Durbar, what durbar – Duryodhana. You can't call our chawl a durbar.

Duryodhana: Ssshhh, optical illusion, yaar. If you don't tell the public you think they'll know the difference between a real durbar and a chawl? Arrey no. If they were so smart, they wouldn't still be watching this play ... Eh, Dushasana, what are you doing here? Go bring Draupadi. Go get her, I'll personally disrobe her with my bare-naked hands.

Dushasana: That's what I'm worried about.

Duryodhana: Worried, why are you worried?

Dushasana: Oh, censor problems, you know. All this nanga-panga stuff. Do you think it will be allowed?

Duryodhana: What do you mean nanga-panga? This is the vastra-haran, the high-point of our rich cultural heritage. Good, so what're you waiting for? Go forth and fetch her.

Dushasana exits. Happy-go-lucky.

Just then, offstage, a loud explosion is heard. Almost immediately, Dushasana comes back. He is a sight; hair dishevelled, shirt torn. Duryodhana and Karna look aghast.

Dushasana (swears): Ayeee … Ayeee!

Duryodhana: What … what happened.

Dushasana: The mad woman, she bit me.

Karna: But if she bit you, why is your shirt torn.

Dushasana (sobbing): I don't know, maybe she was hungry.

Duryodhana: And that explosion?

Dushasana: How the hell am I supposed to know?

Duryodhana: That's strange, what could that explosion be? I hope all is well. Karna, go check up, and bring Draupadi here, at once.

Karna exits. Just then, offstage, a loud explosion is heard. Almost immediately Karna comes dashing back. He is a sight; hair dishevelled, shirt torn. Duryodhana and Dushasana look aghast.

Karna: Ow ... Ow …

Duryodhana: Karna, what happened ... my dear Karna!

Karna: She scratched me ... the mad woman.

Duryodhana: But if she scratched you, why is your shirt all torn.

Karna: I don't know, because like a bolt from the blue, she came up to me and said *'bhala teri kameez mere kameez se saphed kaise'* and then she ripped my shirt off, just like that *(snaps fingers).*

Duryodhana: And what was that explosion?

Karna: I don't know … I thought, it took place here.

Duryodhana: Oh, this is getting to be a serious matter. I think we should re-organise ourselves. Maybe I could go in, and get her personally.

Karna: No, don't do that. She might do something to you, too.

Duryodhana: Then what do I do ... how do we bring Draupadi here?

Dushasana: What do we do?

And then, almost out of nowhere a man pops out. Slick and impeccably dressed in a bow tie and with a peacock feather in his hair.

Duryodhana: Who're you?

Courier Man (CM): It's me. I'm your friendly neighbourhood courier man, I deliver anything anywhere. Just give me your parcel, quote a price, and I'll deliver tomorrow, today.

Karna (in Duryodhana 's ear): Ah, this is a stroke of good luck. We must hire this chap right away.

Dushasana (also whispering in the ear): I really don't think so. We can't just be hiring all and sundry. Even in a free-market economy we must know the *jaat-paat*.

CM: Ha-ha. Have no doubts, my good sirs. We're the best in the courier business. Why, we have even delivered Neil Armstrong to the moon.

Duryodhana: OK, then all things considered, since our own attempts have so disastrously failed. I see no harm in giving you a chance.

CM: Swell, what's the address?

Duryodhana: There, that way out of the stage ... the first left, from the greenroom.

CM: And what do I have to get?

Karna: A woman, and mind you, she is not just any woman.

CM: Then here I go – Vrrroooom.

Courier Man exits.

Even as he exits, there is an enormous explosion, offstage. Duryodhana and others wait eagerly ... and then, slowly – painfully slowly – Draupadi enters, in time and beat to the rhythm of the 'Shanti' mantra. Duryodhana and others exchange lustful smiles. Almost immediately, the Courier Man dashes back on stage.

CM: So, the job is done, the woman is at your disposal. Tip-top.

Duryodhana: But, what was that explosion?

CM: I don't know. *(A beat)* But isn't the suspense damn exciting?

Duryodhana: What were those explosions, Draupadi?

Draupadi: Why don't you ask your Atma?

Duryodhana: What in the name of the Father, and the Son, and the Holy Spirit, is an Atma?

Draupadi: It's so sad Duryodhana that you haven't realised it. The Gods are angry with you, and right now they are getting angrier. Repent and redeem yourself, there is still time ...

CM: Excuse me sir, my pay please.

Duryodhana: But of course! Do you accept credit cards?

CM: No. Instead, I'll make you an offer, you can't refuse. I want Karna's wristwatch.

Karna: Nooooo!

CM: I thought a deal is a deal.

Duryodhana: Take anything else, my friend, but not his wrist-watch.

CM: Why not?

Duryodhana: Ah well, it's a slightly ... hmmm ... delicate matter. You see, he was born with this wristwatch, a gift from his unknown father to him.

CM: Do you expect me to believe this?

Duryodhana: No, I don't.

CM: Then why don't you tell me the truth, and nothing but the whole truth, that his Swiss Bank Account number is written on the back of the watch.

Karna: How did you know?

CM: I know everything.

Duryodhana: Is that so? What else do you know?

CM: Ha-ha, to start with I know what the end of this play is.

Dushasana: Really, tell me what will happen at the end of this play?

CM: The curtains will come down.

Dushasana: Ooooh, you're so clever.

CM: The wristwatch please, or I'll take this woman back from where I got her.

Duryodhana: Give it to him, Karna.

Karna: But ...

Duryodhana: Trust me, Karna.

Karna: Trust you? Am I crazy?

Dushasana: Karna!!!

Karna reluctantly takes off his wristwatch and hands it over to Courier Man, who accepts it gleefully, and zooms off. Vroom-Vroom. Exit.

Dushasana: Ha-ha, now we're all alone. All to ourselves with no one to intervene.

Karna: No Bheeshma, no Drona, no Vidur. And above all, no Krishna.

Dushasana: Shall we begin ... ?

Duryodhana: Yes, what are we waiting for. Take it away, Dushasana, let the show begin ...

Dushasana approaches Draupadi who in turn tightly squeezes her eyes shut, and starts to chant 'Krishna-Krishna-Krishna ...'

But Dushasana, by now like an unbridled horse, unrestrainedly starts to disrobe Draupadi, vulgarly and obscenely (and through mime).

The chorus is chanting Shanti-Shanti ... By now the heavens, start to ding-dong with curious metallic gongs and Draupadi starts to strut around, as if on a catwalk.

Voiceover: Ladies and gentlemen, we take this opportunity to welcome you, to our fashion show; at the same time we regret this interruption to the play, but let us assure you that what you are about to see is extremely vital to the plot development and storyline of the play. And so we request you to watch carefully, and above all, stay awake.

Presenting the ultimate in fashion designing. Draupadi Hosiery, Garments and Apparels. Remember to wear them every day. Easy to wear. Extremely difficult to remove.

For women of all ages, sizes and blood groups, in a wide range of exotic colours and exciting designs.

Dresses specially designed for today's women to make them look ugly, unwanted and repulsive; in order to save them from eve-teasing, rape and marriage.

Yes, for the first time in India, the Magic of Draupadi!

Whenever you see a play. Think of us!

Ting-Tong.

This part of the play was sponsored by Draupadi Hosiery, Garments and Apparels.

In the meantime, Dushasana is feverishly disrobing Draupadi. And with every 'piece' of imaginary cloth that he disrobes, the Chorus throws up another piece of cloth. This is very symbolic; besides, it makes the stage a kaleidoscope of colours.

As for, Duryodhana and Karna, they drool and salivate around Draupadi, as if in a trance. Draupadi struts and catwalks, enjoying herself thoroughly.

Dushasana: Bhaiye, listen to me. I think we should call this thing off. Remember what happened the last time. I believe Draupadi always brings bad luck.

Duryodhana: Absolute rot and bullcrap!

Dushasana: How can you be so confident?

Duryodhana: There's an old English saying 'Lightning never strikes twice in the same place.'

Dushasana: Never?

Duryodhana: Never!

A loud crack of thunder accompanied by lightning. Duryodhana, Karna and Dushasana leap up two feet, let go a heart-rending scream, and fall down.

Dushasana (lifts up head): That is why Dr Ram Manohar Lohia used to say 'Never trust the English.' *(Falls down unconscious)*

ACT II

Fade in. Look, look it's the chorus. But look, they are so different, so solemn. Why have they changed? What that they are chanting? It sounds like the Rig Veda. But hear the words, they are in English!

The Chorus: We have an audience
We even have a writer
We also have a play
Which doesn't know what more to say
Om Shanti! Shanti! Shanti!

This play may get lost
It has to be saved at any cost
So tear up your tickets
If you think something is wicked
Om Shanti! Shanti! Shanti!

After this play, do come and meet
To congratulate us on our feat
If we are dead, then you know it's true
Shanti's no more
Like me and you
Om Shanti, Shanti, Shanti

Om dyauh shaantih
Antariksham shaantih

Prithivee shaantih
Aapah shaantih
Oshadhayah shaantih
Vanaspatayah shaantih

Vishvedevaah shaantih
Brahma shaantih
Sarvam shaantih
Shaantireva shaantih

Saamaa shaantiredhih
Om shaantih, shaantih, shaantih!

Duryodhana, Karna and Dushasana are groggily getting up. Draupadi is warily watching them, hidden behind the chorus.

Karna: What lightning, yaar. Even the Brahmastra doesn't make so much dhamaka ...

Duryodhana (looking around): Arrey, but where is Draupadi? She is not to be seen.

Dushasana: Good riddance to her!

Karna: How can you say that, when we had her at our mercy? With not a single Pandav in sight. Er ... actually, I meant to ask this question long ago, but why are the Pandavs called the Pandavs?

Dushasana: Because Pandu Chacha was their father, that's why ...

Karna: Ha-ha, Pandu was no such thing. Everyone knows it. Dharma fathered Yudhishthira. Indra, Arjuna. Vayu, Bheem. And the Asvini Devas were the fathers of Nakula and Sahadeva.

Dushasana: So ...

Karna: You nitwit, halfwit, *mandhbudhi* ... don't you see it. The Paanch Pandavs are not the Pandavs. They are just a bunch of guys, sticking together – to enhance their brand equity.

Duryodhana: Ssssh – listen to the chorus. Hmmmm, this Shanti-Shanti sounds so much better than ... Yaar, what's it called, Acid Rock. Ooooph, what cacophony. *No taal. No sur.* Complete *apasvaram*. Incidentally, why do they call it Acid Rock?

Karna: Those Americans, if they can call Marlon Brando the greatest actor in the world, and baseball the greatest game in the world, then they can call anything Acid Rock.

Dushasana: I hear, it's all a grand scheme to promote their only export commodity.

Duryodhana: What's that?

Karna: Hollywood!

Duryodhana (taps at forehead): These Yankees are totally Doodley.

Chorus (fading): Shanti, Shanti .....

Dushasana: But Bhaiye .... what IS this Shanti-Shanti that they are chanting?

Duryodhana: I don't know – may be it's some phirang lingo.

Karna: No, I don't think so.

Dushasana: Bhaiye, it might be a code word. I remember Kunti aunty saying it all the time. Shanti-Shanti-Shanti ...

Duryodhana: Oh, this is proving to be serious. Why don't you look up the word in the dictionary.

Dushasana (extracts a pint-sized dictionary, and searches for word): ... Aah, here it is. Shanti ... Shanti is Sanskrit for Peace.

Duryodhana: Peace, what does Peace mean ... ?

Dushasana (reading from the dictionary): Peace ..... Peace is English for Shanti.

Karna: I don't know Duryodhana, but this seems to be some kind of conspiracy, all this Shanti and Peace.

Duryodhana: Dushasana, are you sure that's what is written in that book?

Dushasana: Of course I am, Bhaiye. You can see for yourself if you want.

Duryodhana: What good will that do, huh? You know I am a certified illiterate. Not even Matric pass. So no need to rub it in – OK. *(sighs)* It's all Papas' fault. One day, he decides that of his 100 sons, he can provide schooling and education only to the ten most intelligent ones ... and so, I'm disqualified. Why? Just because I don't score well in the entrance exam.

Dushasana: But Bhaiye, you didn't answer even a single question correctly.

Duryodhana: So ...? So what? I have always been excellent in extra-curricular activities.

Karna (loudly): Guys, watch out! Hide the Pan Parags and Strohs' beer cans. Look, who is coming this way ...

Duryodhana: Bursting bombs, it's Moms!!!

Gandhari (with an uncanny resemblance to the Fairy Godmother) struts in, blindfold and all.

Gandhari: Beta, how many times have I told you to stop swearing in my name.

Duryodhana: What are you doing here, mom? And why do you still have that blindfold on you?

Gandhari: Beta, O beta, how many times have we gone over this? I'm a social worker and it is my duty to wear this blindfold. Because that is the only way I can be a blind visionary, totally out-of-touch with reality.

Duryodhana: But surely you're too old for all this …

Gandhari (clears throat): Ah well, who else is with you?

Duryodhana: Karna and Dushasana.

Gandhari (upset): What is Dushasana doing here? Doesn't he have to go for his tuitions. Phew, that boy, he never studies, always wasting his time. Eh Karna, you must knock some sense into Dushasana's head. He is your friend, he'll listen to you.

Karna: Don't worry about him, aunty. He's doing quite fine.

Gandhari: You'll obviously support him, he's your friend. Who am I, just as old blind woman?

Duryodhana: Mom, you're not blind …

Dushasana: You're only playing blind man's bluff for society's sake.

Gandhari: There, there did you hear him, back-answering me like that. It's all because of watching MTV day in and night out ... he will become a vegetable, I tell you! Come here, Dushasana, touch my feet … enough of your American repartees 'Hi Mom', 'Yo Mum', 'Way to go, Babe', 'Really, swinging it out with Dad, huh?'. I'm your mother, treat me with respect.

Dushasana reluctantly touches feet. Gandhari grabs him by his ear.

Gandhari (sniffing loudly): Thought as much! So you've been smoking once again … ? Why do you do it, you're such a good boy otherwise. Such a bright future. I mean, you had such a brilliant career in Marxism.

Dushasana: It's not my fault if all those countries vanished.

Karna: That's why I told you to not to pay heed to Drona. He wasn't the right kind of Guru for you.

Dushasana: Karna, there is no reason for you to get nasty about Dronaji ...

Karna: No need to get upset? OK. Everyone knew there were serious flaws in Drona's educational policy. Too much stress on archery, wrestling and horse-riding. He never taught anything else.

Dushasana: He is not to blame. That was his area of specialisation. He had a double PhD in it.

Karna: In that case, he should have authorised someone like Vidura to teach the other subjects.

Duryodhana: Chee-chee, not Mama Vidura – he is a socialist, yaar. Very boring.

Gandhari: Boys, boys, boys. Now come on and run home. All this hanging around street corners doesn't do any good for our family reputation. Only today our neighbour, Mrs Draupada was telling me 'Don't your sons have any kaam? Don't they have anything better to do?'

Duryodhana: Mom, how many times have I told you to ignore her?

Gandhari: Of course, I don't believe her, but still ... OK, come on get home. Daddy must also be waiting. Today is his day to be told a story. Have you decided which story you'll tell him?

Dushasana: Yes, mother. The life and times of Hellen Keller.

Duryodhana, Karna and Dushasana exit.

Gandhari: Oooof, these boys, no ambition, no talent. Only capable of becoming non-entities. Look at that Dhoni, so young, and already so successful. So much fame-name, endorsing all those products. A million dollar company. He also plays cricket, I'm told.

Meanwhile, Draupadi, who has been silent, whilst trying to sneak away, makes a noise.

Gandhari: Who be that? Eh? Speak up ...

Draupadi: It's me. Er ... are you really Gandhariji?

Gandhari: To be precise Gandhari Saubali Gandhararajaduhita Saubaleyi Subalaja Subalamaja ... Short and sweet. But not to worry, that's only my pet name. And who are you? *(removes her blindfold. Draupadi gasps)* ... Arrey, it's Draupadi! Still in these parts? Oh jolly good. Come, come, sit next to me. I always wanted to gossip with you. But never could. I was always told that Draupadi Madam has no time. I can understand. With five-five husbands. Oooof, life must have been hell for you. I toh can't even handle one ...

Draupadi: Your blindfold ...

Gandhari: What about it? You like the *karigari* on it? It's absolutely ethnic, I tell you ...

Draupadi: You removed your blindfold!

Gandhari: Yes, of course. How else could I see you? Silly girl.

Draupadi: Oh my Goddess! In one stroke you have re-written history. You have freed yourself, myself and all women from the shackles of the blindfold. You have paved a way for all the stree-jaat, who exist below the blindfold level. This is even more important for women than the 33% reservation at the Panchayat level.

Gandhari (giggles): Nothing of the sort, young woman. It's just that I've a recurring cataract problem. So from time to time, I've to put eye-drops on the retina of my eye. Doctor's orders. But let that be ... Oooh – look at you, lovely earrings! Have even lost a bit of waist! Hmmm, and that look on your face. It's the one thing I admire you and Medha Patkar for.

Draupadi: Oh! You mean our spirit of ...

Gandhari: Both of you look lovely without make-up.

Draupadi: Well ...

Gandhari: And your husbands ... how are they? Still nursing a grudge? Itching for a panga?

Draupadi: They must be OK.

Gandhari: Good. That's good. I hope they are not planning any more expeditions and wars. Tell them things like Mahabharatas are antiquated concepts. No one goes forth on conquests and annexations any more. All that has been done with. The big-time battles are fought on the commerce and financial front. Why, just the other day, someone was telling me that even Attila the Hun has become a financial consultant.

Draupadi: But you know the Pandavs, they are no good at economics.

Gandhari: Oh really? Have you tried talking to either Nakula or Sahadeva?

Draupadi: Oh, they are bachchus. Just a couple of sweet-looking kids, who do jee-huzoori to the other three.

Gandhari: Tut-tut. That's where you're mistaken. Those two, believe me, have real brains. Yudhishthira, Arjuna, Bheem were good for popular rhetorics. For mass support. For image-building. But the twins were the ones who chalked out and planned all the Pandav schemes.

Draupadi: How do you know?

Gandhari: Hmmmm, I don't know if I should be confiding this to you. But before the Mahabharata, the twins came to me for my support in the post-war era.

Draupadi: They did that??? But when?

Gandhari: That was the time when you and the Pandavs were mustering public support for your campaign.

Draupadi: Oh!!!

Gandhari: Well ... when the twins came to me, I said only one thing 'The future is all so uncertain. I'm very worried.'

Draupadi: With the impending war, no doubt ...

Gandhari: Oh no, not in the least. No matter how one abhors the idea of wars, it keeps occurring. Nothing one can do about that. It is integral to human progress. Enhances morale. Distracts the citizenry.

Draupadi: But ...

Gandhari: Also, the blood ... is good for the crops. In fact, it is said that every genuine civilisation has to stage a few wars.

After all, it's because of yesterday's wars that today's tourist industry survives. The only thing war sites and travel guides have in common. Makes perfect sense, no?

Draupadi: What about the loss of human lives. Our very own relatives, friends, near and dear ones ...

Gandhari: Pah, mushy sentimentalism and oversimplification. Come on, Draupadi, you disappoint me. You must learn to be more practical. And realistic. You're renowned the world over for your views. Surely they cannot be so mundane!

Draupadi: What do you mean mundane? Surely one cannot trivialise the untold damage, huh? Property destroyed. Houses burnt. Farms decimated. Palaces pilfered. The ruins, the carnage.

Gandhari: Ah, now you're talking. Economic harm. In other words, losses to the treasury. That's what I told the twins straight. That the basic problem with the *Mahabharata* is that it is an unprofitable proposition. Both the Pandavs and the Kauravs are unworthy victors. I'm not in the favour of one dynasty overthrowing another just for the sake of change, you know.

Draupadi: That was because your sons were ruling!

Gandhari: Ruling, but ruling badly. Their policies were all muddled up. Land reforms, primary education and health were neglected. Industry was demoralised. The workforce was demotivated. No investments. Zero savings. War, war, war was all they thought of. Why, even when iron was discovered for the first time, near the Indus Valley Basins, instead of exporting the stuff, they used it to manufacture armours and helmets. Fortunately, the rainfall was good and the soil excellent, or else the masses would have rebelled long ago ... Nakula and Sahadeva were aware of the seriousness of the situation, and so, they proposed ...

Draupadi: What?

Gandhari: They were willing to give me direct control over all fiscal matters relating to the state – if I backed Yudhishthira's claim for monarchy. All decision-making would be in my hands.

Naturally, due to the precariousness of the situation, this could not be disclosed to the public.

Draupadi: With due apologies, Gandhariji, but what do you know about the nitty-gritty of economics?

Gandhari: A lot. My father, King Subala ensured that I graduated in Economics.

Draupadi: Why that's terrific! One never associated you with being educated. I suppose, it has something to do with the fact that you mothered one hundred sons.

Gandhari: Oh that? That was merely an extension of my concept of mass industrial production. You know, *hum do hamare sau.*

Draupadi: How did Uncle Dhritarashtra react? Was he happy?

Gandhari: Initially, he sulked. Stopped talking to me. Until one day, I told him 'Look jee, as it is, we can't see each other. On top of that, with your *maun vrat* business, we have even ceased *bad-badofying* to one another. At this rate, we will become like any other husband-wife jodi.'

Draupadi: Did he relent?

Gandhari: Of course – he did. After all, it was he, who kept pestering me for a male child. So I said to myself '*Saala, ladka itna hi chaiye – toh ek ke jagah ek sau le.*' ... Arrey, but the best thing is, after the children were born was he never came near me. Not even for a kissey. He was totally terrified that I might knock-up another century.

Draupadi (giggling): I can well imagine. Men have such quaint notions about these things.

Gandhari: Yes, yes. And who will know it better than you – with your five husbands ...? Ahem, actually, I always wanted to ask you about this. How did you cope with them ... *(meaningful winks and shrugs)* you know ... you know ... ?

Draupadi (deep breath): In the beginning, it was awful. Five-five men. And on top of that they never brushed their teeth. Mind you, they were great at everything else – giving long speeches, wearing expensive clothes and perfumes – but they just wouldn't brush their teeth! Ooof – it was unbearable – the stink of garlic and tambakoo!

Gandhari: Poor dear ... I can imagine.

Draupadi: In addition, they would all line up outside my door. Day-in and night-out. Every single moment. Arrey, not a moment of peace. So I told Dharamaputra 'O great and wise one.' Yudhishthira always liked to be addressed thus. It did wonders for his ego. Anyway, to cut a long story short, Dharamaputra decided that whoever was in the room with me, had to leave his Royal Slippers outside the door so as to avoid any embarrassment for all concerned.

Gandhari: I have heard about this.

Draupadi: It was the best thing to happen in my life. You won't believe it – the first thing I did before Yudhishtra would change his mind was – make duplicates of all the Pandav chappals!

Gandhari: Why?

Draupadi: So that, I could always leave one pair of chappal outside my room, at all times. And so, every Pandav thought the other brother was with me! My spies ensured that the system was foolproof. They reported all the moments of the Pandav to me. So I knew whose chappal to place when!

Gandhari: What if one of them had cross-checked with the other?

Drauapdi: It would be below the Pandav maryada to do any such thing.

Gandhari: But ... what about all those rumours about your extra-affection for Arjuna?

Drauapdi: Oh, that was just a coincidence. It's just that I ended up placing Arjuna's chappals ouside my room most often. He was a safe bet. Always practising his archery in the woods. Nobody ever knew his real whereabouts.

Gandhari: Jai Kamasutra. Om Khajuraho. This throws a new light on your sexuality, your feminity. All those lores about your oooooomph, huh?

Drauapdi: That was just media hype. You know how it is with ... us royalty types. People are always curious. Look at what happened to Charles and Diana!

Gandhari: Ssshhh, look who is heading this way ...

Writer barges in. He notices Gandhari and Draupadi. All round gasps.

Draupadi: YOU!

Writer: Draupadiji! Fairy Godmother!

Gandhari: Ah, you. Still around? How is the play coming along?

Draupadi: Have the two of you met before?

Gandhari: But how do you know each other?

Writer: What are you doing with Draupadi? After all, you are my Fairy Godmother.

Draupadi: She is nothing of the sort. She is Gandhariji. Mother of Duryodhana ... at whose mercy, you so callously left me.

Gandhari: Duryodhana! You didn't tell me about that, Draupadi. What has he done – now?

Draupadi: Well ...

Writer: The vastra-haran. All over again! With the assistance of Karna and Dushasana.

Draupadi: How do you know? I never told anybody.

Gandhari: ... Is this true, Draupadi?

Draupadi: It is – Gandhariji.

Writer: That is not all – the Pandavs have also heard the news. And they intend to do something about it!

Draupadi: Oh no!

Gandhari: Hmmm. In that case something will have to be done about it. This *haath pe haath rakhna* will not take us anywhere.

Writer: Yeah! I fully endorse your opinion. And I'm all for any action plan.

Draupadi: You keep out of this. You have caused enough trouble – already. It's because of you – that I've had to endure such woes.

Gandhari: Draupadi is right. It's all your fault. Why in the name of Natyashastra did you have to write a play in the first place? Now look what you have done. Created problems for everyone. That is what is wrong with you writer chaps. Begin to take yourselves and your characters too seriously. And then, when there is a mess, you throw your hands up in despair. Chee-chee.

Draupadi: Come on, Gandhariji, let's leave. There is no point in getting upset over him...

Gandhari: Yes, let's exit. Down stage. Left wing. It's about time ... I have a talk with Duryodhana. he is getting out of hand. Oh dear, all this is such a bother, you know. Just when my career was looking up. Only yesterday, I was commissioned me to pen my autobiography. Oh dear, I even had a lovely name for the book. 'An Eye for an Eye: the Autobiography of an Aai.'

Writer (speaking to the audience): Arrey Gandhariji ... come back, will you? ... Boy-o-boy, this is a big mess! Things really look in a bad shape. It seems I've plunged into some crazy world in which nonsense is the only available sense. And the tragedy is ... I'm the only one to realise it. I mean, why are all these perfectly straightforward people taking my play so seriously? Don't they have better things to do? Take up some other drama of our time ...

Uh-oh, under such circumstances, where am I going to get help from. The UN, The Red Cross, Washington ...? Or can I come up with a good scheme to dissuade the Pandavs? But first, I must find them ...

Fade out.

In another part of the world, the Pandavs are about to hold an Extraordinary General Body Meeting. The four Pandavs are present. There is a smattering of chorus, who form the audience.

Bheem: As convenor of today's meeting, let me tell you right at the outset, that There is Big Trouble in These Parts. As you are already aware, today's meeting is a brainstorming session – to discuss our role in the absence of Draupadi.

For an in-depth analysis of her absence, and its repercussions, I throw open tonight's discussion to our distinguished panelists.

On my right is Mr Arjuna, leading snapshooter for the mafia in Italy. Now on special duty in Afghanistan.

On my left are the youngest yuppies of the advertising, Nakula and Sahadeva, who are also the proprietors of Sachi & Muchi advertising, named thus after the Sachi-Muchi habits of their elder brother.

Well ... ahem ... I declare the panel discussion open!

Nakula: Ladies and Gentlemen, Draupadi, our wife, has been kidnapped, and although the world at large is expressing its sympathy, no one is doing anything about it. But we are not going to let nothing not happen.

Sahadeva: On that solemn but striking note, I take this opportunity to set up the Draupadi Foundation Trust in honour of Mata Draupadi.

Nakula: Yes, and so remember the name, Draupadi Foundation Trust.

Sahadeva: Our motto: You believe ... what we tell.

Echo (offstage): And our ad copy: You buy ... what we sell.

Bheem: Who said that? Who ... *(picks up a megaphone)* Hell-Hell-Hello? Is there anybody out there?

Echo: NO!

Bheem: OH!

Just then, out of the blue, an Echo arrives on the scene. He has a peacock feather in his hair, adjusting his disguise offstage.

Arjuna: What's that, a bird, a plane, or is it superman?

Sahadeva: It's an echo, dumbo.

The Echo struts around the stage, a pale reflection of himself.

Nakula: Ah, a walkie-talkie 3-D Echo.

Echo: And you, what are you? Tourists?

Bheem: Tourists ... no, we're not tourists. We're Kshatriyas.

Echo: Kshatriyas, what's that? A rock group?

Bheem (still shouting): Look Echo Maharaj, is there no other way to conduct this conversation? I mean, in spite of my so-called loud, uncouth manners, I feel having a conversation in this way at the top of my voice is indecent.

Echo: If that's so, why don't you try me on the hotline *(aside)* although I've oft wondered, why everyone starts to shout while talking to me.

Bheem (to Nakula and Sahadeva): Put me down. Oye, Echo Maharaj, what's your number?

Echo: Dial Eeeeh for Echo!

Bheem (takes up a phone receiver): Ow! This thing is HOT.

Echo: Yes, that's why we call it the Hotline.

Bheem: Ah-ha. *(Dials a number)* Ping-pong-doong-dchang-twong.

Echo (in dull monotone voice): All the lines in this exchange are busy. Please dial some other number.

Bheem: Tchonk-dwang-doong-twong-ping.

Echo: You have dialed a non-existent exchange code. Please consult a psychiatrist before dialing your number.

Bheem: Dwook-drack-tookang-whrr-whrr ... Ha, it's ringing!

Echo: Hello-hello-hello.

Bheem: Hello, I'm Bheem.

Echo: Jai Bheem. Jai Ambedkar.

Bheem: Who Bheem? Who Ambedkar?

Echo: Big Mac jaroor khayenge, parantoo mandir wahin banayenge.

Bheem: What mandir ... ?

Echo: Kursi hatao, desh bachao.

Bheem: Hello-Hello ... I think we've got a socio-politically relevant cross-connection.

Echo: Hell-hell-hello.

Bheem: Ah, hello. I'm Bheem. Pandu Putra Bheem. Vayu Putra Bheem.

Echo: Ah-ha, a joint venture.

Bheem: Information, I want information.

Echo: Shoot.

Bheem: Hmmmm ... Echo Maharaj, my wife, actually our wife, Draupadi, is missing.

Echo: Have you lodged a complaint with the police?

Bheem: No.

Echo: Good, that's the most sensible thing you have done.

Bheem: Thank you.

Echo: So, what are you going to do about her disappearance?

Bheem: Well Nakula and Sahadeva have prepared a blueprint, and we are going to work out our strategy based on that.

Echo: Whatever it is, don't do something that you'll later regret.

Bheem: Such as ...

Echo: Well ... something on the scale of a Mahabharata.

Bheem: But ... we don't repent the Mahabharata! Whatever gave you the idea ...

Echo: You know, the Kauravs.

Bheem: Kauravs, ha-ha, we've already vanquished and defeated them centuries ago. Our only real achievement. Oui-oui. And – if we have bashed them up once, we can do so again. Yes Sir – so hear my call.

(in loud oratorical voice) Bhaiyon aur behenon. Long enough have evil forces reigned supreme on these lands. They, the Kauravas, have committed all kinds of anti-national activities. Doing as they please. Saying whatever it is that they wanted about us. Defiling our *izzat*. Denigrating our *maan maryada*. And we've appeased them. Not once have we uttered a word. But now, the Kauravs, have gone too far. They have not only disrobed Draupadiji, but

they have also distributed sweets and burst crackers after that. This won't do. It just won't.

And so, the time has come to fight our rights. It is believed that the Kauravs, once again, are deviously plotting to cascade our downfall through the dastardly act of kidnapping our wife Draupadi. Just as Ravana abducted Sitaji. And so, like Lord Rama, we must prevent them from achieving their goals because otherwise we'll be branded as cowards. In these times, any signs of weakness, will be mistaken for fear, so lest, they overcome us, we shall put a halt to their evil schemes and overcome them. Onward March. Onward Mahabharata. *(A beat)*

Nakula: Very good Bheem! Jolly good. We have scored the first points. Sahadeva, make copies of that speech and send it to all the major news agencies. Pronto.

Echo: What's happening ...

Nakula: PR, my friend. Public Relations An old saying: Behind every successful war is a good PR.

Echo: What about the ... Mahabharata?

Sahadeva: Oh let me handle this, guys. Look, Echo Maharaj, this IS the Mahabharata. Do not be deceived by all that propaganda about war being evil. Or all that spleen about blood and death. That's just to charge up the Janta Log. War is nothing of the sort. In fact, it's quite a peaceful affair. Consider: the Third World War ...

Echo: What Third World War ... I thought there have been only two World Wars ...

Sahadeva: Now, isn't that something? You haven't even heard about the Third World War – the single biggest War of this century. The defence rests, My Lord.

Echo: So, what're you going to do ... ?

Nakula: Nothing. Just twiddle our thumbs and wait. Whilst you echo our cry the world over, Echo Maharaj. Create mass support. Generate hysteria. Initiate a wave – in our favour ...

Echo: I'll do that only on one condition. You'll have to pay me my salary in *makhkhan*.

Sahadeva: Meaning ...

Echo: Actually, even buttermilk will do ...

Bheem: I knew it – right from the outset. He is an undercover agent. An unpatriotic dog. A desh drohi. I knew it all along – he is typical of the lot. Staying on our land – and making fun of our customs and way of life. Mocking all and sundry. No respect. No decency. Thinking no end of himself.

Echo: You're mistaken, dear sirs. My intentions were noble.

Bheem: Stuff and nonsense. Arjune ... Destruction!

Arjuna springs into action and puts the nozzle of his AK-47 into Echo's mouth.

Arjuna: Bhaisaheb, what should I do with this thing? Should I finish him off bang-bang-bang – but wait a minute, is it in my Karma or no? Is it in my Dharma or no?

Echo: No, it's not, my child.

Arjuna: How do you know?

Echo (smiles sweetly and pulls out a flute): Well, let's put it this way, I'm an authority on the Bhagavad Geeta.

Arjuna: You are, are you? Then help me Swamiji, I'm so confused. To be or not to be ...

Bheem: Arjuna, get rid of that imposter. We have a war on hand. Ah, Nakula and Sahadeva, I was wondering ... instead of Hanumanji, wouldn't it be a good idea to have Schwarzeneggerji as our mascot. That way, we can even get some funds from the World Bank

They exit.

Arjuna: Your wish is my command, Bhaisaheb *(Picks up AK-47, and shoots into Echo's mouth. But nothing happens).*

Echo (in a clipped, artificial tone): For strong, healthy, bullet-proof teeth, drink buttermilk!

Arjuna: Oh God ...

Echo: Yes ...

Arjuna: … Have you heard of Dukha? I'm experiencing that right now.

Echo: My child, have you heard of Nirvana? I'm experiencing that right now.

Arjuna: Duh!

Echo starts to play his flute, softly and melodiously. A pool of light surrounds him as he strikes a classical pose.

Arjuna: What's happening ... ? Ow, my head … it's aching. My mind is spinning. My brains are going soft. Oh no – but what is happening to me? My Vacika is coming back. What a tragedy – I was so happy without talking. So much time to practise my archery. To become better than the best sharpshooter in the world. But no more. Now, it's back to the same routine – arguments with the other Pandavas. Small-talk and chit-chat. Discussions and debates. And above all, the Bhagavad Gita with Krishna. Yes – the very same Bhagavad Gita, which confused me so much that I lost my ability to speak. To speak out my mind ... aaah, my eyes are burning, my body is paining, what is coming over me? It seems I'm being transferred to the battleground of Kurukshetra. To the Mahabharata ...

Pauses

Krishna, my Krishna, can you hear me. If you can, then tell me if you can see the warriors, each one of them arrayed in their fighter planes and battleships. Ready to decimate – all that you have so painstakingly created. It frightens me. My limbs are giving away. My mouth is parched, my heart beats too fast, and my pulse has gone weak. Look … my Gandiva drops from my hands, and my skin burns. Even my mind is confused, and I do not know why I am, what I am ...

I mean, why is it that of all the people on this planet, I had to become a cold-blooded professional killer, a mercenary, a soldier of war. Eager to destroy. Unwilling to create. Imparting sorrow – never joy.

No, Kesava, don't remind me of my Karma, or my Dharma. I

don't understand these words in any case. Especially, if I have to kill my relatives and friends on this planet for them.

You say 'Kill your Brother, if Duty calls, without Passion; as long as you have Faith in Me – all Sins are Forgiven.' But then, isn't that what the history of these lands is about? Brothers, and even fathers and sons, killing each other for a throne. My father Indra smashed his father to death. No one applauded him for his deed. How come? Wasn't my father fulfilling his duty too?

It's all very confusing, Vasudeva! All this talk about using the whip when one is in the driver's seat. Maybe you are able to do it, but then you're a God – Krishna. I'm a mere human being. An ordinary Purusha, who if he kills now – will never derive any joy from it. Death will bestride my soul and haunt me. Why, because I've always been taught that to kill another is a sin. To which, You might say that these people, with minds blinded by greed, do not perceive the evil they are perpetuating, or the evil of their own sins. But then, who am I to judge? To pass judgements? To decide what is right or wrong?

Aaaaah, everything is dimming. Swimming before my eyes. I'm passing out. *(Looking at Echo)* Is that you, My Lord? Why are you smiling so mysteriously? Don't you recognise me – I'm your Partha. Your Arjune ... Oh Lord – everything is blacking out!

Arjuna collapses in a heap – at Echo's feet.

Blackout.

When the lights come on again an agitated Duryodhana is pacing up and down. Karna is watching him with bated breath.

Duryodhana: I don't believe our bad luck. We are going to have a major outbreak of war – and at that precise moment, Dushasana disappears. Such irresponsibility. Doesn't he realise this is a crucial period for us?

Karna: Relax Duryodhana.

Duryodhana: How can I?

Karna: No need to get hassled. Everything is worked out. We have the biggest trump card of the Mahabharata. This time around, there will be no problem.

Duryodhana: Yes, I've heard that refrain. But what use is it? I mean, try as I may. I remember that last time round you were useless even with Indra's Shakti.

Karna: Well ... this time round, we have Sanjaya on our side.

Duryodhana: Big deal, yaar. That guy is just a chota-mota wimp. What can he do? Besides, if I'm not wrong, he was on our side even the last time. Wasn't he the one who told Mummy and Daddy all the occurrences of the Mahabharata because of his Inward Eye.

Karna: Spot on, Duryodhana. He not only told them the occurrences, he controlled public opinion about the war. He influenced them. Helped the masses make up their mind. He shaped and modified their beliefs.

Duryodhana: So what?

Karna: Duryodhana, try to understand. War is not about using brute force or flexing one's muscles. It's all about scheming. About out-manoeuvring the opponent. Being one step ahead of him.

Duryodhana: OK. Point well made. But how does Sanjaya fit into this scheme of things?

Karna: Apply your mind, Duryodhana. Consider: Sanjaya is indebted to your father. A ball-by-ball commentator of the Mahabharata. In fact he has whole-sole rights to the broadcast. No other TV Channel or Radio Station is in the picture. And so, Sanjaya stimulates people into becoming obedient tools. For them he is automatically the Truth. The guiding light. A friend-philospher-and-guide. Why, it is Sanjaya who decides on the President of the US; the Prime Minister of UK.

Duryodhana: Oh Yaara, what rubbish you speak – how can anyone (leave alone Sanjaya) manipulate that? These are democratic countries with proper elections. Not Jharkhand or something.

Karna: Jeez-beez Duryodhana, what you saying maan. Look at the man's track record. He is the Badshah of thought control.

Duryodhana: What control?

Karna: Arrey, it was Sanjaya who gave the Pandavs a huge hype. In his reports, they could do no wrong. Just consider, his reportage about Krishna. We all knew Krishna was singularly ill-suited to propound any moral doctrine. At every crisis in the Mahabharata, Krishna's advice won the day by crooked means. Be it the killing of Bhishma using Shikhandin as a ploy. Or the death of Drona through false information. Why, even I was shot down against the rules of chivalry.

Duryodhana: Yes-yes and what about my thighs being shattered by Bheem's mace – on Krishna's counsel.

Karna: The point-to-be-noted is not once does Sanjaya censure Krishna for his deeds. In fact he justified it at the end of the Shalya Parvan, by stating that to overpower the evil, this was the only method.

Duryodhana: What are you getting at?

Karna: That Sanjaya is a genius. He can make the people believe in anything that he wants them to.

Duryodhana: He can ... ?

Karna: Why, it was he who came up with the concept of Pepsi and Coca Cola as rivals, so that they can monopolise the market share. When in actuality, everyone in the corporate circle knows that Pepsi and Coke are just one and the same company.

Duryodhana: But why would Sanjaya want to be on our side? Is it because he feels he has wronged us. And his conscience wants him to undo past injustices ... ? Or maybe he has read our manifesto ....?

Karna: Don't be naive, Duryodhana. Ideology is never an issue. In fact, it never was. History has taught us that. I mean, no ruler is a ruler because he is just and has a good conscience. If that was really the case, you would never have been a king.

Duryodhana: True. But does Sanjaya know that?

Karna: He does.

Duryodhana: But why will he back us? Or rather why should he ... ?

Karna: Sanjaya will back us because he is being paid to do so. Ten per cent of our spoils – after our win. The deal has been finalised. I recently met him at an Iftaar party and convinced him.

Duryodhana: Very good then. According to him, what is our game plan? A quick guerilla attack. Take the enemy by surprise. And pin them down ...

Karna: Not so fast, dear Duryodhana. We have to redefine our strategy.

Duryodhana: Eh ... what ... ?

Karna: Look it's quite elementary, actually. We are going to have a Mahabharata. That is, a war on an unprecedented scale. To achieve our targets, we need the wholesome support of the people.

Duryodhana: Support of the people, pah! That's impossible. We never had any. In fact, I was always everyone's pet hate.

Karna: Exactly.

Duryodhana: This is hopeless.

Karna: There's no need to despair. The time is apt.

Duryodhana: How do you say that?

Karna: Consider the facts. The population is angry and upset, and despises what is going on. Fortunately, they are also confused, very confused. They want good governments. Growth. Jobs. Progress. But they do not have any coherent ideas on how it should be done. We merely have to shape it for them.

Duryodhana: How?

Karna: Most simple, really. Talk about 'values'. Basically, rake up something which has no meaning, like why trains don't run on time and how the Public Sector is so inept; or better still discuss Indian spiritualism and software industry. Or the greatness of rich and glorious heritage and the ineptness of the political class. People like all this. Moreover, it keeps their minds away from real issues – and creates a favourable climate for us.

Duryodhana: This is quite brilliant. But will it be effective?

Karna: Of course, it will be. These findings are based on an immaculate and well-researched survey, conducted by …

Duryodhana: Oh look, who is here, finally! None other than my dear brother.

Dushasana barges in huffing and puffing. He is very excited.

Dushasana: Bhaiye, have you heard the news?

Duryodhana: No …

Dushasana: The date for the Mahabharata has been announced.

Duryodhana: Already? And without informing me! Those uncouth louts!

Karna: Calm down, Duryodhana. Everything is under control. And in our favour. Come on, you couldn't have forgotten Operation Sanjaya so soon.

Duryodhana: Oh my blessed-wretched amnesia. Yes-O-Yes. Dushasana, you will really freak out when you hear this plan. Come, I'll tell it to you whilst we proceed towards Kurukshetra.

Dushasana: What Kurukshetra?

Duryodhana: Arrey, how can you forget the Kurukshetra? The badshah of all battlegrounds – where the Mahabharata will be fought.

Dushasana: Oh! It seems you haven't heard the other news.

Duryodhana: What be that?

Dushasana: There's been a change of venue. It's now Sharjah.

Blackout.

Roll of drums. The tempo is upbeat. It's all happening – in rap.

Voiceover: Ladies and Gentlemen – how do you do?
Myself Sanjaya – I bring the Mahabharata to you.
Not the whole thing – just a little preview.
So that everyone understands the basic issues
This epic *Mahabharata* is between two sides
One big family which is ready to fight
For their maan maryada. For their sovereign rights

Now, Lightman, can we have some lights?

And then there are Lights.

The Pandavs and Kauravs are at the venue in their outfits. Staring eyeball to eyeball.

Voicever: Way to go – this is the Pitch
The wicket is good. And there is no hitch
The money is good – the stakes are a bitch
And either way – everyone will be rich.
So ... trill the trumpets and let the conches blow
For the Shubh Muhurat of our Bloody Show
The theme of the setting has already been set
The Maha-Mahabharata between friend and foe!
Let there be blood. Let there be bones
The losers will groan. The winners will moan
Everyone will try to safeguard their lives
As told by their mothers and wives.

Chaos on stage. Even as the Pandavs and Kauravs attempt to out-shout each other. Waving flags. Breathing heavily. Making faces. Forming military formations.

Just then Gandhari and Draupadi dash onto the stage.

Gandhari and Draupadi: Stop this War!

On seeing Gandhari and Draupadi, each of the other characters on the stage react 'Maate/Moms/Aunty' OR 'Draupadi/Panchali/Tu/Draupi Babe'.

Gandhari: That's right boys. And Draupadi and I beseech you, nay order you, to halt this stupid war, here and now.

Draupadi: Yes, we may not have been able to do a thing the last time. And we regret it. But this time we will not permit this unnecessary bloodshed and loss of innocent lives.

Nakula: How dare these women interfere in our war!

Dushasana: Their rightful place is in the kitchen.

Sahadeva: In the bedroom.

Karna: On the pyre.

Gandhari (bellowing): Sarvanaash – Termination – Apocalypse – Pralay – Termination. I give birth to you, and instead of sons, you behave like sins!

Duryodhana: Hush mother, hush! You're raving like a lunatic.

Bheem (overlapping): Ladies, ladies. Be patient. There is a time and place for everything. Even you ladies will have your moment of glory during the Stree Parvan.

Duryodhana: Yes, yes ... the all-important eleventh book of the 18 books in the Mahabharata – during which you womenfolk can come to the battlefield and lament.

Dushasana: Cry and wail. Shout and faint.

Nakula: Beat your chest. Break bangles.

Karna: Burn your jewellery and clothes. Tear your hair off. And starve for days.

Sahadeva: O yes! Imagine what fun you can have!

Draupadi (pause): Stop khus-phusing stereotypical male responses to each other. We are here to change your decision, and let us hear it.

Bheem: Draupi babe, with due respects to you, we have to go on.

Duryodhana: The Mahabharata is the Mahabharata.

Nakula: It's written in our bhagya. In our karma.

Sahadeva: The izzat of our khandaan depends on it.

Draupadi: Bleh! What do you have to say about this, Arjune?

Arjuna: Duh?

Gandhari (clapping): Ah, that's the most sensible thing I've heard since stepping on this battleground.

Duryodhana: Don't you dare denigrate us, Mama, with your superior attitude!

Gandhari: Hee hee hee. Do not wallow in any such false hopes, because we'll denigrate anything and everything, over and over again, especially if it is in the common good of mankind.

Bheem: With due apologies, Gandhari Aunty, what would you and Draupi Babe know about 'man' kind.

Gandhari: A lot. If you care to recollect I mothered one hundred uncaring male children.

Draupadi: And I have five uncaring men for husbands.

Karna: Bug and humbug. These women are dangerous. Evil sorceresses with diabolic designs! We will have to destroy them. Decimate their thoughts. Disintegrate their being.

Pandavs and Kauravs: Yeah yeah. Can't let the women get out of hand, and all. If you do, they start poking their nose in everything. How can we do our work then. Chee chee. What will our dead ancestors say.

Pause

Gandhari: This is it!

Duryodhana: What, mama?

Gandhari: Long enough have we had to endure this kind of boorish behaviour.

Draupadi: Praise be to Kali Mata! You're absolutely right.

Gandhari: I think the time is opportune.

Draupadi: And so is the venue.

Gandhari: To declare the launch of a new front. The Third Force.

Draupadi: With Gandhariji as Captain.

Gandhari: And Draupadi as Vice Captain.

Bheem: What utter rubbish. How can you form a Third Force?

Draupadi: Why not?

Dushasana: Hey hey hey! There is no mention of it in the Mahabharata.

Gandhari: Ha-ha. Which version of the Mahabharata do you speak of? The one with 8800 slokas? Or the one with 24,000 verses?

Draupadi: I hear there's one Mahabharata with over a lakh verses, which deals with all the subjects there is to be dealt with on

Prithvi. In that, there is a mention of the Third Front, methinks. 'Gandhari Third Front Zindabad. Baki Sab Kuch Murdabad.'

Chaos on stage. Slogan shouting. Pumping of fists. Even as the Pandavs, Kauravs and Third Front attempt to outshout each other. Waving flags. Breathing heavily. Making faces. Forming military formations.

The Writer darts in. He is accompanied by a constable – with a peacock feather in his hair. No one notices them.

Writer: Here, didn't I tell you? They are preparing for the Mahabharata.

Constable: But Saheb, how can I, a petty Constable, stop the Mahabharata?

Writer: You are the law. You must do something.

Constable: Saheb, this is not my jurisdiction. Moreover, you haven't even filed an FIR.

Writer: Oh this is hopeless. *(Barges on to the stage)* In the name of the law, I say, stop this lunacy.

Duryodhana: Oh look, who is here!

Gandhari: Oh no – it's that writer fellow again!

Karna: Duryodhana – shall I decimate him and his entire tribe once and for all?

Dushasana: Yes, yes. Bhaiye, all our problems are his fault. Everything was OK, till this chap came along with his writings ...

Writer: Ha! I am not frightened by your threats. I'm a writer and I'll fight with my pen ... which is far more powerful than your swords.

Once again, chaos on stage. Slogan shouting. Pumping of fists. Even as the Pandavs, Kauravs and Third Front attempt to frighten Writer. Waving flags. Breathing heavily. Making faces. Forming military formations.

The Constable tries to attract their attention, but he is not noticed. He pulls out his flute, and plays a note on his flute. Everyone freezes.

Constable (addressing the audience): Oh oh oh. Problems. Big problems. Namaskaram, my children. This address is to seek your assistance. A last-ditch effort. As you are well aware, things are not going well on 'this' planet ... the story has gone haywire. And totally topsy turvy.

You know, in the beginning, it didn't seem that way. Quite harmless. A bit of wholesome fun, if you ask me, but as things progressed, things got worse and worse. And what bothers me is the fact that everyone – these actors, the characters, you, the audience, the critics – everyone thinks I'm really responsible for this mess.

I mean, I shouldn't be admitting this, but nothing was in my control. You all saw that. The story plotted its own course. The characters decided their own future. Why goodness me, even I'm mouthing someone else's lines.

Not any more. Enough of all that stuff and nonsense about Ved Vyasa and Pandavs and Kauravs. From hereon, I take the reins into my own hands. Erect my own observatory. An observatory through which you will watch the end of the play.

What's that you said? Who am I? Well, can't you guess? Oh, you say I haven't introduced myself. Good Lord! Are the times so bad that even I need an introduction?

The Constable snaps his finger. Everyone comes to Life.

Constable: Ha-ha, Watch the fun. Now.

Arjuna: Er .... duh ... duh ... his face it is so familiar ...

Dushasana: Yes, yes ... it's someone well known. Oh, who can it be?

Draupadi: Jai Om Yama. It's Dharmaraja. King Yudhishthira.

Nakula: Dharmaraja, shame on me, for not recognising you.

Karna: I didn't recognise you either.

Writer: Yes, yes ... that's the tragedy of Dharma.

The Constable plays a note on his flute. Everyone freezes.

Constable: Well. Well. Well. The time has come to move this story forward. I mean, we can skip the hello-how-do-you-do, the wining and dining or any other discussions which the re-united family might conduct. Such as what, you might ask? Oh, the commonplace things which everyone discusses. Like, why are the problems of this country so insoluble? Why is it so ungovernable?

Hmmm. The perils of existence. It's tough, you might say. Our future, they say, is with the collective, but our survival is with the individual, and this paradox is slowly killing all of us.

But let's not deviate any further. And get back to the scene of action. Watch the fun!!!

The Constable plays a note on his flute. Everyone springs to life.

Writer: I've an offer for all of you *(pulls out a pack of cards, and in same tone as earlier)* Hi guys, would you be interested in a game of cards, perchance?

Duryodhana: Yes, yes, why not, my good Yudhishthira. What are the stakes?

Writer: You mean, you want to bet?

Duryodhana: That's exactly what I mean.

Writer: OK, so what do you have to offer?

Duryodhana: The services of the two greatest warriors of our times, Karna and Dushasana, for the next 365 days.

Writer: I think the stakes are too low.

Duryodhana: Why, what do you want?

Writer: The services of both you and your two greatest warriors to serve peace, Shanti, for the next 365 days.

Durodhana: Granted. But if you lose, all that you have, will be mine. Your name, your fame, your wealth, your kingdom, your brothers, your wife ...

Draupadi: No, not me. I refuse to be a part of all this.

Writer: Arrey why?

Draupadi: I will not let our mistakes be repeated.

Gandhari: Vetoed.

Draupadi: Gandhariji!

Gandhari: Yes, I hereby announce that for the common good of Mother Earth, we have formed an alliance with the Pandavs. *Yudh karo*, Yudhishthira.

Writer: Thank you ladies. OK, it's a deal, Duryodhana. Let's play.

Duryodhana: Wait, before we begin, let me inform you, in case you haven't realised that my Uncleji will play for me …

Writer: Your Uncleji, but ...

Duryodhana: It's a part of the Agreement.

Writer: What Agreement?

Karna: (brandishes a legal document): In the small print. For your eyes only, he-he-he!

Writer: What is the meaning of this … ?

Dushasana: A deal is a deal, Dharmaraja. Although you can still back out.

Writer: No, do carry on. In spite of the heavy odds, someplace-somewhere I know that Satyamev will finally be Vijayi.

Duryodhana whistles for Uncle. Eerie music, superseded by an evil cackle. Uncle enters on his tricycle. Duryodhana, Dushasana and Karna salute him.

Duryodhana: Salutations Uncleji, I salute you.

Uncle: Asheerwadams Bhanje … today there seems to be a big audience, lots of familiar faces, what's happening Bhanje?

Duryodhana: History is repeating itself, Uncleji.

Uncle: What do I have to do, in these changed circumstances?

Duryodhana: Play a game of cards, and win everything that I ever wanted.

Uncle: Is that all. Your wish is my command. Bhanje.

Writer: Just a minute, Duryodhana, I think there is a misunderstanding here.

Duryodhana: What misunderstanding … ?

Writer: According to the rules of our Agreement, the winner of the card game is the Real Loser of our game. While the loser of the card game is the Real Winner of our game.

Karna: Says who …?

Writer: It's a part of the Agreement.

Dushasana: What Agreement?

Writer: (brandishes a legal document): In the small print. For your eyes only, he-he-he!

Uncle: Bhanje, what is the meaning of this? Is he speaking the truth?

Duryodhana: What kind of question is that, don't you know that Yudhishthira speaks only the truth.

Uncle: Then what do we do … ?

Duryodhana: Obviously, we go ahead with the game.

Uncle: But we will lose!

Duryodhana: Good, that's what I want.

*Uncle:*No, Bhanje, you fail to understand. I will win the game of cards, and so we will be the Real Losers.

Duryodhana: How …. why…. then why don't you lose the game of cards?

Uncle: Don't you recollect, that once-upon-upon-a-time, long-long ago I received a boon that I could never lose at a game of cards.

Writer: And Duryodhana, don't you recollect, that quite similarly I had been cursed that I could never win at a game of cards.

Duryodhana: Oh no!

Writer: Oh yes, let's play!

The game of cards is played.

The Constable plays a note on his flute. Everyone freezes.

Constable: Well then, that is that. Nothing more. Nothing less. What will transpire tomorrow – nobody knows. No, not even me. Oh yes, there is tremendous confusion and chaos. All of mankind is bewildered.

According to my reports, all this chaos and confusion has been initiated by the cast, backstage crew and audience of a spurious, non-Shakespearean natak 'Shanti, Shanti, It's a War'. If that is the case, it's not good for the Karma of the Universe.

For according to my sources, the Gods and the Devas are really upset. So are the Rakshasas and Yakshas. Even the authorities have initiated a Joint Committee probe into the matter.

Meanwhile the question on everyone's lips is: Who will decide the future of this planet? Will it be the Pandavs? Or will it be the Kauravs? Or will it be a Tie ... you know, a Hung Parliament? So far, no one has been able to resolve this dilemma. In case any of you know the correct answers to this question, please let me know. I'll suitably reward you with a matka of makhkhan. Avjo!

The Constable pulls out his flute and plays a melodious tune. And exits.

Meanwhile a soft chant of 'Shanti-Shanti', counterposed with 'It's a War', builds up and reaches a crescendo.

And then, curtains.

The Boy Who Stopped Smiling

Dedicated to BABA (PRABHAKAR SATHE) for having sold hundreds and hundreds of tickets of this play, before he passed away

Playwright/director: Ramu Ramanathan

Producer: Sanjna Kapoor

Cast: Jaimini Pathak, Divya Jagdale, Nilufer Uchil, Lata Sharma, Shivkumar Subhrahmanyam, Joy Fernandes

Music: Rajat Dholakia

Keyboard: Sanjay Pandya

Lyrics: Naushil Mehta, Ramu Ramanathan

Set Design: Mihir Thakker

Light Design: Sunil Shanbag

Light Operator: Tarannum

Costumes and Production Incharge: Kinnari Vohra

Backstage: Kshipra Jain, Preeti Gaonkar

Photography and Publicity Design: Vinit and Manish

Special Thanks: Shrirang Godbole, Naseeruddin Shah, Mohan Agashe, Sataydev Dubey

The stage should contain a mix of stylistic symbols. The stage furniture should be a playful mix of three-dimensional creations consisting of isosceles triangles, hexagons and circles. Bright colours should be used with a dab of yellow: other example, a massive chess board on a red-black carpet; or a multi-purpose tree that could be used as a black-board.

The stage space is defined into four zones: indoor, outdoor, family space and Malhar's space.

ACT I SCENE 1

The play begins with an upbeat song about The Boy Who Stops Smiling

Rum-Pum-Pum
Pa-Pa-Purum-Pum
Rum-Pum-Pum
Pa-Pa-Purum-Pum

Some little boys are very bad
Some little boys are boring
Some little boys copy their dad
Whenever they are snoring ...

Rum-Pum-Pum
Pa-Pa-Purum-Pum
Rum-Pum-Pum
Pa-Pa-Purum-Pum

Some little boys they love to laugh
Some are always smiling
This is the story of a little boy
The boy who stopped smiling (repeat)

So clap-clap-clap your hands
And tap-tap-tap your feet
When you get ready to meet
When you get ready to greet
The Boy Who Stopped Smiling

Rum-Pum-Pum
Pa-Pa-Purum-Pum
Rum-Pum-Pum
Pa-Pa-Purum-Pum

So clap-clap-clap your hands
And tap-tap-tap your feet (repeat)

This is little Malhar
Not so little by far
Every once in a while
Wonder why he doesn't smile
Why he doesn't smile (repeat)

Rum-Pum-Pum
Pa-Pa-Purum-Pum
Rum-Pum-Pum
Pa-Pa-Purum-Pum

Outside the door, Ashwini and Mallika are playing hopscotch and getting on each other's nerves. Inside the house, Mother is folding napkins, etc., but also listening to the children.

Mallika: Hey! hey! You are out. You are totally out. LBW. Clean bowled.

Ashwini: No-no. You are telling lies.

Mallika (screams): Mummy! Mummy! Look, Ashwini is cheating. *(Sticks her tongue out and makes faces.)* Cheater-pop! Cheater-pop!

Ashwini (retaliating): Aaah aaah ha. You're nothing but a big grand-pop!

Mallika (fake bawling): Mummy! Mummy! Mummy! Look, Ashwini is bullying me ... !

Ashwini (teasing): Mummy, mummy; there is a hole in Mallika's tummy. (*Repeats*)

Mother comes to the door

Mother (falsely stern): Ashwini! I heard that. You must not say such things. After all, Mallika is your friend, no?

Ashwini: But Aunty, I wasn't being nasty. In fact Mallika is behaving like a sissy girl ...

Mallika: You must be a sissy. Mummy, Mummy ... look she called me sissy girl!

Ashwini and Mallika indulge in cross-talk which gradually rises to a crescendo

Mother (hands over ears): Silence! Hush! Ram bhagwaan, can I not have some peace in this house. All the time *khit-khit*. Momma this ... Aunty that ... Oooof – it's getting too much!

Mallika: But Momma ... it was she ... who started all this. I was toh only playing by myself. Why does she always have to poke her nose in my games?

Ashwini: Pah! Silly girlie game!

Mallika: You keep quiet, snot-face! I'm talking to Momma.

Ashwini: Eh, you shaddup, big-mouth. I called Aunty first.

Mallika: So what? She is my Momma!

Ashwini: Chee-chee, she will never want to be the 'momma' of such a boring girl.

Mallika: If I'm boring – then you are ugly. The most ugly girl in the colony. You can never be like Aishwarya Rai.

Ashwini (bawling): Aunty, Aunty, look what she said!

Mallika: But Momma, she started it. You saw it.

Ashwini: If you say such things about me, I'll ... I'll put cockroaches in your hair *(she pulls out a plastic cockroach from her socks).*

Mallika: Cockroaches ... *(lets out a wail)* Momma! Momma!

Mother: OK. Enough is enough! Can I have some silence here? Ooof! Today is Tuesday ... and I'm praying for Malhar ... and I don't want any noise from this room till it is over.

Mallika (sniffing): But Momma ...

Mother (overlaps): Not a syllable. From either of you. For the next 10 minutes – no *awaaz.* No running around. Just sit in one place till I tell you to.

Mallika: Chee yaar. Sitting in one place and doing nothing ... so borrrring, yaar!

Mother: Mallika! What did I just say? No noise. And I'm serious.

Mother exits. Silence. Mallika and Ashwini, very petulantly ***don't*** *look at each other. Mallika continues to sulk. Until ...*

Ashwini (in a whisper): Mallika, Mallika. Your Momma is so strict, no?

Silence – during which Mallika makes a face.

Ashwini: Mallika, Mallika, are you angry with me or what? *(Pause)* Are you *Katti* with me? Oh. But I'm *Batti* with you.

Mallika: Why?

Ashwini: You're my best friend, no. That's why.

Mallika: Really?

Ashwini: Yeah, yeah. God promise.

Mallika: Oh. Then will you let me have two-two turns while playing?

Ashwini (reluctantly): O-K.

Mallika and Ashwini start to play. Even as the two girls get engrossed in their game – Malhar trudges out. He is preoccupied. He sucks on his thumb, and draws patterns on the ground with his big toe.

Ashwini (nudging Mallika): ... Look, look, look ... your brother has come ...

Mallika (playing hopscotch): Hmmm. Leave him alone ...

Ashwini: Cheee! Look, he is sucking his thumb. So *gandhoo*, no?

Mallika: Malhar is like that only. Ignore him ...

Ashwini: Hi Malhar!

No response from Malhar. Uncomfortable silence.

Ashwini: Hi Malhar?

Malhar: Ummmm *(thumb in mouth, staccato speech).* Palaeolithic.

Ashwini: What?

Malhar: P-A-L-A-E-O-L-I-T-H-I-C.

Ashwini: Oh, I see ...

Malhar (stuttering): Early hominids ... known ... known as Australopithecines. A-U-S-T-R-A-L-O-P-I-T-H-E-C-I-N-E-S.

Ashwini (whispering to Mallika): Eh ... Mallika ... what's he saying? Is he mad or what?

Malllika: Arrey, don't give him any bhav. He likes to show off ... !

Malhar (digging his nose): Homo erectus ... known as ... as ... Pithecanthropus.

Mallika: Malhar! Stop digging your nose.

Malhar: Hmmmmm.

Mallika: It's bad manners.

Malhar: Hmmmm.

Ashwini: Eh ... he's so weird, reh. I've never seen him talk, or play ...

Mallika: Oh ... yeah-yeah ...

Malhar: Palaeolithic to hate talking. Australopithecines to hate playing. Malhar to hate talking-playing.

Ashwini: What!!!

But Malhar continues to dig his nose.

Mallika: Malhar, stop giving uncle-talks! And stop digging your nose!

Malhar (digging his nose): Ummm.

Mallika: Malhar? What are you doing ... ?

Malhar (Pauses, thinks, takes a deep breath and then blurts out): Malhar is ... is ... examining ... nasal cavity in ... vertebrate ... to understand how air ... sent to ... lungs ... and smell to ... to ... olfactory nerves.

Ashwini: What? Arrey! What's he saying – all these big-big words?

Mallika: He's like that only. Just acting smart. You don't look at him.

Ashwini: Oh!

Ashwini tries to be involved in the game of hopscotch – but she is very self-conscious with Malhar in the vicinity.

Malhar: Hmmm. Play ... game like ... quadrumanous.

Ashwini: What?

Malhar: Q-U-A-D-R-U-M-A-N-O-U-S ... four-handed primates ... *(demonstrates)* Play game ... like this ...

Malhar pushes Mallika, who falls down with a squeal

Mallika: Malhar – don't trouble us. You better leave us alone. OK?

Malhar: O-K-A-Y.

Mallika: I'll tell Momma that you're disturbing our game. *(Stomps off)*

Malhar (withdraws): Hmmm.

Ashwini: Er ... would you like to play with us?

Malhar: Pah!

Ashwini: What do you mean ... Pah!

Malhar: Pah!

Ashwini: Why? Do you think this is a stupid game? Tell, tell.

Malhar: Y-E-S.

Ashwini: What utter rubbish! Hopscotch is the best game in the world.

Malhar: Hmmmm.

Ashwini: Hmmmm??? What is the meaning of 'Hmmmmm'?

Malhar: Ashwini is ... Ashwini is ... Korchnoi.

Ashwini: What!!!

Malhar: K-O-R-C-H-N-O-I- ...

Mallika returns

Ashwini: Mallika – look he is giving dirty-dirty bad words.

Mallika: Malhar???

Malhar: Ummmm.

Ashwini: Imagine, he called me a Korchnoi. My god, nobody has ever called me a Korchnoi.

Mallika: Malhar – say sorry to Ashwini.

Malhar (pokes his finger into his nose): Ummmmm.

Mallika: ... or I'll tell Momma. *(Calling out)* Momma.

Mallika stomps off again

Ashwini: Yeah, yeah – we'll tell Aunty. Malhar – you better tell sorry.

Malhar: Hmmmm. S-O-R-R-Y.

Ashwini: No. No. Properly.

Malhar: Hmmmm.

Malhar with finger in the nose, walks upto Ashwini. A beat. ... Then Malhar scratches Ashwini, who screams. Mallika joins her. On cue Malhar covers his ears and doubles up. He moans. In a flash Mother and Mallika rush out.

Mother: Arrey baba, what happened? What's all this noise and voice?

Mallika: Momma – Malhar scratched Ashwini.

Ashwini: Yeah, yeah *(sniffles)* ... In fact, aunty, if you had not come, he was going to kill me. Murder me till I was dead *(bawls).*

Mother: Malhar – what have you done to Ashwini? Hmmm? Come on tell me ...

Ashwini: Arrey Aunty, I'll tell you. Like a mad man, he attacked me. (*Snarls*) I'm telling you, Aunty you must send him to Thane Mental Hospital. To Agra ...

Mallika: Yes Momma, you must do something about Malhar.

Malhar has doubled up – and with chin on knee, he is making whimpering sounds.

Mother: Malhar – this is not a good thing to do. Come on – say sorry to Ashwini.

Ashwini: (*overlapping*): Oh no-no-no. What is the need of sorry and all, Aunty. I don't want a sorry.

Mother: Arrey – why?

Ashwini (*touching her scratched visage*): Oh – you know ...

Mallika: Yeah-yeah. Because – when you tell Malhar to tell sorry – he scratches people on their faces.

Mother: Malhar! What is it that Ashwini and Mallika are saying ... ?

Malhar is still doubled up and whimpering.

Malhar: Korchnoi ... not ... dirty word. Korchnoi ... name of ... chess player – who nobody likes.

Mallika (giggles): Look-look ... he is talking all nonsense again –

Ashwini (holding her face): Ow' my face ... !

Mother (to Ashwini): Show me, show me. Oh-oh-oh. Beta, this is only a small injury.

Ashwini: Oh, you can say that, Aunty, but I know that I'm going to die.

Mother: No beta, you are not going to die. You're completely alright.

Ashwini: Yeah, yeah. You'll say that – after all he is your son. You should have seen the way, he tried to kill me. He is my enemy, you know.

Mother: Beta, I'll punish Malhar for that ...

Ashwini: Oh ... it is hurting ... Ow-ow-ow ... I think I'm going to have a heart attack. I better go home.

Malhar: Korchnoi ... not ... dirty word. Korchnoi ... name of ... chess player – who nobody likes.

Mallika (giggling): Look, look – he is talking to himself again.

Ashwini: Your brother is so weird, reh. I'm leaving ...

Ashwini exits. Malhar watches her from the corner of his eyes. A beat.

Mother: Oooof, what am I going to do with this boy?

Mallika: Momma, Momma. Why don't you send Malhar to a boarding school?

Mother: Mallika!

Mallika: Or put him in a jail?

Mother: Mallika, don't you dare say such foolish things.

Malhar (staring into space): Hmmm. Hmmmmmmm.

Mallika: Look look, Momma – he has started again ...

Mother: What, beta?

Malhar: Mikhail Botvinnik. Staunton. Gufeld. Kalinchenko. Alekhine. Mikhalchishin.

Mallika: Eh? What nonsense is he blabbering?

Malhar: Mikhalchishin. Farago. Steinitz. Philidor. Emanuel Lasker. Van Hest. Sosonko.

Mother: Malhar … beta … are you alright?

Even as the Mother tries to console Malhar he lets out a sharp yelp. Mallika giggles. Malhar yelps and then runs away in a floppy, clumsy, way. Mother looks worried.

Malhar (offstage): … Vasili Smyslov. Bobby Fischer. Tigran Petrosian. Boris Spassky. Anatoly Karpov. Gary Kasparov.

Just then the doorbell rings. It is Father at the door. The doorbell rings again.

A pause. Then Mother opens the door.

Mother: Arrey arrey, what a pleasant surprise ji! Home early today? How come? *Naukri chod toh nahin diya, na?*

Mallika (dancing up and down): Daddy has come *(repeats several times).*

Father (irritably): Oooodi Baba – it is so hot outside! Can you make the fan any faster ... Oooof!

Mother: Mallika, go get your daddy some sherbet.

Mallika: Shheeee yaar – so boring!

Mother: Mallika!

Mallika: OK Momma. Which sherbet will you have, Daddy? Lime, orange, mango, strawberry … or a little bit of whiskey sherbet ... ?

Mother: Mallika!

Father: Oh come on. Let her be.

Mother: Yes, yes. That's all very fine for you to say. But I've to live with the two of them the whole day. As it is things are hell. On top of that, these vacations. My God, not a moment of rest! All the time … Momma this or Mummy that.

Mallika exits. A beat.

Father (stretching): And what about our little champion? What has he been doing?

Mother: Troubling me. And bothering his sister! What else?

Father: What has he done – today?

Mother: He scratched Ashwini on the face.

Father: Hmmmm.

Mother: Kyon ji, when will our Malhar beta become alright?

Father: In due course of time. This is just a passing phase ...

Mother: You know ji, it's been six months since Malhar has stopped smiling. Oh, it's been such a long time since I've heard him laugh.

Father: Did he eat anything today?

Mother (clucking her tongue): Arrey, not a single bite.

Father: And did he go to sleep?

Mother: Not at all. Hey Lord Vigneshwara, please save my child. Hey Vinayaka, remove all obstacles. Hey Gajanana, rescue my Malhar from the dark pitfalls of hell ...

Father: Relax. Everything is going to be fine.

Just then, there is a blood-curdling scream from Mallika offstage.

Father: What's that ... ?

Mother: It's Mallika! I hope Malhar hasn't done something to her ... !

Father: Mallika? What happened ... ?

Mother: Arrey beta – are you alright?

Mother exits in a hurry. On cue Malhar enters.

Malhar (unconcerned – makes patterns in the air): Tigran Petrosian. Boris Spassky. Antoly Karpov. Gary Kasparov.

Father: Hello – Malhar.

Malhar: Vishwanathan Anand. A-N-A-N-D.

Father: How are you?

Malhar: Y-O-U ....

Father (*distracted*): What are you saying – Malhar .... WHAT?

(*Malhar pauses, looks at the floor, points at it – and tries to formulate words*) Malhar, Longest game ... immortal ... game ... in Belgrade ... between Nikolic ... and Arsovic ... of ... of 296 moves ...

Mallika and Mother enter.

Mother (petulant with rage): Wonderful. Oh Lord Ganesha – only you can save this household.

Father: What has happened, dear?

Mallika: Daddy, the fridge ...

Father: What about it … has it broken down again? Oh no – it must be that fuse thing again. Don't worry, I'll call the mechanic and have it fixed.

Mother: No ji. There is nothing wrong with the fridge. It is our Karma, our fate which is skewed.

Father: What do you mean – please be more specific. You are talking in riddles.

Mother: Why don't you ask your *laadla* what his latest *kaarnama* has been?

Father: What?

Mother: Ask the little devil? Ask him, just ask him!

Father (sighs): Now, what have you done, Malhar?

Malhar (twisting his fingers into a knot makes an unidentifiable sound): DUYEVBDN.

Father: Tell me, why is your mother so upset?

Mother: Upset? I'm going crazy with this boy.

Father (to Mother): Shhhhh. *(To Malhar)* Tell me beta, what is the matter?

Mother: Pah. Troubling everybody all the time. Tell me ji, what face am I going to show Ashwini's mother?

Father: Malhar. Tell me what happened. Come on, quickly, before I count ten. One … two … three … four … five .. six …

Mallika: Daddy, Daddy, I'll tell you.

Mother: Mallika ...

Mallika: Malhar has taken out everything from the fridge – and put his chess-board and chess-pieces there.

Father: He has put his what ... ?

Mother: You heard what Mallika said. Your darling Malhar has taken out everything from the fridge. Now, tell me what do you intend to do ...

Father (laughing): Hey bhagwaan – did you really do this – you *budmaash*!

Mother: Hain ji – stop laughing – OK. All my vegetables are spoilt. My milk has gone sour. Our *raat ka khaana* has been sabotaged and you find it funny? *Hain ji*, what kind of example are you setting for the kids? *Hain*!

Father: I'm sorry, but ...

Mother: No, this won't do. It just won't. Where is that encyclopaedia-set you bought for Malhar ... ? It is no longer for him – but for Mallika. OK?

Mallika: But – I don't want an encyclopaedia-set, Mummy.

Mother: You will have to have it. It's an order.

Mallika: OK, Mummy.

Mother: And young lady, what are you expected to say when someone gives you a present?

Mallika (petulantly): Sorry!

Father: Mallika!

Mallika (sullenly): Thank you.

Mother: And no more chess for you, Mr Genius. Instead, you will go for your swimming classes – as you have been told. Will you or won't you?

Malhar mumbles.

Mother: Speak up! I can't hear you.

Malhar (under his breath): SJKBHJISD.

Mother: Eh? What?

Malhar (sucks his thumb): Hmmmmmm.

Pause.

Mother: Hai Bhagwaan, now he has put that stupid thumb into that stupid mouth of his ...

Father: Relax dear. You are over-reacting ...

Mother: Achcha? Then in that case, you take care of your boy. OK. Frankly, I don't understand him – or how to deal with him!

Father: Look, I've spoken to Dr Bhuskute about Malhar. He'll be coming home tomorrow.

Mother: Arrey, forget your doctor and all. Now, even Brahma can't save this boy. Oooof. I'm really fed up ...

Mother exits.

Mallika: Momma. Momma, where are you going? Listen to me, I don't want that encyclopaedia-set ... Momma. Instead ... why don't you take me to Fantasy Land.

Mallika dashes after Mother. Silence as Father gazes dreamily at Malhar, who has curled up into a ball.

Father (sighing): Malhar beta, why do you do these things? Why?

Malhar: Hmmmmm. Anderssen ... versus ... versus ... Kieseritsky ... in ... in ... the King's Bishop Gambit ...

Father: Oh, you and your chess ... !

Malhar: C-H-E-S-S ...

Father: Yes – you and your chess.

Malhar (peering through his fingers curled to imitate binoculars) Chess. Hmmmm. Kovacevic ... versus ... versus ... Djuric ... in the ... the ... Sicilian Defence ... with ... with ... poisoned pawn.

Father: But beta, this just won't do.

Malhar: Sendur ... versus ... versus ... Kasparov ... King's Indian Defence

Father (*straining to hear*): What? King's Indian Defence!

Malhar: Y-E-S.

Father: And why did Malhar put the chess-board in the fridge?

Malhar: Hmmm.

Father: Why?

Malhar: Malhar to prepare ... secret ... secret ... new moves for chess match with Vishwanathan Anand.

Father: Anand! Oh!

Malhar: Malhar to practice very ... very hard ... Two Knight's Defence. The Ruy Lopez Opening. Pirc-Ufimstev Gambit. Dragon Variation. Nimzo-Indian Defence ...

Father: What all do you possess in that little head of yours?

Malhar (holding his breath): Demolition Sacrifice at KR7 ... Nimzowitch Opening ... and Reti Opening ... Grunfeld Defence ... and ... and ... Alekine Defence ... and ... Sicilian Defence ...

Father: Enough, beta ... enough ...

Malhar: Sicilian Defence ... One: P-K4; P-QB4. Two: N-KB3; P-K3. Three: P-Q4; PxP. Four: NxP; P-QR3. Five: N-QB3 ....

Father: Malhar ... Malhar ... what is happening ... ?

Malhar: Malhar ... versus ... Anand ... King's Knight Opening ...

Father (laughs – and fondles Malhar's hair): Malhar versus Anand! Arrey beta, stop dreaming ...

Father sighs and then exits silently. Malhar stands up and communes with the imaginary chess-board on the floor. A lone spotlight focuses on him. A game of chess has begun with Vishwanathan Anand. Malhar makes the first move – and starts to sing a chess-song.

Akaram-Pakarum-Rum-Pum-Pum
Chakarum-Pakarum-Rum-Pum-Pum
In the middle of the night
When things are quiet
I play chess
C-H-E-S-S
YES.
I play chess

Akaram-Pakarum-Rum-Pum-Pum
Chakarum-Pakarum-Rum-Pum-Pum
Exchange my pawn
Castle my rook
Rum-pum-bum
Tara-rum-pum-dum
Move my bishop
Bum-bum

Trap your king
Run-run
Yes. Run. Run. Run.
Yeah. Run-Run-Run.

ACT I SCENE 2

Malhar and Mallika's house. It is Sunday morning. Father is reading a newspaper. Mallika is noisily playing by herself.

Father: Sssssh beta. *(Mallika continues to play noisily.)* Mallika!

Mallika: Huh? What?

Father: Will you be silent? I'm trying to read the newspaper ... !

Mallika: But, Papa you're always reading the newspaper. Yesterday. Day before yesterday ...

Father: Mallika!

Mallika: And the day before the day before yesterday ...

Father: Mallika!!

Mallika: And you're always telling me to be quiet ...

Father: Be quiet Mallika!!! Shhhhh! Two-minute silence. Finger-on-the-lips.

Mallika: But Papa ...

Father: And right now!

Mallika reluctantly places her finger on her lips. Ashwini saunters in melodramatically with a bandage on her face.

Father (aside): Oh no!

Ashwini: Good morning Mallika. Good morning Uncle.

Father: Good morning beta.

Mallika (with finger-on-the-lips and in hushed whispers): Arrey – it's not a good morning for me ...

Ashwini: Oh! Why?

Mallika: My Papa is bullying me, yaar.

Ashwini: Oh really, how interesting, yaar ... Actually, my morning is also not great.

Mallika: Why? Is your Papa also bullying you?

Ashwini (fiddling with the bandage on her face): No reh. Doctor's told me I can't play ...

Mallika: OK. Don't.

Ashwini: Actually … I'm not feeling very good.

Mallika: Oh? Why?

Ashwini: Arrey, can't you see?

Mallika: What?

Ashwini: This big hurt on my face.

Mallika (amused): Big hurt ... ?

Ashwini: Yeah yeah ... serious injury because of Malhar. The doctor was saying it was a matter of life and death.

Mallika: Really?

Ashwini: Arrey, all kinds of infection, you know. Tetanus. Sinus. Uranus. Everything ... doctor had to perform a big operation. A surgery with an injection. In fact, the injection was this big ... *(she stretches her arms wide apart to indicate the size of the injection)*

Mallika: Chal chal! Big lies. I've never seen such a big injection.

Ashwini: Oh – this was an imported injection.

Mallika: Achcha ...

Ashwini: Look, look – over here ... *(peels the bandage)* ... all marks.

Mallika (peering): Where? Where? I can't see anything?

Ashwini: In fact, Daadi was saying, now it is going to be very difficult to get a good boy to marry me. Correct, no?

Mallika: No-no – I don't think so ...

Ashwini: Meaning ... ?

Mallika: Why-why-why – I know a boy who is willing to marry you!

Ashwini: Who, who, who? Tell, no? Is it – Virat Kohli? Yuvraj Singh? Oh, I'm so excited.

Mallika: Hmmmm. This boy is in love with you.

Ashwini: Oh? Tell me no, who is it?

Mallika: He is madly in love with you.

Ashwini: How do you know?

Mallika: One day he told me that of all the beautiful girls in the world, the best is Ashwini.

Ashwini: Really ... ?

Mallika: Yes, yes.

Ashwini: But what's his name?

Mallika: Come here. *(Whispers in her ear)* Apna Malhar.

Ashwini (screams): Malhar! You're cracked or what?

Mallika: Arrey no baba, Malhar was saying that he loves you ... madly.

Ashwini: Oh no!

Mallika: In fact ... he wants to marry you.

Ashwini: Oh my god!

Mallika: Good, no? So now you'll become my Bhabhi.

Ashwini: Bhabhi!

Mallika: And I'll become your sister-in-law.

Ashwini: Sister-in-law!

Father: Mallika, can't you be silent? How many times have I told you that whilst I'm reading the news ...

Mallika (with finger on the lips): But Papa, my fingers are on my lips ...

Ashwini: No-no Uncle, she is telling lies and all. Actually, Mallika was saying ...

Mallika: Nothing Papa. Nothing.

Father: In that case, be quiet.

Mallika: Chee yaar, sooooo borrrrring ...

Father: OK. In that case, do something useful. Go get some coffee for me.

Mallika: Filter decoction coffee!

Father: Absolutely!

Mallika (screams): Momma, get some filter coffee for Papa.

Father (covering his ears): Arrey beta, I told you to go to the kitchen and ask Mummy ...

Mallika: Will you have some coffee ... Ashwini Bhabhi?

Ashwini (blushing): No ... I don't drink coffee. I only drink milk. That too, hot, and with chocolate and skimmed cream.

Mallika: Oh-Oh-Oh. Even Malhar drinks only milk.

Mother enters holding a tray with some difficulty.

Mother: Filter coffee. Two cups.

Mallika: The coffee was ground by me – tell that also, no, to Papa ... ?

Mother: Hahn bhai. Coffee was ground by Mallika.

Father: Achcha? Shabash beta.

Ashwini: Good morning, Aunty.

Mother: Good morning, beta. How is Momma?

Ashwini (melodramatically): Arrey Aunty, serious problems. Doctor said that chance of survival was only 1%.

Mother: Oh!

Ashwini: A matter of life and death.

Mother: Oh!

Ashwini: They were even thinking of doing an artificial heart transplant.

Mother: My god! When did all this happen to Mommy?

Ashwini: What Mummy? All this happened to me.

Mother (exchanges a look with Father): Oh? But now you're fine. That's what matters.

Ashwini (to Mallika): We had to buy five bottles of blood for transfusion ...

Mallika: Really?

Ashwini: I swear ...

Father and Mother sip their coffee.

Mallika (expectantly): How is the coffee?

Father: Excellent. Sheer brilliance. The best cup of coffee I've ever had, sir.

Mallika (jumps up and down): Really Papa? Really?

Ashwini (in a jealous tone): Actually Uncle, I also make good coffee ...

Mallika: You're just saying for the sake of saying.

Ashwini: No, really! Ask Aunty. Correct, no Aunty?

Mother: Yes beta.

Mallika: Momma will support you only ... but Papa will tell the truth. Correct, no – Papa. Tell ... no. Tell ... no.

Mallika tries to sit on the father's lap and almost spills the hot coffee.

Mother: Arrey Mallika, be careful. Daddy might spill some of the coffee on his lap.

Father (laughing): There must be a trophy for this coffee. Right, Mallikaji?

Mallika (putting her tongue out at Ashwini): See-see-see ... I told you!

Father: Tut-tut – where is my purse? *(Extracts his purse with some difficulty)* Hmmmm. Rupees ten to the best cook in the world!

Mallika: Ooooh wow! Daddy! You are the best!

Father: And Mummy?

Mallika (reflects): She is the ... super-best!

Mother: Budmash! Being diplomatic, eh?

Ashwini: Aunty, Aunty what is the meaning of diplomatic?

Father (laughs): Foot-in-the-mouth. Foot-in-the-mouth.

Mallika: Yuck, Daddy! Why should anyone put her foot in the mouth?

Father: Well ... my dahling, it's just a figure of speech.

Ashwini: Uncle, uncle, what is a figure of speech?

Father: Well, it's like this ...

Mother (laughing): Kyon ji? Foot in the mouth for you, too.

Mallika: I really don't understand what the two of you are talking. Elders are so complex, you know.

Mother: What? Complex!

Father: Complex? Who taught you that word Mallika?

Mallika: Malhar.

Father: Oh!

Mother: Where is Malhar, beta?

Mallika: In his room.

Mother: Doing what?

Mallika: I don't know. Perhaps playing chess.

Mother: Oh, but I thought he was not supposed to be playing chess.

Ashwini: Why-why – aunty ... ?

Mother: Well beta, it's like this ....

Father: Er, Mallika, can you please tell Malhar to come here. And no fighting, OK?

Mallika: But I never fight, Daddy.

Mother: Of course, you don't darling. Daddy just wants you to be careful. OK?

Mallika: Malhar! Malhar!

Father: Arrey, softly beta, softly. Such a racket you make.

Mallika: But, you only told me to get Malhar.

Mother: Exactly. We told you to 'get' Malhar, not scream for him.

Mallika (nudging Ashwini): Ah, Bhabhiji, *woh aa gaye hain ... !*

A beat. Malhar enters sucking his thumb.

Mother: Ah, talk of the devil and he appears.

Mallika (giggles): Malhar, Malhar, Mummy is calling you a devil.

Malhar (staring intently at his feet): Hmmmmmm.

Father: Malhar, say hello to Ashwini.

Ashwini: ... Er ... hello.

Father: Ashwini's face is still hurting. She had to go to the doctor ...

Malhar: Hmmmm.

Father: In spite of which the brave girl is willing to forgive you and be friends with you ...

Malhar: Hmmmm.

Father: Don't you think you should not have hurt her?

Ashwini: It's OK, Uncle. Malhar did it by mistake.

Father: Look, Ashwini is being so nice. Now, why don't you at least give her a smile.

Malhar (grimly): Hmmmm.

Mother: Come on, Malhar give Ashwini a smile ....

Father: Yes, yes ... beta ...

Mother: If you give Ashwini a smile, your punishment will be cancelled. I'll even allow you to play chess.

Father: Oh, come on, *chodo bhi*. What punishment and all. He is after all only a child.

Malhar (in a distant, older person's voice): It ... is ... interesting ...

Mother: Er ... what?

Malhar: This ... this ... problem.

Father: Eh? What's that you said?

Mother: Which problem?

Malhar: ... of Kachchra in ... city – t-this problem existed ... since the ... 1850s. Be it ... be it ... the Municipality. M-U-N-I-C-I-P-A-L-I-T-Y.

Mallika: Momma, Momma, Malhar is once again talking rubbish.

Malhar: Or be it ... be it ... Metropolitan Board of Works in London.

Mallika: Mummy, Mummy, do something.

Mother: Sssshhhh.

Malhar: Hund .. hundred years ago – 153.8 tons ... of excreta – was ... was ... the nightly average ... carried on ... heads.

Ashwini: Yuck! All that *gandhoo-gandhoo* on their heads! Sheeeee – so dirty ...

Malhar: One ... only mode of transportation – until ... t-the British acquired iron-carts .... for speedy disposal of excreta. T-take ... taken by special train ... mixed with ash and vegetable matter .... dump ... dumped into ... salt marshes. For reclamation of ... of land ....

Father: How do you know all this, Malhar?

Malhar (overlapping): R-E-C-L-A-M-A-T-I-O-N .....

Father: Malhar, listen to me. Who has been telling you all this?

Mother: O Ganesha, what is happening? Listen ji, I think it is better that we tell Dr Bhuskute to come over right away.

Malhar: Hmmm. Botanical garden ... opposite Dr Bhuskute's dispensary in Sewri ... built on ... on ... burial ground.

Ashwini: What is a Sewri?

Father: Malhar! Stop standing like a statue and ...

Malhar (overlapping): Statue ... statue of ... of ... Sir H C Dinshaw Adenwalla ... next to ... to ... Churchgate Station.

Mother: Who?

Malhar: Adenwala ... b-before he was ... statue – he himself unveiled ... statue ... of ... of ... of Muncherji Edulji Joshi in 1938.

Ashwini: Who is a Joshi?

Malhar: J-O-S-H-I ... principal founder of ... of ... Dadar Parsi Colony. Top ... housing scheme in ... in ... Asia.

Mother: Your Nalini Maushi lived in Dadar Parsi Colony – originally.

Malhar: Originally. ... Or-igi-nal name of Mazagaon – Machcha-grama. That is, Fish Village. Original name of Chinchpokhli – Tamarind Grove. Ow. Ow – My head!

Father: Mallika, get a thermometer. Quick. I think ... he is delirious. And some ice and cottonwool ...

Mallika exits.

Malhar: Cotton – C-O-T-T-O-N. .... in 1863 – the Great Peninsular Railway link between Bombay and ... cotton-growing areas of ... Deccan plateau was inaugurated. Ow!! My head!!

Mother: Hey bhagwaan, mere bete ki raksha karo.

Father: Mallika, hurry up.

Offstage, the muffled voice of Mallika can be heard.

Ashwini: Uncle, I think I'll go to my flat ...

Malhar: Flats. F-L-A-T-S ... kind of swampy territory – which ... high tide used to invade. Today, most of ... of ... Bombay lives 'on' these Flats.

Mother: Eh-ji. I think he is possessed.

Malhar: .... like ... great cities of ... world – Bombay has ... the distinction of being raised from ... water. Central London ... built on ... on the terrace of river gravel. New York on rock. Leningrad on ... marsh ... and ... and Bombay's foundation – rests on ... leaves of coconut palm and ... and dead fishes *(winces in pain)* Owwwww!

Father: Malhar, beta, are you – OK?

Malhar: Aaah my head.

Mother (loudly): Mallika, arrey beta, come fast. He is turning green ...

Malhar (delirious): ... t-t-the evergreen game. Adolf Anderssen v-v-v-versus J Dufresne ... with .. the ... the ... the Evan's Gambit ... e4 ... e-5; Nf3 ... Nc6; Bc4 ... Bc5; b4 ... Bxb4; c3 ... Ba5; d4 ... exd4 ...

Father: He's blabbering again ...

Mother: Hey Ram, *yeh shatranj ka bhoot sawar ho gaya hai is ladke par.*

Mallika rushes in, with a vessel full of ice and a towel. By now Malhar is delirious. Mother tries to swab Malhar with ice rolled in the towel.

Mother: He is sweating. *Hey bhagwaan – burree nazar lag gayee.*

Malhar (speaking fast): P-p-paul Morphy versus Karl of Br-br-Braunschweig and Count Isouard ... and ... and ... the Ph-philidor Defence ... e-4 ... e5; Nf3 ... d6; d4 ... Bg4 ... dxe5 ... Bxf3; Qxf3 ... dxe5; Bc4 ... Nf6; Qb3 ... Qe7; Nc3 ...

Mother: Here, Malhar beta, have this medicine – it'll make you forget – chess.

Malhar (rattling off rapidly): K-k-kurt Von Bardeleben versus ...Akiba ... ba ... Rubinstein ... Tarrasch Defence ... d4 ... d5; Nf3 ... e6; e3 ... c5; c4 ... Nc6; Nc3 ... Nf6; dxc ... Bxc5; a3 ... a6; b4 ... Bd6; Bb2 ... 0-0; Qd2 ... Qe7; Bd3 ... dxc; Bxc4 ... b5; Bd3 ... Rd8; Qe2 ... Bb7; 0-0 ... Ne5; Nxe5 ... Bxe5; f4 ... Bc7; e4 ... Rac8; e5 ... Bb6+; Kh1 ... Ng4; Be4 ... Qh4; g3 ... Rxc3 ... a remarkable sacrifice of the queen which cannot be ... be ... refused to Qxe4 ... Qxh2#; gxh ... Rd2 ... it is not enough for ... for ... Rubenstein t-t-to sacrfice his queeeeeeeen. He t-t-to throw a rooook into mix-mixture ... Qxd2 ... Bxe4+; Qg2 ... Rh3 ... and ... and ... checkmate by move ... move 26. Since ... since ... Rxh2 can-cannot be ... be .. avoided ... so ... so ... Rubenstein wins ... *(and Malhar cheers loudly)*

Silence.

Father (anxiously): Malhar? Malhar? I think – I better go and get Dr Bhuskute – myself. You stay here, and keep an eye on the boy.

Exits.

Mother: Malhaaaaaar! Beta? Is everything OK?

Mallika: Malhar. Malhar. *(Pause)*

Malhar (looks up groggily and jabbers): DHUIFWJS.

Mother: What beta?

Malhar (gesticulates): SDJKHBNE!

Mother: What – is it one more of your chess-moves???

Mallika: No Momma, I think, he wants something to drink.

Mother: Oh. Juroor beta. Er ... Mallika go and get Malhar a nice hot glass of milk.

Malhar (groans frantically): YFGDFFEIU.

Mallika: I don't think he wants me to make it. He wants you to go and make it. Please.

Mother: Juroor Beta. Anything for you. But please do get alright. Meanwhile Mallika, take care of Malhar. If he needs anything let me know, I'm in the kitchen. *Hey Bhagwaan,* save my child from evil spirits ...

Mother exits. Tense silence. Malhar gets up and looks around.

Malhar: Hmmmm.

Ashwini: Malhar, Malhar, lie down. Aunty, Aunty ...

Mallika: Sssssssh. Be quiet, dumbo!

Ashwini: Ssssssssh? But, Malhar is not well.

Malhar: Pah.

Ashwini: Pah?

Malhar: Enemy ... camp ... gone ...!

Ashwini: Who, Enemy Camp?

Mallika: Arrey, you dumbo. Momma and Papa.

Ashwini: You must be a big dumbo.

Mallika: Sssssh. Softly, or else Momma will hear us.

Malhar: E-N-E-M-Y Camp.

Mallika: Malhar needs our help.

Ashwini: Oh, but why must we help him?

Mallika: Because he is my brother.

Ashwini: No, he is not.

Mallika: He is not?

Ashwini: No. No, he is not. He is so weird, reh. And ...

Mallika: And ... ?

Ashwini: And, you don't even tie a *rakhee* on his wrist.

Mallika: Ah *rakhee*, that doesn't mean anything.

Ashwini: But everybody else ties *rakhee*. My Yamini Fuiya always ties a *rakhee* round Himanshu-bhai's wrist.

Malhar: Malhar want to know ... what be *rakhee*? R-A-K ... *(he falters)*

Ashwini: R-A-K-H-E-E.

Malhar: Hmmmmm.

Mallika (overlapping): But I do not believe in *rakhees*. And I never will. Why should I take anybody's protection. I'm equally strong. Here, look at my muscles. Good, no? So, if anyone wants to, they can tie a rakhee for me. I'll protect them.

Malhar (cocks his head in the direction of the kitchen): They ... to ... to ... return ...

Ashwini: Yeah, yeah. The Enemy Camp .... Heeeee-Heeeee

Mallika: Sssssh. Be silent. Don't attract attention.

Ashwini: Why, why?

Mallika: Look, you must help Malhar.

Ashwini (meditating): Well, I'll help you, but ...

Mallika: But, what?

Ashwini: First, you must tie a *rakhee* to Malhar. How else do I know you really think him to be a brother ...

Malhar: B-R-O-T-H-E-R ....

Mallika: And, in return you'll help me.

Ashwini: Arrey, Mother's Swear.

Mallika: God Promise.

Malhar: P-R-O-M-I-S-E ...

Ashwini: But, where is the *rakhee*?

Mallika: I don't have a *rakhee* ...

Ashwini: In that case, what are you going to tie ... ?

Mallika: Ummm. Anything.

Ashwini: Anything???

Mallika: Your socks, we'll use your socks as a *rakhee*.

Ashwini: Oh, but it so *gandhoo*. So dirty.

Mallika: Arrey, this is only for the time being.

Malhar: ... t-t-temporary ...

Ashwini: OK. OK. But which socks ... left one or right one?

Mallika: Any. How does it matter?

A beat. Ashwini peels off her socks. Mallika ties the socks (as rakhee) around Malhar's wrist.

Malhar: Hmmm ... Malhar t-t-t-to have *rakhee.*

Mallika (ties a knot): There, now we are 'real' brother and sister.

Ashwini: Hey, congrats!

Malhar: C-O-N-G-R-A-T-U ....

Mallika: Thank you, Mr Brother ...

Ashwini: Three cheers for brother and sister. Cheers! Cheers! And some more Cheers!

Mallika: Ssssh. Be quiet. Speak slowly. Or else Enemy Camp will hear everything.

Ashwini: And, they must not hear everything?

Mallika: No.

Ashwini: Why?

Mallika: Then our plans will be spoilt. Right, Malhar?

Malhar: Sabotaged. S-A-B-O-T-A-G-E-D.

Ashwini: Oh.

Mallika: Look, Ashwini ... Dr Bhuskute is coming to our house.

Ashwini: Who???

Mallika: Dr. Bhuskute!

Ashwini: Who's he?

Mallika: He is the Boss of the Enemy Camp. Very Evil.

Malhar: ... d-d-d-diabolical ...

Ashwini: Really?

Mallika: Yes, he eats children like us for breakfast. That too, kababs. Roasted and all.

Ashwini: Eeeeh, he is non-vegetarian. What a horrid fellow!

Malhar: Non ... non-vegetarian ...

Mallika: Yes, a monster, a dragon. In fact he eats so many children, that now he even has a big office, in which all parents take their children to be eaten.

Ashwini: How do you know all this?

Mallika: Malhar told me.

Ashwini: So, this Dr Kutkute is going to eat you.

Mallika: And Malhar. And you.

Malhar: And Y-O-U.

Ashwini (starts to cry): Mummy, Mummy.

Mallika: Be quiet. Arrey, you are supposed to help me. How will it be if YOU start to cry. Eh, tell me, tell me?

Ashwini: It will hurt a lot, no, if he eats me?

Mallika: But we won't let him eat us.

Ashwini: How?

Mallika: Dr Bhuskute is going to come to our home.

Ashwini (frightened): Mummy ....

Mallika: Oh. You must not be afraid.

Malhar: ... p-p-petrified ...

Mallika: You must not be afraid.

Ashwini: How?

Mallika: Simple. You and I'll stand outside, and tell him there is no one at home.

Ashwini: But will he believe us ...

Mallika: Arrey, at least try.

Ashwini: Why?

Mallika: Because the doctor is coming to kill Malhar.

Malhar: M-E. Me.

Ashwini: So what?

Mallika: He will also kill me.

Ashwini: So what?

Mallika: I'll be dead, you fool.

Ashwini: So what?

Mallikar: Everybody will say, 'Look, there goes Ashwini.'

Ashwini: So what?

Mallika: You will be well known as the friend of the dead Malhar and Mallika.

Ashwini: So what?

Mallika: You'll have no friends, all your life. Nobody to play doll-doll with or hopscotch; or ...

Ashwini: So what?

Mallika: He'll also kill you, and eat you.

Ashwini (hesitatingly): So what ...

Mallika: He'll bite into you with his crocodile like teeth ...

Malhar (demonstrating): CHOMP-CHOMP, CHOMP-CHOMP.

Ashwini: Huh ...

Malhar: Doctor to do CHOMP-CHOMP, and not t-t-to allow Malhar t-t-t-to play chess ...

Ashwini: Huh ...

Mallika: Look, you made a promise. A Mummy Swear.

Ashwini: Yeah, yeah, but, what am I to do ...?

Mallika: Come, I'll tell you ...

Mallika and Ashwini exit. Almost simultaneously, Mother enters. Malhar clumsily heads to bed.

Mother: Arrey, where is Mallika?

Malhar (groans): ... M-A-L-L-I-K-A ... M-A-L-L-I-K-A ...

Mother: Mallika. Mallika ... Ooooof, this girl ...

Mallika and Ashwini are hiding outside.

Mother: Ooof, that girl. I tell her to be around for one minute and she disappears. No sense of responsibility. No nothing.

Malhar (moans): T-t-t-the ... King's Indian Defence ... d2-d4; Ng8-f6; c2-c4; g7-g6; Nb1-c3; ....

Mother: Oh beta, forget your chess for one moment. Take rest. Go to sleep.

Malhar (whines): Ow. My head.

Mother: Here, beta have some milk.

Mother helps Malhar drink some milk. Meanwhile Dr Bhuskute appears on the scene. He has a visiting card in his hand. He is obviously searching for the house. Mallika and Ashwini watch him very intently. Even as Dr Bhuskute identifies the house and is about to press the door bell, Mallika screams.

Dr Bhuskute (shocked, leaps in the air): Arrey, what?

Mallika: Uncle, Uncle, don't even press that doorbell.

Dr Bhuskute: Eh what, you know, you know, who are you?

Mallika: I live next door, Uncle.

Dr Bhuskute: Oh. *(about to press door-bell)*

Mallika (nudges Ashwini): Do something. Say something ...!

Ashwini: Don't. Uncle, don't press the doorbell.

Dr Bhuskute: Why not?

Ashwini: Er ...

Mallika: All kinds of things are happening in that house!

Dr Bhuskute (disbelievingly): Really?

Mallika: In fact, Malhar's Daddy told us to guard this house, till he comes back, you know.

Dr Bhuskute: Why?

Mallika: There is a ... dog inside. With rabies ... and it bites strangers.

Dr Bhuskute: Oh!

Ashwini: In fact, Malhar's Daddy has gone to get the Municipality people to take the dog away.

Dr Bhuskute: What about Malhar's mother?

Mallika: Oh, you don't know what happened to her?

Dr Bhuskute: No.

Ashwini: She is in the hospital.

Dr Bhuskute: My God, what happened? I spoke to her only today morning, you know. She seemed alright then.

Mallika: She was Uncle. She was. Until she was bitten.

Dr Bhuskute: By the dog?

Ashwini: No, no, by Malhar.

Dr Bhuskute: By Malhar? That kid ...

Mallika: Not just a kid, Uncle. He is very dangerous. We call him Mad Max in the colony. He is capable of anything. I mean, how do you think the dog got rabies?

Dr Bhuskute: Through the environment ...

Ashwini: Chee-chee. Mad Max bit the dog.

Dr Bhuskute: What utter nonsense, you know, you know ... !

Ashwini: Uncle, look he also scratched me. Here ... *(points to the bandage)* ... I needed to be operated on.

Mallika: Ten stitches! That too, big ones ...

Ashwini: It was a matter of life-and-death.

Dr Bhuskute (positively perspiring by now): I don't know, if I should believe all this, you know, you know.

Mallika: Then ring the bell, Uncle. But wait till I'm a safe distance away. Or else, one never knows, who will bite you. The dog or Malhar! Wait, wait.

Dr Bhuskute (hesitates): Well ... you know, you know ...

Mallika (at a distance): Uncle, if you have any last wishes, let me know.

Ashwini: Yeah, yeah. Also give us your address and telephone number, so that we can inform your house that you are dead.

Dr Bhuskute: Er ... when is Malhar's father returning?

Mallika: One hour. Two hours. No idea.

Ashwini: You know, how it is with all the grown-ups. No sense of time. No punctuality.

Dr Bhuskute: Well ...

Mallika: But, Uncle, if you want to give him a message, I'll only be too willing to do so.

Dr Bhuskute: You will. Will you?

Mallika: Of course, Of course. Uncle ji.

Ashwini: That's why God has made children, to help the elders ...

Dr Bhuskute extracts a notepad and scribbles a note. Mallika and Ashwini do a jig. Dr Bhuskute looks over his shoulder at the door, anxiously. He hands the note over to Mallika.

Dr Bhuskute: Please, give it to Mad Max's ... er Malhar's father when he comes.

Mallika: I will.

Dr Bhuskute: Thank you. Nice girl, what's your name?

Mallika: Aishwarya. But friends call me Ai..

Dr Bhuskute: And yours ... ?

Ashwini: My name is Tabu. But, you can call me Tai.

Dr Bhuskute: Will you have an eclair, Ai?

Mallika: Thanks.

Dr Bhuskute: And you, Tai?

Ashwini: No, no, I don't accept anything from strangers. Mummy has told me not to. There might be poison in it, you know. So that you can kidnap me ...

Dr Bhuskute: Yes, yes. Of course. OK, bye bye.

Dr Bhuskute exits. Mallika watches him leave. She tears up the doctor's note, and then she and Ashwini do a quick jig. In the house, Malhar is still playacting, groaning and moaning. Mother is seated next to him, fanning him, swabbing him with an ice pack, and muttering prayers. Mallika and Ashwini enter.

Malhar (fake moaning): Ooooooh. Aaaaaah.

Mother (opening the door): Arrey Mallika, *budmash*! Where have you been? I told you to look after Malhar, no? This is really too much. I mean, you are a grown-up girl. Chee, total nonsense!

Mallika (making circles on the floor with her toe): Ummm, well, you know, Mummy.

Mother: Yes, yes, where have you been, huh? Gallivanting all over town?

Mallika: No, I was just outside ... er .. no ... actually at Ashwini's place. Helping her with her craft homework.

Ashwini: Yes, Aunty.

Mother: Arrey, help her all you want, but certainly not at a time when your brother is so seriously unwell.

Mallika: But, Mummy, Mummy, Malhar is OK. He is just pretending to be ....

Malhar coughs hysterically to cover up Mallika's gaffe.

Mother: Arrey beta, what happened?

Malhar: Malhar wants H-2-O. Water.

Mother: Oh God, water, wait a moment, I'll get you some. Just a second.

Mother exits. Promptly, Malhar springs to life.

Malhar (whispering): Malhar ... not ... pretending

Mallika: Oh! I know. I forgot.

Malhar: And ... Dr Bhuskute ...

Ashwini: Sssshhh, Aunty has returned.

Mother (entering): Aaah, beta, here is the water. Have it. You will feel better.

Malhar takes a sip, and spits it out, with a loud shout.

Mother: Malhar. What's the matter?

Malhar: Oooooh. Eaaagh. Pwagh!

Mother: But, beta that's what I got for you.

Mallika: Momma, warm water. I think Malhar needs warm water.

Mother: Oh yes, beta. Hey Ganesha, how can you let loose such injustice on such a small baby. Have you no mercy??? *(Exits)*

Malhar: Where Dr Bhuskute?

Ashwini: He's gone ...

Mallika: Yes. Now, in return what will you give me?

Ashwini: Yeah, yeah, you have to give us something.

Malhar: Malhar can give no-thing.

Ashwini: Nothing.

Mallika: Wait ...

Ashwini: What?

Mallika: Malhar to give ... something ... right, Malhar?

Malhar: Malhar to give something ...

Ashwini: But, what?

Mallika (naughtily): Malhar to give Ashwini Bhabhi a kissey.

Ashwini: NOOOOOOO! Are you mad or what ...

Malhar: Malhar, to give Ashwini Bhabhi a kissey ...

Mallika: Yeah, yeah ...

Ashwini (seeing Malhar approach): Nooooo. This is too much, hahn. I'm going home. Tata. Bye-bye.

Malhar (following Ashwini): Malhar t-t-to give Ashwini Bhabhi a kissey ...

Malhar tries to give Ashwini a kiss. But she is paranoid. Malhar keeps mumbling to himself, and follows her even as Ashwini exits. An exasperated Malhar finally rethinks his strategy.

Malhar: Malhar to give .... Mallika Bhabhi ... a kissey ... Malhar ... to give Mallika Bhabhi a kissey ... *(Kisses Mallika)*

Mallika (screams): Sheeeeeeee, *gandhoo*. Don't try to make romance with me. Kissing me and all.

Malhar: Malhar to give Mallika Bhabhi a kissey.

Malhar tries to smooch Mallika again; she manages to evade Malhar's attempt. Gradually, Malhar ends up chasing Mallika all over the room. Just then Mother enters. Almost, simultaneously Father enters through the main door. There is a shocked look on their faces. Freeze tableau.

ACT II

The following scene is mimed, as though in fast-forward mode:

Malhar tries to give Ashwini a kiss. But she is paranoid. Malhar keeps mumbling to himself and follows her, even as Ashwini exits. An exasperated Malhar, finally rethinks his strategy.

Malhar tries to kiss Mallika again; she manages to evade Malhar's attempt. And gradually, Malhar ends up chasing Mallika all over the room. Just then, Mother enters. Almost, simultaneously Father enters through the main door. There is a shocked look on their faces. The children notice the parents a little late. And Malhar kisses Father. Silence.

Malhar: Malhar to give Papa-Bhabhi a kissey ...

Father: Malhar! What is the meaning of this?

Silence.

Father: Malhar. I want to hear an answer, right now.

Mother: Beta, tell Papa, what is the ...

Father: You keep out of this. Malhar, come on quick, before I lose my patience. *(A beat)* Malhar!

Mallika: April fool, Papa.

Mother: Ssssh .... Mallika.

Father: Malhar, I'm talking to you. Hmmm? Speak up ...

Mallika: Papa, April Fool ...

Malhar (overlap): A-P-R-I-L. F-O-O-L.

Father: Be quiet, Mallika. Not a word.

Malhar: Malhar not to know what April Fool be ...

Mallika (giggles): Malhar to know only big-big things. He not to know interesting-interesting things ...

Father: **Mallika!**

Mother: Arrey, chodiye bhi na ji. Thank God, that everything is alright.

Father: What do you mean Thank God? Malhar, what is the meaning of this, eh! Playing these kinds of tricks.

Mother: Oh let it be, ji. It was only a harmless prank.

Father: What do you mean harmless? I was really scared. So worried. My heart is still thumping loudly.

Mallika: Daddy, Daddy, what is the meaning of thumping?

Mother: Sssssh beta.

Father: And where have you learnt all this rubbish from? Surely, you must be in bad company, to have picked up such ideas.

Silence.

Father: Where did you learn all that from? Hmmm?

Silence.

Father: Phew. This boy will be the death of me. Really. Come on tell me the truth, or else ...

Father raises hand to strike Malhar. Malhar lets out a brief yelp.

The doorbell rings. It is Dr Bhuskute.

Mother (relieved): Oh, it must be the Doctor saheb.

Mallika: Oh no. Mar gayi mein!

Doctor enters. Mallika tries to hide behind Mother.

Father: Welcome welcome, Dr Bhuskute. Any difficulty in finding the house?

Dr Bhuskute: Not in the least. Is everything, alright, here, you know, you know?

Father (staring at Malhar): Well, not really. Some people have been playing nasty pranks. But, we will not mention any names, shall we?

Mother (hurriedly): Doctor saheb, do come in. And please do sit down.

Dr Bhuskute: Well, speaking of pranks, a very strange trick was played on me. You know, you know.

Mother: My God, really? By whom?

Dr Bhuskute: Oh, by two little girls.

Mother: Two little girls ... ?

Dr Bhuskute: And these girls, you know, concocted a most fancy story. That you have a dog that suffers from rabies ...

Father: I hate dogs. I would never keep one.

Dr Bhuskute: ... because it was bitten by ... er .. Malhar.

Mother: By Malhar?

Dr Bhuskute: And Malhar has now bitten you, and so, you're hospitalised.

Mother: Hey bhagwaan, such nonsense.

Dr Bhuskute: But that's not all, you have gone to the Muncipality to inform them about the dog.

Father: Hmmmmm. Who were these girls?

Dr Bhuskute: Well ... they told me a name. You know. Asmita. No. Asawari. No. Arrey, it's on the tip of my tongue ...

Mallika (from behind Mother): Aishwarya.

Dr Bhuskute: Aishwarya. That's right. Oh, thank you, you know. But ... who said that?

Father: Our daughter.

Mother: Mallika, come on stop feeling shy. Show, your face to the Doctor uncle.

Father: Mallika, stop behaving crankily. Come on, out!

Mallika emerges from behind Mother. Dr Bhuskute, lets out a short yell as he recognises her.

Dr Bhuskute: But this, you know, is, Aishwarya!

Mother: No, no. You are mistaken, Doctor saheb, this is our daughter, Mallika.

Dr Bhuskute: My eyes cannot deceive me. This is the same girl, you know, who scared me outside a few moments ago. 'The dog will bite you. And Mad Max is dangerous.' My God, and her friend was equally bad. What was her name ... Tabassum ... Tarannum ... ah yes ... Tabu.

Mallika: No, no. That was Ashwini.

Father: So, you did do all this, Mallika?

Mother: Is the Doctor Uncle telling the truth?

Dr Bhuskute: Of course, I'm telling the truth, Ma'am. What do you mean? First, you let your kids (you know ... you know) loose on me, then you doubt my word.

Father: No no, Dr Bhuskute, you misunderstand, my wife didn't mean it that way.

Dr Bhuskute: Then in what way, huh? Here, I come to your home, and your daughter says all kinds of crazy things to scare me. So, I go away. Then, I see you on the road, you know. Thinking, you might need some assistance ...

Mallika: Mummy, Mummy, what is the meaning of assistance?

Mother: Ssssh.

Dr Bhuskute: ... so, I return to find out if you need some help. And instead of, you know, acknowledging it, you suspect my word.

Father: No, no, Dr Bhuskute, it's not like that. It's just a misunderstanding. I'm sure I can explain.

Dr Bhuskute: Oh, look at your two children, now they are exchanging looks. They perhaps find the whole thing, you know, hilarious. This is it. I'm leaving. OK, bye. If you need my services, please come to my dispensary, OK?

Mother: Doctor saheb, please. I apologise on behalf of my children. But, you must understand, *bachche toh aakhir bachche hi rahenge*. After all, you too must have been a child.

Dr Bhuskute: Well ... I was never a child!

Father: Mallika. Say sorry to Doctor uncle.

Mallika: I'm sorry, Doctor Uncle. *(A beat)*

Dr Bhuskute: It's alright, my dear, you know.

Mallika: But Malhar, told me and Ashwini to frighten you away. Saying that you are the Boss of the Enemy Camp.

Dr Bhuskute: He, said that?

Father: Malhar!

Mallika: Yes, Doctor Uncle. He also said, you eat little children.

Mother: Mallika, will you please be quiet?

Mallika: Mummy, Mummy, now that Doctor Uncle is here, is Malhar going to die?

Mother: Chee chee. Nothing of the sort, beta. Doctor Uncle is a good man. Like Papa. Like your Chandran Kaka.

Dr Bhuskute: Yes, yes. I don't, you know, eat children. In fact, I love children.

Father: OK children, the Doctor Uncle is here to discuss something important. I want the two of you on your best behaviour. Is that understood?

Mallika: But, Daddy, Daddy, I'm always on my best behaviour.

Mother (relaxing): In fact Doctor saheb, you would be happy to know that Mallika is very interested in becoming a doctor when she grows up. No, Mallika?

Mallika (unsure): Ummmm ...

Mother: It is her ambition in life. No, Mallika?

Mallika (uncomfortable): Well ...

Malhar: Malhar ... to be ... a ... a cartographer.

Dr Bhuskute: A what???

Mallika: Mummy, Mummy what's a cartographer?

Father: Malhar. Stop being cheeky in front of the doctor.

Dr Bhuskute: No, no. It's fascinating. Where did the boy learn a word like that?

Father: Oh, he must have picked it up to show off. I'm planning to prepare him for a career in Financial Management. There is tremendous potential in it.

Dr Bhuskute: Excuse me ... do you know the spelling of cartographer?

Father: Er ... spelling, I don't even know what it means ...

Malhar: C-A-R-T-O-G-R-A-P-H-E-R.

Father: Malhar! *(A beat)*

Mother (making small talk): Hee hee hee. Only last week, Mallika got a trophy in school for Poetry Recital, right? Which poem did you recite, Mallika? Tell Doctor Uncle.

Mallika: Well ...

Father: In these days of competition, one has to prepare the children for everything. Poems and all.

Mother: Mallika has also appeared on a TV chat show. Tell, Doctor Uncle about that.

Mallika: Well ... it was like this ...

Father: Keep your hands straight.

Mother: And stand properly. Don't shift so much.

Father: Well?

Mallika (nervous): It was a ... TV show about ... oys.

Dr Bhuskute: Toys or Boys?

Mallika: Toys.

Dr Bhuskute: Oh, really?

Father: You know how it is Dr Bhuskute, these TV shows, any *ghisa-pita* subject. As long as they get their sponsors.

Mother: Why don't you tell Doctor Uncle your poem?

Mallika (scowls): No, Mummy. Not now. I'm not in the mood.

Mother: What, mood and no mood. You are not a maharani or something. Come on, show Doctor Uncle how clever you are.

Mallika: Ummm ...

Father: Ha ha. Normally, she is very extrovertish in front of strangers, but today, I don't know ...

Dr Bhuskute: It's all right.

Mother: Hmmm. So silly of me Doctor Saheb, not to have asked you earlier. But will you have some coffee? Or a sherbet? Mallika makes lovely sherbet.

Dr Bhuskute: No, no. I better be leaving.

Father: So soon ... ?

Dr Bhuskute: Yes, the patients would have started arriving at the clinic.

Father: Yes, yes.

Uncomfortable silence.

Dr Bhuskute: Er ... you know, can I have a word with you?

Father: Sure.

Dr Bhuskute: In private.

Father: Oh, of course. Children, go to the next room.

Dr Bhuskute: Oh, that won't, you know,, be necessary. Let them be. Instead, you could, you know, see me off.

Father: Oh, most certainly.

Dr Bhuskute: OK, bye kids. Bye Ma'am.

Mother: No, no, I too will be coming outside. Malhar. Mallika. Say tata to Doctor Uncle.

Malhar and Mallika, do not respond. Even as Dr Bhuskute, Father and Mother step out of the door to 'talk'. Promptly, Malhar steps up to the door. And soon enough, so does Mallika.

Mallika: What's happening?

Malhar (under his breath): Enemy Camp ... thinking of ... new strategy.

Mallika: Strategy? How do you know?

Malhar: They go out ... to talk about Malhar ... to punish Malhar.

Mallika: And me?

Malhar: And t-t-to punish Mallika.

Mallika: Ssssh. Quiet, Enemy Camp is talking.

They overhear the elders' conversation.

Mother: Doctor Saheb, I hope everything is OK, with Malhar.

Father: Well ... Dr Bhuskute, what does Malhar's report state?

Dr Bhuskute: It's all very strange. Really, you know.

Father: Even then ....

Dr Bhuskute: Look, there's nothing to worry about.

Father: Yes, yes, we know that.

Dr Bhuskute: Well, it's like this, I've consulted Dr Nishith, who is, you know, a renowned neurosurgeon ....

Mother: And ...

Dr Bhuskute: Well, you know, it has something to do with your son's amygdala. Both of them.

Inside, the house, Mallika asks Malhar, 'What is an Amygdala?'

Father: A problem ...

Dr Bhuskute: Well, not a problem in a real sense. The point is, you know, because of this 'different' amgydala, your son's brain has superior faculties.

Mallika (behind the door): What's a faculty?

Malhar (taps his head): F-A-C-U-L-T-Y.

Mother: Hey bhagwaan, what is the meaning of all this?!

Dr Bhuskute: Don't get upset, Ma'am. Relax.

Father: But how did this ... er ... amygdala suddenly malfunction?

Dr Bhuskute: It's like this, to put it plainly, your son's neocortex just took over.

Mallika: What ... cortex ...

Malhar (points to Mallika's head): N-E-O-C-O-R-T-E-X.

Dr Bhuskute: Let me explain. The neocortex is the thinking brain. And, you know, your son's neocortex just jammed the extensive web of neural connections, intercepted signals from the thalamus, and soon enough, you know, rendered the amygdala 'different'.

Mother: Hey Ganesha! I don't understand a word. Please explain all this in English.

Dr Bhuskute: It's like this. Your son's, you know, neocortex has taken control of his whole brain. It's a minor scientific miracle, really, according to Dr Shetty.

Mallika (behind the door): Malhar, Malhar. So many big-big words the Doctor Uncle is using.

Malhar: All part of ... of ... of ... Enemy Camp ... Strategy ...

Father: How is it a scientific miracle ... ?

Dr Bhuskute: The last sample test we ran on your son's brain showed that your son has a very high IQ rating.

Mallika (behind the door): What is the meaning of an IQ? Is it a code word?

Malhar: Intelligence Quotient. Q-U-O-T ...

Mallika: Oh, Malhar, Malhar. You are so clever, no.

Father: So, Malhar has a good brain.

Dr Bhuskute: In a manner of speaking, yes.

Mother: But what has that to do with his not smiling?

Dr Bhuskute: Ummmm. You know, it's like this, he is trying to cope with his newfound mental prowess. Come to terms with it, you know, you know.

Mallika (from behind the door): Doctor Uncle is calling you mental.

Malhar physically tries to gags Mallika. She bites him. He reacts sharply but soundlessly.

Dr Bhuskute: And so, basically, the boy is trying to come to terms with his changing perception about the world. You know, you know.

Father: No, we don't know. Can you be a bit more explicit?

Dr Bhuskute: It's like this, the boy's cerebral faculty has improved. At the same time, his surroundings have remained the same. It is still status quo. And he is trying to undertand this changed environment.

Mother: Hey Lord Ganesha, by not smiling?

Dr Bhuskute: It's just an emotional reaction. He will, you know, get over it. Once he has made the adjustments ...

Father: What do you recommend, in the meantime?

Dr Bhuskute: Sensitivity. I mean, bear in mind that your child is different from other children, and so, he has to be understood in that context. The ground rules are different with him ...

Mother: But, Doctor Saheb, can you give some date, when our Malhar will start smiling?

Dr Bhuskute: The boy will have to discover that for himself.

Mother: Can we not be of any assistance? We are after all, his parents, you know.

By now, Malhar is trying to hit Mallika, in retaliation. A fight ensues.

Dr Bhuskute: Actually, you know, you know, I say that to every parent who comes to my clinic. Parenting is the most difficult job on earth. Almost everybody does it. But nobody knows how it is to be done. You know, you know.

Father: Very true, Dr Bhuskute.

Dr Bhuskute: As regards your child. In fact both of them, be it Malhar or Mallika. Just remember that every child is special. Don't compare one with the other. And above all, don't inflict your views on them. Let them unravel the world for themselves. Bit by bit, you know, you know.

Mother: Arrey baap reh, all this is too much, huh!

Dr Bhuskute (looks at watch): My God, it is late. I better be hurrying, you know, you know.

Mother and Father exchange Ciaos and See yous. Dr Bhuskute exits. Just then Mallika lets out a loud scream because Malhar has hit her.

Mother: Ooooof Ganesha, what have these kids done? Now?

Father: I'm really sick and tired of all their mischief.

By now, Mallika is wailing. Malhar very suspiciously watches his parents enter the house.

Father: What now? What is the matter?

Mother: Arrey, Mallika beta, stop crying. Come on. Hush. Hush.

Father (wearily): MALHAR. What have you done, now?

Malhar: Hmmm.

Father: Malhar!!!

Malhar: Malhar t-t-to do nothing.

Mallika (being consoled by the Mother): Liar-pop. Liar-pop. He bit me, Daddy. Look over here.

Father: What, you bit her, Malhar ... ?

Malhar: Malhar, no bite ...

Mother: Hai bhagwaan, are the two of you dogs or what? Biting each other like this.

Father: Yes, yes. Biting each other, no wonder, our dear little Mallika told the Doctor Uncle that we've a dog who bites people.

Mother: Have you no shame, huh, Mallika telling the Doctor Saheb that I'm in the hospital?

Father: Maybe that's what they want, that the two of us are in hospital. Completely out of their way, so that they can trouble everyone! Hmmmm.

Mallika starts to cry loudly.

Mother: Now, what is the matter, huh?

Mallika: It is hurting ...

Father: Obviously, it will hurt. Biting each other like mad people. The two of you must be kept in the zoo.

Mother: Yes, I'm toh totally exhausted. At this rate I'm heading for a nervous breakdown.

Father: Yes, yes, I think, it will be a good idea to lock the two of them in the bathroom and throw the key into the Arabian Sea. Yes, that will be the right thing to do. It's about time! The two of you need someone who is very strict with you.

Mallika (starts sniffing): Oh my hand. It is paining. It is hurting very much. Here, look *(and Mallika starts crying).*

Mother: Oh, be quiet for some time.

Mallika: Ow, but Momma. It is really paining.

Malhar: Malhar not t-t-to give pain to Mallika ... Mallika t-t-t-o be Malhar's friend.

Mallika: I'm not your friend. You greedy-cock-eyed-fat-pig.

Malhar: Mallika t-t-to say not nice things ... so ... so Malhar t-t-t-to call Mallika an ... an inconsequential-insignificant-invalid cretinous Korchnoi ....

Mallika (wails): Waaaaaah. Mummy, he called me a Korchnoi.

Father: Malhar!

Malhar: Korchnoi t-t-to be chess-player nobody like ....

Mallika: Ow, my hand, it is hurting. Aaaah, I think I've got leprosy!

Malhar: Leprosy. Contagious bacterial disease ... caused by ... by ... bacteria ... that is ... Mycobacterium leprae.

Mallika: Ow, my hand ... *(wails)*

Father: Ssssh.

Mallika: Aaaah, Malhar bit me ... *(howls)*

Mother and Father try to console Malhar and Mallika, but to no avail. Finally, the dam bursts ...

Father (shouting): Enough is enough. If the two of you don't stop this racket, right now, I'm going to make you eat *karelas* for breakfast, lunch and dinner for one whole year.

Mother: Why ji?

Father: You keep out of this, hahn. I'm, I'm sick and tired of all this bakvaas. I mean everybody has children, but I've never heard of anyone's children behave like these two. Really!

Mother: Malhar. Mallika. Look what Papa is saying. You must behave yourself.

Mallika: But Mummy, Mummy, I always behave myself.

Mother: Sssssh.

Father: Pah. Not once have I seen you well behaved. Not that I expect you to, even in the future. It's just that your mother and I have been very decent. Haven't we? Hmmmm.

Silence

Father: Haven't we? Answer me. *(Pause)* Hmmm. Hmmm. OK, I'm quite sick of all these games. Tomorrow, I've to go to work. I've a hectic schedule ...

Mallika: Papa, papa, what is the meaning of hectic schedule?

Mother: Chup beta!

Father: ... and I need to rest right now. OK, where is that mathematics book?

Silence

Father: Malhar, where is that book?

Malhar, sniffles, and gives the book to his father. Father, marks some pages

Father (looking up): OK. Malhar will solve the problems from pages 31 to 45. And Mallika will solve the problems from pages 56 to 69.

Mallika: Pages 56 to 69. When, Daddy?

Father: Right now. I want to see the answers by evening. Neat and tidy. And all correct.

Mallika: But, Papa how can we do mathematics? After all, it is our vacations.

Mother: Ssssh, listen to what Papa says.

Father (to Mother): Come on, let's leave them alone. They have a lot of hard work to do. OK Malhar. OK Mallika.

Mother: There is some milk in the fridge, just in case ...

Father: There's no need to pamper them. Chalo.

Mother: OK beta ....

Father and Mother exit. Tense silence on stage.

Malhar, picks up the book and starts to solve mathematics equations. Mallika, picks up the book, turns pages and starts weeping. No response from Malhar. Silence.

Mallika: I hate Daddy. I hate Mummy. *(Pause)* I hate homework. I hate Maths.

Malhar: Oh!

Mallika: I also hate you. *(Sticks tongue out)* Braaaaack.

Malhar (loudly): One hundred and twenty-two into thirteen is equal to one thousand five hundred eighty-six.

Mallika: Idiot into Buddhu is equal to Malhar.

Malhar: One thousand eighty-six divided by 19.37 is ...

Mallika: Monkey take away Brains is equal to Malhar.

Malhar: Hmmm. According to Boole's mid-nineteenth century algebraic description of logic, it is the differential of the square root of 1.97602.

Mallika: According to Mallika ... in 1998 ... Malhar is a joker.

Malhar: However, according to Godel's theorem of incompleteness ... the fraction of x, less than infinity, is directly proportional to the inverse of y, which is not equal to z.

Mallika: What are you bad-badofying?

Malhar (writing vigorously): Hmmmm.

Mallika: 'No Homework Multiplied by Crying is Equal to Mallika'. Help me, Malhar.

Malhar: Malhar to help ....

Mallika: Yes, help Mallika.

Malhar: Hmm. Malhar help Mallika.

Mallika (opening her exercise book): So, how do I solve this problem?

Malhar: Mallika to say the multiplication table for 957. Start. *(Starts muttering the tables beneath his breath)* 957 ones are 957, 957 twos are .... (*Etc.*)

Mallika: Whoa. You know, multiplication tables for 957, or what? How? How? Hillary Mabel teacher has not taught it as yet.

Malhar: Malhar to know it.

Mallika: But how?

Malhar: Malhar not to know how Malhar to know.

Mallika: Sachi-muchi. Chal-chal, I don't believe you.

Malhar: Malhar t-t-to know table for 23-digit number.

Mallika: 23-digit ...

Malhar: Ten-to-the-power-of-twenty-two ...

Mallika: Tell me, tables of 6666.

Malhar (takes a deep breath): Why?

Mallika: Please.

Malhar (Pause): Six thousand six hundred and sixty-six ones is equal to six thousand six hundred and sixty six ....

Mallika: Wow!

Malhar: W-O-W.

Mallika: Now, why don't you tell me the sums of one million + one billion.

Malhar: Hmmm.

Mallika: Tell, no.

Malhar: Malhar not to tell.

Mallika: Why?

Malhar: Malhar to do maths sums ...

Mallika: Oh! Yes, yes. After all, Malhar is Mummy's Koo Koo Koooooook.

Malhar: Hmmm.

Mallika: Malhar is Momma-Papa's Cutey-Cutey Koootchie-Pie.

Malhar: Hmmm.

Mallika: Malhar is their Mallu-Kallu.

Malhar: Hmmm.

Mallika: Malhar is doing *chamchagiri*. Malhar is their *chamcha*.

Malhar: Hmmm.

Mallika: Malhar is scared of Momma-Papa. Scared-booby. Scared-booby.

Malhar: Scared-booby???

Mallika: Yes.

Malhar: Malhar not scared.

Mallika: Then, then, why are you doing the sums?

Malhar: Malhar LIKE to do sums.

Mallika: Chee-Chee. What lies!

Malhar: Malhar not to be lying.

Mallika: Yes, yes you are. After all, nobody likes to do maths sums. I hate maths. Ashwini hates maths.

Malhar: Malhar to know lots and lots of people who t-t-t-to like to do maths.

Mallika: Such as who?

Malhar: Malhar to know.

Mallika: Name them. Name them.

Malhar: Oh there to be ... no-no, ummmm ... there is Aryabhatta. Bhaskara. Ramanujam. Leonhard Euler. Pythogoras. Fourier. Leibniz. Mobius. Collin Maclaurier. Augustine Louise Cauchy. Joseph Louis Lagrange ...

Mallika: Wait-wait, who are all these people ... ?

Malhar: People ...

Mallika: Yes, who are they ...

Malhar: They are .. are mathematicians.

Mallika: Math-a-magician?

Malhar: M-A-T-H-E-M-A-T- ...

Mallika: Are you a mathematician???

Malhar: ... I-C-I-A-N.

Mallika: Hmmm.

Malhar: Malhar to be a mathematician.

Mallika: A mathematician, who can play chess. Who bites people. And, who doesn't smile.

Malhar: Malhar, not to smile???

Mallika: No, Malhar. Don't you know, you haven't smiled for so many months.

Malhar: Malhar, not to smile???

Mallika: Momma and Papa are so worried ...

Malhar: But why, Malhar not to smile ... ? *(A beat)*

Mallika: How should I know why you don't smile ... ?

Malhar: Oh. Mallika not to know why Malhar not to smile ...

Mallika: No, Mallika not to know. But does Malhar know ...

Malhar (thinks, takes a deep breath): Malhar to know only chess. Malhar to play with ... with Vishwanathan Anand.

Mallika: Who?

Malhar: .. who to .. to also be ... be chess-player ...

Mallika (rushes up to Malhar and hugs him): Oh Malhar. You are so different from everyone else.

Malhar: Hmmmm.

Mallika: And, I love you for that. Because, you're so-much so-much fun.

Malhar: Hmmmm.

Mallika: Hmmmm???

Malhar: Checkmate. You lose in four moves.

Mallika (pauses): Oh!

Malhar: Hmmmm.

Mallika: Malhar, help me with my maths homework, please!

Malhar is engrossed in solving maths equations.

Mallika: After all, I'm your rakhee sister, look I even tied rakhee round your wrist.

Malhar is engrossed in solving maths equations.

Mallika (sweetly): Malhaaaaaaar. I helped you, no?

Malhar is engrossed in solving maths equations.

Mallika: I went, no, so bindaasly, and talked to that Doctor Uncle. To the Boss of the Enemy Camp.

Malhar: Homework over.

Mallika: Homework over?

Malhar: Q.E.D ...

Mallika: So, now, it is your turn to help me. You will help me?

Malhar: Help ...

Mallika: With my homework.

Malhar: H-O-M-E-W-O-R-K.

Mallika: Look, if you help me I'll eat all your *doodhi*, *shalgam* and *kareley ki bhaji* for you.

Malhar: For Malhar.

Mallika: Promise. I'll also not trouble you, ever.

Malhar: Forever.

Mallika: Promise. God's Promise.

Malhar: Promise.

Mallika: So, help me ...

Malhar: Malhar ... to help ... Mallika.

Mallika: With maths.

Malhar: But, maths to be so simple.

Mallika: So simple!!! Are you mad or what?

Malhar: Let, Malhar explain to Mallika.

Slight change in mood. A song about mathematics can be heard.

Mallika: One-Two-Three-Four
Maths is a big bore.

Malhar: One-Two-Three-Four
Maths is not a bore
It helps you tell the cricket score
Tell Sehwag's six from Sachin's four

Mallika: Five-Six-Seven-Eight
Maths, I really hate

Malhar: Five-Six Seven-Eight
Maths, you mustn't hate
It helps you tell your next birth-date
Calculate your grandma's weight

Mallika: Nine-Ten-Eleven-Twelve
Throw the Maths Book down the well

Malhar: Nine-Ten-Eleven-Twelve
Read your maths book very well
It helps you when you buy and sell
And count the ding-dongs of a bell

Malhar and Mallika: Ding-Dong. Ding-Dong. Ding-Dong. Ding-Dong ...

Even as the final bars of the song fade out, Malhar and Mallika, shut books, relieved that homework is done!

Mallika: Mallu, so good, no, I've completed my homework.

Malhar (imitating her tone): 'Mallu, so good no, Mallika has completed her homework.'

Mallika: No, no, you have completed the homework. Yours and mine. Shall I go and tell Daddy?

Malhar: No, tell Daddy.

Mallika: Why?

Malhar: Daddy to come, and say 'Malhar and Mallika, what you ... you doing? I hope you ... you are not doing ... masti?'

Mallika (giggles): Daddy is so strict, no?

Malhar: Daddy strict. Mummy ... strict.

Mallika: Yes, yes. All the time, 'eat this, drink that'. Not like Ashwini's mummy, who goes to work, and never troubles her.

Malhar: Hmmmm.

Mallika: Yes, yes. So Ashwini can watch TV. Eat chocolates. Play video games. Do anything at home, all the time.

Malhar: Total Freedom.

Mallika: But, Ashwini likes our Mummy.

Malhar: Pah.

Mallika: Pah???

Malhar: Ashwini not know anything. She ... not even know that Dicentra spectabilis t-t-t-to be a plant.

Mallika: Ashwini not to know ... but I to know what is Dic... Spec ...

Malhar: Hmmm.

Mallika (conspiratorial tone): Papa and Momma are Big Bullies. All the time troubling us, no?

Malhar: B-U-L-L-I-E-S ....

Mallika: Don't you remember, how in front of that Doctor Uncle, Momma started asking me to say that poem?

Malhar: Poetry.

Mallika: Momma, even wanted me to become a doctor.

Malhar: A p-p-physician ...

Mallika: Two days ago she wanted you to become a microbiologist.

Malhar: Malhar wants to become a cartographer.

Mallika: All the time, behaving as if they don't do any mischief. They must also be doing some *gadbad* at work. Not doing their homework, properly ....

Malhar: Hmmm.

Mallika: Shall, we AKS them?

Malhar: AKS them? OK. Ask them!

Mallika: Mummy. Mummy.

Malhar: Papa. Papa.

Gradual change of mood. Some music. Colourful lights. A fantasy situation. Father and Mother, enter behaving like children. Malhar and Mallika, pretend to be adults.

Father and Mother (child-like tone): Hello Malhar. Hello Mallika.

Malhar: Ah-ah. Come-come. Momma, enter.

Mallika: Hmmm, Papa, you are looking very messy. Have you had your bath yet?

Father: Yes, Mallika.

Mallika: Oh! Then go and have another bath.

Father: But, Mallika ...

Mallika: And this time, go rub yourself properly with soap. Here, come here. Let me have a look. *(Tugs at Papa's ear)* Oh-Oh-Oh. You have not cleaned the back of your ears properly. Tut-tut-tut, and look at your nails.

Malhar: This won't do. It just won't. What will your boss say in office? Quick, go bring a nail-cutter.

Papa: Yes, Malhar. *(Exits)*

Mallika: Oooof, this Daddy. Never taking bath on time. Never looking clean and proper. Look at that Didmishe Mama, so good he looks.

Malhar: So, Momma. Have you taken bath? And cut your nails?

Mother: Yes-yes.

Mallika: Good, in that case you must also tell Daddy to do it. It is your responsibility after all, you are his wife, no?

Mother: Yes.

Father enters with a nail-cutter.

Malhar: Ah, Papa. Have you got the nail-cutter? Good. Now sit down. And cut your nails, carefully.

Mallika: Hmmmm. Look at the mess, you have made of the house. Everything is everywhere. Ooooof. What will the neighbours think?

Malhar: Yes, yes. Listen Papa. Listen Momma. You are grown-ups now; you must know how to behave. OK?

Mother: OK.

Father screams.

Mallika: Phew, what now?

Father: I've cut myself.

Mallika: Can't you be more careful, huh? Can't you even cut your nails?

Father: Aaaaah. It's hurting.

Malhar: Of course, it will hurt. That's why you should concentrate. Not daydream about the stock market all the time.

Mallika: Yes, and what is this, I hear from Naushil Uncle?

Father: Who, Naushil?

Mallika: The head of your Regional Head Office.

Father: What about him?

Mallika: He was saying, you are not coming to work on time. And that, you haven't prepared the structural module for that Industry Report.

Father: But ...

Mallika: No buts. A job is a job. And you must do it properly. Right?

Father: Right.

Mallika: That's like a good boy. Now, cut your nails.

Malhar: And Momma, what is this we hear about you?

Mother (gulps): What Malhar?

Malhar: That you have not paid the electricity bill, yet?

Mother: I'm sorry.

Malhar: You have also not gone to the market to buy toys for us.

Mother: I'm sorry.

Malhar: Even the *doodhwallah* and *dhobhiwallah* were complaining that you have not paid them their *pagaar*, yet.

Mother: I'm sorry.

Malhar: No, no. Saying sorry will not do.

Mallika: Yes, yes. You will have to say A-B-C-D. Ten thousand times.

Malhar: No, no. One lakh times.

Mallika: Malhar, Malhar. Which is bigger? One lakh or ten thousand?

Malhar: Ssshhh. OK, start.

Mother: A ... B ... C ...

Mallika: Oooof, Momma, stop shifting your weight. And stand still in one place.

Malhar: And clearly. And open your mouth, wide, like this. Aaaaaaaah.

Mother: A ... B ... C ...

Mallika: No, no. Not straight. Backwards. Z-Y-X-W, and so on.

Mother (groans): Oh no!

Malhar: Young woman, if you have a problem, let me know. In that case, no Zee TV for you today.

Father screams.

Malhar: What now?

Mallika: This Daddy is really clumsy!

Father: Ow. It is hurting!

Malhar: Really, look at the other parents. So good. So well behaved. But these two! Just not capable of doing anything properly.

Mallika: On top of that, thinking no end of themselves. I'm really tired of them.

Malhar: Yes, I know. The other day, I asked them to take me for a children's movie. They made a face and took me. You were there too.

Mallika: Instead, they took us for a grown-up movie. It was so boring. Only kissing. And talking. Yak-yak-yak.

Malhar: They also did not give us popcorn.

Mallika: And ice cream.

Malhar: I could not even go to do *susu*.

Mallika: Why? What happened?

Malhar: Arrey, I'm so small. And the *susu* pot is so high. How could I do *susu*?

Mallika: And I could not even see the film.

Malhar: Why?

Mallika: There was a Big Uncle sitting in front of me. Like that *(points to an elder in the audience)* ...

Malhar: Hmmmm. This won't do.

Mallika: It just won't do.

Malhar: It's all the fault of this Enemy Camp.

Mallika: The Enemy Gang!

Malhar: I think, we must give them stricter punishment.

Mallika: Good idea. But, what?

Malhar and Mallika think. And then, it is Show Time!!!!!!

Malhar: Welcome. Welcome, dear Friends. To our Special Quiz Contest.

Mallika: Our participants are: on my right, Daddy.

Malhar: Put the nail-cutter down. And smile. Properly.

Mallika: On my left, Mummy.

Malhar: Momma. Don't jump about. People are watching you. Ooof.

Mallika: The rules of the competition are: Daddy and Mummy have to answer the questions. If they don't, they will take us to Esselworld. Yeah!

Malhar: Even, if they do, they have to take us to Esselworld. Yeah!

Mallika: Shall we start now?

Malhar (talking fast, almost chattering): You have five seconds to answer my questions.

Mallika (makes the sound of a beeper): BWAAAMP!

Malhar: Is Papa a Good Boy, or no?

Mallika: BWAAAMP!

Malhar: Is Momma a Good Momma or no?

Mallika: BWAAAMP!

Malhar: If school is so much fun, then why don't Papa and Momma also attend it?

Mallika: BWAAAMP!

Malhar: Who invented lunch and dinner and vegetables?

Mallika: BWAAAMP!

Malhar: What is better, Cartoon Films or Homework?

Mallika: BWAAMP!

Malhar: Sweets and ice cream are the principal exports of Children-land. True or False?

Mallika: BWAAAMP!

Malhar: Who are the most best children in Bombay?

Mallika: BWAAAMP!

Malhar: Toys are cheaper than lipsticks and cigarettes. True or false?

Mallika: BWAAAMP!

Malhar: If Papa, Momma love us, then how come they want to us to eat *karelas*?

Mallika: BWAAAMP!

Malhar (by now very rapid): Malhar t-t-t-to play Vishwanathan Anand. White versus ... b-b-b-black. Ruy Lopez Opening.

Mallika: BWAAAMP!

Malhar: ...e4 ... e5; Nf3 ... Nc6; Bb5 ... a6; Ba4 ... Nf6; 0-0 ... Nxe4; d4 ... b5; Bb3 ... d5; dxe5 ... Be6; c3 ... Nc5; Nbd2 ... d4; Ng5 ... dxc3; Nxe6 ... fxe6; bxc3 ... Qd3; Bc2 ... a good move by Malhar ... Qxc3; Nb3 ... a brilliant new move by Malhar, preserved in the freezer of ... of ... of fridge ...

Mallika: MALHAR!

Malhar: ... Vishwanath Anand t-t-t-to play Nxb3; Bxb3 ... Nd4 ... and Malhar t-t-t-to play Qg4 ... he to play Qxa1; Bxe6 ... Rd8; Bh6 ... Qc3; Bxg7 ... Qd3 ...

Mallika (overlapping): Malhar .... what's happening? You're frightening me! Please, don't do that .... Arrey Daddy, Mummy look what Malhar is doing!!!

By now Malhar is in a frenzied state.

Malhar (very loud, and at breakneck speed): Malhar to play Bxh8 ... Qg6; Bf6 ... Be7; Bxe7 ... Qxg4; Bxg4 ... Kxe7; Rc1 ... c6; f4 ... a5; Kf2 ... a4; Ke3 ... b4; Bd1 ... a3; g4 ... Rd5; Rc4 ... c5; Ke4 ... Rd8; Rxc5 ... Ne6; Rd5 ... Rc8; f5 ... Rc4+; Ke3 ... Nc5; g5 ... Rc1; Rd6 ... and Vishwanathan Anand resigns to Malhar ... he resigns ...

On cue, Malhar starts cheering and applauding.

Mallika: Malhar ... what's happening? You're frightening me! Please, don't do that ... Arrey, don't behave like this. Daddy, Mummy see what Malhar is doing ...! Arrey, Malhar where are you going ... ?

Malhar, flops out of the house. Rattling out chess-moves under his breath. Mallika screams out 'Mummy-Daddy'. Malhar exits. Blackout!!!

ACT III

A sad version of the song is sung by Mallika, Father and Mother.

Malhar, Malhar. Where are you?
Where did you go? Why did you go?
What did we do, to frighten you?
Come home. Come home.
We love you.

Mallika: He made a chess-board on the floor
He really gave me a fright
He danced his way out of the door
Though, we didn't have a fight.

Malhar, Malhar. Where are you?
Where did you go? Why did you go?
What did we do, to frighten you.
Come home. Come home.
We love you.

Mother: Maybe he's gone to the library
To read some special book
Maybe he went to the planetarium
To merely have a look

Malhar, Malhar. Where are you?
Where did you go? Why did you go?
What did we do, to frighten you?
Come home. Come home.
We love you.

Mallika: What are we going to do Daddy-Mummy.

Mother: We don't know what to do!

Mallika: Oh. I think I'm going to start crying. Boo-Hoo-Hoo. Boo-Hoo-Hoo. Ballyhoo ...

Mother tries to console Mallika. Father tries to console the two of them. Changes his mind and exits. Lights come and go: by now it is evening. The opening version of the song is heard. Father enters, looking tired, haggard and hassled.

Mother: Stop crying, Mallika. You have been crying for the past four–five hours.

Mallika: Daddy has come, Daddy has returned.

Mother: Eh, ji. Any *khabar* about Malhar?

Father: None, whatsoever.

Mother: We also called up all the possible places he could have gone to. But no one knows about our Malhar's whereabouts.

Father: I only hope this is not another of his practical jokes!

Mother: Should I get you something to eat? Or to drink?

Father: No, no, I've lost all my appetite.

Mother: What do we do now, ji?

Father: Maybe we will have to lodge a complaint with the police.

Mother: Arrey bhagwaan. (Starts muttering as she uses her prayer beads)

Father: I've also spoken to Singanaloor Sheshadri Venkatramanan at office.

Mother: Who???

Father: The Security Officer. He has some good contacts in the police. He said, he will talk to some people. I have to call him in some time.

Mother: Hey bhagwaan, save my child from the Evil Eye.

Father: I'm really worried. Genuinely, you know.

Mother starts praying. Father starts pacing up and down. Just then the doorbell rings. Mallika runs and opens the door. It is Dr Bhuskute along with Malhar.

Mallika: Daddy, Mummy, look who is here!

Dr Bhuskute: Good evening everybody.

Father: Dr Bhuskute ...

Mother: Malhar, beta, you are here!

Father: How ... er ... where ... ?

Mother (fondly petting Malhar): Malhar, beta, are you OK? Where were you, hahn? Momma was so worried, no.

Mallika: Yes, yes. We were even going to complain to the police. The army. And the CBI.

Father: Sssssshhh.

Mother: Hey bhagwaan, I have to go to Siddhi Vinayak, today. To do an aarti in your name ...

Father: But Dr Bhuskute ... how ...where? I mean, you and Malhar together.

Dr Bhuskute: Relax, everybody. We have a long story to tell. You know, you know. Don't we, Malhar ji?

Malhar: Yes. Doctor Uncle. *(Smiles)*

A beat

Mallika: Mummy, Mummy, did you see that? Malhar smiled!

Mother: The Devas and Gandharvas be blessed, Malhar, my beta has smiled after six months.

Father: But, did he really smile?

Mother: Of course, he did. Won't you do it again, beta? After all it's been so many days since we have seen you smile.

Malhar smiles. There are loud gasps of exhilaration and joy all around. Malhar smiles again. And again

Dr Bhuskute: You know, today has been an insightful day for me.

Mallika: Mummy, Mummy, what is the meaning of insightful?

Father: Ssssssh.

Mother: Kyon, Doctor Saheb, why do you say that?

Dr Bhuskute: You know, you know. As you were aware, today was the Youth Chess Championship at the Club.

Mallika: Mummy, Mummy, Malhar was supposed to play in this competition.

Mother: Hey Ram, we completely forgot about it, ji.

Dr Bhuskute: And that's where I met, nay, saw your son.

Father: At the competition??? But Malhar, I thought you were given strict instructions not to participate in the Championship. Hmmmm.

Mother: Oh, let that be, ji.

Father: But ...

Dr Bhuskute: That's not all.

Father: Meaning ... did Malhar do some mischief there too?

Dr Bhuskute: Mischief ... what mischief?

Father: Oh, you know Dr Bhuskute, Malhar has been missing from home for the past six hours. We were all so worried.

Mallika: Yes, Doctor Uncle, we toh thought Malhar has run away.

Dr Bhuskute: Nothing could have been further from the truth, you know.

Mother: What do you mean, Doctor Saheb?

Dr Bhuskute: I mean, you know, you know, if you only knew what your son has done. He has done you proud.

Mother: Proud??? Malhar?

Father: I hope, you are not being sarcastic, Dr Bhuskute?

Mallika: Daddy, Daddy, what is the meaning of sarcastic?

Mother: Ssssshh.

Dr Bhuskute: Me and sarcastic? Nothing of the sort! You know, you know.

Father: Then ...

Dr Bhuskute: Well ... let me explain. I reached the hall, where the chess championship was being held, you know, you know.

Slight change of lights and mood. A transition to the chess-club. Even as Dr Bhuskute is speaking, a table is set up with a chess-board, and a chair for Malhar to sit in ...

Dr Bhuskute: Who do I, you know, you know, see on the stage? Mr Vishwanathan Anand, in person.

Father: Oh!

Dr Bhuskute: Apparently, he had agreed to play fast-chess with 64 players simultaneously. You know, you know. It was really exciting. On one side, one of the best players in the world, and on the other, 64 local chess enthusiasts!

Mallika: What is the meaning of chess enthusiast?

Dr Bhuskute: Just then, I was distracted by something, and you know, you know, what do I see?

Mother: What?

Dr Bhuskute: That your son, Malhar is one of the 64 players.

Father: My God, Malhar versus Vishwanathan Anand.

Dr Bhuskute: The bell rang. The clock started ticking. Anand started moving around. He was playing black. You know.

Mother: And what was Malhar playing?

Dr Bhuskute: White. Like all the others, you know, you know, 64 players.

Mallika: Did Malhar win or lose? I'm sure he must have made a foolish joker of himself ...

Father: Ssssshh.

Dr Bhuskute: Anand swiftly countered the moves. Some of the participants were in deep concentration. By now, one or two of them had already lost the match, you know, you know.

Father: Was Malhar one of the early losers?

Dr Bhuskute: No. In fact, within 30 moves, things were becoming clearer. There were hardly a handful of players left.

Mother: Oh, Doctor Saheb was our Malhar one of them?

Dr Bhuskute: Yes, he was, you know. In fact, by now Anand was spending the maximum time at Malhar's table.

Mother: At *apna* Malhar Beta's chess-board! *Hey bhagwaan*!

Dr Bhuskute: On the 58th move, only one player was left. You know, you know.

Mallika (whispers): It was Malhar ... !

Dr Bhuskute: The game slowed down. Anand thought. And so did little Malhar. All the experts and pundits started to watch the game seriously. Some of them were even exploring the possibility of an upset win. And then ...

Father: And then, what?

Dr Bhuskute: Anand spoke at length to Malhar. For a full ten minutes. Then Malhar smiled.

Mother: Malhar smiled.

Dr Bhuskute: And then, the two of them agreed to a draw.

Mallika: Wow!

Mother: My beta did that!

Dr Bhuskute: Yes, Ma'am.

Mallika: My brother drew with Anand! Yeah! My brother drew with Anand. Wooh!

Father: Ssssshh.

Dr Bhuskute: Yes, and so, now, we have a new chess prodigy in our midst.

Mallika: Daddy, Daddy, what is the meaning of prodigy?

Dr Bhuskute: And these are not my words, but the general opinion of the Grandmasters who were present in the auditorium.

General feeling of euphoria.

Malhar: L-l-l-ook, Vishy Anand Uncle ... gave ... gave this to Malhar.

Mallika: Show, show.

Mother: Mallika!

Malhar (hands over a small box): This t-t-t-to be Anand uncle's personal ... chess-board. With his autograph ... also ...

Father: And, what?

Dr Bhsukute: And e-mail. So that any time Malhar wants, he can discuss moves with him ...

Father: Oh!

Malhar: Anand Uncle ... also planning t-t-t-to give Malhar ... CD ROM of 'The Best of Chess'.

Mother: Hai Raam, what is a CD-ROM?

Mallika: Malhar, what's a CD-ROM, Malhar?

Malhar: CD-ROM... t-t-t-to contain ... international games. All the moves, with explanations.

Stunned silence, just then Ashwini saunters in.

Ashwini: Hello Uncle. Hello Aunty.

Dr Bhuskute: Hello, Poison Tabu ...

Ashwini (*shocked to see Dr Bhuskute*): Oh, Bye ... I think ... I've some important work.

Mother: Arrey, Ashwini beti ... don't go away.

Ashwini: I can't, Aunty. I must go away. *(Whispers in Mother's ear)* Otherwise this uncle will eat me. Chomp-chomp.

Mallika: No, no, he's very busy. You know, Mallu drew with Viswanathan Anand ...

Ashwini: Really ... what did he draw???

General festivity.

Mother (Clicks her knuckles against her temples to ward off the Evil Eye from Malhar): Oh, my Beta, such a genius. Really!

Ashwini: Yea, yeah, Aunty. I always used to say Malhar is a genius.

Mallika: Achcha, and who called him a *paagal*, and who wanted to send him to Thane Mental Asylum.

Ashwini: Oh, that was like that only. Mistake.

Mother (clears throat): Kyon ji, somebody else also wanted to put Malhar in a zoo.

Father: Eh ... what?

Mother: It's a good thing he disobeyed you. Or else, all this would not have happened to Malhar.

Father: What do you mean disobeyed me? It is you who was trying to impose, all those karate and swimming classes on the boy.

Mother: But I, toh, did that in good faith.

Father: So what ... ? It was quite apparent that the boy hated those classes. Right, Dr Bhuskute?

Dr Bhuskute: Well ... it is a tricky situation, you know, you know. The parents obviously love their children. As the two of you love Malhar and Mallika, but the point is, you could make mistakes.

Father: What kind of mistakes?

Dr Bhuskute: Mistakes that cannot be rectified. I mean, I shudder to think, what would have happened, if Malhar had not gone to the Championship, today. A golden opportunity of a lifetime would be lost.

Father: But I had to punish Malhar for not behaving.

Dr Bhuskute: Which is why, balance is such a fine word in parenting. The parents will have to find the right balance in bringing up their children, properly.

Loud scream from Mallika.

Mallika: Mummy, Mummy, look no, Malhar is not showing me his chess-board.

Malhar: Malhar not give t-t-t-to Mallika. Chess-board ... gift from Anand Uncle to Malhar.

Mallika (sticks tongue out): OK. OK. Showing off. Showing off. In that case, I'll also not allow you to play with Ashwini.

Malhar: Chee-chee. Malhar ... not want to play with Ashwini ...

Ashwini: Oh, but Ashwini want to play with Malhar.

Mallika: But, you're my friend.

Ashwini: No, no, now I'm Malhar's friend.

Malhar: F-R-I-E-N-D. Friend. Amigo. Companion. Bum-Chum. Side-kick ...

Mallika: Momma, Momma, look, no, nobody loves me. Everybody hates me.

Mother (consoling Mallika): Nahin beta, you must not say such things.

Mallika continues to bawl, even as Ashwini joins Malhar for a game of chess, which has already been set up.

Father: Ah, Dr Bhuskute, now how would you handle a situation like this? By tolerating the kids or shouting at them?

Dr Bhuskute: Well ...

Father: Yes?

Malhar (to Ashwini): Checkmate. You lose ... in four moves ...
Ashwini reacts. Malhar smiles.

Dr Bhuskute: By smiling, what else ...

Malhar smiles. Everyone laughs.

An upbeat song about The Boy Who Started Smiling plays.

Rum-Pum-Pum
Pa-Pa-Purum-Pum
Rum-Pum-Pum
Pa-Pa-Purum-Pum
Some little boys are very bad
Some little boys are boring
Some little boys copy their dad
Whenever they are snoring ...

Rum-Pum-Pum
Pa-Pa-Purum-Pum
Rum-Pum-Pum
Pa-Pa-Purum-Pum
This is the story of a little boy
The boy who started smiling (Repeat)

So clap-clap-clap your hands
And tap-tap-tap your feet
Rum-Pum-Pum
Pa-Pa-Purum-Pum
Rum-Pum-Pum
Pa-Pa-Purum-Pum
So clap-clap-clap your hands
And tap-tap-tap your feet

Rum-Pum-Pum
Pa-Pa-Purum-Pum
Rum-Pum-Pum
Pa-Pa-Purum-Pum

Curfew

Dedicated to JAIMINI PATHAK (who tolerated me – and the pager pings from GBS – for more than ten plays)

Director: Jaimini Pathak

Production: Suruchi Aulakh, Shruti Rao, Ahlam Khan and Pooja Asher

Cast: Romi Jaspal, Manoj Agrawal and Jaimini Pathak

Music: Suruchi Aulakh

Lights: Ramu Ramanathan

An over-dressed, forlorn, down-and-out musician enters the stage. He begins an invocation.

Kiss the earth, and smell the dark
We have arrived on schedule today,
The time has come to put on a mask,
To shout a vow, to chant and pray
Mumbling-Bumbling-Rumbling-Tumbling
This is the beginning of our religious jumbling
Moksha is the object, Prakriti our means
This along with some philosophy is ingrained in our genes
O noble gods of Upanishads, O sacred lord of Puranas
We hope for Dharma, Artha, Kama, Moksha
And the blessings of Shri Ganesha
O Vighneshwara, Vinayaka, whoever and whatever-a
We stand unprotected on your land
We want Thee to bless our Nataka
Give us strength, bless us with your hand

Bahuroopi, Baul, Burrakatha,

Chau, Gondhal, Terrukoothu,

Samagrih, Karika, Nirukta,

This is the end of our Ranga Puja

Three times OM is also OM

This here is our home sweet home

Once upon a time, and the time is now, there is a room – any room. A is consulting a huge cloth map. From time to time, he jabs at the map with a drawing-pin and with a lot of passion. A beat.

A (clears his throat): Swagatam. Shubh swagatam. Brothers & Sisters, I welcome thee gentlemen ... and ladies, I salute the cosmic atoms in thee. For your information, ladies and gents, at this moment in history, we are here (*jabs at the map*) ... which in a sense is an inappropriate venue for me ... In fact, every venue is dishonourable after the first few hours. I'm a traveller. Always on the move. And like Marco Polo, Christopher Columbus, Huan Chang, Vasco Da Gama, and so many others before me, I strive not to stay in a place for more than ...

A harassed looking B barges in with a pooja thali, muttering 'Ahara Ahara' (an invocation for Lord Shiva) under his breath.

B: Ahara. Ahara. Lord Shiva I invoke you. *(Noticing A)* Ah, you. Is there milk in the house? *(A nods)* That pancha-patram which was made in honour of our birth? Remember? *(A nods)* I need to make some sacred tirth in it. It's imperative. *(A nods)* Ahara. Ahara. Lord Shiva, I invoke you ...

A: This is my twin brother. He was born three microseconds after I was born. There is not much of a resemblance ... but unknown to the rest of the world our umbilical cords were once entangled. We even have identical birthmarks. This big in size – like a nice nipple. Two of them. Double-trouble. And like the two of us. Inseparable. From an early age, our Daiva, our destinies have been intertwined. It's a thing we have grown accustomed to. Although every 14th year, we try to part ways, at every Kumbh Mela, but somehow, we can't. That was how, we became travellers. We had to. It was a search. A process of discovery for body and soul. Travelling across the longitudes and latitudes of the world. Along historic trade routes, exploring continents and nations and cities and towns and villages and streets …

B peers out of the door – and screams.

A: What happened?

B: Our travel plans will have to be scrapped, postponed ...

A: Why?

B: They have imposed a curfew.

A: Again?!

B: Yes.

A: How do you know?

B: Listen ... they had clamped it when you were asleep ... *(A beat)*

A: That's the tenth curfew for the month. At this rate – life will become totally meaningless. You tell me – how can normal people like us survive???

B: Yes, I know. Such an ill-fated moment. I mean, what a time to have a curfew.

A: On top of that, they never tell us what these curfews are for. Just clamping it left, right and centre – without so much as prior intimation, huh. Arrey, there is something called basic human decency. About informing law-abiding citizens like us ... *(a gunshot)* ki *'Bhai, we have decided to have a curfew, so please do the bandobast for your chai-paan and tambakoo.'* Huh, you tell me – is that too much to ask for? You tell me ...

B (distressed): Ahara. Ahara. The future is so uncertain. To top it all, there is no milk at home! Oh, what will I do now ... ?

A (angrily): Arrey, the ages have inundated us with all kinds of sufferings and you blather about milk. This is an unmitigated disaster. Never before in the history of this planet have things been this bad. What about my travel plans, my grand schemes of embarking on a journey, of conquering new peaks, trekking through a desert, of ... *(B frantically rings the bell in the puja thali)* What are you doing???

B: Lighting a diya.

A: Why?

B: Well ... it's like this ... there is a bit of trouble with my future, with my existence. My life is in the doldrums.

A: So is mine. In fact – it is a millennium hangover.

B: Yes, yes, I know all that. This is different ... but let it be ... you won't understand.

A: Oh.

B: Well ... it's like this ... I'm going to die.

A: So ... I mean, so am I ... so are all of us.

B (makes a point): I'm going to die tonight.

Silence

A: Really? How do you know ... ?

B (fidgets, clears throat, etc): I've consulted Baba Alladin Bhavnagarwallah. Apparently, he is a great ... futurologist.

A: You mean, an astrologer, a horrorscopist. How could you?

B: I want to live ...

A: But surely, as a rationalist, you know very well that we should have no contact with spurious fortunetellers and crystal ball gazers. How could you be this irresponsible? So careless ....

B: ... Baba Alladin Bhavnagarwallah is different. He is spiritual, you know.

A: Sounds like a Sister-Ephing-Chillum-Sucker!

B: Look here, Baba Alladin Bhavnagarwallah is not a fraud. He is real. He connects with your mind. He then probes into your Atma, and only then does he predict your future.

A song (in Gujarati).

Aavya, Aavya, Baba Aavya

Bhavnagar Thi Ganthiya Lavya

Mahan Baba Ne Ghani Khama

Amari Taraf Thi Jhuki Salam

Aavya, Aavya, Baba Aavya

Bhavnagar Thi Pendha Lavya

Mahan Baba Ne Ghani Khama

Amari Taraf Thi Jhuki Salam

All hail the mighty Baba Alladin Bhavnagarwallah.

All hail his presence.

By now, the scene should replicate the encounter between Baba Alladin Bhavanagarwallah.

B: All hail the mighty Baba Alladin Bhavnagarwallah. All hail his presence.

A (in the persona of Baba Alladin Bhavnagarwallah): Dikra, how many times have we been through this. Don't state the tautological. Remember, I can read your mind.

B: A thousand and one apologies, oh wise one.

A: Alright. Alright. Now push my swing ...

B: What swing, Baba Alladin Bhavnagarwallah. I see nothing!

A: Ha-ahmmm. Dikra, life is an illusion. It is all Maya. Here, feel the swing. Ha, ahmmm. Feel the wood, it is genuine Kathiawadi from the forest of Sasan Gir. Ha-ahmmm. A gift from a Tirthankar. Dikra, push a little harder. *(A beat)* Oh-oh-oh. This is life. Now tell me, what seems the problem? Is it that indigestion thing again ... ?

B: No, no, Baba Alladin Bhavnagarwallah ...

A: Dikra, how many times must I repeat, don't fritter your life's source energy in conversation. It is an utter waste. I can read your mind ...

B: A thousand and one apologies Baba Alladin Bhavnagarwallah ...

A: Will you have a mango? Ha-ahmmm. Don't answer. Remember, I can read your mind. *(Even as the imaginary swing is being pushed, they both suck on an imaginary mango.)*

B: Apoos. Wah! It is sweet. And juicy.

A: Yes, yes, good, no. Ha-ahmmm. All nature inasmuch as nature is good. This is especially true of mangoes.

B: Is it from Ratnagari?

A: Ha-ahmmm. Mine is from Ratnagari. Yours is from Valsad. Ha-ahmmm ... So, as I see it, due to the conjunction of Rahu with Ketu, it seems you're going to die in this lunar month.

B (swallows the imaginary mango seed): What? This is totally unexpected. What am I to do, Baba Alladin Bhavnagarwallah?

A: Dikra, keep pushing the swing. Don't slacken the momentum. Remember, life is a series of ups and downs.

B: But what about my life?

A: Ah life. Ha-ahmmm. Dikra, you've been a good disciple. Regular habits, clean conscience, no garlic. In other words, I'm pleased with you. *(A beat)* Say something, dikra.

B: Oh, I thought you could read my mind. I'm profusely indebted to you, oh Baba Alladin Bhavnagarwallah ...

A (mulls over the matter): Ha! Alright, alright.

B: What should I do?

A: Listen carefully. The only way you can guarantee your survival is, if you can convince Yama, the Pitripati, the king of all the spirits of the dead to be benevolent and generous, and let you keep your soul.

B: But Baba Alladin Bhavnagarwallah ...

A: Light a diya, invoke the name of Lord Shiva. Keep an offering of milk and water ready in a pancha-patram. Ha-ahmmm. Try all the tricks in the book. It is all a matter of time. Remember – Lord Yama is Kaala, the controller of time. He is also Antaka and Kritanka, that is, he who ends life, but also he who can bring about a release from the sufferings linked with the wheel of birth and death in this illusory world. For example, this swing. Come here. Sit. Look, how illusory it is ...

B falls down with a thud from the illusory swing.

B (burps): Er ... Baba Alladin Bhavnagarwallah, the mango was it also an illusion???

A: Haahmmm. Dikra, you've learnt fast. Now, if you can

outsmart Yama, you can outlive your present cycle of birth and death. Remember, however innumerable beings are, I vow to save them. But it is for me to tell the Way, it is for you swelter at the Task ...

A song (in Gujarati)

Gaya, Gaya, Baba Gaya

Badhana Ganthiya Khai Ne Gaya

Gaya, Gaya, Baba Gaya

Badhana Pendha Khai Ne Gaya

Gaya, Gaya, Baba Gaya

Badhana Maatha Khai Ne Gaya

And so, it is back to now.

B: To cut a long story short that was what happened with Baba Alladin Bhavnagarwallah ...

A: And you believed him. Why? Right now, the son off a chillum, he must be tripping his medulla oblongata to high heaven. *(Imitating Baba Alladin Bhavnagarwallah)* 'What to do Dikra, Mata Bhavani come from Dada Hari. Bring top stuff. Like nectar and honey. Jai Bhavani. Jai Bam Bhole. Jai Boom Shanker. God Bless all the wells in Dada Hari.' Arrey, where are you going?

B (exits): To find milk.

A: In the curfew? Are you cracked in the head or what ... ? I really don't think it's such a good idea to go out now. The times are pretty bad. No chance for survival.

Loud noises offstage. Unidentified sounds. Loud scream from B. Shortly after, B barges in.

B (entering): ... the mother-ephing curfew – it's outside, out there!

A: I told you already. But nobody listens to me ...

B (panting): There is a big crowd out there creating havoc. Breaking into people's houses and all! They are interrogating everyone ... beating them up. It's too much ... !

A: Any known faces among them ... ?

B: Yes, yes ... Arrey, just now, I saw Mrs Sashital K Jambusaria, the fat one in the nightdress, walking towards the booth on Kutchi Dasha Shrimaliwadi for some milk for her cat – when there was a thunderbolt like a shot from the blue – and BANG she was dead with her mouth open ....! Arrey, this is too much, can't even get a simple commodity like cow's milk these days ... !

A (sighs): All because of this curfew... Oh, this is hopeless. Such a big universe and we are all stuck with this mother-ephing curfew ...

B (falls on knees and pays obeisance to the musician in his new avtaar: The Peepal Tree): ... and this Peepal tree.

A: Yes, this senile, doddering, Peepal tree.

A song. The musician springs to life.

(Oh Yeah, I'll show you)
Well, they promised a good role to me
And they told me I'll be there in every scene
They said I'll tower above everything
Oh look at me, please look at me
I ended up being part of the scenery
Mummy look at me, Daddy look at me
They fooled me into playing the Peepal tree

A: (all round exultation and applause): Yes, yes, yes. What we have is the magical, musical, mythical Peepal tree.

B: The magical, musical, mythical Peepal Tree.

Plucks a leaf from the peepal tree (which responds with appropriate ouches).

B (picks up a leaf): And a leaf from this Peepal tree.

A (also picks up a leaf): And, you are right, a leaf from the Peepal Tree.

B: ... which has an inscription.

A: That states '*The Arabian Nights*'. What does your leaf say?

B: This one states '*The Tales of Panchatantra*'.

A: Here's another leaf with an inscription. It says *'The Saga of Ulysses'*.

B: Ah – and listen to this leaf *'The Complete Works of Walt Disney'*.

A: This is a blessing from the Gods. A sign from the Muses above. A sign – to tell a story.

B: But which story?

A: Any good story, which is dictated by a leaf on the Peepal tree. A story which has been passed on from generation to generation. Through Time. And Nature. I say, let's create our own stories. Here and now, on the spur of the moment.

B: But – why stories?

A: Don't you see??? This Peepal tree and its stories are a divine ordinance which is going to save your life. The stories that branch out from it will change your destiny. Its stem will stem the tide which is against you. Its root will show you the correct route to a long and prosperous life. Yes, this Peepal tree is the only way you can outsmart, outmaneouvre, outmatch Yama, the God of Death.

B: But where are we going to find these stories, fables, parables?

A indicates the peepal tree.

B (picks up another leaf): Whoa – this leaf has a story etched in golden letters.

Peepal Tree (sings): Jolly good – 'what are you waiting for. The moment is auspicious. Your Karmic accounts are fit. Your existence is blessed. Om. Oṃ. Om ... (cubed).

A: Let's move. Quick. Right now. On the double. Pronto. Time is running out ...

B: Wait-wait-wait! What are you talking about?

A: Ooof, as a fellow traveller, is that all you have to query? Come on, I'm speaking of the beginning of a new journey. A journey in which we chart out our own paths, make our own destinations ... *(A escorts B to the huge cloth map. He jabs at it, and the map lights up)* ... look here – this you.

B: Me! What do I have to do?

A: You will sleep my child, for the leaf from the Peepal tree says so.

B: Why – sleep ... ?

A: For sleep is that great pacifier. It has calmed tempers, passions, history. As it will calm you ... so that when you awaken you will be a new you.

B: And, what will the new me be called?

A: Ooof, this persistent need for classification. How does it matter – what you're called? A name is just a name. Mispronounced, misspelt, misunderstood.

B (thinks it out): Can I be called *Kaala*? That way I'll be a controller of Time. You see, Time is precious for me ... I want to free myself from its shackles and plunge into Antaka ...

A: Yes, yes, what a timely idea! For then, ours will be a journey through this *Kaala*, through Time. A journey which will be a continued progress of incidents unfolding one after another in Time. A set of events which will affect your past, present and future.

B: Sure. And you, what will you do?

A: I'll also travel through Time with you. I'll play a since-time-immemorial role which has been allocated to me by the time-honoured Peepal tree.

B: Oh, in that case as timekeeper, I beseech you to get on with it and exit ... Tick tick tick ....

A: Tick tick tick .... and I request you to sleep and dream the dreams of a baby ... Tick tick tick ....

B sleeps even as A exits. The lights come and go. Once. Twice. Blackout.

This is followed by an announcement.

Attention. Attention. Ladies and Gentlemen. Bhaiyons and Behenjis. We regret to announce that an indefinite curfew has been declared in your locality. I repeat – a curfew has been imposed under Section 144. This is an order to remain indoors till further notice. Anyone found outside will be considered a threat – and shot at sight. To prevent any such occurrence, we request all inhabitants to co-operate with us – and prevent any untoward incident …'

A song.

He'll be riding on a buffalo when he comes
He'll be riding on a buffalo when he comes
He'll be riding on a buffalo
He'll be riding on a buffalo
He'll be riding on a buffalo when he comes

All the dogs will be howling when he comes
All the dogs will be howling when he comes
All the dogs will be howling
All the dogs will be howling
All the dogs will be howling when he comes

Fade in. B (now Kaala) is asleep. Silence. A gun shot. Kaala wakes up. Looks around.

Kaala (scared): Ahara Ahara. Who be that? Stand and unfold yourself ...

Yama is at the door. A brilliant shaft of light. A (alias Yama) emerges from it. A medieval face with a rope slung around his shoulders. Sniffs the air. Sprinkles magic dust.

Yama: Mr Kaala?

Kaala: Yes. More or less.

Yama: Myself Yama the God of Death.

Kaala: Good God. A real God!!!

Yama: Yes …

Kaala: Nice to meet you, sir.

Yama: I sincerely hope so …

Kaala: Yes, yes. This is the most metaphysical out-of-body experience of my life. I mean, I've never been confronted by a Hindu God before. They are all over-busy these days. You see, we have a revival of Hinduism in these parts. Really good fun. But let that be. Why are you bestride on thy soul on my threshold? Pardon my inhospitality. But I'm so nervous. After all, it's not every day that the God of Death comes home. This way, please …

Yama: Thank you.

Yama and Kaala enter the room.

Kaala: Pray, good sire. To what good fortune do I owe this visit? Is it some ennobling deed on my part? Oh, I'm so excited! How can I serve you?

Yama: You can do nothing for me. You're merely an inconsequential Purusha.

Kaala: Well … er … that I am.

Yama: And I'm Yama, the God of Death.

Kaala: Are you?

Yama: Now, what is that supposed to mean?

Kaala: How do I verify you're not a fake something? That you're really the God of Hindu Death?

Yama: Tchsk. Tchsk. The Hindu God of Death.

Kaala: Isn't it one and the same thing?

Yama (confused): It's not … well, actually, let me see …

Gunshot. All of a sudden, the lights come and go. Once. Twice. On cue B clambers onto the drum and peers through the broken window.

B: .... Oh no, the curfew has still not been lifted. And look, look over there, that Mrs Jambusaria K Sashital, the fat one in the nightdress, her body is still lying unattended. Unclaimed. We must contact the municipality, the Ward Officer …

Peepal tree stops the story by blowing the whistle.

A: You fool! Like some doddering amateur you've disrupted the story! How could you have done it, huh? Bear this in mind – the story must never be interrupted. It must reach its logical conclusion …

B: I say, should we carry on? I mean, the story seems to be taking on deathly proportions. I mean, consider this business between Kaala and Yama ... it all reeks of pessimism ...

A: Ah ha! When we started telling stories, we gave our lives a new dimension of meaning. Of apprehension, comprehension, destination.

B: Sounds more like suffocation, asphyxiation and depression.

A: Please clarify.

B: I mean consider, Yama. He is supposed to be repulsive with his red garments, green colour, and blue crown. A pucca RGB. Looking menacing on a four-eyed buffalo, a mace and noose. The Yama of our story seems a pale imitation of this reality. An imposter, a fraud.

A: O despair not. You take things too literally. Everything is not what it appears to be. Come here, lick my feet, tickle my ear, twirl my moustache, scratch the lice out of my hair, blow into my armpit, and get on with the story. Alright. One. Two. Two-and-a-half. Start!

Peepal tree blows the whistle.

A: Well ...

Kaala: It's your line, Yamraj ji.

Yama: It is. Very well. Look Purusha. I had an appointment with you.

Kaala: OK, so what is on the agenda? What do you want?

Yama (roars): What do I want? Ha, mankind when will Thou progress. *(Clicks his tongue)* Since the beginning of the human race, every time I've approached a man, he has always quivered and queried 'What do you want, Yamraj ji?' ... Come on, be serious. What can I, Yama the God of Death want. Your life, ye lifeless one. Give it to me or I'll send you to the worst of the twenty-eight Hells.

Kaala: But what have I done?

Yama: You've lived, isn't that enough?

A song (The Yama Mantra as a tribute to Elvis Presley)

Mahisastha Yamagocha Dandahasta Mahabala

Raksa Tvam Daksinadvaram Vaivasvata Namostu Te.

Kaala: Ah, well said. Never was a truer word spoken. But your chanting is meaningless to me. Not my fault though. I'm convent-educated, you see.

Yama: Your time is up. The moment has come to depart for that quieter and better world. Come on, off with your soul. Discard your Atma. For this is the Supreme Law of Creation. Of Ordination. Obeyed by multitudes upon multitudes, men and women, heroes and cowards. All of whom have gifted their lives to me. Their only possession. The only real thing. To me – Yama the lonesome God of Death. Ha ha ha. Pay heed as I speak. For there can be no longevity before me. Just as there can be no life before death. This is the way of the world. From birth to death. From womb to tomb. I see all. I'm omnipresent. The other Gods might shirk from their earthly duties. But not me. It is written in my Karma, in my Dharma. There's no way out. Whether there is birth or not. Whether one has lived or not. Whether one is ailing or ageing. Yama reigns. It's the Dicta of the Mother Goddess of Earth. A curse which has to be with the old times. Mourning in death and disillusioned at birth – where every second shall hurt. But the last one will kill.

Kaala: Hmmmm. All this is very fine ... But er ... why am I dying?

Yama: It's a gift from the Devas of the Vedas. Only they know. Unless even they know not.

Kaala: What! There are no reasons?

Yama: Such is life.

Kaala: I mean ... look at me. Perfectly perfect. Not even a common cold. Nothing. Pathologically, my health is first class. Not even bad breath. I just had a medical checkup. No infection. BP is OK. Mentally, I'm fairly stable, except, I watch a bit of India TV. No drinks. No smoke. Oh yeah, I use coconut oil on my hair. But I haven't heard of anyone popping off because of that.

Yama: Neither have I.

Kaala: Very well then, Yamraj ji. I hope you realise what you are doing. You're trampling on my fundamental right to exist. My right to breathe. My pulse to pulsate. My veins to be vain. My heart to be hearty ... it's a human rights violation. I could even report you to the Amnesty International for this....

Yama (takes a deep breath): Look here, the universe has laid claim to your soul. I'm merely the messenger. The courier boy. There is no denying that. The number of deaths are monitored elsewhere. No one knows by whom. Some say it is the Creator. But if it is the Creator, why would there be deaths? No one knows. And this is how we have survived for so long. Ha ha. Firmly believing that where there's life there will always be death ...

Kaala: Is this ... er ... religion at its bestest?

Yama: Oh oh oh. Look at you, poor dear. Rotting away, like the bad meat of a carcass. Ye hear-hear, your metabolism is breaking down. Ye feel-feel, your fingers are growing crooked. No longer can you poke your nose. Ah ha, you are beginning to symbolise death so well ...

Kaala: I hope this is a dream, or worse still, a nightmare. Somebody wake me up. Mummy, help me. Mummy ...

Gunshots. Pause. The lights come and go. Once. Twice. Thrice. A beat.

Yama; Be mum. What was that?

Kaala: What was what?

Yama: That sound.

Kaala: It was a cry for mummy of mine.

Yama: No. Not that. The other sounds.

Kaala: Ah, it must be the curfew.

Yama: The – what?

Kaala: The curfew – what else?

Yama: What is a curfew?

Kaala: You haven't heard of a curfew? Ever?

Yama: This is the first time.

Kaala: Your debut?

Yama: In a manner of speaking, yes.

Kaala: My first curfew was with my mother *(loudly)* Mama, can you hear, or are you completely mummified ...

Peepal tree stops the story and blows the whistle.

Kaala (alias B): Er, do you think the time has come to consult the Peepal tree. I don't like this meeting between Kaala and Yama. As far as I can see, there seems to be a bit of *chaos.*

A: Not in the least. On the contrary, we have just succeeded in transforming the *chaos* of Kaala into an experience. Making sense of it. And from the look of it, even domesticating it.

B: But – we are intruding into his life. His privacy. His thoughts. It's unfair.

A: Remember, the greatest stories are those that pry and spy. Come on, let's get on with our journey into the narrative. It's flowing like a dream.

B: You don't think it might be *dangerous.*

A: Ha, ha. Stories are meant to be *dangerous.* Shit Yaar, that is how they become liberating in a search for their destiny.

B: OK. OK. OK. Blow your own trumpet.

The Peepal tree blows the whistle.

A (plucks leaf): Since ours is a story of Kaala, a journey through Time, we can weave it any which way we please. *(Rushes to the huge cloth map)* Hmmm. Come here. Let's begin at the very beginning of a newer journey from here ... for which we have to travel backwards ... this length of distance in time to meet a very, very young Kaala ...

B (excitedly): ... a very, very young Kaala – hey that's me.

A: As I was stating, a young Kaala and his mother, who are going to school in a vehicle.

A song.

Come–come–come
Come–mummy–come

Go for a drive now
Have some fun
Come–come–come
Come–sonny–come
Go to the school now
Oh little one
Come–come–come (repeat)

Once upon a time, and the time is now, a very very young Kaala is going to school with his mother or Mama (alias A) in a car.

Kaala: A for Amitabh. B for Bachchan. C for ...

Mama: Tut tut. Arrey beta, you must not waste your energy saying such rubbish things. You're a good boy. Very intelligent. You must be goody goody. Hope for nice things...

Kaala: But ... Momma. All my friends, Chungu, Mungu, Dungu talk this way.

Mama: Hai bhagwaan, you must not mix around with those boys. How many times have I told you this. They are troublemakers. Fit to be only bank clerks. Look at you, such a bright future, even your teacher was saying so .... !

Kaala: But Chungu is already doing big-big things. Only last week, he delivered a talk – at the International Education Conference on the Structurality of the Semester System.

Mama: Total nonsense person, that boy. He should leave all these things to the grownups. Why do you think God has made elders? To do these things. Today's young generation. Ooof – no direction. No nothing ...! I wonder what kind of upbringing this Chungu has? Arrey baba, wipe that snot from your nose. How many have I told you not to salivate through your nostrils ... and why are you giggling? How many times have I told you – do what you want, but don't giggle. Only girls giggle ... !

Kaala: Ow, will you stop tweaking my cheeks. That too, in public.

Mama: Ah ha, my beta is growing up. Feeling embarrassed and all. I must start looking for a Sweetie-bahu for you ...

Kaala (changing the topic): ... Only yesterday Mungu was caught in the girls' susu room – doing some drawings on the wall.

Mama: Chee chee chee. Don't you dare tell me any more!

Kaala: Really damn cool drawings. The drawing Sir said, you can't understand the drawings, unless you read John Berger.

Mama: Won't a *Femina* or a *Cosmopolitian* do?

Kaala: No Mama, this is modern art. You can't make head or tail out of it. A bit like your cooking ...

Mama: Arrey beta, you mustn't talk to Mama like this ...

Kaala: Why ya! After all, Mungu's drawings are sold for thousands and thousands of rupees. Even the drawings in the susu room will be sold – along with the walls. It's the latest trend in avant garde. The interdiscipline of the sublime with the slime.

Mama: Arrey Deva, you are even beginning to say incomprehensible things like an art critic. No-no, beta, not an art critic. You can even become a cricket selector but not an art critic. Beta – listen to me – there is still time to repent. It's still not too late.

Kaala (overlapping): Mama, why is it that susu rooms are always so stinky?

Mama: Hush! Will you ever be quiet? All the time muttering–puttering dirty things. Look at your friends. They have gone so far ahead in life. Whereas you, all the time troubling! Don't eat on time. Don't take your bath when told. Dirty goose. And here Papa and I – take so much interest in your upbringing.

Kaala: OH YAAH–YAAH. Five o'clock – in the morning – Private Tuitions. Six o'clock – Swimming Classes. Seven o'clock – Cricket Nets. Eight o'clock – GK Orientation Program with Low–Calorie Breakfast. Nine o'clock – School. One o'clock – Zero-cholestrol Lunch. Three o'clock – Tennis Sessions. Four o'clock – 30 minutes surfing on the World Wide Web – followed by Yoga. Five o'clock – Tutorials in Sanskrit, Chinese and Swahili. Six o'clock – 30 minutes Transcedental Meditation. Six-thirty – Vocational Guidance in Cooking, Carpentry, Plumbing and Fuse Repairs. Seven o'clock – Sauna and jacuzzi at the Club. Eight o'clock – Homework – alongwith Dinner. Nine o'clock – 10 minutes relaxation. Nine thirty – Crash course on Initial Public Stock Offering on the global stock exchanges. Eleven o'clock – Play a round of Golf. Twelve o'clock – Continue the research on Teutonium for Industrial purposes.

Mama: And at one o'clock instead of practising to become a solo tanpura player – you go to sleep. ... Beta – I hope you realise that the competition is so much. By going to sleep at one o'clock – you're frittering away vital man hours. Beta, it won't do. Just won't. Look at your colleagues – they have all gone ahead of you. Whilst you are all the time creating – mischief. And all the time asking questions – *'Mama, what is the meaning of Ontological Etiology'* or *'Mama, what is the difference between a Gramscian intellectual and daddy?'* How often have I told you leave all these things to the Uncle log. You just sit and do your homework, and you will also become one. Then you can do all this Uncle-talks .... And don't yawn when I'm talking to you, understand?

Kaala: Mama, you really look ravishing when you get angry. I swear.

Mama: Naughty, naughty. You're getting too much for your age.

Kaala: In fact, Dungu was telling me the other day that, yaar, of all the mothers in the school – you're the sexiest.

Mama: That 12-year-old *bachcha*! What does he know about all this?

Kaala: It's not Dungu's fault. You see, he has a massive Oedipus complex. Apparently, it originates from penis envy. So said Freud.

Mama: What!

Kaala: Yes Mama. The poor fellow. You must adopt him.

Mama: Who? Freud?

Kaala: Don't be a dumbo. I meant Dungu.

Mama: Penis envy and what not. Holy Lingam, who is telling you all this bunkum ...? And what about studies and all? Arrey, somebody tell me what is happening to our education system? I spend time and effort and give birth to a baby boy – that too, through a caesarean – so that he grows up to learn Geography, Arithmetics, PT, Moral Science ....

Kaala: All that is old hat, Ma. Things have changed. Already, we are planning a series of civic upheavals. It's all worked out. An underground movement. I'm in charge of Removal of Air from the Car Tyres Squad.

Mama: Oh bhagwaan. Please protect my son! What weird ideas he has!

Kaala: Don't be a proper bore, Ma ...

The car screeches to a halt. A pause. Lights come and go.

Mama (piercing screams): O Hellish Hell. Look ahead. There is a huge crowd. There seems to be some mischief going on. See, see, over there. Can you spot them? Oooh, I'm getting disoriented. My head is dizzy ...

Kaala: I sense trouble, Ma. It cannot be the October Revolution. Nor the Peasant's Uprising. Not even the French Revolution. Or the fight for Independence. Oooh – what could it be now ... ?

Mama: It's the curfew. They have clamped a CURFEW.

Kaala: A curfew? What is a curfew ya? Mama, Mama, tell me, which extraordinary brain invented it?

Mama: Beta, come, turn around. Hurry. Into the galis and alleys. Let's go to home-sweet-home.

Kaala: Mama, when and where was the first curfew imposed?

Mama: Arrey baba, no time for questions!

Kaala: What ya – tell me, is a curfew the will of the people? Or is it the desire of the masses?

Mama: The garbage is overflowing. The bandicoots are all around. Broken glass pieces. Shattered dreams. Ah, how it all begins. Didn't we pass this dead manhole some time ago? Come beta. Run.

Kaala: What ya – this is irresponsibility run riot, I swear. I mean what about my future?

Mama: I understand, beta. But what to do? You'll have to make a compromise. A national sacrifice. Circumstances are such. Bad times. Bad days.

Kaala: What ya? Do you realise, you are snatching my Fundamental Right to Education from me?

Mama: Shaddup. Be quiet – you sonoffabitch!!! OK. Will you throw your tantrums, some other time? Ayyo, was that a bullet shot?

Kaala (wailing): YAH – I'm katti with you. I swear. God promise.

Mama: Will you be quiet for a moment? Here, we are fighting a battle of life and death, and yet, you go chatter-chatter. Be silent, or I'll tell Papa to beat you ...

Kaala (running): A for Amitabh. B for Bachchan. C for Curfew ...

A song.

Run-run-run
Run-mummy-run
Save your own life
And save your son
Run-run-run
Run-sonny-run
There's CURFEW out there
And it ain't no fun
Run–run–run *(repeat)*

The Peepal tree blows the whistle.

B: Er ... should we carry on with our story?

A: Now – what's the matter?

B: Here look here *(points to the huge cloth map)* ... It's just that ... our story about Kaala seems to hurtling towards a *tragedy*.

A: Ah, but isn't that good. It's said that only those who have suffered profoundly and known the *tragic* penumbra of things tell truly wonderful stories.

Yama: In the larger realm of things, not much. It's just that o. I got into an affray, a fracas with Shiva. It was terrible, what he did to me. Here, I was on duty. Ready to solidify the soul of a 16-year-old devotee of Shiva .....

Kaala: 16-year-old!

Yama: Let that be!!! And so, when I threw my lassoed noose of death around the neck of this kid – Blooming Narakas, I missed.

Kaala: Oh.

Yama: Instead, the lasso fell around Shiva's neck.

Kaala: Oh no! You were caught necking Shiva of all the Gods.

Yama: It was a complete disaster. He opened his Third Eye. And Zip–Zap–Zoom.

Kaala: Was it serious? I mean, did you die ... ?

Yama: Yes, yes. No scope for hope.

Kaala: That must have been an interesting situation for you as the God of Death. Tell me, how did you get back from the dead?

Yama: I really don't know. One day, I just resumed my earthly duties. In fact, I'm still trying to figure it out. There's no mention of it in any of the scholarly texts ...

Kaala: What happened since then?

Yama: Imagine. Not a word of apology. Or even so much as a by your leave. Nothing. And mind you, I'm a fairly senior kind of God. In fact, I'm, how shall I utter it, good enough to get a cabinet rank in the Hindu Ministry. And yet, after all these years of Karma, such is my reward. Shiva Om ... Shiva Om ...

Kaala: Ahara ... Ahara ...

Yama: Ahara?? Ahara???

Kaala: What now, Yamraj ji ...

Yama: I was wondering, Purusha ...

Kaala: What about?

Yama: That all this is a devious trick. That history is repeating itself.

Kaala: Meaning ....

Yama: Do not try to fool me. After all, even I can understand things. I mean, are you not the very same devotee of Shiva? You utter the same sentences, when I pronounce a death sentence. You do not fear me, instead you riddle me. Have you been reincarnated? What is your star sign? Show me your horoscope ...

Kaala: What kind of suspicion is this? I'm in your service – forever. It's just that the circumstances are victimising ...

Yama: The same words. The same tone. Gosh, the naked transparency of the thing is evident. How could I have overlooked it?

Kaala: What ...

Yama: This curfew is a newer word for Shiva – The Destroyer – The Destructor – The Demolisher ...

Kaala: Preposterous. The curfew is nothing of the sort. It's just a sort of ... er ... sociopolitical disaster. As you stated, a kind of man-made death.

Yama: I hope you are not trying to hoodwink me. Remember, there is no escape from death. Like the pre-genital desire of urinating, death is a fait accompli.

Kaala: Oh, it's nothing serious. We'll merely have to be patient. Wait a while for the trouble storms to blow over. Let things settle down.

Yama: But what about Shiva?

Kaala: What about Him?

Yama: As it is, He is angry with me. To be precise, enraged. I'm the only God, who conducts my activity without the Ganesh Sutra. I don't need it. I have to end things, not begin them. And so, I fulfill my Dharma with the Yama Mantra. I don't think, He approves of that. Ganapati is His favourite, you know ... all this nepotism among Gods too, it's not fair, they always pick on me. What do they think I am ... a *kachcha nimbu*?

Kaala (overlaps): Er, relax Yamraj ji. Be cool. Stay calm. Have a cup of chai. It should soothe you.

Yama: Chai? What's that? A newer version of soma rasa?

Kaala: No. This is part of the T-series.

Yama: In that case, a big cauldron of chai for me. No sugar. Got to watch my waist.

Kaala: Make yourself comfortable, whilst I make you a Special ....

Yama: Oh I see – trying to abscond. Making an attempt to prolong your life. Seek a long life, like a tortoise ...

Kaala (exiting): No Yamraj ji, no. You grievously misunderstand me. I'm merely trying to be a good host, before I turn to a good ghost ...

Loud scream offstage.

Yama: Arrey, what happened? Are you dead or what? *(Momentarily reflects; in an aside)* But surely that cannot be possible, if I'm here ...

Kaala (rushes in): It's that damned CURFEW!

Yama: What happened?

Kaala: There's no water in the house.

Yama: So?

Kaala: And when I tried to turn on the taps, blood flowed out, as in the River Tiber.

Yama: Blood! Yummy! Which blood group?

Kaala: How does it matter? *(A beat)* What do we do now?

Yama: How am I to know? I may be a God, but this is your house.

Kaala: What a mess! Good God!

Yama: ... Yes?

Kaala: What?

Yama: Er, you called me ... ?

Kaala: When?

Yama: Right now.

Kaala: I did? Well ... then help me.

Yama: How?

Kaala: I've to get to work. My future hinges on it. There's no money in my pockets, and my bank account is bankrupt.

Yama: So go to work.

Kaala: I can't.

Yama: Why not???

Kaala: Because of the curfew ... it's all around. The circle is tightening. Can't you feel it? It's suffocating ...

Yama (tentative): Are you certain this curfew is not another name for Shiva ...

The Peepal tree blows the whistle.

B: Look, we are stuck. That much is evident. Hmmmm, do you think the time is appropriate to turn to the Peepal tree for guidance?

A: What further guidance do you need? Look, Kaala our main protagonist has been able to hoodwink Yama, The God of Death. If he can survive for a few moments more, he will have new lease of life! That is the only thing which will keep this journey going ...

B: Yes, I know all that. What I'm saying is why don't we get a few tips from the Peepal tree. After all, we are new to this business of storytelling, aren't we, eh?

A: Pah – that's a feeble argument.

B: Explain.

A: Look, we are *Homo fabula*. That is, storytelling beings. Part human. Part stories. Surely, we need no assistance.

B: But ...

A (plucks a leaf): I suggest like a leaf from the Peepal Tree – you leave for the next story.

A song

What is the most globalised, privatised,

Multi-internationalised

Thing in the world
A CURFEW
What is the most beautiful, wonderful,
Extra-ordinaryful
Thing in the world
A CURFEW

Once upon a time and the time is now, we are in the presence of Kaala who is in the presence of his boss (alias A).

Boss (heavily accented): Come in .....

Kaala (enters hesitantly): Er ... how are you?

Boss: Look, I'm a busy man. Don't have time to fritter. Because time is money. And every second that I waste is a dent to this company's turnover ...

Kaala: Yes. Of course ...

Boss: So? Who are you?

Kaala: I ... well ... work here.

Boss: You do? Very strange, I don't recollect interacting with you. Ever.

Kaala: That was because I couldn't come to work for some time ...

Boss: And pray why, may I ask?

Kaala: They had er ... imposed a curfew in the vicinity of my home. There was no chance of stepping outdoors.

Boss: How then do you explain your presence – today?

Kaala: Oh – with great difficulty. Er ....

Boss: Excuses excuses excuses. It's people like you, who are responsible for the state and being of this country. No sense of responsibility. No initiative.

Kaala: It's not that, sir ...

Boss (Rings a bell. A beat. Talks to an invisible peon): ... Arrey Shinde, what is happening to that Bill of Loading. Check it, maan. Also, send someone to the warehouse, and grease the officer. Our consignment is held up. Client has already signed an LC for next order. Come on, hurry up ... *(dismisses peon, turns to Kaala)* ... Ah, so what were you stating? Quick. I've no time to waste. Time is money, you know. Every second is precious.

Kaala: Well sir, even my name no longer exists in the official records ...

Boss (grunts): I'm not surprised. If you make a guest appearance after all these months, what else do you expect? A red carpet welcome? Tell me, tell me. Huh. Look mister, this is a private company. And not some public sector dinosaur. We're on the Go. In these times of recession, we cannot let our productivity suffer ...

Kaala: Recession, Sir? Aren't we going through an inflation? Everything is so costly!

Boss: You dare contradict me. Do you know who I am? I'm a regular contributor to the *Times*. An expert on fiscal matters. A guest lecturer at management schools. And you dare contradict me!

Kaala: But sir, everything has changed so drastically. The layout of the office. The interiors. The cloakrooms have been airconditioned. Even, the people are all unfamiliar. I mean, what's happening? Where's everyone?

Boss: We've gone in for major restructuring. This is the multi-nationalisation of wealth. Enough, of all that hollow talk about Gandhism and all ...

Kaala: Who, this Italian one?

Boss: Arrey, no no that Khadi fellow.

Kaala: Yes. What about him?

Boss: Root cause of the trouble in this country. Stunted our economy. Created misconceptions, with his talk about self-reliance, social justice and what not. One number troublemaker, I tell you!

Kaala: Sir, but what about my job ... ?

Boss: What? You dare interrupt me! Don't you know who I am?

I'm a freelancing advisor to the Executive Secretary in the Ministry of State of Finance. In fact, my revised paper '*The Appreciation of the Currency due to the Creation of Depreciation in the Land of Vitiation*' is going to be presented at the International Finance Trust. In that paper, I argue for whatever it is worth, that Gandhi was a no-gooder.

Kaala: Gandhiji was a no–gooder, sir???

Boss: Yes, yes. For instance, look at this curfew business. Haven't you learnt from it? It's all Gandhi's fault.

Kaala: What has Gandhiji to do with the curfew?

Boss: Everything. All that rubbish about civil disobedience and satyagraha – to what avail? What was wrong with the East India Company? An efficient profit-making organisation. Clean management. Goodish returns. And reasonably high turnover. Now, what more can the economy want???

Kaala: Well ...

Boss: Anyway, all that is the past. The East India Company is back. OK, the brand name is different. But then, as whats-his-name-Willie-the-Shakes said 'What's in a name?' Ha-ha. Just to show you that some things remain the same ...

Kaala: But – sir ...

Boss: Stop arguing like a Lohia-wallah, OK?

Kaala: But sir ... what about me, sir?

Boss: What about you?

Kaala: Am I employed or no?

Boss: I don't think so. The official records don't have your name.

Kaala: But that's strange. After all, how can it be? I've worked here for the seven best years of my life.

Boss: Really? How strange! Because the company hasn't been in existence for that long! Your case is closed, pal!

Kaala: But ... you can't expunge my name from the files without any prior notification. Please reconsider, sir.

Boss: I don't know about all that. You talk to the legal chaps about it. But, as things stand, my personal reading is, we cannot re-hire you.

Kaala: What about my qualifications? Even my credentials are impeccable ...

Boss: All that is fine. But it's a no-win situation. We've received a directive from our overseas headquarters in Salzburg that in the name of modernisation and automation, we cannot recruit any more personnel. Babe, downsizing is the name of the game!

Kaala: And me, what do I do, huh? Where will I get another employment, at such short notice?

A gunshot.

Kaala: Good God, what is happening?

Boss (rings the bell; talks to an imaginary peon): 'Arrey, What the hell is happening – Shinde. What's all this noise and voice? Eh, what. Speak up, yaar. Whoa, stocks have been burnt up! There is a riot in the factory? Sonoffagun, how can this country progress if there is daylight vandalism. That too, bloody blatantly. What'll happen to our growth rate. Our output ... Achcha, listen Shinde, you tell my PA to contact the Ministry. Get me Mr Shourie on the line ... and tell him to impose a curfew *in these parts. A shoot-at-sight. That's the only language those goondas and Mawalis understand.'*

Kaala: A curfew ... ? But the curfew is already in existence.

Boss: So what, we can always impose another curfew. What difference does it make?

A song.

Tell me more, tell me more, tell me more about it.

Have black coffee, have iced tea,

Let's discuss debt traps, the equity

I'm ok with the inflation–recession

'Cause I prefer it to the Great Depression

The fiscal deficit, the bankruptcy

We need a drastic change of policy
What is the most globalised, privatised,
Multi-internationalised
Thing in the world
A curfew
What is the most beautiful, wonderful,
Extra-ordinaryful
Thing in the world
A curfew

The Peepal tree blows the whistle.

A (blowing the trumpet): Ooooh la la la, our story is really getting interesting.

B: It's getting confusing. I genuinely don't see any *point*.

A: Look yaar, is there any *point* to human existence, eh?

B: That is a facile argument – if I may say so.

A: See. Stories – at least great legends have to resonate our beginnings and intuit our endings. It has to tell the story of Life. It has to dissolve Origin and Destiny into One. It has to keep tabs of the Time. And our story is doing that – it is keeping a close eye on Kaala ...

B: Sounds like some impenetrable paradox. Anyway – get on with your journey.

A: Oh, don't sound so despondent ... in our line of business it's always said no matter how important the other things are ... the completion of the journey is most crucial. And, look here, we are so close to our final destination.

The Peepal tree blows the whistle.

Yama: OK, Purusha forget your chai and blood from the taps ... I've duties to attend to. Appointments to keep. This, here, is not the only sphere of my activity. There's a world on the other side of this living void. And that world is my whole-sole responsibility.

Kaala: Yamraj ji, the CURFEW is not in my hands. In fact,

it doesn't seem to be in anybody's hands.

Yama: Look, don't you realise the seriousness of the task? I have to get back to the dead. Spend some time with them. Or else, they might start vanquishing the living ones. Because if, by chance, I overshoot my deadline, it will be uglificating! A demonic blow to DEMONgraphy. To the balance between life, birth and diseases ... And pray, may I ask, what statistical activity are you now indulging in?

Kaala (tinkering with a telephone): This is deadly.

Yama: What?

Kaala: This telephone, it is dead.

Yama: That is impossible.

Kaala: Why?

Yama: I did not do it. Nor do I recollect sending my agents to collect the Atma of this phone.

Kaala: Phew, this is exasperating! Every time there is a CURFEW, the phones go dead. It's all part of a ploy. They are deliberately trying to instill tears and fears in our minds ... the entire system is phoney! The phone is instrumental in it. Nothing works when you want it to. *(Pause)* Come to think of it, you could help us – by rectifying the phone. Here and now.

Yama: Me? How?

Kaala: You're the God of Death, aren't you? You take away the soul of living things, don't you? Well then, by the same quantum, you could even restore it back, couldn't you?

Yama: Hmmmm ... let me see. The phone might be handy. I have to contact Headquarters Yamapuri and get the latest update on deaths on Yama–TV ....

Slight change in mood. Telephonic sounds and colourful dream-like lighting. Kaala and Yama, not only converse on their respective phones, but with each other as well. They must speak rapidly and with staccato evenness. Every attempt should be made to retain the illusory quality of the scene.

A song.

Senorita, Margurita, Paparazzi, Mona Lisa,
Oh Sunita, Vinita, Kavita ... My Papita
Doobie–Dooba, Dooba–Kuda, Kuda–Dooba, Dooba–Tera
Oh My Pizza, My Bournvita, My Bambalita,
Too thi, Main tha – Senorita
Doobie–Dooba, Dooba–Kuda, Kuda–Dooba, Dooba–Tera

Kaala (on a phone): Tring–Tring–Tring ...

Yama: What's happening?

Kaala: Sssssh. You have broken through to the other side. The first known instance of telecommunication between Prithvi and Swarga. Sponsored by Yama-TNL.

Yama: Hell–Hell–Hello ...

Kaala (in a fake, high-pitched female voice): Dahling, is that you. I'm so worried. Where are you speaking from?

Yama: I'm speaking from the mouthpiece. And you ...

Kaala: My sweetie-cutie-fruity-cooh, you're so clever.

Yama (to Kaala): What's happening, Purusha, who be that strange creature?

Kaala (to Yama): Fear not, it's a regular occurrence. A cross-connection.

Yama: A cross-connection? Jesus Christ!

Kaala (henceforth a lady): Dahling, are you there, or are you not. The question is tying me up into knots.

Yama: Look Sister ji ... I'm not who you think me to be.

Lady: Why? Who are you – handsome?

Yama: I'm Yama, the God of Death.

Lady: And I'm the Rani of Jhansi. What great fun, no?

Yama: Please understand, this is an emergency. I have to contact someone urgently. This is no time to joke.

Lady: Arrey baba, what happened? Is there some fighting-lighting in your area? Someone killed someone or what? Our galli has become quite peaceful, after the curfew. It's so boring. But last night it was too much ...

Yama: Why – was there some trouble last night?

Lady: Hai Toba, 365 heads in all ... head a day. No discrimination, you know. Equality for all – no matter what the shape and size of the head.

Yama: But what happened?

Lady: That's what I'm telling. Why don't you see it right away? The cable fellow is showing an LD print. It's – so exciting ... they have even found sponsorship for the curfew. This part of the curfew is sponsored by Die-Soon Undertakers!

Yama (appalled): A sponsorship for the curfew???

Lady: You are mad only. Not knowing all this. Why? Where have you come from, the village or something ... ?

Yama: No. I'm Yama from Yamapuri.

Lady: Travelling on a Yamaha ... ?

Yama: No. I travel on my buffalo..

Lady: Sheeee, what a dirty fellow! You're too much of a weirdo for words. Eh, you are too much, hanh. I'm going, reh. TaTa. Buy-Buy. Reliance. Sell-Sell.

Yama: Hold on. Hold on. Just a minute. I desperately need to talk to you.

Lady: Achcha? First behaving like a village bumpkin, then flirting! Look Mister, if you act funny, I'll shave your eyelashes off. Got it, no?

Yama: But ...

Lady: Look mister – I'm going through a bad patch in my life. So don't try any hanky-panky with me, OK?

Yama: Sister ji, there seems to be some ...

Lady: Let me give my fundas straight, huh. I really don't like men. I hate the category. Every single one of them. In fact, I'm even going to divorce my husband. Any moment. Phuta phut ...

Yama: A divorce?

Lady: Absolutely – useless fellow! Why? I haven't even seen the fellow for two years.

Yama: That's 730 days!!!

Lady: And 730 nights as well, my good sir. The chap says he can't come home because of the curfew.

Yama: The curfew?

Lady: For two years I had to fend for myself. Oh Lord, tell me why, of all the blessed-wretched things did I have to marry a husband!

Yama: Things are not that bad – Sister ji. Consider this: If there were no husbands, there would be no wives.

Lady: Yes, yes. What you say is also true.

Yama: Supply and demand.

Lady: True, true. But you forget – that it is this that makes life so full of tension! The search for a good husband. A companion in life. A friend in need. Arrey baba, for a woman, it is a vital need.

Yama: Well spoken. 'Cause even the laws of Manu and Kamasutra say this.

Lady: But how to get your hands on the right husband, at the exact moment you require him? It is big problem. All those big-big books and PhDs on the subject, but still, no way to find a good husband. In fact even the Yellow Pages omits the profession 'Husband'. They just mention all the worthless trades. All kinds of dhandawallahs – who are supposed to be of assistance in a midlife crisis. But, you tell me, what use will I ever have of Zari Products and Turnkey Projects, Earthmoving Equipment and Unani Specialists, and such rubbish. I want a husband. Arrey, even an average fellow will do. But no, there is no mention of a good husband. Pah, all a money-making racket. Hahn, hahn. They will tell you how to find an Electro Galvanising Anodiser, as if anyone knew what to do with an Electro Galvanising Anodiser once you possess it. They give the telephone numbers of Angadia

Services, when you don't even know what it means. That's the problem with this country. Good husbands are unavailable. What to say about such a mentality ... phew, the kind of things we wives have to undergo! And the kind of men we have to marry ... Ooooof!!!

Yama: Sister ji, you sound delirious. Is it that time of the month for you?

Lady: Achcha, a below-the-belt attack!

Pause. The lights come and go. Once. Twice. Thrice. Four times.

Yama: Hush. Can you smell it?

Lady: What? My ....

Yama: The whiffs of the curfew.

Lady: Hey, what are you a poet or what? The whiffs of curfew and all. Hey, you are really an intellectual type. Superb, yaar. Hey, you listen to my poem too! I'm sending it along with my divorce petition. Want to hear, no? This is the way to go.

A song (in Punjabi)

Baari Barsi Khatan Gyaasi – Ki Khat ke Leyan Da?
Khat Ke Leyan Da CURFEW.
Do Baras Gaye Guzar Na Aaya
Ud Gaya Mera Fuse
Ki Main Jhoot Boliyan? – Koi Na
Ki Main Kufar Toliyan? – Koi Na
Baari Barsi Khatan Gyaasi – Ki Khat ke Leyan Da?
Khat Ke Leyan Da TALAQ.
Pati Ka Bistar Gol Kiya
Ab Nipple Hue Azad.
Ki Main Jhoot Boliyan? – Koi Na
Ki Main Kufar Toliyan? – Koi Na

Yama (shocked): Hello Sister ji?

Kaala (no longer Lady): Yamraj ji – the worst has occured, my wife has divorced me.

Yama: She has? How do you know???

Kaala: Why Yamraj ji, you just heard her ...

Yama: What? That woman of exquisite taste and refinement was your wife?

Kaala: Yes, Yamraj ji ... but not any more. And all because of this curfew. That makes it the one millionth divorce in these parts for this week.

Yama: I say this Curfew is unnerving me. I've never witnessed anything like this before.

General pandemonium. Alarm bells go off.

Yama: Look, look, look how the past, the present, the future are all converging together and creating a complete breakdown of all the things that have been created by the Creator.

Both scrutinise the huge cloth map.

Kaala: Look here, there's been a communal conflagration here. And over here too ... the authorities have imposed a curfew in Jallandhar. According to official reports, it's all because that Barnali Bhowmick was trying to fly a kite on his terrace. It seems the kites were a secret signal to the enemy. The officer on duty said the administration hopes to introduce an ordinance KATA which will ban flying kites on all days except Makar Sankrati ...

Yama: And a **curfew** in Imphal because Puneet Dhar Das sold his Impala. ... Ah, and what have here, the Battle of Kalinga, that's strange ... an unusual anachronism, but let that be.

Kaala: Look, look a curfew in Mandu as a result of that spice merchant Lavang Elaichiranjeevi wanting to set up a Mirchi Manufacturing Plant in honour of his wife Kadi Atta Patta Nahin. ...

Yama: Ooooh, this one's a beauty: a curfew at Ranikhet because Papachan Kutty Cherian and his cousin Thomas Kutty Varkey refused to speak in Hindi to their Jharkhand guide on the foothills of the Himalayas ...

Kaala: Oh, and what have here: the Mutiny of the Sepoys in 1857! Arrey, that sounds a bit out-of-place ... Ummmm, look here, a curfew because Tanaaz Tantra who resides in the mentally handicapped centre in Ranchi broke the nib of his fountain pen before he could pen a revolutionary draft about the land reform bill.

Yama: … and one more curfew on 123, Karappa Gounder Street where RVN Raghavan and his thirteen-and-a-half relatives ate all the Idlis, Vadas and Dosas that the AIADMK was hurling at the DMK ... Arrey, this one is genuine fun! A curfew in Aligarh because Wafa Hakim Thorat's son-in-law Khalid Halim has ceased overseeing the preservation of the Hazarduari Palace in Murshidabad ... and this one's a bit hazy, can you make it out, something about two countries criss-crossing in 1947 … heee-heee-hee. And see this, a curfew in Guntakkal where Charit Rao's mother has stopped breastfeeding him at the age of 32 ... yes, and here, no-no, not there, over here we have a curfew in Shekawat because the caretaker of Gulab Rai Ladia's Haveli has a toothache … and, look here, Yahya Khan is busy signing a treaty in 1972 in Dhaka! I wonder what is the significance of that ... ?

Kaala: Oh my my, we even have a curfew in Gwalior, because Parama's daughter, adorned in her marriage costume, jewellery and mehndi is waiting in the lobby of a cinema house for her Bundela husband to appear on a horseback ... and bhalo-bashi, a curfew has been imposed on Kunju Bihari Bose Lane of Tollygunge because a group of 17-year-olds are unable to decide which is better, Mohun Bagan or hilsa with mustard ...

Yama: And look, over here, there are other curfews too. Agartala, Ajmer, Alappuzha, Amritsar, Ayodhya, Andaman & Nicobar ... I could go on.

Kaala: Enough enough enough!!! *(Silence)* Yamraj ji, how do you propose I should meet my end?

Yama: Ah ha, you who were so defiant, now you choose to die.

Kaala: What to do? Things are utterly hopeless. This curfew ... it ... it controls my existence. I mean, the curfew has made sure that I've failed in every stage of my life. When I was very very young the curfew ensured that I could not complete my education, and my duties to my mother – my *dharma*. And then, the curfew was an obstacle between me and my work, my sole source of employment – my *artha*. The curfew even guaranteed that I do not perform my husbandly duties – my *kama*. And so, today, I'm isolated from my mother, my family. I've no job. No job. I dread to think of the morrow, what with this curfew having permeated every pore of my existence. I genuinely don't know what other tragedy awaits my living being. Oh, what hope do I have now of ever attaining moksha? Oh Yamraj ji, let me cast off this worn body and start again. *(A beat)* Give me my death ... death ... death ...

A song.

When Kaala was a young boy,
In the year who knows when
Determined to go to school
In his Momma's Mercedes Benz
He was hoping to excel
In whichever class he went
But when the CURFEW came
He ended up being spent

He wants to die
Everybody knows he wants to die
Kya kare bhai,
Dimag ka ho gaya bheja fry

Kaala had a regular job
With lots of perks at that
Meanwhile no one ever knew
What the CURFEW was really at
Kaala had a big house
Which was totally bullet-proof
Till he lost his job

When his Boss hit the roof
He wants to die
Everybody knows he wants to die
Kya kare bhai,
Dimag ka ho gaya bheja fry

In his later years
Kaala wanted a son
This CURFEW messed me childhood
May be me son can have one
But his wife she had other plans
And she clearly stated so
She took all the cash
And then she hit the road
He wants to die
Everybody knows he wants to die
Kya kare bhai,
Dimag ka ho gaya bheja fry

Kaala (who has aged): Beware! Beware! Beware of the storyteller who is not fully conscious of the importance of his gift. Do not trust the Peepal tree and its stories so completely. It is a dangerous thing to do. I've been paying heed to the stories all my life – but now, I've come to the conclusion that this Peepal tree is very slowly and consciously poisoning this nation and its people – with its stories. After all, a people are only as healthy and confident as the stories themselves. Remember, unhappy lands prefer utopian stories. And happy lands prefer unhappy stories.

Yama: Sssshhh!

Kaala: What?

Yama: Listen can't you hear it. The sound of sounds. The earth has become overcrowded with living beings.

Kaala: I do not comprehend.

Yama: Don't you realise? There hasn't been a single death whilst

I've been whiling away my time with you. It was bound to happen in my absence. Oh, this curfew will not only be the end of me, but of this planet. *(Lies prostrate on the ground)* The number of living beings have trebled. Perhaps quadrupled. The earth can no longer bear their weight. Can't you feel the gravity of the situation? The earth is sinking. It has already sunk 13 yojanas! And at the rate at which incidents are unfolding, it will sink another 100 yojanas, at least!

Kaala: But ...

Yama: If that happens, ye foolish Purusha, the earth will shift to another solar system, to a dark age.

Kaala: Yamraj ji, this might shock you. But unknown to you there is a world outside of here. And out there, the situation is vastly different from what you think it to be. According to available reports, deaths are occurring even in your absence.

Yama: Preposterous! What a thought!

Kaala: But it's true. I have the facts with me. Here – peer through these binoculars. What do you see?

Bright blue lights. Naturally – to indicate a change of scene – even as Yama peers at the audience.

Pause. The lights come and go. Once. Twice. Thrice.

Yama (staring into the audience): Arrey, Purusha, where have all these corpses come from?

Kaala: Sssshhh! Do not disturb them. They are the Souls of the Gods.

Yama: Souls of the Gods. In that case, why are they residing in these earthly forms?

Kaala: Can't you see, it's a graveyard? An assembly of dead Gods.

Yama: No, no, they cannot be dead. Listen, I can hear the sound of their breathing ...

Kaala (cocks his head): It is more like the sound of breeding.

Yama: What? Breathing and breeding. Breeding and breathing.

Kaala: More and more Gods in heaven breeding into dead earthly forms ...

Yama (a despairing cry): Hai Rudra, what is happening? It seems like big trouble! Perhaps the end. Yours. Mine. And, perhaps the universe's. How come I was unaware of all these deaths, all this while ... ?

Kaala: It's because of the curfew ...

Yama: Is this curfew the beginning of the Kaliyug? O sky, that's lurking all over and round – bring light to us. See, how unjustly we have become mere shadows. Is this curfew the promised end? Ye sky, don't you think the time has come, when someone–anyone tells us the truth. Here we are seated with immaculate intelligence, contemplating on the distance our species has trvelled, and yet, we don't know what might happen. Whether the curfew is prevalent, or it has subsided. Whether it is good or bad. Whether it can be questioned or not. *(Snaps)* This can't go on. It will be a great tragedy. After all, I monopolise death. So state the laws of the universe. I've to be departing.

Kaala: You cannot depart without me. Remember, I'm supposed to be the departed soul.

Yama: Ssssshh.

Kaala: What?

Yama: Be quiet. Your soul is about to be relieved of its bodily duties ...

Yama sprinkles some magic dust – and chants 'Mahisastha yamagoccha dandahast mahabala raksa tvam daksinadvaram vaivasvata namo stu te'

Kaala (falls on the floor and freezes, arms akimbo): Well ...

Yama: You are dead.

Kaala: Is that all? It cannot be. I feel the same. No change.

Yama: That's how it is with some souls. There's no life before death.

Kaala (intently scrutinising a white sheet on the floor): Say, is that my corpse on the floor?

Yama: It is!

Kaala: Good heavens, don't tell me I used to look so ugly. Really horrible. Look at those ears, they are as crooked as the mafia! And that nose .... Gosh, I really empathise with the folks who had to see me day after day. What do you think, Yamraj ji?

Yama (after a beat): Shall we leave?

Kaala: Is it safe?

Yama: You mean, that curfew ...

Kaala: What else ... ?

Yama: Enough of all this. Attention. Look sharp. On-your-mark. Get-set. One-two-three. Go. Lights. Music.

Brief blackout. Gunshots.

Since it is the beginning of the end, we return to the beginning.

A and B wake up.

A dramatic announcement: Attention! Attention! An indefinite curfew has been declared in your locality. I repeat – a curfew has been imposed under Section 144. This is an order to remain indoors till further notice.

Just a short while ago an extremely dangerous, and notorious terrorist has been shot dead in your locality ... whilst he was trying to escape on a buffalo ...

Right now, there is no reason to panic. But we request all citizens to please abide by the law – and not believe in rumours to the contrary. We have all things under control – and the curfew should be lifted shortly.

In the meantime, anyone found outside will be considered a threat, and shot at sight. To prevent any such occurrence, we request all inhabitants to cooperate with us – and prevent any untoward incident ...

A song.

And so, even Yama – the God of Death, had to die

As the CURFEW cast its spell on these two Bhais

We have reason to worry, every reason to brood

With Yama's death, this CURFEW is up to no good

Once I told stories, full of rhyme, full of tune
But now I think, I've reached the ... dark side of the moon.
So please hear my death wish, my dear friend
Make sure this CURFEW is not part of a fashionable trend
Well, it's late, so you better go home straight
Before this CURFEW transforms your future and fate ...
Freeze tableau.

Mahadevbhai (1892–1942)

Dedicated to APPU KILLI and BACHUA SHEESH
(for instilling an iota of Gandhian thought in me
even before I was born)

Premiered on 15th November (2002) at the Prithvi Theatre Festival, Mumbai

Director: Ramu Ramanathan

Performed by: Jaimini Pathak

Research and Music Design: Kinnari Vohra

Production: Suruchi Aulakh

Set Design: Nikhil Khadilkar and Vinesh Iyer

Lights: Kavi Bhansali and Rama Ramanathan

Sound: Pragya Tewari

Backstage: Rishi Mazumdar

Publicity Design: Bobby Chhaya

There is a Gandhian baithak at stage left (an exclusive area for Mahadevbhai); a special area for the Dadaji encounters (stage right with lots of books for reference); and a central area for the young actor. Two cane stools are present -- one is used for discussions and the other to highlight Gandhiji's two ideological adversaries: Jinnah and Ambedkar.

There is a standing mike up front (stage right). Key political speeches (Gandhi, Tagore, Amdedkar) are delivered at the mike.

The set design should be spartan but neat and elegant; in effect, Gandhian.

ACT I SCENE 1

Actor, reads from a scroll.

Whenever I think of Mahadevbhai

This play was first published in *Collaborators and Mahadevbhai* by Ramu Ramanathan, ed. Alok Bhalla and Anju Makhija, Sahitya Akademi Publications, New Delhi, 2006.

I am reminded of the following verse:

Who will not bow to him;
Who always has a smiling face;
Who has speech full of sweetness
In a compassionate heart
And whose deeds help others!

(looking at the audience for the first time) ... So said Vinayak Narhar Bhave, Vinoba ... about Mahadevbhai.

ACT I SCENE 2

The actor speaks

Mahadevbhai! But who is Mahadevbhai? And why am I, a meek and humble, subservient and lowly actor, talking about him! Wait! For patience is a great virtue, mon ami! Hold your fire. Hang on to those horses. We will pass time, together. Me and you. You and me.

But who am I?

Well, as aforementioned on one occasion, I am a meek and humble, subservient and lowly actor. For those of you who know me there is no point in disclosing my identity, since that would be a waste of time. And for the millions and millions of masses who don't know me, there is no point mentioning my name, since it would not make the least difference. After all, they did say, 'He can't be a high-quality actor. If he is performing a play, at best he can be an out-of-work actor.'

But just because I'm out of work you must not undermine my creed. Coz, like everyone else I have a gotra. Like everyone else I have a father who has a father who has a father who has a father ... ad nauseam, ad infinitum, etc. etc. As many fathers to fathers as there are stars in the Milky Way. But wait a moment ... I've gone ahead. Because my father's father had a brother. Yes, that is to say, my grand-uncle of sorts.

(Actor refers to an old black-and-white photograph)

Ah, here he is ... in this old black-and-white photograph. Here can you see him, my grand-uncle. Next to him stands Mahadevbhai ... and that over there is Mohandas Karamchand Gandhi ...

And so, although I'm a meek and humble, subservient and lowly actor, *as afore mentioned on two occasions,* I have considerable standing in the world because of this photograph. I'm **well connected**, you see. Me ... my father ... my grandfather ... my grandfather's brother ... Mahadevbhai ... and Mohandas Karamchand Gandhi ... waah! In other words, me and Gandhiji have a direct connection. This photograph is precious. So much so, instead of approaching producers of TV serials with pictures from my portfolio, I carry this photograph. Me and Gandhiji. But no one gives me work. Instead they ask, *hahn babua, yeh sab toh theek hain, but beech main yeh Mahadevbhai kaun hain? (Spits out paan)*

Mahadevbhai kaun hain???

So I asked my father, *'Arrey Daddyji, yeh Mahadevbhai kaun hain?'* So, my father asked his father, *'Arrey Papaji, aah Mahadevbhai kaun che?'* To cut a long story short, my Dadaji sent a letter to my Daddyji.

Actor reads letter.

The letter, ah, here it is, said:

Chi Dikra,

Gadheda tane aatlie pan khabar nathi ... ki Mahadevbhai kaun hutta? Too diwali maan aiyaan awish toh taro udhado lehi naakish!

Haveh – ek pag par ubha raheineh – waach!

(Actor ad libs) Baap re baap, *bade boozurgon ke liye ... kya kya karna padta hain.*

(Clears throat, etc.) Mahadev Desai born on 1st January, 1892 at Saras, Taluka Olpad, District Surat. Father – Haribhai Surbhai Desai. Mother – Jamnaben Haribhai Desai. Married – Durgaben Khandubhai Desai of Kaliawadi, near Navsari, at the age of 13.

Gadheda sambhle che ki nahin. Terah varas ni umar ma lagann thaye gaya tha ane haveh taro olo suputra ane maro putra ... tees varas noh ghodo thaiye gaya che ... pan lagann karta nathi. Tanne joiye toh ayan ek mast nih chokri che. Sundar ane viveki. ... ane gadheda pag upar kar.

In 1907, Mahadevbhai was admitted to Elphinstone College in Mumbai to study literature and philosophy. He wrote poetry in the college magazine *Elphinstonian* under the name of Bhola Shambhu! Mahadevbhai passed his final LLB in 1913 and stood first in the university in 'Equity'.

Arrey Mishraji, aap pooch rahe the ki Mahadevbhai kaun hain – yeh dekhiye!!!

Translations in Gujarati and English, five biographies, 20 volumes of diary. Journalistic editing of *Harijan*, *Navjivan*, *Young India*, *Independent*, *Harijan Bandhu*. Twenty miles of walking per day. And so on. And so on. Oooof, these Gandhians! Tireless and indefatigable.

Ah, but as usual, I'm jumping the gun. Let's pause for a moment and travel ... back in time ... when India was a prisoner.

ACT I SCENE 3

My mother and me used to visit Dadaji during Makar Sankranti so that I could fly kites on their terrace. At that time, Dadaji told me stories about the freedom movement along with liberal offerings of doodh-pak, mohan-thaal, shrikhand and basundi.

The reason Dadaji talked about the freedom movement was because of a pencil on his desk.

'*Dadaji, aah shoo che? Aah* pencil? What is this ... thing? This pencil, which you have been safeguarding? It doesn't even have any lead?'

'Arrey beta, be careful. That's not any second-rate pencil. That is the pencil gifted to me by Gandhiji at Premabhai Hall. Personally. And you remember your Rajani Kaki from Porbander? He gifted her an apple.'

Just then Dadiji entered with doodh-pak, mohan-thaal, shrikhand, basundi ... for sampling purposes.

In the midst of this aristocratic company of food, Dadaji would speak about this-that-and-the other. 'Did you know,' Dadaji said 'Rabindranath Tagore believed that India's shackles were self-made. He wept at seeing his India, the eternal ragpicker at other people's dustbins.'

'Dadaji, tamhe pan magaj noh laddoo lo ne ... saras che ...'

Dadaji continued 'Did you know that Tagore once wrote: Prisoner, tell me who was it that wrought this unbreakable chain? It was I, said the prisoner, who forged this chain very carefully.'

'Dadaji, but why are you telling me all this ... ?'

'Because like me, Mahadevbhai was 24 ... when he wanted to break the unbreakable chain! At that time he heard of Gopal Krishna Gokhale's prediction about Gandhiji: 'This man can make men out of dust.' '

That was the first time I had heard of Mahadevbhai. But at that time I had not paid any heed to Dadaji ... since he was always name-dropping. Rajagopalachari of Tamil Nadu, Motilal of Allahabad, Chittaranjan Das of Bengal, General Smuts of South Africa.

'Sambhal dikra,' Dadaji began once again. This time, he started telling me about General Smuts' sandals.

'Dikra, did you know, Gandhiji returned to India on 9th January 1915.'

'Yes, my history teacher – Madame Priscilla – is always telling me something like that!' I replied polishing off the last of the shrikhand.

Mahadevbhai, like everyone else, had heard about Gandhiji's accomplishments in South Africa: the night at Maritzburg station. Then there was the Appeal for Indian Franchise in Natal; the use of **satyagraha** for the first time in Transvaal till the Indian Relief Bill was submitted to the Union Parliament in Cape Town; ... and ... and presenting a pair of sandals, which Gandhiji had made in jail for his old adversary General Smuts.

Speaking about the gift of those sandals ... many years later ... General Smuts remarks: '... I have worn these sandals for many a summer since then, even though I may feel that I am not worthy to stand in the shoes of so great a man.'

Then Dadaji allowed me to touch the pencil he had received at Premabhai Hall. I touched it. Hmmm. It was not as exhilarating as General Smuts' sandals. Nor I imagine as yummy as the apple presented to Rajani Kaki.

Later when I found the black-and-white photograph in the family album ... you know the one with Gandhiji and me ... I realised that Mahadevbhai had attended Gandhiji's lecture at the very same Premabhai Hall. In fact that was the first time Mahadevbhai had set eyes on Gandhi Saheb, according to Mahadevbhai's friend and confidante, Narhari Parekh in his book, *Mahadevbhai-nun Poorvachairitra*. Ah here, it is, *Mahadevbhai-nun Poorvacharitra*. English translation. Third edition.

Actor reads.

'Like Tolstoy Farm and Phoneix Farm in South Africa ... Gandhi Saheb ... (which is what Gandhiji was called then) ... began a Satyagraha Ashram on the western bank of the Sabarmati River. At that time he published a pamphlet about the aims and objectives; and rules of the Ashram. This was distributed in the entire country. The List of The Rules was the basis of character building for Ashramites and highlighted the individual virtues of truth, non-violence, non-possession, non-stealing ... as well as, other revolutionary social values.'

Actor intervenes.

Arrey waah! The same values that Dadaji kept telling me about. Hai na Dadaji?

(Actor still intervening) Since Gandhi Saheb wanted these rules, or vows, to be discussed he distributed the copies. In this sense, he sent some copies of the pamphlet to the Gujarat Club. Acceding to Gandhi Saheb's appeal, Narhari Parekh picked up a copy of the List of Rules and read it with Mahadevbhai. The two lawyer-friends, then drafted their reaction in a letter to Gandhi Saheb.

Narhari says:

'Then one day, Gandhiji came to address a public meeting at the Premabhai Hall (the same public meeting in Premabhai Hall which was attended by my Dadaji and Rajani Kaki from Porbandar). When he was leaving, we – Mahadevbhai and me – reminded him of our letter. He said: "Yes, I've received a letter signed by the two of you. Come, let's talk if you have the time." Gandhiji then took out the letter and talked. He talked for 90 minutes. We interrupted with our arguments, but mostly we did the listening.

Later, we walked for a few miles in silence and when we reached Ellisbridge, Mahadevbhai said, 'Narahari I've half a mind to go and sit at the feet of this man.'

Around that time, Mahadevbhai had completed his translation of Lord Morley's 'On Compromise'. He felt it was necessary to seek Lord Morley's permission before publishing it. So Mahadevbhai had drafted a letter. Mahadevbhai felt it was best to show this letter to someone who had recently returned from England and was conversant with the manners and etiquette of that country. And so, Mahadevbhai showed the letter to Gandhi Saheb.

Gandhiji did not like Mahadevbhai's letter to Lord Morley:

'It is not for nothing that the Englishmen call us flatterers ... who are unfit for Swaraj. Such high praise for Morley is out of place. Besides why should your hand quiver and pen falter whilst writing him a letter? You have to write a simple business letter. Here, come here, I shall dictate the letter, if you want. Come sit here. Here take this pencil. Now write.'

Hmmm. After this, Dadaji tells me, Mahadevbhai endeared himself to Gandhiji because of his goodness and hard work and skills in translation. Gandhiji invited – nay ... *Gandhiji ne mangi lidha* ... Mahadevbhai to join him ...

There was a lot of soul-searching, until Mahadevbhai procured a train ticket. He was travelling in the Frontier Mail, which was the fastest train in those days. Mahadevbhai was going from Mumbai to Godhra.

ACT I SCENE 4

It was 1917, and Gandhiji had organised a Political Conference at Godhra, the most backward of all areas in Gujarat. Gandhiji made the Conference at Godhra unique in many ways.

It was at Godhra that Gandhiji spoke about Hindu–Muslim unity. He said:

Actor speaks into the microphone.

I've only one object in view and it is a clear one, namely that God should purify the hearts of Hindus and Muslims and the two communities should be free from suspicion and fear of one another.

This testimony was endorsed by Vallabhbhai Patel, Lokmanya Tilak and others.

Among the stalwarts of the Panch Mahaal movement, was an unexpected speaker. He was a Khoja Muslim from Kathiawar. He was six feet tall, weighed nine stone and had a monocle dangling from a black cord. He smoked cigarettes, and he was wealthy and cultured. This was Mohammed Ali Jinnah, who considered himself Gandhiji's opposite number. When not speaking, Jinnah would pull in his chin, tighten his lips, knit his big brows. The result was a forbidding earnestness. He rarely laughed. Not only did Gandhiji convince Jinnah to be present at Godhra, he made Jinnah address the masses in Gujarati.

When Jinnah spoke in Gujarati there was tremendous applause. Godhra was seen as a symbol of Hindu–Muslim unity. Sarojini Naidu said she couldn't fathom which among the two was the bigger achievement – getting Jinnah to speak in Gujarati or Hindu–Muslim unity!

Actor speaks into the microphone.

Gandhiji concluded the Godhra Conference with the following words:

'Yes, as Tilak Maharaja says, ours is a struggle for Swaraj, a yearning for Swaraj. But what is Swaraj if the mind is not free from prejudices. For this, there must be a change of heart among

Hindus and Musalmaans. Before Hindus and Musalmaans think of freedom, they must be brave enough to love one another, to tolerate one another's religion, even prejudices and superstitions, and to trust one another. I'm not interested in freeing India merely from the British yoke. I am bent upon freeing India from any yoke whatsoever!!!'

Mahadevbhai was present throughout this Conference. He was attentive. But his mind was fixed on the thought of joining Mohandas Karamchand Gandhi.

Gandhiji had told Mahadevbhai: 'I do not call anybody like this. You're the only one I'm asking for.' And so, when Gandhiji saw Mahadevbhai with his wife Durgaben at Godhra, he asked:

'So when do you intend to join me?'

'Whenever you ask, sir!'

'Are you ready to join right now?'

'We are ready.'

'Both of you?'

'Yes, indeed.'

'Can the two of you join me in my travel?'

'Certainly.'

'All right then, come along.'

Mahadevbhai realised that that was the beginning. As he followed Gandhiji, he hummed the words of Tagore:

Our pilgrimage has commenced,

O Captain!

Come wind, come storm,

Return we will not.

'Arrey Mahadev, what are you waiting for, come along!'

And saying this, Gandhiji started walking. Mahadevbhai followed him. But Gandhiji was walking very fast and therefore Mahadevbhai and Durgaben had to run to catch up with Gandhiji.

Since that day, Mahadevbhai and many others have been trying to catch up with Gandhiji.

It's true, haven't you noticed, whilst others ran, Gandhiji walked.

The Actor imitates Gandhiji walking while others ran – to the beat of Ekla chalo re by Tagore!

ACT I SCENE 5

Mahadevbhai, pencil in hand, went to Champaran in North Bihar from Godhra on 6th November 1917.

The first jottings in Mahadevbhai's diary began on 13th November 1917. Since that day, Mahadevbhai maintained a daily diary till 14th August 1942, the day he died with his head in Gandhiji's lap at the Aga Khan Palace in Pune. Mahadevbhai was so immersed in Gandhiji, that his 21-volume diary has no mention of the day his son, Narayan was born. Hmmm. Whenever he was away from Gandhiji, the pages in his diary were blank.

But wait, I'm running ahead. And the events I have to discuss are being left behind.

So where were we, ah yes, with Mahadevbhai in Champaran.

'Chaaaampaaaaran ...,' as Madam Priscilla, my history teacher in school (who had spent one year in Paris) used to say ... 'Chaaaampaaaaran had ... aaaaarable laaaaand in the district. And this laaaaaand was divided into large estates by Englishmen and worked by Indian tenaaaaaants. The chief commercial crop in Chaaaampaaaaran was ... indigo. The laaaaaandlords compelled aaaaaaall tenants to plaaaaaaant three-twentieths or 15 per cent of their holdings with indigo aaaaaand surrender the entire indigo harvest aaaaas rent. This was done by long-term contract, known as ... you there ... tell me??? ... *I don't know Miss ... the tinkatiya arrangement ... the what ... the tinkatiya arrangement, Miss!*

'Pay attention and write down every word I say. There will a 5-mark question on Chaaaampaaaaran in the Unit Test.

'Hahn, so where was I? Ah, in Chaaaampaaaaran. So Mohandas

Karamchand Gandhi launched a mass civil disobedience movement in Chaaaampaaaaran. He collected thousands of signatures in Chaaaampaaaaran. The officials felt powerless in Chaaaampaaaaran. Their foe was a man who was polite and friendly. He was willing to plead guilty and go to jail in Chaaaampaaaaran.'

'But Miss, why did Gandhiji prefer to go to jail, rather than pay the fine?'

'I don't know.'

'Miss, is it because going to jail was the prevalent fashion of those days?'

'Don't ask stupid questions, you dim-witted bombino! So where was I? In Chaaaampaaaaran. Ah, because of all this activity by Mohandas Karamchand Gandhi the *tinkatiya* arrangement was abolished. The poor peasant saw that he had rights. He learnt courage.'

Tttttrrrrrring. *Chutti*! Tomorrow we will study the Rowlatt Act!

But staying with Chaaaampaaaaran for a while ... Gandhiji was not satisfied. After the Champaran agitation he wrote a detailed letter. It said:

Actor mimes certain parts of the letter.

What I did in Champaran was a very ordinary thing. I declared that the British could not order me about in my own country. The point is, I take up activities as they come to me. In Bihar, besides overseeing legislative activity, I'm opening and managing schools. The teachers are, as a rule, married, and both husband and wife work. We teach the village children, educate the men about hygiene and sanitation. We enlighten the women and persuade them to discard the purdah and send their daughters to schools. We provide free medical services. There are innumerable diseases but we have the remedies. We, therefore, do not hesitate to entrust work to untrained men and women, as long as they are reliable.

Mahadevbhai was one of these untrained men and he saw the

miserable health conditions in Bihar. According to Mahadevbhai ... only three medicines were available: castor oil, quinine and sulphur ointment. Anybody who showed a coated tongue was given a dose of castor oil. Anybody with malaria fever received quinine plus castor oil. Anybody with skin eruptions received ointment plus castor oil.

Gandhiji continued: Kasturba, is working at one such school, and she distributes medicine, free-of-cost. To date, we have cured 3000 malaria patients. We clean village wells and build village roads and thus enlist the villager's active co-operation. Three new schools have been opened. And they train over 250 boys and girls. In all this, it is my good fortune that I'm assisted by Narhari Parekh and his wife, Mahadevbhai and Durgaben ...

Rajendra Prasad (the first President of free India) who was part-observer part-player in the Champaran agitation saw the community activity in the villages and commented: 'Gandhiji has read our minds correctly. He has taught us a lesson in self-reliance. For this is true self-reliance. This alleviating of the distress of large numbers of poor peasants.'

ACT I SCENE 6

I don't know much about peasants. Sure, like everyone else, I've seen peasants from the train window when I'm travelling from our home to our hometown.

Once we had to travel, because my elder brother had procured an appointment. That way, my elder brother was smarter than me. Me ... I was a meek and humble, subservient and lowly actor as aforementioned on three occasions. My brother had completed his MBA. He touched my Dadaji's feet with his characteristic swagger. Although Dadaji disapproved of rituals, he blessed him and said:

'Congrats! You've a job, dikra!'

'Yes, Dadaji. In a Big Business Corporation.'

'Shabash. You know, at your age I had quit my job! Or else, who knows, I might have had a lucrative practice as a barrister.'

'Yes, Daddy was telling me about it. Don't you ever regret quitting your profession?'

'I don't regret a thing, dikra. People far more important than me left the British courts, Nehru, Vallabhbhai, Das, and even your Meera Mami?'

'What? Meera Mami?'

'Your Meera Mami made a great sacrifice. She rebelled against her father, her family, her people. When Gandhiji started the non-cooperation movement, there were six hundred men and women. Meera Mami was one of them.'

'That's so awesome.'

'Not just that. Later, thousands of students dropped their professional studies.'

'Ah, I would like to quit my studies, too. It will be so kooool! Sit at home and totally chill out!'

'No chill out, dikra! 'Coz after renouncing their studies, these students went into the villages to teach literacy and non-co-operation?'

'Non-cooperation is like a hartal, a bandh, no?'

'Dikra, in those days, non-cooperation for the peasants meant not working.'

'So?'

'Not working meant non-payment of taxes to the British government. It also meant a ban on intoxicating liquor from which the government derived a large revenue. Here, have some boiled groundnuts! Or would you want some grapes and raisins?'

'In our MBA class, we had a professor who taught us Mr. Gandhi was against development. Why was Mr. Gandhi anti-development?'

'Dikra, Gandhiji was opposed to the craze for machinery, not machinery as such. Moreover, Gandhiji manufactured something very important.'

'What? Khadi?'

'Yes! Mahadevbhai said Bapu was a manufacturer of souls.'

'A Manufacturer Of Souls!'

Hmmm.

Speaking of Mahadevbhai did you know how Gandhiji manufactured Mahadevbhai's soul. Mahadevbhai recounts the incident in his diary:

Actor reads from Mahadevbhai's diary.

'In 1917, I was with Mahatmaji in Betia. At that time, he did not entrust any special work to me ... but one day, the day I was reborn, he told me to prepare chapatis. Chappatis??? I did not know how to make chapatis, so I asked him: 'Bapu, I ... er ... don't ... know how to make ... chapatis.' To which, he replied: 'It's very simple. *(Actor assembles the necessary props)* Here is the rolling pin, here is wooden board, here is the water and here is the flour. Now, if you start doing it, you will learn, somehow.' I accepted the order and tried to prepare the dough ... *(Actor is very clumsy with the ingredients and is finally left with atta on the face)* ... but it was a big mess. So I had to ask someone else to prepare the dough and I started roasting it on the griddle. Mahatmaji returned from his bath. Only one chappati was ready. He saw me and laughed. Then with a twinkle in his eyes, he said: 'Mahadev, if I wanted to eat chappatis prepared by someone else why would I have told you to make them?' Before I could say anything, he started rolling the chappatis and roasting them. That day I ate one of the most delicious chappatis of my life.'

Actor shuts the diary

And Dikra, Mahadevbhai's training did not stop there. Later, Gandhiji taught him to wash clothes, scrub toilets, clean roads. Here, have some of this goat milk, dikra!

Hmmm.

And so, Mahadevbhai besides being a secretary, a journalist, a diarist, a translator, and an apostle to the **cause** was also a bavarchi. In fact Mahadevbhai was a pir, bawarchi, bhisti, hamaal.

Mahadevbhai's initiation through the song about Pir, Bavarchi,

Bhisti, KHAR (using rolling pin/wooden board as musical support)

ACT I SCENE 7

Mahadevbhai was engrossed in his work. This took him across the country. Very rarely did he remember his ageing father in Dihen, or his wife who was waiting for him at Sabarmati. Gandhiji realised this so he penned a letter to Mahadevbhai's father Haribhai.

It said:

Actor reads the letter

Sugna Bhaishri,

I had decided a long time ago, to write to you whenever I could seize a chance, but I have been busy for some time ... with certain issues concerning our nation ...

You will please forgive me.

Let me beg to state that you have committed no error in entrusting Mahadev to me. The experience he is having here is quite a necessity for his development.

I (too) was on the lookout for a helpful companion who should also be a man of lofty character, compassionate heart and profound learning. Mahadev has fulfilled all these requisites.

All I wish and pray is, you cease to have any worry ... and that you give your blessings in this march of life.

Respectfully yours,

Mohandas Gandhi

Sixteen days after this correspondence, Haribhai met Gandhiji while he was travelling from Bombay to Delhi. There is a mention of this meeting in Mahadevbhai's diary. This in itself, is a singularly extraordinary event because Mahadevbhai never recorded personal incidents in his diary. But this time, he might have been compelled to do so, since his father was meeting Bapu. *Arrey waah*, Father–Bapu. Bapu–Father!

Similarly, Gandhiji wrote to Mahadevbhai's wife Durgaben en route to Nadiad from Vasad. He admonished her gently.

Actor reads letter

Chi Durga

Maybe you've forgotten me. After all you're so busy. But let me say, I've not forgotten you.

You've been separated from Mahadev much longer than I expected. I've told him to visit you whenever he feels like it. If you wish, I'm prepared to send him immediately.

However, at the same time I must let you know that Mahadev is having an elevating experience here, and he, and I'm sure you, are certain to gain through it. Perhaps your awareness of this fact can assuage the sting of separation.

There is yet another risk. If I happen to get involved in a struggle which is much more serious than the one I've been involved in so far, then Mahadev cannot be spared. If you want Mahadev at that time, it may not be possible. So this may be the last time for you to pay him a visit.

I'm at your disposal and will always follow your wishes.

Blessings,

Mohandas

Within a short time of joining Gandhiji, Mahadevbhai's activities increased. Besides being Gandhiji's secretary, Mahadevbhai maintained meticulous notes of Gandhiji's speeches. In fact Mahadevbhai simultaneously translated Gandhiji's speeches on the dais. Dadaji said that at times, Mahadevbhai jotted a sentence in English on his notepad even before Gandhiji uttered them in Gujarati.

So be it.

But besides these letters, editorials, speeches and meetings, Mahadevbhai never gave up his own study. Sometimes this led to rigorous debates with Gandhiji or C F Andrews.

Actor refers to diary

Once, there was an earnest discussion with Gandhiji about a

play by Dolatram Pandya. This was about the phrase 'clumsy', as recorded in Mahadevbhai's diary:

Gandhiji said: 'Mahadev, *Amasatra* is a good play. The Sanskrit shlokas are good. The play is well-written, but the plot is worthless.

I demurred: 'His style is ... er ... clumsy!'

Gandhiji asked: 'Mahadev, what's your definition of clumsy?'

I replied: 'A style is clumsy when any thought which could have been expressed in simple language has been deliberately cloaked in convolutions and complexities, so that no one understands the real meaning of the sentence.

Gandhiji responded: 'But Mahadev, whatever is difficult to understand is not necessarily clumsy.'

I let that pass, instead I asked: 'Bapu, among the English writers, who do you think has a clumsy style?'

Gandhiji thought for a moment: 'None comes to mind. The British have been careful that we've not studied any clumsy writers.'

'What would you say about Samuel Johnson, Bapu?'

'I would certainly not call him clumsy, Mahadev!'

'Then Bapu, could Austin's *Jursiprudence* be termed clumsy?'

Gandhiji mulled and said: 'I didn't find it tedious. It is ... ummm ... interesting.'

'But Bapu, does it have the same felicity as Dicey's *Law of Constitution*?'

'You're right, Mahadev. Austin does not have the same flow.

'And Bapu, what's your view on Karl Marx's *Das Kapital*?'

'I think I would have written it better, assuming, of course I had the leisure for the study Marx put in.'

'And Bapu, what about the Bible?'

'Mahadev, as you know, I've read anything and everything in Gujarati. I'm willing to go through the worst trash if it is in Gujarati. But I cannot stomach the Gujarati translations of the Bible. It goes against my grain to see a book which is a masterpiece in English being rendered into a parody in Gujarati. It's so shameful! Now, go to sleep Mahadev. It is late. You need to rest too.'

ACT I SCENE 8

'Children, finger-on-the-lips, it is 1918.' That was how Madam Priscilla began her history lesson. The First World Waaaaaar has ceased. The French have won. The Germans have lost. God Save the King!'

'God Save the King! Dadaji, God Save the King!!!'

'*Gadheda*. God save the king! Which king? Whose king? Tell that *babauchak* teacher that I was present during those times. The Indians suffered many things under the waaaaaartime administration. Prices rose shaaaaarply. Wages laaaaagged behind them. There was no attempt to check profiteering or to ration necessities. The influenza epidemic of 1918, with its total of ... thirteen million deaths ... revealed the depressed conditions of the Indian people.'

That was when the Report of the Rowlatt Committee on the repression of the seditious movements was published.

'The Rowlatt Act? Does anybody in the class know what is the Rowlatt Act? Quickly.'

'Miss, Miss, Dadaji tells me that the Rowlatt Act is a bit like MISA, TADA, POTA ... with a subtle difference ... the Rowlatt Act was tabled by a foreign government.'

To which Madame Priscilla said 'MISA, TADA and POTA are not in the syllabus and so don't waste our time.'

'Children, pay heed to the Rowlatt Act. Fill in the blanks. 100%. The Act, please write it down, clearly stated that political cases were to be tried without a jury, and power was conferred on the Government to intern suspects, you know goondas and badmashs, indefinitely without a trial. '

When Gandhiji got the news, he prepared a campaign of satyagraha.

During this period, Mahadevbhai recorded one typical, normal day in Gandhiji's life in his diary.

Actor starts to walk on the spot, slowly, at the outset. He gradually increases speed till he reaches a frenzied pace.

'Bapu is in full form. He works for 14 to 15 hours daily and does not seem to get tired. Today, he got up and walked. Later at five o'clock, Bapu sent a telegram and scolded everyone at Calcutta. He had an interview with Sir Pattani from six to eight. He sent a message to Montague with Sir Pattani. There was a lot of tension when he gave the message. At nine, he gave an hour's sermon to Jamnadas on hygiene and a healthy diet. At ten, a sermon to Umar Subhani on how to tackle the Hindu–Muslim vexations. At eleven he wrote an article about Swadeshi for publication. At 11.30 another one on Hindu–Muslim unity. At 12, he translated the Satyagraha pledge during which he counselled a brother and sister. At 12.30 he gave a sermon on 'How to spend your money for a good purpose' when some people came and contributed their money for a good cause. Then he dashed across and visited Anandshankerbhai who is on his deathbed en route to the station. At the station, he provided some guidelines to Satyagrahis till the train's departure. Then on the train, till he reached Palghar, Bapu translated the Swadeshi letter into English. Then he gave me the letter and tried to sleep in the train compartment, third class, in the middle of all that crowd. This was at four o'clock in the afternoon.'

Half the day was yet to come. Water!

As Dadaji used to say, the thing with Gandhiji was 'during his struggle, he used to come across leaders, be it South African or British or Indian, and face them. Irrespective of age or stature.'

And so it was that Gandhiji reached Allahabad during the non-cooperation movement. Mahadevbhai has this to say:

We stayed with Motilal Nehru in Allahabad. I had never seen such extravagance. The Nehrus lived with greater pomp than a king. They must be spending a lakh of rupees every year.

Gandhiji has been labelled as a Corruptor Of Youth. The same charge which was levelled against Socrates in Athens! Jawaharlal Nehru has signed the non-cooperation pledge in protest against the Rowlatt Act. This was against Motilal Nehru's wishes. Bapu tried to calm the mother and father. Motilal Nehru said: 'My only son is a barrister and a great scholar. He has been brought up in great luxury. How can he withstand the sufferings of non-cooperation?' To which, Bapu replied: 'Would you like to see your son riding fancy horses, or would you like to see him challenge a formidable Government as a leader of thousands of men?' That was not all. Bapu told the mother: 'Aren't you ashamed to be so oppressive to your thirty-year-old son? I would be terribly ashamed. When are we going to free ourselves from the family fold? Our mothers give birth to babies and then pamper their sons like babies all through their living life.'

Events moved rapidly after that. The Jallianwallah Bagh Massacre. Gandhiji's arrest. Riots in Bombay, Ahmedabad, Gujarat, Punjab, Delhi. Consequent police oppression. Suspension of the non-cooperation movement. And Gandhiji's fast as penance for the massacre for Chauri Chaura.

On February 5th in the small town of Chauri Chaura, an Indian mob committed murder. When news of this atrocity reached Gandhiji, he said: *(Actor speaks into the microphone)* it was '*a bad augury*. And although a drastic reversal of practically the whole of the non-cooperation programme may be unsound and unwise, the suspension is necessary. Chauri Chaura shows the way India may easily go, if drastic precautions be not taken.'

Around that time, Mahadevbhai wrote to Narhari Parekh from Bombay:

The condition is grave. The crowds that were chanting *Gandhiji Ki Jai* a few days ago are showering abuses on him. Every day we receive abusive letters. The letters says: 'Beware that your condition does not become like Mrs Besant or Dinshaw Wachha'. Or 'The British Government has a free police officer in Gandhi. What else should we expect from a *bania*.' Or 'Gandhi has been overpowered by the Government, he does not have the guts to convene meetings. But we are not indebted to Gandhi or his *bania* ancestors. We're not Gandhi's slaves nor are we slaves of the Government. We shall strike and conduct meetings, shout slogans.'

This is a sample of some of the letters. Bapu's heart has broken. And yet not once has he hesitated. He continues speaking to people. He tells them: 'Even such a mighty government will have to yield if we're true to our pledge. For the pledge is no small thing. It means a change of heart. We may no longer believe in the doctrine of 'tit for tat'; we may not meet hatred with hatred, violence with violence, evil with evil; we have to make a continuous and persistent effort to return good for evil ... I believe, nothing is impossible.'

So, as you can see, at present, ours is a fight against darkness, against dark forces. Perhaps you understand the agony I'm undergoing. Sometimes I feel that our frenzied crowds will take Bapu's life. And that Bapu would prove the victory of his truth and duty by sacrificing his own life.

Hmmm.

Shortly after this, Mahadevbhai was served a notice ordering his own arrest. He was going to be tried under Section 170 of the Criminal Amendment Act and Section 117 of the Indian Penal Code.

Mahadevbhai was in heaven. As he said: 'At last I'm fortunate!'

Like all good Gandhians, Mahadevbhai craved to be in prison. His enthusiasm and excitement knew no limits.

When the case was being conducted, the Magistrate asked Mahadevbhai, 'Do you want to cross-examine the witness?' Mahadevbhai replied, 'No, thank you. They, the police officers, cannot commit mistakes. How can one cross-examine them?' Then Mahadevbhai made the following statement: 'I'm going to help you. Not to oblige you, but to be able to go to jail. We all are revolutionaries and the most amazing thing is that instead of conducting a trial for that main offence of not abiding by your law, you are trying to arrest us for small, negligible offences. I am prepared to accept the greatest punishment you can give me. I am only afraid that you are not going to be able to remove the attitude of tremendous revolt against you even if you push us into the deepest valley of hell, nor are you going to succeed in implanting in our minds, the hypocrisy of loyalty towards your rotten government.'

Gandhiji wrote a letter to Haribhai when he heard of Mahadevbhai's arrest:

Actor reads the letter with a touch of humour.

Sugna Bhaishri,

It is good that Mahadev is jailed. He will get some rest, thereby. With me the work has been so demanding that I was afraid he would fall ill. Besides, jail has its good side. There's only one warden, whereas in free life there are many. No worry about food. The hard work keeps the body healthy. No vicious habits. Moreover Mahadev has a special knack for charming people wherever he goes. Please be patient and do not worry.

Respectfully yours,

Mohandas Gandhi

In jail, Dadaji said, Mahadevbhai had started learning Urdu from Khwaja Saheb. Yes, Mahadevbhai did undergo a lot of hardship on account of the Chauri Chaura massacre and the subsequent resolutions by Gandhiji, which was accepted with **reluctance** by the Congress Working Committee. But Mahadevbhai was busy. He wrote letters, proof-read, tried to spin khadi on the charkha and generally worked hard. He also translated Sharadchandra Chattopadhya's *Biraj Bahu* and three stories during his jail term. Dadaji used to joke that if Mahadevbhai had served a longer jail term, he would have been the next contender for the Nobel Prize of Literature, after Tagore.

Perhaps.

But Mahadevbhai was released. On 2nd July 1923, Mahadevbhai's father passed away in Dihen. Mahadevbhai received a telegram on 3rd July, even as he was editing a new issue of *Navjivan*, a publication which had become a habit with his father.

Mahadevbhai and Durgaben set off for Dihen. In a letter to Narhari, Mahadevbhai conveyed his grief:

If the supplement of Navjivan was not to be published on Thursday and if I had not received a letter from my father asking for books about indigenous colours, I would have visited him. As always, serving the country came before my serving my father.

There is more.

After death, there are some gruesome rites to be performed by our community. I had to put a stop to it. I decided not to feed my relatives nor was any Brahmin to be fed after the rites. Many did not like this. But how can I **not** *practise my belief? How can I falter from my course?*

There is more.

I've received Rs 1000 for my translation of Morley's On Compromise. I've decided to set aside half the amount for scholarships in memory of my father. Four boys and preferably four girls can master the art of cloth-making with this amount at the ashram.

There is more. A letter from Jawaharlal Nehru.

Dear Mahadev,

I received the news about your father's demise as I was descending from the train at Nagpur station. Ramdas informed me.

I've had the good fortune of having experienced the depths of a father's love. Many times I've wondered as to how I could repay this love and affection. This has troubled me a great deal.

I did not have the privilege of meeting your father. However, I can imagine him being proud of his son. Mahadev, you distress yourself needlessly. The lessons of service you've inherited from your father have been shared with the world. Your father would never grudge you this. He would never have preferred the narrow boundaries of domesticity for you ... to the wider service of the nation.

Affectionately,

Jawaharlal

ACT I SCENE 9

Soft chants of Raghupati Raghava Raja Ram play in the background

With Haribhai's demise, an important chapter in Mahadevbhai's life drew to a close. A new one was about to ensue.

As always, Mahadevbhai received a telegram – this time a happy one – announcing the news of Gandhiji's release from prison.

Mahadevbhai was ecstatic. He wrote in his diary:

Today, my joy is boundless. I had to deliver a lecture on Bapu's Philosophy at Gujarat College, but it was cancelled. Laddoos and guud were distributed. The boys took out a procession and moved around the town. There were fifty to sixty cyclists. The whole procession was chanting Raghupati Raghava Raja Ram; and the cyclists were marking time with the cycle bells.

Actor sings the Raghupati Raghava song ... with brief interludes of 'Gandhiji zindabad' in the song.

ACT II SCENE 1

'Arrey Babu, where are you? Come here.'

'No, Dadaji, I'm playing.'

'Look, what I've got for you.'

'What? Cricket bat?'

'No! Books. Books on literature, aesthetics, history ... '

'Not history, Dadaji! Madame Priscilla is constantly boring us with history.'

'Hmmm. It is because of your Madame Priscilla that history has become a travesty.'

'What is the meaning of travesty?'

'Hmmm. Here read this, dikra:

Q: What is this foul substance? Ans: This foul-smelling substance is history, sir!'

From Allan Sealy's *Trotternama*. Below which we find Gandhiji's

My Experiments With Truth, which has been translated into English by Mahadev Desai.

Arrey, **apna** Mahadevbhai!

And below that, a copy of Mahadevbhai's *The Story Of Bardoli.*

This book is rated by scholars and pundits as exceptional. *The Story of Bardoli.* It is a creative work and a rare document, all the more, since Mahadevbhai was a witness to the unparalleled Satyagraha at Bardoli.

But as usual, in my impetuosity, I've jumped the gun. I need to control it. It has got me in trouble in the past, and now I've given away the suspense. So let's rewind, spool back, reverse, back-track ... and have a look at what Mahadevbhai has to say in *The Story Of Bardoli.*

'I never had the privilege of being a 'combatant' in the Bardoli Satyagraha ... but I had done enough work. It was in 1917–18 that Vallabhbhai Patel came under Gandhiji's influence and learnt from him the first principle ... India lives in the village and that the peasant is at the heart of it. No scheme for freedom, or any programme would be possible, unless it is framed with special reference to the peasant.

And it was Vallabhbhai who best understood this lesson from Gandhiji.

In 1928, Vallabhbhai was the Mayor of Ahmedabad. At Gandhiji's suggestion, he left the post and went to Bardoli, to guide the 8000 peasants in a peaceful revolt.

The villagers, responding to Vallabhbhai's leadership, refused to pay taxes. The collector seized their buffaloes. Cultivators were driven off their farms. Kitchens were invaded and pots and pans were confiscated for delinquency. Carts and horses were taken.

The peasants remained non-violent.

Months passed. Bardoli stood its ground. Hundreds were arrested. The Government was accused of lawlessness. India began to take notice. Voluntary contributions flowed in for the maintenance of the struggle.

'Why not barricade the roads' some peasants whispered to

Vallabhbhai, 'or place spikes on the road to burst the tyres of official cars.'

No, Vallabhbhai admonished, your fight is not for a few hundred thousand rupees, but for a principle ... you're fighting for self-respect, which will ultimately lead to Swaraj.

On 6th August 1928, the British Government capitulated. The weapon had worked!

The master was a non-peasant philosopher-saint who enunciated the principles. And the disciple was a born peasant who looked into the practical applications of those values.

The people of Bardoli demonstrated they knew how to live, how to fight ... and above all, how to die.'

Hmmm.

After reading *The Story Of Bardoli*, Rabindranath Tagore wrote a letter to Mahadevbhai:

Dear Mahadev,

I've read your 'The Story Of Bardoli'. It has the spirit of the Epic in which we witness the triumph of moral right over the arbitrary power through a just fight. Such a thing is unique in modern times.

I thank you, and the leader of the non-violent fight, Sardar and the fighters, as well as your great guide, Bapu. My blessings.

ACT II SCENE 2

Many years ago, in tenth standard, I had acted in a nautanki. As aforementioned on four occasions, I am a meek and humble, subservient and lowly actor – and so, that school production was my big break!

We could have done Shakespeare, which is every actor's ultimate destination. But Madame Priscilla said NO! I told her, Ma'am there are sections in heaven, wherein actors are denied entry if they haven't played a part in a Shakespeare play. Even an ordinary foot soldier will suffice. But Madame Priscilla was adamant. She said we will do a nautanki play written by one Mr Anonymous.

In my school we were always doing plays by one Mr Anonymous. He is our favourite writer. So there I was playing an ageing Shahenshah. I know, tenth standard is kind of young to play a Shahenshah, but with a beard I looked … Shahenshah-ish. The plot was simple. I have three daughters, and I ask them:

These days I'm not on top of my health

And I'm going to distribute my wealth

Now, tell me, how much do you love me, my dears?

Give me your answer, without any fears.

The oldest says Papa, I love you more than money

The second says I love you much more than milk and honey

The youngest says, I love you as much as food loves salt

Begone from my kingdom, you ingrate,

Coz you have a grievous fault

Dadaji had come to Bombay to see me star in this production. Post-show, when I asked him how it was. He thumped my back. Said this was the first time he had seen a Shahenshah with a sofa set and suit-boot. I was embarrassed. You know the thing with talent is, it is never appreciated within the family.

'Ah, but dikra, that thing about the youngest girl telling that crack-pot father of hers that she loved him as much as salt … that was a good touch.'

'Crack-pot? How can you say that Dadaji? The Shahenshah is an … is an … ideological analysis of power and the re-distribution of wealth in a classless society which is weighed by capitalist ambitions …'

'Pah! English Medium! … Reminded me of Gandhiji!'

'My Shahenshah (beard and all) reminded you of Gandhiji!'

'No, dikra, the salt. A brilliant theatrical touch.'

'Ah, you know Mr Anonymous … a dramatic genius …'

'And dikra, you know Gandhiji, a real-life genius …'

'How so?'

'Consider: if Gandhiji had gone by train or motor-car to make salt in Dandi, the effect would have been considerable. But to walk for twenty-four days and rivet the attention of all India, to trek across the country-side, subsisting on channa-mamra, and saying, "Watch, I am about to give a signal to the nation" and then to pick up a pinch of salt in publicised defiance of the mighty Government, required imagination, dignity and the sense of showmanship of a Great Theatrical Artist.'

'Perhaps ...'

'It appealed to the women, who use salt everyday. Day after day.'

'Perhaps ...'

'It appealed to the hard-working, perspiring poor man for whom salt was as essential as water in the tropical heat.'

'Perhaps ...'

'It appealed to a sophisticated critic and fierce opponent of Gandhiji like Subhash Chandra Bose who compared the Dandi march to Napolean's march to Paris.'

'Perhaps ...'

'It appealed to the middle-class youth because of the underlying principles of namak-haram and namak-halal.'

'Perhaps ...'

'Dikra, admit it, even your Mr Anonymous would have been proud of Gandhiji.'

Saying so, Dadaji laughed heartily and said: 'Am I rubbing salt in your wounds?'

A month after Gandhiji touched salt at the Dandi beach, India was seething in angry revolt. But except at Chittagong there was no violence. Or let me add, no Indian violence.

Meanwhile the Viceroy Lord Irwin filled the jails with no less than sixty thousand offenders. Estimates ran as high as hundred thousand. Mahadevbhai was one of them.

Mahadevbhai was arrested on 23rd April. He describes his arrest:

Twice I heard rumours about my arrest. On both occasions, they turned out to be false. On the first occasion the rumours were so viscious that I read my own obituary in the newspapers.

Here let it be said I did not leave a single opportunity of preaching sedition. In the last seventeen days I broke the Salt Law. I instigated thousands to do the same.

Finally, I was arrested. En route to the jail, a crowd wanted to garland me. But the white sergeant disregarded them – and drove off the prison van. One misguided person hurled a stone, which hurt the sergeant's chin. The sergeant abused me. I replied, 'You can hit me with that stone, or give the stone to me so that I can hit myself, if that gives you peace of mind.' The sergeant understood the satyagrahi's attitude and started talking about pleasanter things.

At the gates of the jail, the sergeant tried to return the pen, which he had borrowed. I insisted that he keep it as a memento. In return I asked for the stone. When he gave it to me I threw it out of the window, saying, 'Please throw away the bitter memories of the incident'. The sergeant smiled and replied, 'That has already been forgotten, olde fruite.'

As Dadaji had said once: 'The purity of a satyagrahi's methods made it difficult for anyone to oppose him. Victory came to the satyagrahi not when the opponent had no more strength to fight him but when he had no more heart to fight him.'

ACT II, SCENE 3

Gandhiji was in Yervada Jail. When Vallabhbhai Patel was arrested, he too was lodged in Yervada Jail. Mahadevbhai was transferred from another jail to Yervada Jail. Gandhiji had requested for his companionship. When Mahadevbhai arrived he lay his head at Gandhiji's feet.

In Yervada, Gandhiji read the newspapers carefully and aloud. Sardar analysed the political situation. Mahadevbhai made notes. All three, washed their own clothes, spun, studied the stars, did gardening and read voraciously. Besides all this, the trio enjoyed numerous conversations.

Mahadevbhai wrote fifty-odd letters in his fine, precise handwriting. He continued learning French and Urdu. At times, Gandhiji and Mahadevbhai locked horns over correct spellings and the etymology of words.

Once, whilst penning a letter to Miraben, Gandhiji asked Mahadevbhai, 'Is there an 'h' in inexhaustible?' Mahadevbhai checked the dictionary and said that there was an 'h'. Gandhiji and Mahadevbhai then examined the root, so as to seek a clarification. This led to a longish discussion on roots and origin of words, and the things one can learn from Latin.

Now, Gandhiji had a habit of putting sodium bicarbonate in every cooked dish, so as to aid the bowel movements. And so, when Sardar, who was striding up and down, did not see an end to the 'inexhaustible' discussion on the Latin origin of words, he said in his inimitable style, 'Bapu, why, don't you add some sodium bicarbonate into the word. It's meaning and spelling will not seem as 'inexhaustible'.'

Besides letter writing, Mahadevbhai had taken over the responsibility of cooking. As he said, he used to prepare some 'experimental' *khichri* and vegetable dishes.

Once Gandhiji was reading a newspaper article in which there was a derisive mention of Gandhiji's 'constructive vacuity'. Mahadevbhai queried, 'I wonder, what constructive vacuity means?' Sardar said, 'Quite elementary, Mahadev. It's something like the dal you burnt this morning.'

One day, Gandhiji woke up at three in the morning. Sardar was disturbed. He said, 'Bapu, why are you brushing your teeth so vigorously. The few that remain may fall off.'

In the midst of Sardar's wit, Gandhiji continued his spinning. As Gandhiji explained to Sardar, with the charkha, he was trying to bridge … brain and brawn, to unite city and village, to link rich and poor. The charkha was presented to the nation for giving occupation to the millions who had, at least for four months of the year, nothing to do …

Sardar knew this. One day, when Gandhiji's right hand ached, due to undue spinning of the charkha, Sardar challenged him.

On cue, Gandhiji, started practising to spin with his left hand. Soon, he could spin 131 yards of yarn in three hours. Then Sardar asked what Gandhiji would do, if both his hands started aching. Gandhiji replied he would use his feet. Next morning when Sardar woke up, he found Gandhiji practising the spinning of yarn with his feet.

Sardar sat bemused, and helped Mahadevbhai in preparing envelopes for letters written the previous night. Gandhiji asked, 'What portfolio should we give you in Swaraj?' Vallabhbhai replied, 'I shall wander the streets with a *chimta* and a monk's bowl.'

To which Gandhiji replied, 'And I'll be a *bhangi* with a *bhangi* and a *dhed* with a *dhed* and do their work with equal ease. If untouchability is not destroyed during my lifetime, and if it is ordained that I should take a second birth, I wish to be born a *bhangi* and none else.'

ACT II SCENE 3

This was the scourge of untouchability.

It was the Anguish of September 1932. On 17th August 1932, Prime Minister Ramsay MacDonald announced Britain's intention to grant a separate electorate not only to Hindus and Muslims, as in the past, but to the untouchables and Depressed Classes, as well.

This meant that not only Hindus and Muslims but the untouchables too, would elect their leaders from within their community.

Actor speaks into the microphone

Gandhiji responded: 'Mr PM, I've to resist your decision with my life. The only way I can do it is by declaring a perpetual fast unto death from food of any kind save water.'

The Prime Minister was not alone in his bewilderment. Many Indians, and most orthodox Hindus were perplexed. They felt, independence was the central issue. Untouchability was a side issue.

Tagore explained Gandhiji's fast:

Actor speaks into the microphone

'The penance which the Mahatmaji has taken upon himself is not a ritual but a message to all India and to the world ... let us try to understand the meaning of his message ... no civilised society can thrive upon victims whose humanity has been permanently mutilated ... those whom we keep down, inevitably drag us down ... Mahatmaji has repeatedly pointed out the danger of these divisions in our country ... against such deep-seated moral weakness in our society Mahatmaji has pronounced an ultimatum ...'

Tagore understood that this was the language of non-violence. Tagore also envisaged the possibility of losing Gandhiji through the fast.

Meanwhile Gandhiji lay on a white iron cot in the shade of a low mango tree in Yerwada Jail. Sardar and Mahadevbhai sat near him. Several deputations met him. The Government permitted many religious and political leaders to see him in jail.

One of them was a distinguished lawyer with international experience. He owned a powerfully built body and a strong, stubborn, superior intellect. Like me, he too had a father who had a father. But the similarity ended there. For his grandfather and father served in the British army. The accumulated bitterness against Hindus that rankled for centuries in millions of **Harijan** breasts found expression in Dr Bhimrao Ambedkar's hatred. He preferred British Raj to a Hindu Raj. He preferred Muslims to Hindus. He had once thought of leading the untouchable community, as a body, into the Mohammedan Church. Lifelong Hindu cruelty to his brethren filled him with anger and spite.

If any one could have contemplated with equanimity the death of Gandhiji, it was Dr Bhimrao Ambedkar. But he called the fast unto death 'a political stunt'.

When Dr Ambedkar's statement was being read, Gandhiji said 'I do not feel angry. He has a right to say all that he is saying. I deserve all that he and the other untouchables are doing out of anger. We all deserve it.'

Discussions and parleys began. They continued till 24th September. Dr Ambedkar renewed talks with Hindu leaders and they agreed that the Depressed Classes would have 147 seats instead of the 197 Dr Ambedkar demanded and the 71 McDonald ordered.

The document was signed.

Mahadevbhai has recorded a key exchange during this period:

Towards the end of the negotiations, as Ambedkar came to Gandhiji, Thakkar Bapa said, 'Bapu, look, Ambedkar has changed!'

To which Gandhiji replied, 'That is what you say, not Ambedkar.'

Immediately Ambedkar intervened and stated, 'Yes, Mahatmaji, the change has taken place. You have been a great help. You've tried to understand me more than your people tried to make me understand. I feel there is more similarity amongst both of us than amongst them.' Everyone laughed.

At 5.15 on Monday evening, in the presence of Tagore, Sardar, Mahadevbhai and the negotiators, Gandhiji accepted a glass of orange juice from Kasturba and broke his fast. Tagore sang Bengali hymns.

Dr Ambedkar made an interesting speech at a press conference in Bombay. He said:

Actor speaks into the microphone

'I must confess that I was surprised, immensely surprised, when I met Mahatmaji, that there is so much in common between him and me. I was astonished to see that the man who held such divergent views from mine at the Round Table Conference came immediately to my rescue and not to the rescue of the other side. I am very grateful to Mahatmaji for having extricated me from what might have been a very difficult situation.

My only regret is, why did Mahatmaji not take this attitude at the Round Table Conference in England? If he had shown the same consideration for my point of view then, it would not have been necessary for him to go through this ordeal.

However these are things of the past. I am glad that I am here now to support this resolution of ratification.'

So was the Mahatma's torment necessary?

The answer to this question, according to Mahadevbhai, is crucial to an understanding of Gandhiji's role in Indian history.

On 13th September, when the fast was announced, to the afternoon of 26th September, when it was broken, Gandhiji made each Hindu personally responsible for his life. Gandhiji told Mahadevbhai:

'No patched up agreement between Caste Hindus and Rival Depressed Classes would have answered the purpose. Without a fast, the bill would not have had an effect on the nation. It might have redressed a legal Harijan grievance but it would have remained a dead letter as far as the Hindu's personal treatment of untouchables was concerned. Most Hindus would never have heard of it.'

Mahadevbhai agreed. And so did Dadaji. In fact Dadaji had a scrapbook in which he kept track of the events surrounding the fast.

It was amazing. *(Actor refers to a huge scrap book)*

Page 1: Whilst, the negotiators parleyed, a billion Hindus experienced an upheaval.

Page 2: In the very first week, the famous Kalighat Temple in Calcutta, and the Ram Mandir of Benares which were a citadel of Hindu orthodoxy, threw their doors open.

Page 3: Twelve temples in Allahabad were made accessible to Harijans for the first time.

Page 4: All temples in the native states of Baroda, Kashmir, Bhor, Kolhapur cancelled temple discrimination.

And look here: Newspapers printed the names of hundreds of temples that lifted the ban under the impact of Gandhiji's fast.

And over here, **page 38:** Mrs Swarup Rani Nehru, Jawaharlal Nehru's very orthodox mother, let it be known that she had accepted food from the hand of an untouchable. Thousands of prominent Hindu women followed her example.

Page 49: At the strictly Hindu Benares University, Principal Dhruva, with numerous Brahmans dined publicly with street cleaners, cobblers and scavengers. Similar meals were organised in hundreds of other places.

Page 103: Villages and towns allowed untouchables to use wells. Hindu pupils shared benches formerly reserved for untouchables. Roads and streets were opened to Harijans.

And finally, a note by Dadaji, on the last page, 'Naturally, the fast did not exterminate the curse of untouchability, which was more than 3000 years old.'

That got me thinking. So I asked Dadaji, 'But, access to a temple is not access to a good job. And Harijans continue to remain the dregs of our society, more now than ever.'

Dadaji sighed a sigh, and stated with infallible logic, 'True, beta. But after the fast, untouchability forfeited its public approval, the belief in it was destroyed ...' So be it.

ACT II SCENE 4

And so, it was. Gandhiji – and Mahadevbhai with him. Gandhiji travelled extensively across the length and breadth of the country. He talked, he walked. Mahadevbhai made notes. At meetings whenever Mahatma saw a sector of the grounds set apart for untouchables, he squatted among them and challenged Brahmans and caste Hindus to do likewise. Once he told Mahadevbhai, 'My Mahatmaji is worthless, if the people don't understand the meaning of my simple message.'

People thronged to see the Mahatma. Audiences were large and Gandhiji had to be careful that there was no stampede.

Dadaji said once ... In Dakha, a man of seventy was brought to Gandhiji. He was wearing a photograph of Gandhiji around his neck. He approached Gandhiji, kissed his feet, and thanked him profusely for having cured him of paralysis. 'When all other remedies failed,' the poor man said, 'I took to uttering Mahatma Gandhi's name and one day I found myself cured.' Gandhiji was distraught. 'The people should understand that meaningless deification can do no good either to them or to me. It will only intensify the superstitious nature of the simple people.'

But the people were immune to words of caution. One day, Gandhiji's train stopped with a jerk. Somebody had pulled the emergency cord. Crowds lay down on the tracks and refused to get up till they had a darshan of the Mahatma. Gandhiji was asleep after a gruelling day. A chant began. Mahadevbhai who was accompanying Gandhiji was in a quandary. He did not want to disturb Gandhiji. So he stood at the door of the bogie and shouted *'Aah rahyo, tamharo Mahatma (Look, this is your Mahatma).'* The crowds dispersed, and the journey continued.

That was perhaps why Gandhiji thought of the Maun Vrat. The travelling, the crowds, the meetings, were taking their toll. He wanted rest for one day in a week. So he instituted fifty-two silent Mondays. When he met his colleagues he would communicate through chits of paper. But he could not do that on the days, he had to deliver a speech. So I asked Dadaji what did Gandhiji do?

'It was simple, really. Gandhiji would arrive. The crowds would be very noisy. So Gandhiji would sit on the dais till the audience, which sometimes numbered two lakh became quiet. He then continued to sit in silence, and everyone sat in silence. Once there was pin-drop silence, he would lift his left hand and open up the five fingers. Taking the first finger between two fingers of his right hand he would gesture. Some people didn't understand, but others in the audience would explain. 'That is equality for the untouchables.' Then the second finger. 'That was spinning.' Then the third finger. 'That was sobriety: no alcohol, no opium'. Then the fourth finger. 'That was Hindu–Muslim friendship.' Then the fifth which was equality for women. The hand was bound to the body by the wrist. Gandhiji would point to the wrist which was non-violence. These five virtues would free the body of each one of them, and hence, India. He then continued to sit in silence, until he touched his palms together, smiled and departed.'

ACT II SCENE 5

The Battle for Swaraj was on. There was a flurry of events. The Simon Commission, The Cripps Mission, World War II, a toughening of stance by the British Government, the stand-off between Gandhiji and Winston Churchill.

Gandhiji threatened to launch a fast unto death when he realised the British had no intention of going away.

Mahadevbhai dissuaded him. The Congress held an AICC Session on 8th August 1942. They were planning to launch a civil disobedience movement: **Quit India**. It's slogan – **Do Or Die**. The next day, Nehru, Patel, Maulana Azad were arrested. Gandhiji was also arrested along with Mahadevbhai and they were quarantined in the Aga Khan Palace, near Poona. Kasturba got herself arrested by announcing that she would speak at the rally at which Gandhiji was scheduled to speak.

For Gandhiji, this stay in prison was an unrelieved tragedy, due to the widespread violence and his inability to deal with it made him unhappy.

This tragedy was deepened by personal loss. Six days, after entering the Aga Khan Palace, Mahadevbhai had a sudden heart attack and lost consciousness.

'Mahadev, Mahadev, get up,' Gandhiji called out.

'Get up Mahadev,' said Kasturba, 'look Bapu is calling you. You've never disobeyed him in your life. How can you not obey him now?'

But Mahadevbhai was no more. He had accomplished in fifty years, what others would not be able to perform in a hundred.

Here, I could also speak about so many other things, my grand-uncle in the old black-and-white photograph, Mahadevbhai, me and Mahatma Gandhi. But since I'm a meek and humble, subservient and lowly actor as aforementioned on five occasions, I'll end this thing where I began.

Arrey Mishra, ab toh aap nahin kahenge ki Mahadevbhai kaun?
Actor hands over black-and-white photograph

Waah, kya baat hain! Main soch rahan kuch historical banaaon. Aaj kal patriotism ka bahut bada market hain. Arrey Munna, tujhe bhi photo dekhna hain kya ...? He-he-he ... yeh mera su-putra hai. Mere ladke ka ladka. Hamare khandaan main sirf ladke paida hote hain ... arre, sambhalkar kar, beta.

And then, that suputra tore that old black-and-white photograph. If I had not heard of Mahadevbhai I would have indulged in un-Gandhian behaviour and beaten up that three-year-old. Instead I smiled, and said, '*Koyi baat nahin, bachcha hai ...*' and started picking up the pieces ...

In any case, fifty years ... maybe twenty years from now, this old black-and-white photograph would not matter. People would have better things to do. They would have forgotten about Mahadevbhai, my grand-uncle, Mohandas Karamchand Gandhi, **me**. All that will remain will be the pieces ... these pieces. The one thing in common. See, how it connects, and inter-connects! Dadaji, Rajani Kaki, Meera Mami, even Madame Priscilla who taught history. Aren't all these events intertwined? Haven't we shared the same processes? Surely, we cannot disassociate ourselves from things, can we?

But this is not the time and place, to bring it up.

It is time to bid Mahadevbhai good-bye. The final entry in Mahadevbhai's diary was on 14th August 1942. One day before he passed away. If he had written a diary on 15th August 1942, this is what it would have said ...

Actor reads Mahadevbhai's diary for the last time

My only prayer to God was 'take me away before Bapu'. And God has never refused my prayer. Today, in one stroke, I fulfilled two duties. I died with my head in Bapu's lap, as it was destined. And I realised my duty as a patriot by fulfilling the slogan of the Quit India struggle. Do Or Die. Both these processes have merged, this morning on 15th August 1942.

Mahatma Gandhi dictated a telegram 'Mahadev has died a yogi's and patriot's death. No sorrow permitted.'

Music. Fade out.

Collaborators

Dedicated to MADHUKAR DESAI and
T M P NEDUNGADI and VIJAY TENDULKAR
(three first-rate men; one better than the other)

Presented by Out of Context and British Council Division; premiered at Prithvi Theatre / NCPA during August 2004.

Playwright/Director: Ramu Ramanathan

Executive Producer: Kinnari Vohra

Production Incharge: Dnyanesh Madgaonkar

Music design: Krishnan Anantha

Sets: Vinesh Iyer, Nikhil Khadilkar, Supriya Thyagarajan

Publicity design: Karan Arora

Light design: Hidayat Sami. Jasvinder Singh

Sound + PRO + Rehearsals: Preeti Gaonkar

Cast: Joy Sengupta, Suruchi Aulakh, Satyajit Sharma, Lubna Salim

Production: Partha Akrekar, Monish Talpade

Licenses: Chandar Patil

The set should be ultramodern and the furniture extremely uncomfortable, symbolically challenging the rule book.

When the curtain rises, there is a huge backdrop (20 feet wide) with Kranti's distorted face, with red ants all over. In the latter half of the play, the image disintegrates and the remaining three characters (wife, best friend, best girl-friend) enter Kranti's mind-scape. This should be done through little windows in the landscape. At the point where Kranti is suggesting, that nothing is worth fighting for, he should dance with a TV held aloft. The TV symbolises the boulder Sisyphus pushed up the mountain.

The stage setting could generously use artifacts from unexpected eras and representative of consumer culture.

This play was first published in *Collaborators and Mahadevbhai* by Ramu Ramanathan, ed. Alok Bhalla and Anju Makhija, Sahitya Akademi Publications, New Delhi, 2006.

ACT I SCENE 1

Husband sighs

Husband: It was an evening like ... today? ... It was an evening dedicated to bridge ... which as they say is an unfriendly sort of game. But it was appropriate for the sort of evening that ensued.

The doorbell rings.

Husband: This is my home.

The doorbell rings.

Wife: Coming!

Husband: This is my wife, Arundhati! My name is Kranti. When I was seven years old, I returned from school and asked my mother what was the meaning of 'Kranti'. She said, I was named 'Kranti' by Nana. It meant revolution. I told my mother but I'm too small to revolt. She said, beta, one can revolt in small ways through little things. After all, as Nana used to say, it's the little things that make a man. *(Sighs)* Ever since I've returned from that prison in Faizabad, I've realised, I've let down Nana, my mother, and ...
The doorbell rings. Music plays in the background.

ACT II SCENE 2

Music plays. The doorbell rings. Man enters. Kisses in the air. Man hands over a bottle of wine/flowers. Wife speaks a staccato, unfaltering speech.

Man: Hey Arundhati!

Wife: Hey, Himanshu. Thanks for coming. This means so much. Did you have any difficulty in finding the house?

Man: Not really. Things have changed since the last time. The slums have proliferated. The yuck-and-muck. The number of people.

Wife: It's getting crazy. Big time. The city is becoming one big slum, you know. But I should have mentioned the birds and the baobab. It's a real beauty, a saving grace. Sooooo very beautiful.

It's the only one of its kind in the suburbs. I'm hoping the municipality does not chop it down. We are planning to register it as a city heritage. Ummmmm. That's a divine tie you are wearing! Very classy.

Man: Did you get my postcard from Switzerland on your anniversary?

Silence.

Wife: You're certain you don't want tea. I have two varieties. Assam and Darjeeling. I love tea. Daddy had commented that once upon a time, tea was a banned product, like heroin. And that you could even be jailed for drinking tea. Ah Daddy. I wish all men were made like Daddy. He was always getting involved with the high-end of corporate life. Yes. That was good. Money does wonders for the blood flow. Really. It's such a coincidence, everyone on earth does these clever things. Oh dear.

Man: I sent a postcard from Amsterdam. A miniature Van Gogh.

Wife: The past seems so much nicer ... and now, what have I been doing. Ageing!!! Growing Wise!!! Putting on weight. I've to watch out. We have a history of diabetes in the family. A tendency to put on weight. All Tata Sumos.

Man: You look pretty ... nice.

Wife: Daddy was really worried. So he enrolled me in an aerobic class. The other thing is, I cycle. At home. You cannot cycle in Mumbai any more. So I cycle at 33 km per hour for 15 minutes minimum. Those being the standards my dietician has set for me. Oh, he's so cute.

Man: He's a carbon copy of Deve Gowda. A lookalike, no?

Wife: I heard about Srikanth.

Man: Hypertension, I'm told.

Wife: Medical science must do something about all this cholesterol and blood pressure. Srikanth was so young. What was it? Forty-one?

Man: ... Forty-two?

Wife: I met him at a wedding after he had divorced Tanya. He looked burnt out. He was telling me that he was surviving on Betacard, Combiflam, Alprax, Digene, black coffee.

Man: Mostly cigarettes ...

Wife: Yes, cigarette smoking is injurious to health.

Man: Arundhati, I sent a postcard from Brussels, too.

Wife: Oh that was you. So sweet!

Man: In what way can I be of assistance to you?

Wife: Srikanth should have taken a break. Gone to Greece or Prague. It is so beautiful. The mountains, the clean air, the fresh water ... I wish Srikanth had paid heed to my advice. Oh, what a waste.

Man: The office organised a condolence meeting, the other day. Everyone paid their tributes. Everyone wept buckets of tears.

Wife: Yeah. Right. OK.

Man: Salunkhe gave a moving speech.

Wife: The time has come to serve cappuccino. Would you care for some wine. I've a Chateau Petrus. Meanwhile you can peer through the window pane and see the baobab; and the days gone by. Yeah. Right. OK.

Man: Srikanth hated Salunkhe, you know.

Wife: Ummm. Thanks for coming. This means so much. So much. You know.

Music plays.

ACT I SCENE 3

Husband, Wife and Man sit still. Everyone sighs loudly.

Husband: Pause. Then Himanshu asked me if I was ok.

Man: Are you like ... ok?

Husband: Sure, I said. I'm ok. Thanks. Then I asked him, what about you?

Man: I'm ok. Kool.

Husband: There was a pregnant pause. Then he asked me, are you genuinely ok?

Man: Are you, like, genuinely ok?

Husband: Sure, I said. Sure. There was one more long pause. So, to cover up ... he told a story. Himanshu was never at a loss for words.

Man: I must tell you ... this. It's just that strange things have been known to happen in prison. You know, the company wanted to set up a plant in Malabo, Equatorial Guinea. Bizarre country. People are rounded up, paraded before the TV, and then they disappear from prison! Good thing it did not happen with you, no?

Husband: Sure. Short pause. Himanshu proceeded, again.

Man: The thing is, in Malabo, no one is allowed to protest or oppose. If you do, you're eaten, alive. Buried without your testicles and brains. Good thing it did not happen to you, no?

Husband: Sure. A pause. Himanshu added, oh, it must be painful.

Man: Oh. It would be so painful to live in Malabo. Good thing we're a democracy. Right?

Husband: Sure. Of course.

Husband, Wife and Man sit still. Everyone sighs loudly.

Husband: So that was that ... my best friend and my only wife ... as I had stated, in a vague sort of way, even today, I recall every single detail, including what it was I said ... *(The doorbell rings)*

Wife: Coming!

The doorbell rings

ACT I SCENE 4

Woman enters. The Wife and Woman kiss in the air. Then Woman and Man embrace and kiss in the air. Man, Woman and Wife reflect.

Man: Hey Shivani!

Woman: Hey Himanshu!. Hey Arundhati!

Wife: Hey ... Hey ... Hey Shivani. This is ... you know ... whatever ...

Woman: I agree. It's too much, I swear it.

Man: Uh-huhn, awright, yeah. Had to park my E 220 outside. There's an ambulance in the compound.

Wife: That must be Mr Mahalonobis. He is critical. Very critical.

Man: Mahalonobis? What a curious name? What is he? A Bong?

Wife: I don't know. I could ... like ... find out.

Woman (overlaps): It's so warmish, these days, no. Means ... the humidity and all. Oh dear. Really hottish. Sweltering. It's too much, I swear it. Oh shucks!

Man: Every year it gets worse. Uh-huhn, awright, yeah. So what's up?

Woman: Oh, the usual. You know a little bit of this and a little bit of that. What about you?

Man starts to speak in an over-pronounced, highly accentuated manner.

Man: It's really too much. Surana is making my life arduous and strenuous and laborious.

Woman: Pour que (if my French is right)? Hee hee hee.

Amused chuckle from all

Man: Oh yeah ... Surana's gone and become the President of his Industry Association. So every fortnight they have a get-together. And because of that loan I've to write the man's speeches. Quid pro quo. It's so painful. So far I've written speeches on laughter is the best remedy, a small family is a happy family, the Holy Ganges, Amartya Sen is not sane, yoga and aerobics to prevent a heart attack, Bhagavad Gita for the Soul, and military rule is the answer to India's problems. Ah yes. There was one for snoring in which I included two jokes. Ques: Do men always snore? Ans: No. Only when they're asleep.

Wife: Ha ha. You're so funny, Himanshu.

Woman: So witty. You know, like Birbal.

Man: Ah, you got it? Because Surana didn't.

Wife: What are you saying! This is too much.

Woman: No way. I swear it!

Man: There was another joke: Doctor, doctor, I snore so loudly I keep myself awake! Doctor: Sleep in another room then.

Wife: You're so funny, Himanshu.

Woman: Really.

Man: The thing with speech writing is one has to enter the mind of the other person. Cloak your thoughts and intermingle with the principal. That's very difficult with Surana. To start with he thinks like a Marwari from Rajasthan, which is what he is. The other day, he was to deliver a speech on hair. I had written something about hair being lustrous. And Surana in all his wisdom mentioned something about hair being lusty.

Wife: What are you saying, Himanshu! I'm so shocked!

Woman: People are so illiterate in this country. It's just too much! Too much!

Man: Last Wednesday there was a seminar on Central Excise. Surana invited me, so that I could report the proceedings in a 32-page bulletin for members only.

Wife: Enchanting.

Man: There were 367 of us – bundled in a hall. The hall could seat 275 perhaps? Earlier they used to meet at Juhu Centaur. But due to economising, they meet in this new club. Oh yeah. Zero taste. Hideous chandeliers. Ghastly service. Purple carpets. Stink of phenyl from the floor. Belongs to the Deputy CM's nephew. I'm told Surana gets 10% commission on the hall booking ...

Woman: Get on with it, Himanshu. Don't digress.

Man: The session was supposed to begin on the dot at 19.03. This was notified by Rustom Kateli, the Association, Executive Secretary who had begun to resemble a vulture. Surana's step-uncle Premchand Popat Chandaria arrived. He was recuperating from his trip to Palitana. Mulchand Khiamsia was not present since he had ... loose motions.

Wife: Ummm. So enchanting.

Man: Premchand Popat Chandaria kicked off the proceedings. Oh yeah. Right at the outset, he said, The Association must make a strong representation to oppose the planned Parliamentary legislation which will debar those who collaborated with the British in the 1940s.

Woman: Ummm. Really. What for?

Men: So that collaborators could not hold high constitutional posts and become the ... the ... Prime Minister. Of course members of the audience had no clue as to what collaboration he was referring to. Immediately, Premchand Popat Chandaria pulled out a red-coloured document which proved how certain people were being falsely implicated for opposing the three mass movements – non-cooperation, civil disobedience and Quit India. Once again – a ditto reaction from audience.

Woman: Ummm. Really. They must keep politics out of all this, no? It's so silly.

Man: Then Premchand Popat Chandaria said the persons who have published the erroneous red-coloured document can't sing the Vande Mantram without referring to a chit of paper. Under such circumstances how can we, the people, trust their untruth. Then he proceeded to sing the Vande Mataram.

Woman: I adore the Vande Mataram. Such a lovely tune, no? So catchy, so hummable!

Wife: It is our national song, no ...

Man: There was a question–answer session in which members wanted to know the difference between insecticide and pesticide; between bubble gum and chewing gum; between exercise book and notebook; between snow and ice.

Woman: Snow and ice ... well ... let me see ...

Man: Don't even bother, Shivani. Because Sudhakaran, who was the moderator, pointed out that the seminar was an exercise in futility. He explained that this was because the city has seven commissioners for seven zones and that each of these commissioners abide by their own law of interpretation. That set the cat among the pigeons. After some hullabaloo, Shekaran, asked the audience to define a tomato – was it a vegetable or a fruit? The unanimous opinion was fruit. What do you say?

Woman: Ummm. A fruit.

Wife: Well ... you know ... whatever ...

Man: A vegetable. Sudhakaran brought to our notice a Supreme Court ruling which after eleven years of dispute stated that a tomato is a vegetable since ... it is sold ... in the vegetable market.

Wife: Ummm. .Fascinating.

Man: Oh yeah. So at the end of seven-and-a-half hours of talk-talk-talk what my pea-sized brain understood is – the notification issued by the finance department is 'erroneous' and is **not** fool-proof. And that everything under the sun which is movable, marketable, and manufactured is excisable. From a spaceship to a pin. Probably, the maternity ward is the only manufacturing unit which has been spared from the clutches of excise duty. Which is why, producing babies is duty-free.

Woman: And ... what about that chap ... the one you wrote the speech for ...

Man: Surana began his vote of thanks. He mispronounced the names of the dignitaries on the dais and then proceeded to maul a couplet by Mir. Then he invited everyone for cocktail dinner and to partake of the melodies of an orchestra. And I stumbled out of the room gasping and groaning. Dashed to the cloakroom; and popped a Crocin; whilst Daler Mehndi filtered through the sound system.

Man / Woman / Wife: Uh-huhn, awright, yeah.

Husband: Bridge, anyone?

Man / Woman / Wife: Uh-huhn, awright, yeah. Oh yeah!

Music plays.

ACT I SCENE 5

Music plays. The doorbell rings.

Wife: Coming!

Husband: Many days later. It was an evening like ... the previous one? ... again, an evening dedicated to bridge ... and once again, to conversation ... to wining-dining.

The doorbell rings.

Wife: Coming!

Man: Arundhati, hey!

Woman: Hey, hey!

Wife: Himanshu, Shivani, we're so glad you could make it. We were afraid you might not be able to come. Everyone is so busy. Some salted peanuts? Would you like to have some whisky? There's also some cognac. Daddy's client got a bottle from Europe. Daddy's so popular amongst his clients. So popular. Really popular. One of them got those little windmills from Amsterdam. So cute.

Woman: Yeah. Right. Ummm. Let's talk ...

Man: Yes, yes, by all means ... Uh-huhn, awright, yeah.

Woman: Yes-yes, no? It will be very much fun. Eeenie-meenie-mynie-moh. Hee hee hee. Your turn.

Man: Me? Hmmm. The education system is so faulty. The problem, I think, lies with the students. They don't value the thing. It's all this subsidy. Look at the IIMs and IITs.

Wife: Yes ... you know ... whatever.

Man: May I remove my shoes and relax? Sweetie, could you please blast the music?

Wife: Cannot do it. Mr Mahalonobis is unwell. The building secretary has issued a circular to maintain peace and quiet.

Man: Oh no. What a bother!

Woman: Himanshu, behave yourself. Don't be inhuman.

Husband: Hmm. There was a short pause. Himanshu queried, Mahalonobis? What a curious name? What is he? A Bengali?

Man: Mahalonobis? What a curious sort of name? What's he? A Bong?

Husband: And Aru said, I don't know. I could find out.

Wife: I don't know. I could ... like ... find out.

Husband: Then Himanshu said, Hey Kranti!

Man: Hey Kranti! Wasn't he the gent we met in the lift?

Husband: I said, yes. Yeah.

Man: Do you recall what he said? I didn't comprehend a word ...

Husband: Mahalonobis talked about the Great Bengal Famine in 1943. Himanshu said, oh that! How does it matter, today?

Man: Yeah. Right. OK. How does it matter? Today, we're shining. Things are looking up. Whassay?

Husband: I said ... Mahalonobis says, the Great Bengal Famine could have been prevented, if the Government of the day had officially accepted there was a famine. Same as today. On cue, Himanshu shouted ...

Man: What famine? Where's the famine? These Bongs are intent on bad-mouthing our country. Satyajit Ray, Jyoti Basu, and this chap. What's this guy, a loony?

Husband: He is an ... economist. Chairman of an Independent Famine Inquiry Commission.

Man: Ah, that's one and the same thing, no?

Husband: Everyone laughed. Then there was a pause.

Woman: You're so hilarious, Himanshu. The funniest man on earth, I must say.

Man: Oooh. Shivani, how's your baby?

Woman speaks in a high-pitched, attention-seeking tone.

Woman: Ooooh la la laah. I'm feeling fine. Purshottam is such a pleasure. A dear. Really too cute, I swear.

Man: Ah, you decided to call him Purshottam?

Woman: Yeah, right. Absolutely. Aditya was hoping I'd give birth to a girl. He wanted to call her Indira. You know, how Aditya's dad and V C Shukla uncle were such good pals in the seventies. Uncle had got Aditya's dad to invest in Sanjay's Maruti project.

Wife: How was the labour? You were saying ... !

Woman: Ooooh. The labour was OK. The epidural was simply brilliant. I enjoyed every bit from then on and had more energy after birth to interact with him. I was a first-rate star pusher. Two reasons: my level of flexibility (all the squatting till my date of delivery) and my determination to make sure that Purshottam was out before the epidural wore off. The nursing staff was excellent. At one stage the nurse asked me if I would like to see Purshottam's head when I pushed. That was an excellent strategy as it helped focus my pushing. Aditya is so proud to have cut the umbilical cord, though in our birth plan he had mentioned that he did not want to. There he was with his flashing 1000-watt smile and yellow roses, holding him, commenting on how handsome he was. Etc. Etc. He was there when they gave Purshottam a bath, treatments, all of which has been instrumental in Aditya's confidence when dealing with Purshottam.

Wife: Really. Great. Wow, I mean!

Man: Can you imagine?

Woman: And ooooh la la laah. He (most often) has a 2–3 hour night pattern and during the day, he maintains a similar pattern. We bought a sling which cost Rs 950/- but it is nothing but a westernised version of a jhula. And the diapers and the baby food, baby soap, baby powder, baby toys, baby music, baby therapy. And so on. Everything is so exorbitant too. I've bought ear-muffs for Purshottam because of the sound pollution. You know, the traffic sound from the street. Too many cars on the road. One night I caught the poor dear having a flutter. Phew. Raising a baby in this day and age is so difficult, no.

Wife: Yeah. Right. OK.

Man: How's Aditya?

Woman: And ooooooh la la laah. We – Aditya and me – have been going out with him so often that at times I forget that I have a month-old baby. We try to do something special with him every Saturday. And Aditya and I have our dates every Sunday. Of course our 'dates' are a day in Alibaug, but hey, they are magical. Yesterday, Purshottam and I went to the bank to fill my ATM forms and trust my luck I had a woman who did nothing to assist me. Means ... halfway through my test, Purshottam needed to be fed – no rest rooms, raining outside, the woman pissed off. Really angry and agitated. So I just held him to my breast and fed him. The lady was shocked. She better be, the breastless thing, no. Hopefully if a few of us do this, support for breastfeeding might change.

Wife: Yeah. Right. OK. How interesting!

Man: How's it at the new home? The shift, eh?

Wife: Have you settled down?

Woman: Oooooh la la laah. I cannot believe it's been six months since I moved to Altamount Road. I am shocked that I have not missed that side of life. I'm doing this yoga course. It is so soothing. So uplifting. That's why our sages did yoga, no. It has kept me active. Nivedita, my girl-friend commented on how soon I have begun to enjoy Purshottam. I know the reason is because I have engaged with a lot of non-parenting activities and time and space to myself. Aditya and his mother have been so very supportive of this and, that I even managed to start some exercises a week after Purshottam's birth.

Wife: Yeah. Right. OK. How's breastfeeding?

Woman: And oooooh. I love every moment of breastfeeding, even at night. Fortunately all the reading and classes, cabbage leaves and creams and etc. etc. helped in the initial process. I hate burping. I love it when he coos which he does in the sling. Cooing is the equivalent to burping being an acceptable sign of appreciating food! It's really gorgeous, I swear.

Wife: Yeah. Right. OK.

Man: Wow. Maan! So kool!

Woman: Next week Aditya and me plan to get Purshottam admitted into a pre-school. It's very good. There's such a huge waiting list. We intend to pay seven lakhs as donation. The office is soooo supportive. One has to plan these things right away, no. Got to give the child a proper education. And Purshottam is so clever. He can even say 'paapaa' ... you know. Good, no?

Music plays.

ACT I SCENE 6

Man, Woman and Wife get ready for a game of cards.

Husband: And so, the evening unfolded ... It was time for bridge ... a kind of ritual. But it was appropriate for the sort of evening that ensued.

The bidding for bridge begins.

Man: One club.

Woman: One diamond.

Wife: ... Er ... what shall I say.

Man: Say something, Arundhati. You must.

Wife: Ummm. One heart.

Man: What! Are you certain? Take another peek at your hand!

Woman: Hey, cheating. Cheating is not allowed. You cannot change your bid.

Husband: One no trump.

Man: Two ... diamonds.

Woman: What?

Man: I said, two diamonds.

Woman: Two diamonds? Pass. Its your turn?

Wife: Yeah ... I know ... I say, pass.

Husband: Likewise! Pass!

Man: Let's play.

Wife: Shall I get some brownies, and French fries with cheese batter?

Man: Ok.

Woman: Ok.

Husband: Ok.

Music plays.

ACT I SCENE 7

The game of bridge is in progress. Wife speaks staccato, unfaltering speech.

Wife (sighs): Oh dear oh dear oh dear – things have become so hectic.

Man: Right, city-life is so crazy. So many meetings. Running from one appointment to another. Ridiculous.

Woman: It's too much, I swear.

Man: How's the dog?

Woman: The dog's fine. We have changed its name.

Man: Again?

Woman: This time he is called: Underdog. He has such a silly smile on his face. I think he is in heat. We are planning to neuter him.

Wife: Yeah. Right. OK. Fascinating.

Woman: I swear it!

Wife: Big Timc.

Man: I met Halari Oswal Jain, yesterday, whose annual turnover is Rs 8.5 crore approx and he spoke about how his karma tripped his dogma, after he attended a Murari Bapu show. He had lived his best years in Burma before the military regime extradited him. Now, he wants to return to Rangoon.

Husband: Your turn!!!

Woman: Neutering is very much fascinating, you know. In fact we should neuter all males in this country ... especially those in heat. It will solve the population problem. Whassay!

Wife: Yeah. Right. OK. So fascinating, I mean.

Husband: Your turn, again!!!

Man: Halari Oswal Jain says Rangoon is any time better than ... this. He said 'Ame Surat-Amdavadna Jainone ane akhi duniyane amaru pani badadi didhun. Ane have gauravbher fariye chhiye.'

Wife: I mean this is ... you know ... whatever ... Indians are never treated properly in India. It's so sad.

Woman: The house looks celestial. Really lovely.

Wife: Really. I'm so glad you noticed. It's all Daddy's doing. Daddy is such a gem. He has spent so much time on the little things. Poured a lot of his sweat into it. Of course, thanks to Daddy's business friends, we have good contacts amongst the antique dealers and collectors. Isn't it nice?

Man: It is nice.

Woman: Very nice. Indeed.

Man: Rather nice.

Woman: Nice. Quite so.

Wife: Seriously, I didn't expect things to turn out so well. But it has. The house has a definite character. It's not just relics and old things. One has to know how to procure them and then arrange them along with your modern furnishings. A blend of the contemporary with the historical. You won't believe the luck we had with a cinema theatre in Kerala. A small town near Ernakulam. They were disposing off their chairs at a throwaway price. It was teak ... and a century old. So Daddy spoke to the proprietor and procured a dozen of them. We had them transported by a truck. I hope to place them in the library. The only problem is the books. But the chairs are gorgeous.

Man: Yes, yes. Dazzling.

Woman: Truly elegant. Yes.

Husband: Your turn!!!

Woman: Is it my turn?

Man: Your turn.

Wife: Your turn.

Woman: Is it my turn, again?

Husband: Your turn!!!

The doorbell rings.

Wife: Oh oh oh, that must be a message from the bai. There's been a death in her family. TB. Apparently thirteen TB deaths in the past seven days in the slums. It's a crime. Did you know, instead of a doctor, these poor people consult the paanwallah for medicines. We must do something for the poor people. And the newspapers don't even report it!

Woman: We must, we must.

Man: Yeah, right. Absolutely. No question about it.

Wife: Can you procure a job for my bai's husband? She needs the money. Her daughter is spastic. And the bai's husband sits at home and abuses all and sundry and beats up the bai and the daughter. His company shut down. See if you can get him a job? Anything. Watchman, courier-man, anything. Ask Aditya? His name is Mahadik. I've even told Daddy about him. But Daddy is so busy. We must help these poor people, no? Whatever.

Woman: Uh-huhn, awright, yeah. I can donate some of my old chiffon sarees, you know. Anything for charity.

Man: Yeah, right, we must do something. Absolutely. No question about it.

The doorbell rings.

Wife: Coming!

Wife exits. Music plays.

ACT I SCENE 8

Music plays.

Husband: Exit Aru. Sigh Shivani. Himanshu analysed the game. He always did it. Thought he was Omar Sharif. Dashing and debonair.

Man: What a round that was! I should have forced a bid from you guys. What a super-idiot.

Woman: True-true.

Husband: Slight pause. And then Shivani asked me ...

Woman (to Husband): How are you, Kranti?

Husband: She always took my name. Kranti. But before I could respond, Himanshu said ...

Man: You know, I got swayed by that no trump! I should have calculated at least 11 points, there. Good touch, yaar!

Woman: What they did in there was unpardonable. Oooooh. Arundhati told me that it was terrible. You must have been devastated, no?

Man: Oh yeah. Absolutely.

Husband: And then their questions which had been bottled up, began! It was Shivani's turn, first.

A beat.

Woman: So how was it in there? Can our sort bear it at all? Must have been terrible, the hygiene? So you have to do your potty in the jail, eh, in front of the others? Oooh, maan that's so not happening, no! I could never do it.

Man: The main thing is Arundhati ... how is she taking it? Is she on medication? She needs serious counselling. Kranti, you must do something about it!

Woman: Arrey Himanshu, but what is Kranti expected to do about Arundhati?

Man: He has to lift his little finger! Be supportive. He's her husband! Lawfully-awfully wedded.

Woman: So?

Man: Yeah. You won't understand. Arundhati is so vulnerable, you know.

Woman: Yeah. Right.

Man: You know what Arundhati did the other day? It was shocking! And just because she is depressed. Why else would she be slitting gas tubes? A good thing, the windows were open. Or else ... it would have been terrible. Of course she says it was a freak accident.

Woman: Arundhati should have been more careful. She's so ... scatter-brained, you know.

Man: ... It's a good thing Arundhati's dad dropped in. Or else Arundhati would have been dead ...

Woman: Nothing was going to happen. Surely you know that, no? Arrey it was all drama baazi.

Man: Don't 'arrey' me, Ok?

Woman: Arrey.

Man: Arrey to you.

Woman: Relax. Some ice for your drink, Himanshu?

A beat

Husband: Himanshu had an Arundhati obsession. Rumour had it, if I had not married Arundhati, it would have been Himanshu.

Man: Kranti, are you allowed to play cards in jail? Something intelligent like bridge or something?

Woman: What kind of a stupid question is that?

Husband: Hmmm. Shivani loathes Arundhati. It's a college thing. One of those juvenile rivalries. One day, Arundhati compounded things by asking Shivani, if Aditya is still having an affair with Gayatri.

Woman: Oh. That Gayatri. Don't be silly. Preposterous. Hee hee hee.

Man: You know when Nehru was in jail, he had all sorts of privileges. He really freaked out. Writing, walking, wheat bread. Maan, those times! The Brits had class. Real kool. Their jails were so well provided for.

Woman: Kranti, you should have paid the police off! Aditya would have done that. A little bribe. Did you explain that it was a terrible misunderstanding?

Husband: So it was. I tried to talk but no one paid heed. I wanted to tell them about the mutilated body in the jail. He was one of the protestors. Perhaps. Just as I was getting accustomed to sleeping, the jail gate opened. Someone walked into our cell in the middle of the night. He urinated on the mutilated body. Sliced the ears. Rubbed them with oil. To lure red ants.

Man: Yeah, yeah, ants, red ants. Listen yaar, you must let us know, if there's anything we can do. We are your friends. We are. Really!

Woman: Yes-yes. Absolutely. Aditya sends you his regards. He couldn't come to meet Arundhati after the accident because they are in the midst of shifting their office to the Bandra-Kurla complex. Today, they have a *gruh-pravesh pooja.* Have you been to Bandra-Kurla? It looks like a science fiction movie at night ...

Man: You must not let all this get you down. You must not get depressed.

Woman: Perhaps you must consult an astrologer. That is the only way to counter this ... this thing. Whatever it is ...

Husband: Next day, the face was covered with hundreds, thousands of ... red ants.

Music plays.

ACT I SCENE 9

Music plays. Wife enters with a note that is being circulated in the building.

Wife: Oh no. Oh no. Oh no. We have a tragedy in the building. Mr Mahalonobis is dead.

Woman: Mr Mahalonobis! Who Mr Mahalonobis?

Man: Oooh maan. Death. Life's final reward. I wish I'm not around when it happens to me. Say, how old was this chappie?

Wife: Mr Mahalonobis lived on the sixteenth floor. Or is it the seventeenth floor? He was grey-haired, suffered from Parkinson's or some sort of myocardial infarction ...

Woman: Oooof?

Man: Ah!

Wife: I can't seem to recollect what it is. We've to send our condolences and commiserations. Frankly, one is befuddled about utterances at such times. Ideally, silence should prevail. However, we have been bequeathed words ... and so, they should be uttered.

Woman: Yeah, you're so right. Death is so ... so deadly, if you know what I mean.

Man: Uh-huhn, awright, yeah. Absolutely.

Wife: You know there are people who live in the same building for God knows how many years and do not know who their neighbours are. It's such a shame. I'm different ... in a nice sort of way. In fact, of late, things are becoming important to me.

Man: Oh yeah. Oh boy. This is so kool!

Woman: Really! Soooo sweeeet.

Wife: I need to show to people that I care when they are alive. Often my behaviour borders on indifference even though I think I am what can be called an affectionate person.

Woman: Soooo charming. Come here, give me a hug!

Man: There you are ... isn't that lovely ... ?

Woman: Ooooof. I know how it is. My grandfather died recently. He was 92. He collapsed on his writing table after he completed his essay which he had to submit to *The Tribune*.

Wife: Means, he couldn't have selected a better death, no!!!

Man: Oh yeah. Absolutely super.

Woman: I suddenly realised that I would never be at peace with regard to him because there were a zillion things left unsaid. His gentleness, his humour, his mischievous eyes. So now I say things to the living, through gifts. Little things, you know. There's this lovely curio shop in Juhu. Means, I know, it is not the best way to shower affection, but it is the best way I can think of. Right, no?

Wife: Fascinating.

Man: Oh yeah. Absolutely.

Woman: Ooooh ...

Man: Yeah ... right ... kool ...

Wife: Come, come. I have a new CD of Baazi. Daddy got it from Toronto. It's memorable. Have I mentioned ... Guru Dutt is my favourite director. Dev Anand and Geeta Dutt are adorable. You agree, no? Come, let me show you some of the furnishings in the bathroom. I have a beautiful stained glass, cast-iron washbasin. I could place an order for some food. There's a cute Vietnamese joint round the corner. It shouldn't be long. Ah, look it's a full moon. Look at the poor thing, alone and isolated, trying to create a space for himself.

Man: Bridge, anyone?

Music plays.

ACT I SCENE 10

Silence. Blackout

Wife: Oh dear ... a power failure ...

Man: It must be load-shedding ...

Wife: ... It's become so frequent, these days ...

Woman: Even we have been experiencing it. The city is going to the dogs, I swear.

Man: Hey, it's an overload on the grid. Plus there's the pilfering and theft. Something must be done quickly or else Mumbai will become like Bihar ...

Woman: Do you have candles ... ?

Wife: Candles ... I can't recollect where I've ...

Man: Oh yeah, that will be a good idea. Absolutely. Romantic, hunh?

Woman: Oooof ... where's that torch Aditya gave me ... ? *(Pause)*

Husband: And ... that was when I was alone for the first time in the evening ... that is ... all alone ... I wrote some lines of poetry ... after ages ... at the moment ... one feels like Humayun ... a bit like a hyphen ... sandwiched between a mighty father ... Babur ... and a mightier son ... Akbar. I've ... been reading ... a thing which has been absent ... for all these years ... It's with a heavy heart ... that one chose poetry ... It is my aspiration ... to have the largest collection of poetry ... and to read all of it ... meticulously ... only when I'm old and disabled. It's like my dad ... he has this thing about heaven ... an empty room with a mattress ... *agarbatti* and candles ... and Bade Ghulam Ali Khan – the greatest of singers – rendering an *alaap*.

ACT II SCENE 1

Husband: And ... that was when I was alone for the first time in the evening ... me and Bade Ghulam Ali Khan rendering Raga Adana Bahar ... it was my father's favourite ... he used to listen to it whenever he caused an unrest in other people's lives ... It was Lala Lajpatrai's anniversary and father had to deliver a keynote ... To attract a crowd, the organisers had promised lunch after the keynote ... When father entered the lunch room, he noticed the women were not being served ... when he asked one of the organisers, he was told, its protocol, first men and then women ... after all, a custom is a custom ... Father was furious ... he sat down to eat ... as per convention, the others could start eating only after the guest of honour had begun ... so, everyone waited for father to begin ... father took a handful... threw it over his shoulder ... second handful, over the shoulder ... third handful ... the organisers were outraged ... Father explained, he was following a protocol ... he always fed the great characters from history (Gandhi, Nehru, Sardar, Bose, Ambedkar, Bhagat Singh) before he began a meal ... after all, a custom is a custom ... Naturally, father became unpopular and was never invited for a keynote ... but it seems, the next year when they hosted Lala Lajpatrai's anniversary, the organisers served the men and women, together ... hmmm ...

A beat

Man: Hey, I've a super idea. Another round of bridge? In candle-light?

Music plays.

Husband: And in this way, another game ensued. And another day. And yet, another evening. Followed by yet another round of amateur bidding. Pass.

Wife: Pass.

Man: Three no trump.

Woman: Four no trump.

Husband: Pass.

Wife: Pass.

Man: Five no trump.

Woman: What??? There is no response like five no trump? Let me sms Aditya.

A beat

Husband: Years ago, Arundhati and me had won a grand slam. She was just learning the nitty-gritty of bridge. May be she has forgotten, those days. We were a team. Unbeatable at the club.

Wife: We were a great team. Unbeatable partners. What happened, Kranti?

Husband: What happened, Aru? Pass.

Wife: Pass.

Man: Six no trump.

Woman: Seven no trump.

Wife: Today, life is ploughing on. Everything seemed so different a few years ago. Daddy treated Kranti like a son. Daddy had confessed to me that he never wanted a daughter. When I said I was like a son, he joked that I was eyeing the family business.

Husband: Her daddy was obsessed with his business.

Wife: Daddy wanted Kranti to take over the family business.

Husband: Before our wedding, her dad took me for a drive with two of his friends near Jamshedpur. It was one of those bonding exercises. There was a chap called Grover, who wanted to click photographs of tribal women. Almost got beaten up by the locals. Grover is now a professor in MIT. When I ask her dad 'in what?' he replies, 'pornography'. It's his favourite joke. These days, he treats me like a son. He has to. He lost his only son in the Kanishka plane-crash. So I'm his newfound son. Which means, he expects me to execute his last rites when he dies.

Wife: I told Daddy, I want to do something like the Shroffs in Bhuj. So Daddy put me in touch with a colleague in UP. It was to be a new beginning. A fresh start, for me. The dusty roads, the sultry days, I loathe being mistaken for a foreigner. In India, they always ask me for my passport!

Husband: I'm horrified by Hindu death rites. In fact whenever her dad was seated in front of me in the car, I used to stare at the back of his skull, and think to myself, one day, I'll be smashing this skull to smithereens.

Wife: But my mind was elsewhere. My own home. My dream castle with its magical dust. My own special garden with its bonsais and ferns that admits family, friends, newer acquaintances. Things seemed so simple.

Husband: Her father trying to control our lives. He wanted us to examine a possible centre for setting up a new unit. So we went to Bulandshar, Etah, Pilibhit, Baghpat, Saharanpur.

Wife: Daddy had warned me about him. Daddy had said he would make me unhappy. But at that time I thought Daddy was being .. well .. 'Daddy'. Over-cautious, protective. But ours promised to be a lovely marriage!

Husband: Pass.

Wife: Pass.

A beat

Man: Her dad had asked me my opinion about Kranti. I told uncle that he was not 'our sort'. Uncle tried to talk to Arundhati. But at that time Arundhati thought her dad was being .. well .. 'Daddy'. Over-cautious, protective. She told me, it is going to be a lovely marriage!

Woman: Arrey, it was one of those open secrets: their marriage was doomed right from the outset. They were totally not happening. Incompatible.

Man: Like maan, Arundhati should have married me. Yeah.

Woman: I had given it three-and-a-half years. Tops.

Man: I'm hoping to marry Arundhati after she divorces Kranti! And then migrate to New Jersey, New Zealand or even Nairobi. Get out of this country, before a civil war erupts. Yeah. Right!

A beat

Husband: Pass.

Wife: Pass.

Man: Eight no trump.

Woman: Nine no trump.

Man: I had penned a fresh poem for her.

Wife: I felt so very happy, in a cashmere sweater and the promise of mint tea. I briefly worked in an agency. Kranti barged in with a fresh poem with which he had proposed to me.

Husband: Look, a poem which I have penned. It's sentimental, foolish ...

Wife: He asked me if he could read it. It was for me ...

Husband: Can I read it? It is for you.

Wife: I nodded.

Husband: She nodded.

Wife: He read the poem.

Husband: I read the poem.

Man: Oooh maan, the poem sucked. I penned better poetry than Kranti. I'm a proven-pedigreed speech-writer, after all. Surana will testify.

Wife: It was one of those without a head-or-tail things – and had a long title: 'Why I Want To Conceal Myself In A Sovereign Attire.'

Husband: I recall the poem had a pretentious title.

Wife: It had a melodious title. The poem was sweet.

Husband: She said the poem was sweet. But it was she who was being sweet. The poem was heavily influenced by the poetry I used to read in those days. Those were the days.

Wife: Those were the days. Perhaps I should have paid heed to Daddy. To Himanshu. Yes, may be. I don't know. Whatever.

Husband, Wife, Man and Woman sigh.

Woman: The fact of the matter is, Arundhati was muddle-headed, mousy and a no-hoper. Kranti married beneath himself. Arrey, he needed someone like ... me.

Man: The fact was, Kranti was a weepy, weak-kneed, sneering bastard. Arundhati wedded beneath herself. She should have married ... me. We had longstanding family connections. Oooh maan, what a waste. Ah, marriage, a thing that does not live up to the promise of the first night. Oh yeah. A contract in which love is quarantined.

Woman: Pass.

Man: Pass.

Wife: Pass.

Husband: Pass.

Man: Hey maan. That was a very so-so game. Quite ordinary. Arundhati, it seemed you were not quite there. You know, mentally? One more round?

Music plays.

ACT II SCENE 2

Music plays.

Husband: And so, that's how things are when we meet. We play, we chit-chat, we corroborate, and we collaborate.

Wife: Pass.

Husband: Pass. Hmmm. But instead of proceeding along the beaten path, let me interrupt the flow of things and remind oneself of that day.

Wife: Yes, please do that. Let's clarify it, once and for all.

Husband: It was D-day and what a D-day it was. I was to head for Faizabad. You see, Arundhati had some fancy notions of starting a rural set-up like the Shroffs. Her dad proposed. This meant I had to play out the role allocated to me. I was getting late. I had a flight to catch.

A beat

Wife: It was a perfectly normal day in my life. He walked into the breakfast room, chatting on his cell phone. He was leaving for Faizabad. It was a big day for him.

Husband: I had told her, it was a big day for me.

Wife: He intended to sign the deal and return. Daddy said, it would do him good. As usual we did not exchange a word. There was no water in the house and the kitchen stank. Our pea-green dustbin, the one I had purchased in Singapore, had not been emptied for days. There was a Municipal Workers strike. In the old apartment blocks in Pydhonie, Daddy used to topple the contents of a bin which then would rush through the vertical disposal ducts, plummeting down to the dark vaults at courtyard level. But over here ... nothing like that. And so, and one had to live with well known drawbacks of evil-smelling accumulations like rotten eggs, bloody sanitary pads, stale food. Oh dear oh dear oh dear!

Husband: What's happening to the house!!! Why does everything smell of rotten eggs, sanitary pads and stale food, eh?

Wife: There's a strike. Don't you read the newspapers?

Husband: I read the cartoons. The rest I ignore.

Wife: For some reason, he never read the newspapers. So I filled him on the details of the Municipal workers strike. And he said ...

Husband: Ah yes, bloody rascals. BMC, BEST, banks, the unions. Always going on hartals. Constantly disrupting the lives of decent citizens like us. Why do we pay taxes so that this lot can feed off us!!! I say, all bandhs must be declared illegal. Lock up these chaps for a few weeks then they will come to their senses.

Wife: Last night he threw a party in honour of our anniversary. After the evening's visitors had gone, I had to quickly open the windows, rinse the beer glasses, empty the ashtrays, the tea leaves, leftover biryani, squeezed lemon. It's amazing how every day, we carry out this ritual knowing fully well that the following morning we may begin the new day without having to touch a thing. This is a generation that casts off things.

Husband: Have you seen my socks? The striped ones?

Wife: No.

Husband: Where is the bai?

Wife: The bai left us two weeks ago. I had told you about it.

Husband: The new bai? Oh damn, why do you fire all the bais? I've an important meeting. Oh damn. Those were my lucky socks ...

Wife: Perhaps it would have been a good thing, if he had not gone to Faizabad. But it was supposed to be a new chapter in our life.

Husband: It was a regular deal. Easy come. Easy go. Sign papers. Finalise deal. Come home.

Wife: Like I said it was supposed to be a normal day in my life.

Husband: I took the flight and then drove down to Faizabad. I had got a rubber stamp with a signature on a registration form from the Sessions Court. When I presented myself, I was ruefully told that the triplicate copy of the form might have been misplaced. After six months of doing-the-rounds-and-follow-ups! Bloody red-tapism. I explained my position to Shri Chaubey ji and his assistant secretary. It was easy to make them understand. Meanwhile some peons set out on the valiant task of hunting for the forms. I was told to wait.

Wife: Then he wandered outside. Why?

Husband: I sauntered outside for fresh air. At the maidan I watched preparations for a rally. There was a lot of shouting into the mikes. I purchased some *moongphali* – for old times' sake – and was watching the *tamasha*. It's been the same nehruvian bull-shit for the past fifty years.

Wife: That's what he said. Daddy said the whole thing smells fishy. Especially the bit about a sudden lathi charge ...

Husband: ... And suddenly there was a lathi charge. Before I realised what had happened I had been hit on my head. I fell down. The next thing I knew, I was shoved into a police van for ... for the crime of rioting and destroying public property.

Wife: Daddy says he is lying. His photograph is there for all to see in some local edition of a Hindi newspaper.

Husband: At the prison I notified the officer-on-duty that I had inadvertently been sent to prison. He refused to pay heed to me. I tried to bribe him. He abused me, and said I was the mastermind behind the rally. That I had instigated the locals.

Wife: Daddy says the police do not treat people like us shabbily.

Husband: All my rights were annulled. I was put in a common cell. Later I was produced before the additional chief metropolitan magistrate who directed the police to reject my bail plea since I had created a near-riot situation in the district.

Wife: That was Friday. There was no word from him on Saturday and Sunday.

Husband: That was Friday. The next two days were Saturday and Sunday. That night I shared my cell with Mr Mishra who had been arrested for attempting to smuggle Rs 1.93 crore worth of cell phones. Besides Mr Mishra, there were under-trial prisoners, one black-marketeer from Nepal, a drunk, the six hundred and eighty striking rally-wallahs, and one mutilated body in the centre of the room. The mutilated body offered me a seat. The six hundred and eighty rally-wallahs sang patriotic songs which were composed by Ramprasad Bismil.

Wife: Daddy said he was the mastermind of a Shaheed Mela in Ghaziabad. We expected the worst. Daddy called the local MLA, the Deputy Commissioner. They said things were in a state of confusion. Three revolutionary organisations ... er ... what were their names? Er ... Daddy had given them to me. I asked Daddy, why do people want to revolt? I mean people should be content with life, as it is. Look at me, I make the best of my situation. Don't I? Well. Whatever.

Husband: On Tuesday morning, the rally-wallahs were released.

Not me. There was no one to vouch for me. I noticed that the mutilated body did not move. Mr Mishra was unconcerned. I was appalled. I spoke to the official at the desk. I told him the mutilated body was dead. The head constable behind the desk smiled a smile. He said deaths are common in prisons.

Wife: Daddy said he had been charged under Sections 107, 116 and 151 of the Indian Penal Code. He along with 400 men, 240 women and 40 young children. All troublemakers who had tried to disrupt the peace in Faizabad. Dear Kranti could be anywhere. Faizabad, Sultanpur, Mau, Ayodhya.

Husband: Finally her Daddy's *chamchas* found me. I was told by them that I had breached the magistrate's order of Section 144. I was puzzled. After all, most of the people in the jail were women, students, daily wage workers, labourers, musicians. The *chamchas* informed me ...

Wife: '*... the rally-wallahs were troublemakers and anti-national revolutionaries.*' Daddy said he had got mixed up with this lot. That he had been stupid. Very stupid. Oh dear oh dear oh dear.

Husband: I informed her father's *chamchas* that the rally-wallahs wanted to build a memorial in honour of the martyrs who had died during the Mutiny of 1857. And that the police wanted to prevent it. Daddy's *chamchas* told me things were not so simple and straightforward. They never are! Until I found out the truth. That things are relatively uncomplicated. After all the Awadh region, of which the twin cities Ayodhya and Faizabad are a part, had been a centre for revolt against the British in 1857. A monument in the honour of the people of the land seems ideal ...

Wife: He lives in an ideal world. Yes, the basic problem is his idealism. He is very naive. He does not understand politics. Daddy says, he is ...

Husband: Daat ka kachcha! That's what her dad thinks of me.

A beat

Wife: When he returned home he had become obtuse. Very obtuse. He walked around in a blur. The poems stopped. May be I'm no longer pretty. These days, it's just pain. And worse still ... politeness.

Husband: I started to think. What do things like Article 19 and Article 21 really mean? Am I genuinely part of an open society as codified by our Constitution? I wonder? I wonder?

Wife: The last poem he wrote was ages ago.

Husband: Pretty clear, eh! In this world, all of us have no rights. When I came back, her dad was at the airport. None of my friends were present. Probably too embarrassed. It seems, the head office wants to disown me. Why? Just because perfect procedural justice is rare, if not next to impossible. Ah, I wish I was Ramprasad Bismil. Then I could write songs which were sung by the people of the land. I would speak the people's language. I would be heard.

Wife: In that poem he had said: *Once all this is over / There is ... rest*

Music plays.

ACT II SCENE 3

Woman: Hey Himanshu. I must thank you for meeting up. For these ... bridge tutorials. They are invaluable.

Man: How are you?

Woman: OK. How's Kranti?

Man: Well. No idea, I guess.

Woman: The other day, I met him he was reading all these strange Hindi-wallahs. What were the names: Ramprasad Bismil, Faiz, Nagarjuna.

Man: Strange.

Woman: He should have stuck to Shelley, Keats, Browning! What's wrong with them?

Man: Nothing. All great poets!

Woman: You know, I did some numerology. The basic problem is his name: Kranti. He must change it. No?

Man: A leopard cannot change its spots.

Woman: Still, I wish we could do something for him. Whassay?

Man: Yeah. I dropped him at the airport, you know, on that day. May be I could have ... done something ...

Woman: So could I ...

Man: Our office had donated a sizable sum for the Dr Ambedkar Udyan in Lucknow. Along with seventeen memorials and *parivartan chowks*. We collaborated on the electrification of the project. I'm sure someone from head office could have spoken to the officials. It could have been sorted out.

Woman: Yeah, yeah. And I could have spoken to Aditya's dad who could have spoken to Arunji.

Man: You know, in 1997, or was it '96, when the UP Government installed 15,000 statues of Dr Ambedkar, I had met the CM, twice, you know.

Woman: Aditya's dad knows the other Arunji, too. Something could have been done.

Man: Hmmm.

Woman: Hmmm.

Man: Ah, well. Let's begin ... the bridge tutorials. So, Shivani, do you recall the First Rule in Bridge?

Woman: Er ... no ...

Man: The First Rule in Bridge says Make One Allowance For Bad Break. Pass.

Woman: Hmmm.

Man: Hmmm.

Woman: I feel so guilty about Kranti.

Man: You mustn't ...

Woman: But what could I do, I was so so so busy. That week, when all this happened to Kranti. I was so caught up. I received a warning from the BSES. Aditya was not in town. The warning stated that their personnel cannot take the meter readings since there is a motorbike parked in front of the meter cabin. Imagine.

So I went to meet Hingorani, who owns an old 350 cc Rajdoot to request him to shift his bike. The gent invited me for a very sweet cup of tea and started berating Mr Desikan who is the building secretary, the neighbouring Masjid and its Mullah who does five 'besur' azaans in a day, Medha Patkar; SC/STs, the doddering watchman, bandicoots, voltage fluctuations, water-cuts; socialism, and so on. You know ... everything. There was no mention of the bike being shifted. Meanwhile BSES threatens to cut my electricity supply if necessary action is not taken. Imagine. Hey. How are you, Himanshu?

Man: OK. And how's Kranti?

Woman: Arrey, no idea, I guess.

Man: I wish we could do something for him. Whassay?

Woman: Yeah. I spoke to him the day he was leaving for Faizabad. Or was it Ghaziabad? Oh, it's all the same, no? Maybe I could have, but I was so caught up with what to do with Purshottam's diapers ... and there was that kachrawallah's strike ... er, what is it you said about Rule Two. Simple Play Is Difficult.

Man: Yeah right. What a mess those kachrawallahs created in the city on that day! The municipality goes on a strike for a few days and the rubbish is piled up at our doorways. The city is transformed into a corrupted dunghill; far more quickly than anyone could have predicted. This Diwali I'm not going to pay them any baksheesh when they come to pick up their tip.

Woman: Me too.

Man: That will show them. Oh yeah.

Woman: True, true.

Man: Hit them where it hurts. Oh yeah.

Woman: True, true.

Man: Rule Three. Gain Valuable Time with Key Play. Pass.

Woman: Rule Four. Praise Partner To Cover Own Fault. Superb aftershave, yaar.

Man: Thanks. How is Arundhati taking it? OK and all? Kool?

Woman: She will manage ... I guess. I got a call from her. She wanted me to sleep at her place on the Saturday and Sunday Kranti was missing. I said I'll try. After all, what are friends for!!! Right? How's Surana?

Man: Oh yeah. Yesterday's meeting with Surana was an eye-opener. I had to write a speech on The Art of Eating. Surana was fasting. Some religious thing. Apparently, he has become a member of the Sangh. He told me to become a member. He said it would improve my personality. Give me peace of mind. Make me a better person.

Woman: Oh!

Man: He asked me for a donation for the Sangh. I gave him a hefty cheque. Rule Five. Players Should Be Selfish. I had to. Surana and his uncle blessed me.

Woman: Oooh la la lah, I must tell you this. I went to the Pachauris the other day. They were hosting a prasad festival. It was such a spiritual experience. So cleansing. Peda for Ganapati, plain halwa for Durga. Dal halwa for Holi and Diwali. Moti choor laddoo for Lakshmi. Yellow sweet rice for Saraswati on Vasant Panchami. Kheer for Rakhi, Teej, Sindhara and Sharad Purnima. Dhania panjiri for Krishna. Atta panjiri and suji halwa for Satyanarayan, Churma for Hanuman. It was awesome. Such a lot of ghee. It is a crime.

Man: You know, I'm planning to quit. Migrate to Canada. I have a business contact. My papers are being processed.

Woman: Ooooh Canada. That's near California ... no?

Man: It's very pretty. You must drop in.

Woman: But what will you do in Canada? The usual ... I mean ... whatever it is you were up to ... the last time we met ... ?

Man: Yeah. Right. Surviving. How's Aditya? Once upon a time, he and me had the same enemies. Is he busy?

Woman: Very much so. You know, Aditya has three free days in November. Ha ha. Three free days. We can plan a vacation. Umm. Himanshu, I had meant to ask you something ... personal ... may I?

Man: Shoot, yaar.

Woman: Have you heard anything about this ... Gayatri?

Man: Er ... Who?

Woman: Arundhati was mentioning something about Gayatri ...

Man: In that case, why don't you ask Arundhati about it?

Woman: Arrey, how can I, at a time such as this?

Man: Absolutely. Rule Six. Don't Waste Tears When Play Is Bad. What does Arundhati say about Kranti ... after he returned ... from Ghaziabad or is it Faizabad?

Woman: She says, I wish Kranti had not got involved in something political and all. Arrey, I totally fail to understand ... all this politics. May be you should give me tutorials on politics, too. Ok, I've to hurry. Have to pick up Aditya's suit from the dry cleaner.

Man: Rule Seven. Don't Use One Suit If You Have Two.

Woman: Hmmm.

Man: Hmmm.

Woman: Rule Eight. Don't Play Against Mind Readers! You know, Aditya's been so busy. This vacation to Goa is a godsend.

Man: Rule Nine. Don't Listen To Table Talk. You think Arundhati will get a divorce?

Woman: Rule Ten. Unlucky Players Should Not Guess.

Man: Ok. Bye. Hey Sheebu, give me a bye-bye huggie.

Woman: By the way, have you ever wondered, where do the Goans go when they need a vacation?

Music plays.

ACT II SCENE 4

Music plays.

Husband: Ever since I've returned all I've heard is talk-talk-talk! Firstly, there is Arundhati.

Wife: Kranti, everything is falling apart ... I've not even had a proper bath in all these days. And then there's been that stupid cousin of yours, Damayanti, who has gotten married and had fourteen functions to celebrate. Which meant I had to wear seventeen-and-a-half dresses. Really! And she is such a big bore. Which made it harder for the rest of us to drag ourselves and say – Congratulations!

Husband: There's more to come.

Wife: On top of it, you didn't come for a single function. Daddy says it's a sign of guilt. That you're putting on an act.

Husband: And there's more to come.

Wife: And then there is ... I mean ... all these chores – paying the MTNL bill, paying the credit card dues, the house loan, shopping, getting the deposit, speaking to the Orange people, the newspaper, the cable guy ... even Daddy did not get a Rajya Sabha seat because of your antics in Uttar Pradesh ... you know what I mean ... whatever.

Husband: And still more to come.

Wife: Even that day when I was in the kitchen ... Daddy called ... he was petulant, angry ... Delhi had said, no ... I opened the windows ... I stared at the baobab. I wondered where you were!!! I had got a call from Himanshu. He said you hadn't reported to work for a week? The last thing I remember was the flowers on the baobab tree. They stink, you know. And baobab flowers blossom only once. For one day. That day, I saw one of them on the floor. Crushed. I inhaled the stench from the flower. And your poem returned to me. I recall it ... *above all, there was rest ...*

Husband: Ever since I've returned all I've heard is unsolicited advice. Have you noticed, we the nation, expertise in offering unsolicited advice to all and sundry. There's Himanshu.

Man: Listen Maan! Forget what happened. The poor people do exist. They always have. But that's not our fault, is it? A person lives the way a person lives. You cannot change that. OK, there is injustice in one corner of the world and you feel shit about it. But that's life, you know. I mean this is an exciting time in the company. Mergers, tie-ups, roadshows, technology transfers. We've even purchased four extra units at Vapi. It's marvellous.

Husband: And even Shivani.

Woman: There's no reason why you should make these trips to Faizabad for the hearing. Ooof. All these summons. It is so humiliating. Just pay and get out of the situation. The wrong-doings prick your conscience. But you think the world out there cares. Nobody in this world owes anybody a living.

Man: Freedom and equality and human rights, are fine words, mon ami, but they also sever the primary bonds; the attachments. Where will you be without your duplex flat; your to-and-fro vacation to Seychelles; your daughter's education in Harvard? This identity with your family, clan, religion gives you your security. Eh? You are wealthy and that is the way it has to be. It is your money which gives you a sense of moral virtue and justice. Without it you, your pretty wife and child, will be living in a *jhopadpatti* in Dharavi.

Woman: Come here, Kranti, you poor dear. You've suffered so much. Let me mother you. Oooh my poor dear baby. Do you want to place your head on my chest – like in college – when we watched films at Akashvani? No? Don't be shy? Purshottam does it all the time.

Man: You know, Kranti, everyone's wondering how long you are going to wallow in self-pity ... out-of-sight-and-all-that ... Arrey, I know what tragedy means ... you remember, no ... I lost my uncle and aunt in that tidal wave ... when they were in Andhra Pradesh ... although, god alone knows why anyone would want to go to Andhra Pradesh ... you remember, no ... ?

Husband: Tantalising pause. And then there was music.

Music plays.

Woman: By the way, there's some good news. Tell them, Himanshu ...

Man: No, no. You tell them.

Woman: Ok. The thing is, Himanshu and I've decided to live together and basically get married ...

Man: Yeah. Right. Like you know.

Woman: Purshottam needs a daddy, no?

Man: Absolutely.

Woman: Aditya is not available. He is ...

Man: He is a bastard.

Woman: Don't say such things about Aditya. He's Purshottam's father, after all.

Man: Oh yeah.

Woman: Aditya's living with that ... Gayatri.

Man: What a total bitch, maan.

Woman: Forget her, Himanshu. Now, I have you and you have me.

Man: Made for one another.

Husband: They kissed. Dispassionately. The music faded out. There was silence. They held hands. Awkwardly. A presumptuous pause.

Wife: We must like celebrate this ... I have some *chikki*. Kranti purchased it from Faizabad. He had a hearing in the court. Last week. He had to make an appearance. You know, the whole prison thing still haunts him. He has stopped sleeping.

ACT II SCENE 5

Sound of hammering. Husband moves his lips.

Husband: When in prison I was utterly unable to understand what had happened and why. I more than ever clung to whatever had given me self-respect up to that moment. My job, my family, my religion. Yes. Even whilst I was being abused, I assured everyone that I had never disobeyed the law. In fact, even though I was unjustly imprisoned, I dared not oppose my oppressors in jail. If I had, even in thought, then I might have got the self-respect I badly needed. But all I did was plead and grovel on my knees.

Wife, Man and Woman sit sighing. Awkward pause

Husband: Within three days, I became shiftless. I acquired the characteristics of the group. Petty, quarrelsome, wallowing in self-pity. In prison no one acknowledged the fact that I was Director – Business Development. No one had heard of my Nakamichi and Valentino and Rolex. In fact, no one had even heard of my organisation. I had to make my own rules; or submit without question to the ruling group. I could not ask my PA to screen calls or draft faxes. This was a real situation. It was then that I realised that I had no internal resources to fall back upon. No consistent philosophy of life. No political or social integrity. Nothing.

Wife, Man and Woman sit sighing. Intermittent hammering

Husband: In jail, the mutilated body spoke to me. On the first night. It spoke in a whisper. It told me about a Thakur who had a huge *jagir*. It seems, two weeks ago, the Thakur had held a magnificent funeral for his right leg which had to be cut off. On the second night, the mutilated body spoke of a former MLA. This MLA had won elections for twenty-six years. When he finally lost an election, by his side sat a skeleton on a chair, decked out in Rajput armour. On the third night, the mutilated body spoke of Jogi Prasad, who had invented a pendulum to detect snake and scorpion poison in the blood. That's not all. Fifty-two years ago, it seems, Jogi Prasad's father had draped the streetlamps of his village in red paper, so as to defeat an epidemic of hunger.

Wife, Man and Woman sit sighing.

Husband: The mutilated body did not speak of wars, or the repression of woman and children or about the number of children who fled their lands. The mutilated body merely narrated stories. Until finally, it stopped speaking. The next day, there were red ants. Hundreds, thousands. Red ants.

Long pause

Man: I say.

Husband: What?

Man: Have you become a socialist?

Husband: What!

Man: ... like you know, Lenin-Stalin ... the USSR ... socialism ...

Castro and all that ...

Husband: Oh that.

Man: Oh yeah. *(Pause)*

Husband: Hmmm. You know, on the day I was released, an old man from Jharkhand started talking to me. He asked me what I had done. I said nothing. He asked me what I was fighting for. An issue, or some cause. I said, no, I was here by mistake. The old man looked perplexed. I asked him what the matter was. He replied 'How can that be? There's always something to fight for ...'

Sound of hammering

Woman: What's with this hammering?

Man: Oh yeah. How can you put up with this noise? It's excruciatingly painful.

Woman: Indeed.

Wife: Those are the Bhilakhias. They have purchased the top two floors. Now they are remodelling it. Mrs Bhilakhia fabricates children's furniture. It's an enormous market. 300% margin. The Bhilakhias host exclusive supper-shows for which they invite celebrities. It is rumoured V S Naipaul once attended a dinner ...

The hammering continues

Woman: Ooof. This is terrible. It's so ... insensitive.

Man: Oh yeah, so ... insensitive.

Woman: I mean Aditya would have given those people a piece of his mind. Oh dear. But Aditya is in Singapore. With Gayatri. Horrible.

Man: Abominable.

Woman: Oh dear oh dear oh dear. Hai toba!

Man: Ditto.

Intermittent hammering

Woman: Ooooh la la laah. Come, Arundhati, let's go and shop. Let's escape all this. It will get you out of your depression. There's a lovely boutique on Peddar Road. They get their stuff from Hyper Hyper and Ghost in London. The quality is guaranteed. Gucci and DKNY. Say, why don't you get yourself a Louis Vuitton or a Sandy handbag. Ooooh, it will be charming.

Man: Or better still. I say why not a cosy dinner for four at the Rotiserrie & Sea Grill. I could book a table. My brother-in-law knows the chef. It can be arranged. It will be perfect. Oh yeah.

Woman: Splendid.

Wife: Yes ... right ... you know ... whatever.

Man: Imagine. Fresh trout flown in from Norway. Succulently seared. Served with a fresh young French wine. Ummm. Super.

Wife: Right. Right. Right.

Woman: Oh dear oh dear I hope I've something nice to wear. Perhaps I can inaugurate my Manolo Blahnik shoes. I'm so elated. Oooh. Perhaps Purshottam can accompany us. He's never been to the Rotiserrie & Sea Grill before.

Man: Super. Wonderful. Brilliant.

Wife: I mean ... it would be lovely ... you know after all this ... whatever ... it's ... it's ... what it is ...

The hammering is all-pervasive.

ACT II SCENE 6

Husband, Wife, Man and Woman sit sighing. Then they collectively sigh. On cue, there are sounds of wailing. It is shrieky, screechy and soulful.

Wife: It is Mr Mahalanobis. He is leaving.

Woman: Oh no, oh no, oh no.

Man: Can't they be a trifle discreet? You know, we make such a hullabaloo about our dead.

Wife: Yeah right. True, true.

Man: Oh yeah, absolutely. You know what happened when Surana was shot dead. Last month? They declared a bandh. There was mayhem. Surana, dead as a duck on top of a truck. Thousands of people attended the funeral. All of them with lathis. So noisy. So vulgar.

Woman: Aditya used to say Hindu rites have profound significance. You know the symbology and all that.

Man: Absolutely. Surana owed me two crores. That's gone up in smoke.

Woman: Oh. Dahling. You must be careful. You must not lend money to people who are going to die.

Man: Right. Yeah!

Wife: Mr Mahalanobis' body is being flown to Kolkata. The funeral is in their ancestral crematorium. The son will be flying in from Heidelberg. He is a member of the faculty.

Woman: Really! So sweet.

Man: Oh yeah, absolutely.

Woman: What a tragedy ... I mean ... Oh dear ...

Man: Right.

Wife: The coffin has been custom-designed by Gonzales & Bros. It's made of genuine pine. Double rimmed with six-inch hinges. Supposed to be exquisite. They even scent the coffin, I'm told.

Woman: Oh dear. What a divine touch. What a sweet send-off for the departed soul.

Wife: He was a lonely man.

Woman: Oh I see.

Wife: Lived all alone.

Woman: Right.

Man: I hope the coffin does not ruin the elevator. In my building, the new Staedtler lift was damaged by a bunch of incompetent *pall-bearers*. The lift was irreparable. Damn.

Wife: Really?

Man: Oh yes, oh yes.

Woman: You must instruct them to use the staircase. I mean the man's dead. It doesn't make a difference to him, if he uses the staircase. I mean, Aditya would give the workers a piece of his mind ...

Man: Oh yeah.

Uncomfortable silence. Husband moves his lips.

Husband: I had met Mr Mahalanobis in the *same* elevator. Once. Long ago. There was a power failure, and the elevator had stalled. The others in the elevator panicked. Mr Mahalanobis was calm. He spoke about life, about food, eating habits. He explained why he had filed a public interest litigation. And why he would not withdraw it even though he was receiving death threats. He was not perturbed when a woman could not pronounce his name. He was not irritated when a man could not recall his profession. Oh boy. Mr Mahalanobis understood their babble, because he spoke innumerable tongues. He conjured words and phrases and narrated several stories that passed the time ... Oh boy ... With each smile and laugh, I began to dread my stay in that elevator. I felt I was floating. I was flying away from my parentage, upbringing, community. In that darkness, I was anonymous and a caricature for my lot. The word is – generic. That's it. Nothing more. Nothing less. The only thing that appeared to unite me to the people in the country was the census, which counts all of us together. *(Pause)*

Woman: So sensitive. So deep.

Man: Oh yeah.

Wife: Right.

Woman: So fascinating.

Man: Quite so.

Woman: So intriguing.

Man: Oh yeah.

Wife: Right ... whatever ... you know ...

The sound of wailing can be heard. Gradually, it trails off.

Woman: Hmmm, it's raining. This is so unexpected. Oh dear. Look. Now, what will they do with the body?

Man: See. They are shifting it into the underground garage.

Woman: Really? Oh dear. I've parked my car there.

Man: This is such a bother. I like the Eskimo custom. They put their old parents in a kayak and push them into a cold water lake. No fuss. No emotional brouhaha. Arundhati, can't we ask them to shift the body elsewhere?

Wife: Yeah ... but you know ... how can I ... we will have to wait for the rains to subside .. whatever ...

Woman: Can't you speak to the building secretary or something ...

Wife: ... But-but-but ... you know ... it is a passing shower ... Look.

Man: Mahalanobis. What a curious name? What was he? A Bong?

Wife: Perhaps ... whatever ... you know ...

Man: Right. Right. Of course.

Husband: A generation is passing by. If we have to survive, the words, phrases, languages which sustain the lie have to be disinterred. Or else, we live our lives, like collaborators. *(Pause)*

Woman: I say, let's forego our table at the Rotiserrie & Sea Grill.

Man: But ... meanwhile we are trapped ... here.

Wife: ... I could prepare some *garama-garam bhajiyas* at home.

Woman: Delicious.

Man: Oh yeah. Capital suggestion.

Woman: Oh dear oh dear oh dear ... I better inform the bai.

Man: ... and some more of your single-malt scotch, please.

Woman: Hello. *Kaun? Bai? Main memsaab bolti ... tum Purshottam baba ko soola dena ...*

Man: Ummmm. I love the smell of rain. It sort of drowns the stink of this city, of death ... Ummmmm ... Lovely ... Ummmm ....

Music plays.

3, Sakina Manzil

Dedicated to HIMANSHU VOHRA and RAJANI VOHRA
(for the gupshup at Verma Villa that gave me the confidence to write such a play)

3, Sakina Manzil opened at the Prithvi Theatre Festival, Mumbai on 13th November 2004.

Research and guidance: Amrit Gangar

Cast: Suruchi Aulakh and Jaimini Pathak

Director: Jaimini Pathak

Lights: Kavi Bhansali

Sound: Pragya Tiwari

Production: Shahana Goswami, Rishi Majumdar

The play celebrates the Gandhian spirit of things. Hence the staging should be simple, elegant and dignified. Movement is minimal and should be used as a last resort.

The voices of the actors should communicate everything. Pauses and silences are permitted. Light should be deployed sparingly and undramatically.

An empty stage. Two olde worlde comfortable chairs, placed on elegant rugs, next to two distinguished looking lamps, placed on either side of the stage. Lights focus on one side of the stage where the Woman sits.

Woman: Seventy, today. Happy birthday to me. *Janam din mubarak.* Haiyya ho, getting older and older. But look here. Still beautiful. *A husn ki malika.* Sound as a bell ... *(wheezes)* ... except for some respiratory trouble. But I'm covered, medically, that is. All those years as a nurse has benefited me. Look here ... *(extracts a wooden pill box)* ... Let me show you. Pinkish purple pill for catarrh. Henna green pill for painful urination. Amethyst blue pill for sclerosis of the joints. Carbon black pill for vertigo. Battleship grey pill for apoplexy. Arctic red pill for cachexia. And mint white pill for cataract *(she grins)*. All these I swallow, and this one I have to chew. It's easy. *(Shows off her teeth)* Not a single false tooth. Tip top condition. *(She gulps down the medicines)*

A beat

Woman: I told the doctor saheb, he is a solid-looking Parsee boy, it is geriatrics. But he continued to prod my torso, with his stethoscope. Hmm. The thing with medical science is it has not come to terms with old age. And my problem is old age. Nothing else.

Burst of music. Old woman thumps walking stick on floor. Music ceases.

Woman: Neighbours. Have to keep reminding them, there are others who live in 3, Sakina Manzil. That 3, Sakina Manzil is not their whole-sole property. It has a sense of history. Of tradition. It cannot be contaminated with modern music. See, I've nothing personal against modern music. Like everyone else I hope that someday it will turn into melody, sargam. But does it happen? No, never! *No mukhda, no antara. Bas shor.*

A burst of music. Once again, old woman thumps walking stick on floor. Music ceases.

Woman: Arrey, if I had the will I would pour water on them from my balcony. Water with ice cubes. That would show them. The gods must let ordinary people like us select our neighbours. If that's not possible, we should be able to alter their music sense. *Mere bas main hota toh sab ko ek line main bitha kar main unko music sunati. Zabardasti.* There was a film called *Chal Chal Re Naujawan* whose dialogues were written by that chap who used to come to Baba's shop. *Kya tha uska naam*? Hahn. Saadat Hasan Manto. *Usme ek bahut pyaara communal harmony-wallah gaana tha. Bolo Har Har Mahadev Allah-O-Akbar.*

She swallows her medicine.

Woman: When I told my plan to that solid looking Parsee doctor boy, he laughed. *Kya karta, baccha hain. Bahut nervous tha.* He hadn't diagnosed old age, earlier. And he had no sense of history. Or else he would have known about the bearing of old age on women.

A beat

Woman: He touched my feet when I paid him his full fee. In crisp one-rupee notes; no longer printed, but available, if you need to offer them to the deity at Bhuleshwar temple. I told him not to worry, no tension. They tell me the Parsee boy is related to Burjorji Cooverji Motivala who used to live at Kukana House in Dhobi Talao in Girgaum. *Ladka khaandani hai.* Burjorji Cooverji Motivala had returned the gold bar, which fell through his building roof to the authorities for which an award of Rs 999/- was given to him. Burjorji Cooverji Motivala promptly donated this sum for relief work. That was in 1944. Ages ago.

She thumps her walking stick on the floor.

Woman: That's not for the music. That's to scare away the rats. There are three of them. I've classified them. The *chhachhunder* is Robert Clive. He's so cute. The bandicoot is General Dwyer. Very *khadoos.* The female rat is Mrs Lord Mountbatten. She is most dangerous because she can breed a hundred million Mountbattens. At the moment, General Dwyer and Robert Clive are both trying to woo her. But Mrs Lord Mountbatten is not interested. Thank god.

She thumps her walking stick on the floor.

Woman: See, this walking stick is useful. Three-in-one. It can stop the music, scare the rats ... and one other thing, which I cannot recollect.

A burst of music. Once again, old woman thumps walking stick on floor. Music ceases.

Woman: Wapas music. Ooof. That's from the east side. MTV. Northeast is Hindi film. *Wahan se*, re-mix. Over there, it's classical. *Ooos taraf par, purane Freye Road se, shor aur awaz.* And beyond that the dockyard. There was a time I could see the farthermost boat in the horizon. Not any more. The solid-looking Parsee doctor boy says it's presbyopia. But what does the young man know? I can spot, even today, Elephanta Caves, the North Star in the dusky sky, the mixture of water into the milk by our *doodhwallah bhaiyya*, whose family had been providing milk to 3, Sakina Manzil for three generations. With a bit of effort, I can see, all. That way, I'm ok. The brain's consumption of oxygen has not diminished. The thoracic cage is solid. The motor nerves are tip-top. Perhaps, an iota of fatigue has set in.

Disregarding all that, I pick myself up, and go to the ophthalmologist's clinic. I have an appointment with Dr Bhavna Parekh.

Cross fade

Man: I had an appointment with Dr Bhavna Parekh. Cataract operation. On 14th April 1994.

Woman: It was 14th April 1994.

Man: My cataract had humble beginnings. A painless blurring of vision. Then there was glare, or light sensitivity, compounded by poor night vision and double vision in one eye. Now, I have all of it. I recall reading about cataract at the Asiatic Library. Dharamsey bhai recommended an excellent book to me. The book said the most common type of cataract is related to ageing of the eye. The book diagnosed the cause of my cataract. So, when I met the doctor I was prepared. She asked, family history? I said, yes. Medical problems, such as diabetes? I said, yes. Injury to the eye? I said, yes, a jackfruit fell off the tree, bounced on concrete and rebounded on to my eye. Medications, especially steroids? I said, no. Long-term, unprotected exposure to sunlight? I said, yes, could not afford sunglasses. Previous eye surgery? I said, no. The doctor was pleased. That way books are wonderful. I mean, life is beautiful. But books are wonderful. I prefer books to life. When in doubt I recommend books. You cannot always trust life. Anything happens.

Woman: Hai tauba. Usually, the clinic is over-crowded, but today there is one solitary old man. All wrapped up.

Man: I've been waiting for 47 minutes. A lady enters huffing and puffing. She looks a hundred years old. But she is behaving five times her age.

Woman: Suddenly, I feel so old. Ancient! Keeping pace with the changing world is taking its toll. Today, I paid Rs 65 for the taxi.

Rs 62 actually, but the cab driver had no change. Another Rs 50 to return home. Fifty years ago, with a salary of Rs 50–100 a month, a family lived royally. *Shuddh ghee, shuddh teil, sab kuch shuddh aur sacha tha, bhaiyya. As the Kutchi business people used to say, ke pachhi e badhi pari katha to nahoti? Pari katha, pari katha aney shaher ni pari katha!*

Man: I'm sitting quietly. Minding my business when I hiccup.

Woman: The old man who is all wrapped up, hiccups.

Man (hiccups): Why am I hiccupping?

Woman: The old man hiccups, again.

Man (talks to himself): Stop it. Behave yourself. That's why I don't like to take you out. You're so embarrassing. Sshhh. Chup.

Woman: Just then the sweet girl at the reception says, next. I stood up.

Man: The old woman stood up. *(Talking to himself)* Now, now, act like a gentleman and give the lady a chance. *(To the old lady)* Aap jaiye. Ladies first.

Woman: The old man lets me go first. Maybe he is scared of doctors. Maybe he is a flirt. Maybe he thinks I'm as gorgeous as Devika Rani. Hee hee hee.

Man: I let the old woman go before me. I say, Ladies first. She smiles. Where had I seen such a smile?

Woman: I smile. This calls for celebrations. Half a kilo of *garama-garam jalebis*. You know, these days, I rarely smile.

Man: The old woman is gone. I look out of the doctor's dispensary and see the railway station through which I entered the city in the winter of 1940. Things were brewing. I had come to Bombay during the riots. Kaka, who had a small factory in Bhavnagar said riots in Bombay were bad for *dhanda*. In our village in Saurashtra we had a rating system for riots. Bombay, Ahmedabad, Dhaka, which city had the most brutal riot.

A beat

Man: Kaka had jotted down all the riots in a little black book. He was an amateur riotologist. And Bombay was famous for its riots. Hindu–Muslim. Parsee–Hindu. Shia–Sunni. Mumbaikar versus Outsider. Dalit versus Brahmin. Sikh–Hindu. The point is, I was entering the city during a riot. History moves in cycles, no? As a rule, riots don't need any validation. But this riot could be traced to Lahore. The Muslim League at its annual convention in 1940 had passed a resolution, which came to be known as the Pakistan Resolution. That was the first time we heard of Pakistan. No one took it seriously. After all, we had a phenomenon called Bapu on our side. As I got down from the train, I took the name of God and Bapu to save me from the madness of the mob.

A beat

Man (hiccups): Kaka said he had heard good reports about a new college in Bombay. When I attended the first day of college, I realised I was the only male there. My Kaka had admitted me in the newly inaugurated, all-girls' Sophia College. I wandered along the Backbay Area, which was opened up for residential sites. I used to walk around Marine Drive from Churchgate Reclamations to Chowpatty, where uniform, similar-looking buildings, housing residential flats had come up. Everyone said they were fashionable. But I thought they looked like matchboxes. The city was over-crowded. There were 15 lakh people. Everyone who was anyone was complaining about the influx of refugees. About the slums. The sickening smell of decay. The beggars, rummaging for food in the drains, in dustbins. That was fifty years ago. Nothing much has changed, no? *(Silence)*

Man: The old woman, returns. She hobbles.

Woman: The old man is waiting. He has stopped hiccupping. Just then, I hear a melody ...

A song plays softly as if at a distance.

Man: That song. It sounds familiar.

Woman: Hai rabba! They are playing my song. My theme song.

Man: When and where did I hear this song? Ah. I recall. I was out of work. After the fiasco at Sophia College I had got admitted to Elphinstone College. I needed extra money to support my studies. Kaka told me to meet Gala Seth who owned three provision stores. The address was 3, Sakina Manzil.

Woman: I adore the song. In fact every time the song was played I used to pull out my ribbons. I love ribbons. My goal in life is to have the largest collection of ribbons. Here, see, all kinds of ribbons. In each and every colour. *Nava rasa, nava bhava, nava ratna.* Every single emotion and mood. You know, just as every word was once a poem, every ribbon has a story to tell. Like this ribbon. This is a ribbon about my ancestral home. A village called Gulalipur in a district called Lyallpur in Pakistan. They call it Faisalabad, now. I don't know why. When I ask Mother about those days, she replies, Comrade beta, the past is a foreign country; things are different there. My mother calls everyone comrade. Comrade Baba, Comrade doodhwallah, Comrade paanwallah, Comrade Viceroy, Comrade Governor General, Comrade Nehru, Comrade Jinnah, Comrade Bapu, and even, Comrade God. It had something to do with her father and his father. All communists. Baba used to tease mother. He would say, *Bayein mud*! *Ek-do-teen-chaar!* Communism is the opium of the Asses. Mother would say, Comrade Baba would never understand. He was so used to exploiting the weak that he could never be sympathetic to the exploitation of the weak by the strong. To which Baba would counter that mother's communist father was a zamindar. The only good thing he did was to educate his seven daughters. All of who married into rich families. Mother pooh-poohed Baba. She said, he was over-simplifying things. A lion is not a mere lion; he's made up of the goats he digests. They would trade proverbs till the middle of night. *Sawal-jawab.* I don't know how Mother and Baba met. A traditional, illiterate Kutchi businessman marrying a communist girl with an independent point of view on every subject on earth. It was unheard of! When I used to pester them, Baba would say, nothing much to it, *Kutchi Ne Bachchi se shaadi kar liya.* That was that.

Man: It was a typical rainy day in Bombay. I reached 3, Sakina Manzil. Gala Seth was not in the shop. I was directed by an assistant to a young woman who was embroidering a ribbon. The ribbon was pretty. The girl was ... prettier.

Woman: Which thread should I use?

Man: Which opening line should I use?

Woman: What should I embroider on the ribbon?

Man: How should I attract the attention of this pretty girl?

Woman: What does my violin teacher, Benny Satamkar, who lives down the lane, tell me whenever I make a mistake? A man is not old until his regrets take the place of dreams. Apparently, it's a well known Yiddish proverb.

Man: My heart is thumping.

Woman: Ho. Who is this medium-built, so-so looking, unintelligent sort of man?

Man: I'm being drawn to her.

Woman: Why is my heart thumping?

Man: She blushes. She flutters her eyelashes. Her cheeks are pink and rosy.

Woman: Hai rabba. I'm being attracted to him. Perhaps.

Man: I think it's love at first sight.

Woman: Am I falling in love at first sight?

Man: I'm a great advocate of love at first sight. It's a great time-saving, labour-saving device.

Woman: May be I should ask this medium-built, so-so looking, unintelligent sort of man? As they say, every man is a volume if you know how to read him. But why isn't he saying a thing?

Man: Er ... Oh ... Eh ...

Woman: I must wait for him to make the first move. Or else he'll perceive me to be forward-looking, a wench.

Man: I'm trying to speak. But all my efforts result in ... Er ... Oh ... Eh ... *(starts to talk to himself)* Come on, mouth, don't let me down. This is important for me. You've been doing this sort of thing. For years. Bagged me a runner's up prize in the Debating Society. Speak up, maan. Uh-oh. The mouth is responding. It says, if a man will begin with certainties, he shall end in doubts; but if he will be content to begin with doubts, he shall end in certainties. What? What?? What??? Mouth, don't do this to me. The pretty girl is staring at me. I've to say, something. Anything. But the mouth has other ideas. It informs me: Love is like a game of chess. No one ever won a chess game by betting on each move. Sometimes you have to move backward to get a step forward. What? What?? What??? The mouth concludes the argument with: love is like music, it cannot be translated into words. The mouth shuts up. I'm left with Er … Oh … Eh …

Woman: You know, I've never heard a finer rendition of … Er … Oh … Eh …

Man: Er … Oh … Eh …

Woman: Such eloquence. Such oratory. *Waah, kya baat hai*. Irshad, irshad.

Man: Er … Oh … Eh …

Woman: You've obviously done super-specialisation in … Er … Oh … Eh … which university?

Man: I was about to say Er … Oh … Eh … But I pinched myself. Stop it. I was making a fool of myself. So I took a deep breath to clear my mind. My Kaka has told me to meet Gala Seth. The pretty girl says, Oh I see. I want a job with a salary. Because a salary is very important. And everyone who has a job draws a salary. In fact, according to the Ranganekar Board of Conciliation, wages must register a rise because of DA being linked to the cost of living index. What? What?? What??? According to my mouth, which had taken control of all the words pouring out of my mouth, the period 1934–1937 witnessed a cut in wages from Rs 34.56 to Rs 27.25. Now, due to World War II, for which I'm not responsible, the wages are what Gala Seth deems fit. So I would want a salary and a DA and a bonus and … and … and …

Woman: A glass of water?

Man: Yes. My throat was parched. What had I said?

Woman: I preferred his Er … Oh … Eh … As I was about to give him a glass of water, I asked him, are you an economist? You know, like Adam Smith?

Man: Even as I was gratefully gulping my glass of water, I heard the song. *(A song filters through)*

Man: Aur ek glass.

Woman: Zaroor.

Woman hands him a glass of water. He gulps it down at one go.

Man: Aur ek glass.

Woman: Zaroor.

Woman hands him another glass of water. He gulps it down at one go.

Man: Aur ek glass.

Woman: Zaroor.

Man: Aur ek glass?

Woman: Kya aap sukhe-grast illake se aye hain?

Man: I returned the glass of water. I had never drunk so much water in my entire life. Shyly, I asked her her name.

Woman: Bashfully, I asked him his name.

Man: What a coincidence, we shared the same name ...

Woman: Shashi.

Man: Although, technically, I was Shashikumar. Popularly known as Shashi.

Woman: I prefer Shashi to Shashi ... kumar ... look, Baba has come.

Man: Just then, Gala Seth entered. He knew Kaka from the good old days. The terms and conditions of my contract were discussed. Gala Seth owned three shops. One in 3, Sakina Manzil, and two more in Musafir Khana and Prabodh Mansion. Recently, he had opened a new store in the police barracks. He needed me because I was educated and could speak English. The thing is, Gala Seth had British customers and it was important to speak to them in the King's language. I thought the job was simple, until Gala Seth gave me a long list of items – I had to find English counterparts for Indian names. Gala Seth explained. Shashi saab, you know, *doodh* = milk. *Dahi* = curd. *Malai* = cream. *Ghee*

= clarified butter. There was a burst of laughter. Mrs Gala Seth asked, what on earth is clarified butter? If my daadi offered me clarified butter for my roti, I would never eat it. Gala Seth told her to be silent when she guffawed on hearing that khoya, mawa was called solidified milk. For some reason, Mrs Gala Seth called everyone Comrade. And so, I became Comrade Shashi.

Woman: Comrade Shashi is so cute. He was so dazed. Especially, when Mother guffawed and gave him a whack on his back.

Man: I took their leave and went to my *wadi* in Girgaum. For some reason, my back was hurting.

Woman: You know, in all these years, no man has ever said, Er ... Oh ... Eh ... to me.

Man: It was the middle of the night. I returned to my *kholi* for which I was paying Rs 6 a month. This included five chappatis, *dahi* and two *badaams*, *chai*, every morning. I wanted to make a good impression on Gala Seth and his daughter. So, I worked on the translation. *Badam* = Almonds. *Saunf* = Aniseed. *Heeng* = Asafoetida. *Tulsi* = Basil. *Elaichi* = Cardamom. *Dalchini* = Cinnamon. Shashi = Shashi. What must she be doing, now?

Woman: Ering ... and Ohing ... and Ehing.

Man: Laung = Clove. *Dhania* = Coriander seeds. Jeera = Cumin seeds. I wonder what is the English equivalent of Er ... Oh ... Eh?

Woman: I met Comrade Shashi the next day.

Man: I met Shashiji the next day. She was all dressed up!

Woman: I was well-dressed. I was going to the theatre.

Man: The theatre? Er ... Oh ... Eh ... Don't you think, the theatre is such a gross waste of time? It is just a way of fooling the people with false pretences. A place where bad ideas go, when they die.

Woman: I was not going to have the theatre belittled. So I retorted, my dear Comrade Shashi, the drama's laws its patrons give. In other words, a play is only as good or bad as the intellect and taste of the people of the land.

Man: Shashiji, you know, Gandhiji does not have a high opinion about the theatre. It's considered a distraction from the activity of nation-building.

Woman: But he saw *Harishchandra*.

Man: He must have gone to hear the story. Gandhiji is a great admirer of truth. He probably sat through the play with his eyes shut.

Woman: That's the point isn't it? One glance at a play and you hear the voice of another person, perhaps someone dead for a thousand years. To see a play is to voyage through time, no?

Man: You're being charitable to the uncharitable. The theatre is an insidious beast like Medusa, which freezes its audience to stone every night, staring fixedly. It is like the Siren, which sings and promises so much, and ultimately leads people to their doom.

Woman: Say what you want. Today, I'm going to the Baliwala Grand Theatre Playhouse. The locals call it Pila House. It's so exciting, the way a play opens. A loud bang of exploding anaar, the curtain is raised, a hush in the auditorium. The occasional shouts from the vendors. *Pista-Badam – Chopdi – Punkha – Uthao Jaldi*. The incessant extolling of the ticket-seller *Khel Abhi Chalu Hua*. You know, last week I saw a play. It was a big bore. But something exciting happened. As you know, the drama companies bring their own curtain. This curtain has eight heavy stones to weigh it down. This whole contraption is operated by two *mazdoors*. Usually, the curtain pulling *mazdoors* doze off, so, the cue to bring down the curtain is a shrill blast of a whistle. During last week's show, the doddering king, played by a particularly ghastly ham, died. The corpse was lying on the floor. But the curtain pullers were asleep. They were awakened by a shrill whistle, and so, they hurriedly brought down the curtain in the middle of the scene. When the dead king saw the eight heavy stones rushing towards his head, he got up, and ran for his life! Later, it was found out that the whistle was not blown by the prompter but by a tram traffic conductor on the street. Oh, how I miss the glamour and spectacle of the older dramas!

Man: Well.

Woman: Now, what is that supposed to mean?

Man: Well, I should have shut up. But my mouth began, again without taking any cognisance of poor me. The mouth was its bombastic best. Everyone can act. It's easy. We do it in real life all the time. By the same quantum, everyone can eat. But do we watch someone eating, with pleasure? No? When I'm hungry I may do so but that's because I wish I were eating. That's savoury. But people don't climb onto the Opera House stage, grab a fork and spoon, start eating, and then charge tickets, do they? We don't put a fork on a wall on an art gallery and call it art? Or we don't make noises with the click-clank of spoons and call it, music? No. No! **No!!** On cue, I put my fist in my mouth to prevent my mouth from speaking.

Woman: Comrade Shashi, you're an Aurangzebi.

Man: My fist was still in my mouth. I extracted my fist from my mouth, since it is improper to talk to a lady – and a mighty fine one at that – with one's fist in the mouth. Promptly, the words poured out. Do you know, Raksha Kaki, she is the woman who serves lunch and dinner to 30–35 people, daily at our *khaanaaval*. *Khaanaavaalis* like Raksha Kaki have no holidays, ever. Except on *ekadashi*. She makes beautiful *rangolis* in seven colours to welcome us. She says, that a *rangoli* is true people's art. Rich and poor, Brahmin or Harijan, man or woman, everyone does it. Not like the theatre, which is the pursuit of the wealthy and the squanderer. Highbrow stuff. A place where they find out what you don't like and give you plenty of it. Get it? Get it? Get it!!!

Woman: Comrade Shashi, you know nothing about life in Bombay. I've seen *maidani khel*, *dashavatar*, *naman*, *tamasha*, *lezim* competitions, *bharood*, the great *shahirs*, *kushti*, bullfights, *jatras*. Ask your Raksha Kaki about it! There is nothing highbrow about the real Bombay, my sweet man. I've attended a double *baari* by a *bhajan mandali* in which the two competitors sang insulting things about one another, like we are doing right now. I attended a show in which they sang a gan to Bhimrao Ambedkar instead of the traditional invocation to Lord Ganesha. What do you have to say to that???

Man: I refused to extricate my fist from my mouth. My mouth was bound to get me into serious trouble.

Woman: Comrade Shashi, remove your fist from your mouth. It's bad manners.

Man (with fist in mouth): No!

Woman: Why? I'm training to be a nurse, and in my short medical life I've never come across anything like this ...

Man: I could not explain to her that my mouth was a proponent of free speech and democracy. And like all such proponents, completely irresponsible.

Woman: I've heard of foot in the mouth, but this ...

Man: Just then Gala Seth entered.

Woman: Baba came in with a letter.

Man: That's the first time I heard about Yajuvendra.

Woman: I was engaged to Yajuvendra. A childhood communion. Yajuvendra's father and Baba had common roots in Bhuj. Baba had done it secretly. Mother was in Lahore in those days. When she returned she did not speak to Baba for three weeks. Yajuvendra was the only person in the world Mother did not call Comrade. Yajuvendra was out there, somewhere, fighting for a brave new world. I had not met him for ages. Just the occasional telegram or letter.

Man: After I heard about Yajuvendra and Shashiji being engaged, I understood why the great thinkers frittered away such a lot of their time and energy on love. A complex kind of warfare: love.

Woman: Comrade Shashi looked pale. I suppose it has something to do with putting his fist into his mouth.

Man: Ah, love: a book of which the first chapter is written in poetry and the rest, in prose.

Woman: It was time to go out. Should I see *Pundalik* the play or *Pundalik* the film, which is based on *Pundalik* the play?

Man: Heart-broken I immersed myself in work. All food supply was measured in *khandy*. My mantra was: one *khandy* is 40 pounds. And 40 *tolas* is one pound. Gala Seth was a fine employer. Like all Kutchi businessmen, he was thrifty, commonsensical and resourceful. One day, I heard him speak Kutchi to a Kutchi tradesman from Mandvi. I was struck by the multiple Kutchi dialects being used in the radius of the port area in Bombay. Bhatia Kutchi, Memoni Kutchi, Khoja Kutchi, Lohana Kutchi, Bania Kutchi. Each with regional variations. Then there were the Maplahs, the Jews, the Nagoris, the Marathas, the Mahars, the Mathadis, the Kunbis. There's so much of plurality. The way people talk, walk, eat. I met a Vadiyar from Madurai and saw him drink his *kaapi* from a tumbler without touching the edge of the tumbler to his mouth. He said it's the one true test for a person from Tamil Nadu. No one in the world drinks *kaapi* in such a manner. Hmm. What sculpture is to a block of marble, education is to the human soul. Oh. I must jot it down.

Woman: I didn't see much of Comrade Shashi. It's all Baba's fault. Barging in with that stupid letter from Yajuvendra. And Comrade Shashi appears to be one of those over-sensitive types. A bit like Prithviraj Kapoor in New Theatre's film Manzil. Oh. Imagine, Comrade Shashi as Prithviraj and me … Kanan Devi. And P C Barua is directing us.

Man: Gala Seth had a nose for *dhandha.* Let me give you, an example. A new product had entered the market. It was called ACE limejuice. It was nothing but cordial concentrate of sun-ripened limes prepared and packed in the factory in an actual orchard. I told Gala Seth, ACE limejuice will be a flop, because every housewife worth her salt made *nimboo-paani* at home. In principle, Gala Seth agreed with me. But he said, high theory does not translate into good business practice. So, we sold ACE limejuice; chewing gum, which was a dentally improper sort of thing; Vinolia, white rose soap, which was supposed to keep you cool, fresh, exhilarated; and a noisy gadget called radio. It was on such a radio that I heard that the Government had increased milk prices by two annas per seer, from 12 to 14 annas a seer. There was an uproar. Gala Seth was unperturbed by the potential loss of business. In fact, he saw an opportunity in it. He purchased milk from the black market and used it in the preparation of ice-cream and kulfi. It was irresistible! It was a roaring success!

Woman: The outbreak of war and the extension of hostilities by the Japanese in December 1941 created problems. Bloodshed, loss of lives. That was the time I decided to become a nurse. Men are so juvenile. Don't they understand, war is a racket? It has never determined who is right, just who is left. Yajuvendra was part of this madness. Silly goose. He was obsessed with the thought of getting little badges and medals stuck on his shirtfront.

Man: The war caused problems, but it did not deter Hajjis and their travel plans. Gala Seth used to arrange a 15-day ration for them. The gunnis would be delivered on a *haath-gaddi* to the steamer at Zibutti Bunder. Special rates: a chotta gunni, that is, 70 kg, of rice for Rs 6 and a bada gunni of 100 kg for Rs 6.50 only! The Hajjis preferred rice from Burma. Pulses, sugar, coconuts, and so on. Once they disembarked, everything was loaded onto camels, and they began their trek to Mecca or Medina. One morning, when I cycled back from the barracks, I met Shashiji. She had lost weight and the lustre on her face. She wanted to visit a ship, and see how the Hajjis cook food in their makeshift kitchen underneath the hull.

Woman: I wanted to see the kitchen in the ship. Also, I wanted to meet Comrade Shashi. Somehow I missed him.

Man: Gala Seth was a worried man. There were indirect requests to export opium to Hong Kong and China. He had refused.

Woman: Baba was under stress. Due to World War II, there were huge withdrawals from the banks due to panic. It was understandable. Mother used to mention how the People's Bank of Lahore and the Credit Bank of Bombay were liquidated during World War I. There were rumours of how bank officials were resorting to malpractice like creating fictitious debtors and indulging in cotton share speculation. We travelled in a bus. Due to rationing of petrol and car tyres during the war period, many car owners used to travel by bus. Comrade Shashi was as quiet as a mouse. I tickled his ribs and said, 'Comrade Shashi, I prefer a tram to a bus.'

Man: Trams are too slow.

Woman: Why should things be speedy? What's the hurry?

Man: Trams don't exceed 5 miles an hour.

Woman: I like the two-storey trams. They are sort of cute.

Man: The BEST has introduced double-decker buses in 1937. They are nice, too.

Woman: That's different. Tram is cheaper than bus.

Man: That's true. Perhaps you're right. A tram is better than a bus.

Woman: The conversation came to grinding halt. We visited the dock. Comrade Shashi introduced me to Mr Kanwar, a pilot and Examination Service Officer. For some reason Mr Kanwar took it upon himself to explain Port Rules and Dock Bylaws to me. He wanted to impress me.

Man: Shashiji was getting impressed by Kanwar.

Woman: We walked to the Wayside Inn for jam toast and coffee. Mr Kanwar accompanied us.

Man: I walked behind Shashiji and Kanwar. When we sat down Kanwar told Shashiji that we were sitting at the same table at which Karanjia and his friends had decided to launch the anti-fascist newspaper, the *Blitz*, in 1939. Shashiji was thrilled. She fluttered her eyelashes, and exulted, how charming, sooo fascinating!

Woman: Mr Kanwar was a big bore. I had to look interested. I kept fluttering my eyelashes and said, how very charming and sooo sooo fascinating!

Man: Just then, Keshavji Naik entered. Kanwar went to his table to pay salaams.

Woman: We got rid of Mr Kanwar. Touch wood. Er ... Comrade Shashi isn't that Keshavji Naik, one of the biggest cotton merchants in the city? They say, he is bankrupt ...

Man: Sssh. Don't say it loudly. Someone may hear you.

Woman: Comrade Shashi clasped his hand over my mouth!

Man: In any case, the bankruptcy is just a rumour. Spread by Naik's business rivals. You know, what Naik did to counter it? He promised to repay each and every debtor. So the next morning, he assembled bullock carts from one end of Chinchbunder to the other. Each and every cart was stacked with gunny sacks filled with coins. It was a massive show of strength. No one has doubted Naik after that day.

Woman: Isn't the water fountain in our *galli* built by him? I've seen workers washing in it when they come out of the docks. They sing. There's this one chap who sings Kundan Lal Saigal songs. What is it? *Do naina matware.*

Man: She hummed the song.

Woman: The song filled the room. We sipped our coffee in silence ... I wanted to say something to Comrade Shashi.

Man: I had a hundred and one questions to query. And today, seemed like an opportune moment ...

Woman: Comrade Shashi ...

Man: Shashiji ...

Woman: On cue, Mr Kanwar returned. He asked us a riddle, what is a restaurant? His reply: a place where one goes to rest and rant. Then he laughed at his own joke. Ah well. How it ends. And life goes on.

Man: I didn't meet Shashiji for a long time. It seems her mother was unwell.

Woman: Mother was unwell. How hard and painful are the final days on an aged woman! She grows weaker, day after day. Eyes dim. Ears go deaf. Strength fades. Heart no longer peaceful. Oh, to have seen parents being reduced to ill health. Oh, to have witnessed parents being reduced to living skeletons. Oh, to fight with unknown diseases. When I tried to give Mother medicine, she would say, he's the best physician who knows the worthlessness of most medicines.

Man: It was 1942. Yusuf Meherali presented Gandhiji a bow bearing the inscription, Quit India. That became our slogan for independence. The AICC session was held at Gowalia Tank Maidan on 7th August. Sadoba Kanoba Patil, the uncrowned Union badshah of Bombay made arrangements for the sessions. Gala Seth knew Patil Saheb. We got an opportunity to render services for a great cause. That's how I got to see the VIPs, the hundreds of Indian and foreign correspondents, an audience of 20,000. I heard Abul Kalam Azad's opening address. I heard Nehru's historic resolution drafted by Gandhiji, which sought the end of British Rule in India. Gandhiji spoke for two hours. He was ebulliently witty, and effective. He culminated his talk with a simple cry, Do or Die!

Woman: Frankly speaking, Mother didn't believe in the idea of a free India. She said it was going to be a mere transfer of power. Instead of being fleeced by the British bureaucrats and Government, we would be deceived by our own people. A thing which would be much more heartbreaking. Mother felt Gandhiji would not be able to prevent the Partition. First it would be a Partition amongst Hindu–Muslim, then class, then caste. Hopefully, if good sense prevailed, there would be a Partition on gender basis. That is, men and women inhabiting different nations. It would be the best thing to happen to women in India.

Man: The British Government had declared all Congress Committees unlawful. It gagged the press. And yet, the news reached us. A desh sevika scribbled messages on our road.

Woman: The Congress-wallahs had turned the city into a riot zone. It was madness. *Na ek pai, na ek bhai*. No one gained a thing. No one was concerned about the Germans or the Japanese. For me, that was a bigger threat. They had bombed Cocanada and Vizagapatam. There was firsthand information that the Japanese were planning a Pearl Harbour type bombing in Madras or Bombay.

Man: I heard about the Japanese threat. Shashiji's Yajuvendra was fighting the Japanese onslaught in Burma. Where was he?

Woman: Where was Comrade Shashi?

Man: Gala Seth told me she was nursing her mother.

Woman: Mother was my first and toughest patient. In spite of her ill health, she would sing in front of the mill gates. She and her friends, Ahilya Rangnekar, Durga Bhagwat, Mridula Sarabhai would giggle like little girls. They demanded equal wages for women. One of them exhorted me to gather girls and protest. I did so, and got rusticated from college! I was arrested on 26th January 1943. And placed in Arthur Road Jail. I was a prisoner in a Class II jail. I had committed the crime of getting caught.

Man: I courted arrest on 26th January 1943. Instead of Byculla, I was taken to BDD Chawl, which had been converted into a makeshift prison for political prisoners. I was so impressed with myself. I was a political prisoner.

Woman: When I was released, I learnt mother had passed away.

Man: The day I was released was an anti-climax. The movement had lost its fizz. The others were gaining strength. Ambedkar, Dange, Randive, Rajaji, Jinnah, Savarkar.

Woman: I was busy at hospital. One late night, in the early months of 1944, I heard a hiccup. It was Comrade Shashi.

Man (hiccups): I was returning from Gangeru. Nine of us were selected for a mission. It was supposed to a sabotage of a truck carrying ammunitions and military cargo. We walked 19 kilometres to our destination, guided by torches covered with handkerchiefs. We reached the truck. The driver and his helper, saw us, and ran away. We opened the fuel tank and tried to set the truck ablaze, but we failed. We tried to topple the truck, we failed. Then, we tried to deflate the tyres, we failed. Just then, we saw a searchlight. The driver and the help were returning with military support. We fled. Into the night. And escaped.

Woman: May I ask what you are doing ... here? At this unearthly hour? Are you wooing a pretty maiden? Sweeping her off her feet?

Man: I ... er ...

Woman: What's in your hand?

Man: Well ... It's just a cyclostyled sheet of paper.

Woman: What's this? *Congress Patrika!* How interesting? I've unearthed an underground movement. Yooo Hooo.

Man: Don't Yooo Hooo. You will attract attention.

Woman (in a whisper): Who gave it you?

Man: Himmat, my college friend. Many students are involved.

Woman: I'm not a student but I want to get involved. I can distribute it ... to patients at the hospital. Some light reading!

Man: Don't mock. This is an underground newspaper. It is circulated in defiance of the British. If you're caught, you will be given a ... death sentence.

Woman: I'm a woman, no one will suspect me. Can I write? I have some groundbreaking ideas about self-determination and sovereignty.

Man: I don't know. I'll have to ask ...

Woman: Whom will you ask? Who's the editor?

Man: I don't know. No one knows the editor. In fact I don't where it gets printed. Every issue they shift the venue. All I know is, the *Congress Patrika* disseminates news about the freedom movement and sets guidelines for Indian citizens. Most of the newspapers support us and carry our news. Except for the *Evening News* and *Times of India*. They are anti-national. I suggest you stop reading the *Times of India*. OK, bye.

Woman: Where do you think you're going? Don't you know it's unsafe, outside?

Man: I intend to distribute the *Congress Patrika* in Safiya Manzil and Lucky Mansion, and later the chawls at Kalbadevi.

Woman: There's heavy patrolling. You'll be caught, red-handed.

Man: I'm willing to ... Do or Die!

Woman: Arrey, you cannot even halt your hiccups, how can you Do and Die? The only thing that can save you and your cause is the theatre.

Man: The theatre, but ...

A roll of drums. Festive atmosphere

Woman: It's showtime, folks. The ceremony is about to begin. An actor is born. Let the coronation begin ...

Man: Meaning ...

Woman: We change your appearance. Look here. This monkey cap will make you resemble a monkey when you go to Jhaveri Bazar. A Parsi topi and a chota beard when you go to Dava Bazaar or Dana Bunder. A little medical gauze around your head and a band-aid when you visit VJTI or Khalsa College. A man of many parts. A man who changes faces in order to live.

Man: That's how, it was. Exhilarating. Invigorating. Stimulating. Breathtaking. With my many disguises, I got associated with 42.34 metres, that is, *Congress Radio*. The transmitter was located in Ajit Villa, somewhere in the middle of Bombay. The main brain of the radio broadcast was Usha Desai, Achyut Rao Patwardhan, Chandrakant Baboobhai Javeri. The broadcast used to start with the words 'This is Congress Radio calling on 42.34 metres.' We educated the people about the modus operandi of the revolution. We provided graphic accounts of revolutionary activities in the North Western Province and Bihar. Listeners were informed about the Red Shirts and the Khudai Khidmatgars. We included pre-recorded messages and talks by leaders of the national movement. *Congress Radio* broke the news of the collapse of the German Defences and the Japanese bombing of Chittagong and East Assam.

Woman: I heard about the Japanese bombing on *Congress Radio*. Yajuvendra was in the line of fire. Weeks ago, he had written a letter from Kohima. The Japanese were in Burma. They had surrounded Bishenpur-Sikhar. Kohima was the main target of their operation. I was in a quandary. Baba was in Kutch to settle some family property dispute. I sent a message to Comrade Shashi.

Man: That night, I returned home. I recall the day. All of us were still mourning Kasturba's passing away in Aga Khan Palace in February. I had attended a *shoka sabha*, which was actually a secret political meeting. I hadn't eaten a thing. But my disposition received a cheery boost on seeing a note. It was from Shashiji. It said: Meet me at 5 pm at 3, Sakina Manzil on 14th April 1944. Urgent.

[Interval]

Woman: Like Before Christ and After Christ, my life could be neatly divided into pre-14th April 1944 and post-14th April 1944. A new dance ballet called *Kovalan* was coming to Bombay in April. It was supposed to have a bit of Kathakali, Bharatanatyam, Manipuri and whatnot. One of those 'modern' *khichdis*. Very fashionable. The story of *Kovalan* was the story of my life. It was about a man, Shankara Panniker, who is torn between two lovers, Mrinalini Sarabhai and Nandita Kriplani. But that was art. In real life, I was Shankara Panniker and the two women were Yajuvendra and Comrade Shashi.

Man: Wasn't 14th April Shashiji's birthday? May be she's having a *sheera* and *powa* birthday party? May be I should stitch a new bush shirt for the occasion? May be I should carry *pedas*? May be I'm not thinking straight! May be Yajuvendra has returned? Or may be Gala Seth is not happy with my work and wants to substitute me with his nephew from Bachchau? That reminds me. I better go and meet Kanwar Saab and get a list of ships visiting the docks. That way we can plan our provisions supply. Ooof. These are difficult times. The black market is flourishing. One gallon of kerosene costs one rupee. Imagine? The war must end. Mountbatten is planning to make an all-out effort on Japanese positions in Burma and Malaya. The Bombay Port resembles a military headquarters with officers and men of the fighting wings of the Allied Forces. Armed with my special permit, I take the train from Wadala to Ballard Pier on 12th April. This is a special train. Otherwise my third class monthly train pass of Rs 8 from Churchgate to Khar would have sufficed.

Woman: Love is such an irregular idea. It is so difficult to express it, honestly. Why? I mean, look at man and his progress. He is planning to travel to the moon. Explore the depths of the ocean. Discover a cure for TB. Do jugglery with numbers at the stock exchange. And yet, man has not been able to come up with a better option than ... I Love You. It is so unfair to reduce all the great whirl and twirl of grand emotions to three bland words, I Love You. Plus when do you utter it? In the beginning? After three meetings? After a lifetime? There should be a handbook, especially for first-timers like me. Unless ignorance more frequently begets confidence than does knowledge. *Hai, kitna* complicated *hain sab kuch*. Love is too hazardous a business to leave to the discretion of humans.

Man: I examined the ships in the manila folder in Kanwar Saab's office. He returned for lunch, hungry and angry. Apparently, he had examined a British ship, the *Fort Stikine*. A single-screw, coal-burning vessel of 7,142 tons. The ship had unusual cargo. Kanwar Saab had made a meticulous list. He showed it me, boastfully. It said: In Hold Number One – sulphur weighing 325 tons and cotton weighing 268 tons. Above the sulphur bags, there lay fish manure. And 13,163 pieces of timber. In Hold Number Two – 187 tons of category C ammunition. Plus cotton weighing 769 tons. Then there were 11,537 timber pieces, scrap iron, 42 old dynamos, cases of wireless sets, and 168 tons of super-sensitive category A ammunition, 1089 small drums of oil. Hold Number Three – 573 tons of lubricating oil and 58 tons of category A ammunition and 20 tons of RAF's inflammable aircraft dope along with 214 drums of oil. Hold Number Four – 523 tons of explosives and 405 tons of cottons along with dry fruits. Hold Number Five – 196 tons of cotton, dry fruits + resins, pieces of timber and 6,220 drums of oil. But what grabbed my eye was a tiny detail, which mentioned that Number Two Hold had an interesting consignment. Gold. One million pounds sterling. Addressed to a bank in Bombay. Thirty-one wooden crates of gold.

Woman: Love is like gold. And all that glitters is not gold, I suppose. One of man's genuine failures has been: **love**. He hasn't been able to remedy it or find a solution. Man has had three grand failures: he hasn't discovered a saucer and cup from which tea does NOT spill; a pressure cooker in which the handle does NOT come off; and a proper protocol for love, with rules and regulations.

Man: Kanwar Saab was furious with the Captain of the *Fort Stikine* for not abiding by Rule 46 of the Port Rules of International

Code, whereby a ship carrying dangerous cargo should display a red flag. But Captain Naismith of *Fort Stikine* did not want to advertise the cargo of the ship to the enemy. Everyone was expecting a Pearl Harbour type attack on Bombay Port. A few days ago, Madras Port had been bombed.

Woman: That evening on my way from the hospital, I picked up ACE limejuice from the shop. That along with *batata powa*, *bhel puri* and *chiwda* would be a fine *nashta* for Comrade Shashi. D-day arrived. It was 14th April 1944.

Man: It was 14th April 1944. There was something unusual in the air. German Defences had collapsed. The Black Sea Coast was about to fall into Russian hands. Gandhiji had malaria. While I was reading the newspaper, I noticed a very young chap. His name was Devdutt Pishorimal Anand. He had left Lahore in 1943, got down at Bombay Central Railway Station with thirty rupees in his pocket. He had managed to get a clerk's job in Military Accounts Office. He wanted to become a movie star. Pah! What a thought. He had nothing going for him. Except he jumped all over the place, talked a lot and hummed in *sur*. I thought Nehru was much more handsome than him. Anyway, this Devdutt was raving about a film called *Jawab* by a P C Barua chap. I asked wasn't Barua the director of *Devdas*? I failed to understand why anyone should make a film about a drunkard. Baburao Pendharkar told me I'm a *buddhu*. He said, *Devdas badi hit hai*. Naach, gaana, pyaar, tragedy. Even hundred years from now, public will say, *Paisa bolto ahe*. That was the name of Pendharkar's film. He never lost an opportunity to publicise it.

Woman: 14th April 1944. It was a sweltering hot Friday. Every year, it gets hotter. Something must be done about the pollution from the motor cars, the mills. Really, *bardasht ki bhi hadh hoti hai*. I was stuck in a procession in Dadar. It was the 51st birthday of Dr Ambedkar. There were huge crowds. I followed a group of women. Perhaps with a bit of enterprise I could have placed a garland of flowers around his neck. Mother would have been proud of me.

Man: 14th April 1944. I mustered up courage and entered Derby

Talkies. The name, it was rumoured, came into being because the owner had won a jackpot at the Derby. The movie was *Jawab*. This was my first movie. I could have watched V Shantaram's *Mali* at Novelty, but that was not be. Fate played a part. Anyway, it's not as though cinema lost a big *rasik*, in me. Subsequently, I saw one other film, *Gandhi* by Attenborough. I never sat through either film. In *Gandhi*, I left the movie theatre. I could not tolerate the assassination of Gandhiji in the first two minutes. It was very real. That's why, art must never imitate life. It's not good for the health.

Woman: 14th April 1944. I was passing through the streets. Everything was as it should be. Automobile spare parts, Kanti photo studio, *anaaj ki dukaan*. Two men were sipping chai and discussing how Bhoiwada United defeated Maccabi Sports Club by one goal because the match was fixed. That the referee was purchased. Hmm. Men will be men, no?

Man: 14th April 1944. *Jawab* was ok. It had a rich hero called Manoj who is sent to his future father-in-law for a rest cure. But Manoj loses his way and is offered shelter by a railway stationmaster. This master has a pretty daughter called Kanan Devi whose main objective in life is to make funny faces and sing songs. Manoj falls in love with the girl. Even as the love story was about to climax, there was a huge explosion. The screen was ripped apart.

Woman: 14th April 1944. It was five minutes past four. I had reached Razzak Chamber. Just then, there was a tremendous explosion. A hawaldar was standing on the pavement. His head was chopped off by a piece of metal that had flown through the air. I was stunned. People were running, everywhere.

Man: 14th April 1944. It was ten minutes past four. There was a stampede in the theatre. Somehow I managed to jump over the gates. The sky was filled with flying white hot metal.

Woman: 14th April 1944. It was ten minutes past four. Buildings were trembling. Splinters of glass flew from shattered windows. Flakes of hot livid ash and fire were falling, haphazardly. I couldn't recognise Bhujwalla. A few minutes ago, he had lovely wavy black hair. Now he was bald. He kept shouting, the Japs have come, the Japs have come. *Bhago. Bhago.* I believe he ran all the way to Bandra. Full speed.

Man: 14th April 1944. Burning bales, naphtha, debris, dense smoke and one huge boiler blocked the road. I ran and ran and reached an open garden. Burnt limbs, soot was falling all around me.

Woman: 14th April 1944. I limped and scrambled over the rubble. I wanted to get to 3, Sakina Manzil.

Man: 14th April 1944. There was a second explosion. Thirty-four minutes after the first explosion. Louder and much more brutal.

Woman: 14th April 1944. In front of my eyes, 3, Sakina Manzil was crumbling. There was a big hole in its centre. A piece of molten lead had crashed on its roof, and fallen through and through, all five floors, from roof to ground floor. Baba's shop was no more. Where was Baba? Where was Comrade Shashi?

Man: In the open garden, my mind was racing. Someone mentioned the explosions were from a British ship at the docks. I put two and two together. It must be *Fort Stikine*, with its hundreds of tons of explosives, bombs, oil, cotton, timber, sulphur. *Fort Stikine* was a time bomb. Kanwar Saab was right. The ship laden with explosives should not have been allowed into the docks. It was illegal. An accidental spark would have triggered off the ammunition in the hold.

Woman: I was hurt. *Bag main se thoda iodine laga diya. Aur ek painkiller.* I needed to get to a hospital. St George was the closest. But it was in the Dock Area, *kya patta wahan kya aafat aayi hogi.* So, I decided to go towards GT Hospital.

Man: In the gutter, there was a dead man clutching a copy of *Mumbai Samachar.* He had been charred by the heat. I picked up the dead man's cycle. It was scorching hot. I raced to 3, Sakina Manzil. It had a hole ... in its heart. Where was Shashiji ...?

Woman: At GT Hospital, I was treated. There I heard, the ARP, which used to organise drills as prevention against air raids was hiring temporary nurses. I volunteered. I was taken in a fancy

Victoria to Byculla. *Sab kuch tabah ho gaya tha. Log idhar udhar bhaag rahe thay, apni bachi-khuchi cheezon ke saath.* I reached the dormitory. We were short-staffed. So, unmindful of the glass cuts in my face, I got to work. Every minute, more and more injured persons were brought in. Every fourth person would die in front of us. Oos waqt sab kuch narak lag raha tha. The Bombay Dock Explosion.

Man: Even today, at six minutes past four, I have nightmares about the Bombay Dock Explosion. If I'm sleeping, I wake up. I'm trapped in a fire. Everything is ablaze. Me and five black skeletons, which dance. Flaming drums of oil hurtle towards me. My hair bursts into fireworks. I run. But blazing bales of cotton chase me. I dive into the sea and a huge fire envelopes the ships and warehouses. From a cloud, Comrade Shashi appears like Kanan Devi and tries to rescue me. Just then there is a blast and a tidal wave lifts *Fort Stikine* sixty feet into the air and smashes it down on Comrade Shashi's head. Both drown in the sea. Forever. Hmm. This nightmare plays and re-plays in my head, daily. That's why I've stopped sleeping. It's easier. Rather sleepless than anguished.

Change in tone. In a staccato voice, underlining the Bombay Dock Explosion.

Woman: 14th April 1944 was the day of the Bombay Dock Explosion. The official count was 336 dead. 1798 injured. Two days later, I saw some men, come crawling towards me. *Giddon ki tarah. Mujhe laga budmashi kar rahein hain.* When they were near, I realised they had lost all their limbs. No hands, no legs. Day after day, the flow was unabated. As usual, the unofficial guesstimates were ten times the official count. All bodies, except those identified were buried at Worli.

Man: The Bombay Dock Explosion. When I visited the docks to search for three of Gala Seth's *mazdoors* and Kanwar Saab, the whole area was filled with European bodies. When examined it was found out, all of these were Indian dockworkers and fire staff. Their outer skin had peeled off. That's why, they looked white.

Woman: I shifted to Kutch. This after I had helped Nehru's daughter give birth to her firstborn. They named him, Rajiv. Bonny baby. While sitting in the first class bogey and being cooled by ice slabs, Baba told me the Bombay Dock Explosion had transpired on the thirty-second anniversary of the day the *Titanic* struck an iceberg. *Dekho, oon logon ne apne Titanic ka kitna dhindora peetha. Aur ek hum hain ...*

Man: Almost all the fire engines belonging to the Bombay Fire Brigade were destroyed by the first explosion. Firemen were moved in from Poona, Thana, Nashik. Soldiers destroyed specific buildings with army tanks to prevent the fire from spreading to new localities. Petty Officer T Lewis of South Wales steered a truckload of ammunition out of the docks. The truck had no windows, no windscreen, no tyres, no steering wheel.

Woman: The Bombay Dock Explosion. *Sach kabhi bahar nahin aaya. Angrez toh theek hain. Unka agenda tha.* But why were we so careless. *Kyon? Kaise?* The whole thing was shrouded in security because of the War. News was suppressed. *Har baar woh hi drama-baazi.* Innocent lives were lost. Beggars, workers, street entertainers, hawkers, street women, family, friends, foes. Dar lagta hain. The trouble with the world is that the stupid are cocksure and the intelligent are full of doubt.

Man: The Bombay Dock Explosion. The Sheriff Shantidas Askuran requested people not to pay heed to rumours. But people did not pay heed to the Sheriff. One man was arrested in Sholapur for rumour mongering. Food godowns which were built in 1875 were destroyed. 55,000 tons of food grains were lost. Lorries fitted with loud speakers informed two million Bombaywallahs there would be an uninterrupted supply of food grains. No one believed them. There was another irony. Merchants who were engaged in the black market lost heavily because they had kept items, illegally, in the godowns.

Woman: The Bombay Dock Explosion. I recall, the overhead tram wire snapped. Local train services to VT Station was suspended at Byculla. It was a boom period for taxi drivers. Baba says a meteorologist in Shimla recorded a tremor on the station's seismograph. I can believe it. On that day, the world shuddered. I lost a piece of me.

Man: My soul lost its stirrings. The Government couldn't ever compensate that. But it was keen to compensate owners and tenants of ruined buildings, and so it decided to forego paperwork and proof. This was because it wanted to earn the goodwill of the people during the war. One, Harshad Bhai took advantage of the loopholes and made an unscrupulous claim for a non-existent building. Up to that time, the Government had paid 85,000,000 rupees against claims for damage by fire or blast. Traders like Gala Seth, who had shops on the ground floor of the buildings, never locked the cash-petty. In the days after the Bombay Dock Explosion, he lost his money, valuables, jewellery due to vandalism. Since then, the sellers of safes, locks and keys have profited.

Woman: The Bombay Dock Explosion. There was fire on the horizon for three months. All the buildings in a couple of mile radius of the docks smouldered. The fire had spread, rapidly. Although, everything was wrecked, people showed courage and fortitude. The city bounced back to life. But not me.

Man: After 14th April 1944, my life was tattered. I'm not a strong person, in any case. So I just did enough to keep body and soul together. I left the city. Travelled for many years. There were so many disasters, since. But the Bombay Dock Explosion was the worst. Everything turned into a dull shade of grey. My night had begun.

Woman: I never saw Comrade Shashi, again.

Man: I never met Shashiji. She must be living happily. With Yajuvendra. Must have raised a family, opened three more shops, built one more building, got insured for health, started a nursing home, managed finances, become religious at a late age. *Hai bhagwan*. What a calamity! What a mistake my life has been. Come on, mouth. You must not utter such despicable things. Can't go around with such a negative outlook. Shaddup. This is not the time for regrets. I've seen worse dumps. Terrible tragedies. Mine is a fairy tale, in comparison.

Woman: One, I loved. And the other I lost. Sad, no? Comrade Shashi was the apple of my eye. And Yajuvendra was Missing in Action, near the Naga Hills. The two men in my life. Both vanished into thin air.

Man: My dear mouth, strange as it may sound, unbeknownst to you, good things happened too. You recall that filmi chap, Devdutt. He didn't report to work on 14th April 1944. Touch wood. I'm told he became a movie star. Changed his name to Dev Anand. I hope he's earning some money in the movie business. It's such a fickle industry. But much more importantly, there was the **gold**. Ah, I see you're waking up. Sitting bolt upright. Should I get on with it, my dear mouth? Here goes. Due to the Bombay Dock Explosion, the gold bars in the thirty-one crates in *Fort Stikine* flew into the city. Yes sir. It rained gold bars. The rich, the poor, the cheerful, the unhappy, so many people benefited as gold bars crashed through their roofs, and onto their heads! As it's said, *jab uparwallah deta hai, to chhappar phaad ke deta hai.* Burjorji Cooverji Motiwala, who was a retired civil engineer in Bombay Dyeing, returned the gold ingot. I know, since I used to pass his building Kukana House in Girgaum. He was rewarded by the authorities. Shashiji would have said, *Burjorji bahut khaandaani tha*. But the fact is, of the 130 gold ingots, only 43 were found. That too, after a three year search of the docks, the surrounding locality, houses. So, what do you say to that, my dear mouth! 83 ingots and perhaps 83 millionaires are out there, somewhere. As for me, I was half deaf after the explosion. I never married. Remained a *brahmachari*. I've loved, once. And for me the first was the best. Unless, there's a miracle. *Choomantar kalikalantar*! The tattered screen at Derby Talkies comes alive. And the lady with the funny face sings a song and brings my Shashiji to me.

Woman: That was then. 14th April 1944. It's now, 14th April 1994. I told Dr Bhavna Parekh, I'm a birthday girl, today. She wished me happy birthday. And said, I'm still beautiful with beautiful eyes. *A husn ki malika*. Sound as a bell ... *(wheezes)* ... except for some respiratory trouble. But I'm covered, medically, that is. All those years as a nurse has benefited me. See, see, I'm repeating myself. Bad girl. Then, even as I'm exiting the doctor's clinic, I hear the sound of hiccupping ... Comrade Shashi ... That must be Comrade Shashi ... No, no. I've become senile. Comrade Shashi must be a happily married grandfather with 101 grandsons. Or did he pass away at the Bombay Dock Explosion? I never heard about him, since. No, no. Perish the thought. Oh, to hear him talk after he had downed a glass or two of ACE limejuice. Talked as though he was Gandhiji the Second. Today, if he were alive, we would be walking, out of the dispensary, together. Hand in hand. He would say, *Chalo, Shashiji, ghar jaana hain. Ya hum latest film dekh sakte hain. Soona hain Devdas wapas ban rahi hai.* Er ... Oh ... Eh ... *Kya, itni raat ko taxi milegi* ... Hai, the inexhaustible reservoir of sorrow. *(Exits)*

Man (hiccups): Why am I hiccupping? *Shukar hain*, that old woman has left. Or else it would be so embarrassing. Sshhh. Chup. What's that? The old woman has left something, behind. Er ... Oh ... Eh ... what's this? Ribbons. So many of them. *Nava rasa, nava bhava, nava ratna.* It reminds me of .... someone ... Shashiji. Ah, don't dream your impossible dreams, silly chap. The girl must have married Yajuvendra and must be living happily ever after. Ah. Now, now. Don't wallow in self-pity. Eyes, cry your last. The drying up a single tear has more of honest fame than shedding seas of gore. Often have I wondered what if Shashiji and I had kept our appointment on 14th April 1944. I would have lived a different life, no? But promises are like the full moon: if they are not kept at once they diminish day by day. May be one day I should go to 3, Sakina Manzil. I'm told it was renovated and is up-and-about. Perhaps, one day in the near future. To relive old memories, the possibilities, the missed opportunities. But time is passing by in a hurry. And men like me cannot see their reflection because the water runs, rapidly. I need still water. Still water. That's why I swim, in this day and age, in the sea. Er ... Oh ... Eh ... How I wish this hiccupping ceased. Hmm. That must be the doctor. It's my turn, finally ... Coming, doctor. Don't go away. Do wait. Arrey, at least someone wait for me ...

Shakespeare and She

Dedicated to Khan Saab and Pa Pa Pagali (for rehearsing – and freezing – on the terrace during Mumbai's coldest winter)

Premiered on 16th February (2008) at the Hamara Shakespeare Festival, Museum Theatre, Chennai

Playwright/Director: Ramu Ramanathan

Actors: Ahlam Khan, Medha, Pooja Asher, Akshata Sawant

Music: Akshata Sawant, Ahlam Khan

Producer: Kinnari Vohra

Stage design and production: Samir Lukka, Sudeep Naik, Sudeep Modak

Photographs: Arko Provo Mukherjee, Biju Neyyan, Hashim K Basheer, Maitri Dore, Tapan Maharishi

Lights consultant: Arghya Lahiri

The play is a counselling session which transpires in real time. All the other characters and elements - come and go.

The stage is empty to start with. The set is determined from Insomnia's point of view. There is a blank canvas at the outset; later, since Insomnia is an animator, the stage space should fill up with simple props, fabric, visuals and chairs.

There should be lots of lights and naked bulbs -- bright, white, harsh lights for the counselling sessions and a contrasting setting for the Aisha scenes and the songs.

SCENE 1

There is a huge white screen in the background. Four women – Insomnia, Aisha, Insomnia (Alter Ego) and Counsellor, are standing at the side sipping beer from cans and talking among themselves.

The third bell rings ...

Insomnia (Alter Ego) walks to the front and begins to hum. The other three continue to talk. After a few bars, Insomnia joins Insomnia (Alter Ego) in the front and they hum.

A dot appears on the screen. Many dots appear. It finally transforms into an image of Shakespeare!

Insomnia, Aisha and Insomnia (Alter Ego) look at the image of Shakespeare and begin to twirl, still humming. Counsellor walks to the front looking at her notepad.

SCENE 2

Counsellor enters. She asks a series of questions in a staccato, emotionless tone.

Counsellor: Shall we begin?

Insomnia: Yes.

Counsellor: Your name?

Insomnia: Insomnia. My name is Insomnia.

Counsellor: Sex?

Insomnia: Sex!!! Ha Ha. Whatdoesitlooklike? I'm a woman. In her thirties. Waiting for the right guy.

Counsellor: Is that why you are an alcoholic?

Insomnia: Alcoholic! Oh, that's harsh! I ... like to drink.

Counsellor: Daily?

Insomnia: Hourly!

Counsellor: Is it because of an unrequited desire?

Insomnia: If I was in a position to be picky, I wouldn't be here in the first place.

Counsellor: What would you want to do?

Insomnia: Ideally, I would like to retire. With a desired pension. 185,000 dollars a year plus stock options. Me – under a coconut tree having tapioca chips and local toddy. The sea breeze going through my ears. Whoooooooooooooosh!

Counsellor: Education?

Insomnia: Yes.

Counsellor: What sort?

Insomnia: The usual dullish stuff. School, college.

Counsellor: What sort of college?

Insomnia: Intellectually unhygienic.

Counsellor: What did you graduate in?

Insomnia: English Lit. Marlowe, Chomsky, Edward Said. Shakespeare. Post-colonialism. Post-structuralism. Our teacher was a bully. She was the laughable dimwit of self-righteousness. She claimed she had a vocabulary of fifty thousand words but the word Fun was absent in her dictionary. She had a zero sense of humour. Locked us out of her classrooms – even if we were thirty seconds late. She was OK with Falstaff being a fart but couldn't handle us having an attitude.

Counsellor: You hated her.

Insomnia: It was the other way around. I was a target for academic bookish hostility.

A beat

Counsellor: Your most notable achievement?

Insomnia: My collection of pens and post-it notes on which I created miniatures. I loved to draw pigs.

Counsellor: Pigs? Why?

Insomnia: Simple. They are easier to render than alligators and giraffes.

Aisha and Insomnia (Alter Ego): Oink, oink!

Counsellor: Is that how you became an … artiste?

Insomnia: Hmm. Mine is a life without a script. I stumble from one pig sty to another.

Counsellor: As a child did you have any special skills?

Insomnia: Yes, I was a great winker. *(Demonstrates)* Although I haven't quite mastered the art as yet …

Counsellor: What else?

Insomnia: At the age of fourteen, I could drive a car. I love cars, car parts. Zero offset steering. Positive crank-case ventilation valve. Multi-port fuel injection. Every time I hear these words, I get an orgasm. It's poetry.

Counsellor: Do you smoke?

Insomnia: When I'm working, no. On my breaks, yes.

Counsellor: Who is your father?

Insomnia: He is a prick. A dick-head.

Counsellor: And your mother?

Insomnia: She is dead. Childbirth. That's why my dad hated me. And I loathed him. Quid pro quo.

Counsellor: I see.

Insomnia: You do?

Counsellor: I do.

Insomnia: My mother was a blind woman. Like Helen Keller. Ha-ha. Do you know how Helen Keller met her husband? Through a **blind** date! Funny, no? What happened when Helen Keller fell into a well! She screamed her hands off. Not funny, na?

Counsellor: Yes.

Insomnia: My mother had fallen into a well. The thorns bruised her eyes. If my father had been vigilant, her eyes could have been saved.

A beat

Counsellor: Hmmm.

Insomnia: Regrets. That's what our lives are reduced to. My regrets, my mother's regrets. Perhaps my father has regrets, as well. Do you have any regrets?

Counsellor: All the time.

Insomnia: But you handle it with such … equilibrium! Such grace! Such equipoise! Such calm …

Counsellor: Why did you try to kill yourself?

Insomnia: I don't know. That's for you to find out. Isn't that why you're being paid?

Counsellor: I'm not being paid. I'm trying to help you.

Insomnia: Ok.

Counsellor: Relax.

Insomnia: Can I have a sip of … cognac?

Counsellor: No.

Insomnia: Umm. Because that's what I was sipping when I heard the news about one of the Pongas.

Counsellor: Excuse me?

Insomnia: Pongas! Hoo! I was watching a Russian animated film, *The Snow Queen*. Two animators, I admire. Yuri Nordstein from Russia and Frederick Bach from Canada. Nordstein truly deserves to be called an artist. He is something. You must see his work.

Counsellor: I will.

Insomnia: I can lend you a DVD.

Counsellor: Thanks. What happened, then?

Insomnia: When?

Counsellor: When you were watching *Snow Queen*?

Insomnia: I got an SMS.

Counsellor: What did it say?

Insomnia: Ponga is dead. It's over!

Counsellor: What did you do?

Insomnia: Drugged me.

Counsellor: What did you have?

Insomnia: My Paanch Pandavs.

Counsellor: I don't comprehend. Explain.

Insomnia: I'm Draupadi and my Paanch Pandavs are: phenylalanine, tyrosine, tryptophan, 5-hydroxytryptophan and choline. I have them. One at a time.

Counsellor: It's a heavy dose of anti-depressants. For what?

Insomnia: For what? For my balding. For my impotence, my

wrinkles, my obesity, my insufferable insomnia. For this bitch of an existence.

Counsellor: Relax.

Insomnia: I could have if you let me have a sip of cognac.

A beat

Counsellor: What is a Ponga?

Insomnia: A Ponga ... is a ... is a...

Counsellor: Yes?

Insomnia: Is a ... Ponga!

Counsellor: Meaning?

Insomnia: It has no meaning? No definition whatsoever. Yet, it is full of meaning!

Counsellor: How does one become a Ponga?

Insomnia: You take the Ponga Oath!

Counsellor: Which is?

Insomnia: There are three types of rings. Engagement ring. Wedding ring. Suffering. Therefore a true blue Ponga will abstain from marriage till the dying day.

Counsellor: Interesting.

Insomnia: On 8th August, with a touch of irony, we assembled at August Kranti Maidan and formulated a resolution. Quit Wedding Day or Shaadi Chhoddo Andolan. When parents or relatives asked us to marry, we said we can't, it's our civil disobedience movement. Our motto: Don't Do. Therefore Don't Die.

Counsellor: How many Pongas were you?

Insomnia: Many.

Counsellor: You still in touch?

Insomnia: No.

Counsellor: Why?

Insomnia: I think they are dead. All gone. Deader than dead.

Counsellor: Except you.

Insomnia: No. Excluding me. There's one more Ponga. Aisha.

But she got married.

Counsellor: I see …

Insomnia (Alter Ego) begins to hum. Aisha gets ready. Counsellor gets a call on her cell phone.

Counsellor: Hello? Ye … Hel … But … Yes ... N … I ca … Ok … But … Tom … Ok … Ye … Ok... Ok …!

Cross fade

SCENE 3

The scene is enacted between Insomnia and Aisha. Insomnia (Alter Ego) continues to hum and strum the harp. Counsellor hangs up the phone.

Counsellor: I'm sorry. Tell me about Aisha.

Insomnia: The first time I saw Aisha, she had a bruise on her cheek!

Aisha: I have no memory about that first meeting.

Insomnia: She said she banged into a hand loom in the dark. Hand loom? What's a hand-loom?

Aisha: I was playing with Ali. He was Mukhtar Begum's son. Ali leaped out of my arm. He bounced off his head onto the road. **Boing Boing Boing**. Like a pinball. Bhaijaan whacked me on the face. You're tinier than Ali? Why did you have to carry him? What if Ali's skull had cracked? Ali's brains would have oozed out …

Insomnia: We sat on the same desk.

Aisha: Brains? I said. Ali has no brains! It's empty in there!

Insomnia: The class teacher whacked me.

Aisha: That's when Bhaijaan whacked me.

Insomnia: I was contemplating.

Aisha: She was a day dreamer. She had a felt-tipped pen with which she did spontaneous life-size portraits in real time. She had done mine on a huge sheet of glass.

Counsellor (cross talk): This is fantastic! Like that artist Franco

Magnani! He made these amazing memory paintings – you must see them ... Wait a minute, I'll show you!

Insomnia (overlapping): I was contemplating about the strange man in my house. I don't know who the hell he is. When I rang the bell, he opened the door, and said, yes, what can I do for you? I told him this... er... is my house... er... this is my father's house.

Aisha: I took the portrait home. No one liked it. Mother said I'm prettier in real life. In this I look like a *daayan*!

Counsellor: So who was the strange man?

Insomnia: The strange man is my father's friend. Hmm. I don't like my father's friends. That's why I shift my mattress near the main window. That way, I can jump out of the window, especially, if the strange man tries some monkey business. Except I'm located on the twelfth floor. I wish I was a cat. I could walk on ledges and parapets. That didn't prevent Mussolini from falling off the seventh floor.

Aisha: The weather is abnormal.

Insomnia: Why would anyone name their cat, Mussolini?

Aisha: I feel sick all the time.

Insomnia: My walls are purple. I want to render it alphonso mango yellow. Perhaps with a nice green kota floor. A Paul Klee on the wall.

Aisha: I miss my classes.

Insomnia: I miss Aisha.

Aisha: My asthma attacks are acute. I inherited it from mother.

Insomnia: Aisha smiles at my jokes. I call her Dabloo because that's how she pronounces the alphabet, Dabloo! Last week, I told her it's Etch and not the way she says it.

Aisha: We don't know what to do with mother's health. It's a worry! She has fibroids in her stomach. The doctor says it needs surgery. She works so hard. All the cleaning and managing. Plus the daily shifting. In the day, the workers are in the workshop. Mother does her domestic chores – upstairs in the loft. By evening, we go down; and the workers move up to the loft.

Insomnia: I seek a quiet life. No strife. I'm planning to shave my hair?

Aisha: Why, I ask her?

Insomnia: Why? Aisha asks. Ooooof. Aisha is so traditional in her outlook.

Aisha: I tell her, imagine the number of people who will make fun of you. As it is, that Aarti is always mocking you.

Insomnia: People! I loathe people. I prefer Crocin to people.

Aisha: One day, she introduced me to her cousin. She says she loathes her cousin.

Counsellor: Have you always sketched with your left hand?

Insomnia: These days, I try to sketch with my left hand. I realise with a bit of practice I can be better than R K Laxman. I had a leftie auntie, who used to brush her teeth with her left hand. Sew and eat and use the remote control with her left hand. My leftie auntie is my hero.

Aisha: Her cousin is from Cape Town. She is very tall: 6 feet 3 inches. She says tying her shoelaces is a problem. She gives me foreign chewing gum. I get *malai-khaja* for her.

Insomnia: The *malai-khaja* is brilliant. Hundred times better than Kit Kat. Aarti doesn't think so. Aarti is a retard.

Aisha: Aarti passed away.

Insomnia: One day, Aarti died. Just like that. Weird.

Aisha: Memories!

Insomnia: Unpleasant memories.

Aisha: These days, we hardly meet.

Insomnia: Aisha and I hardly meet, these days.

Aisha: I work in a small PHC, near Aurangabad.

Insomnia: She works in some god-forsaken place. Aisha had an all-knowing husband? I wonder what happened to him.

Aisha: He ran away. Abandoned me.

Insomnia: It seems he ran away – and abandoned her? That's what she told me!

Aisha: She said, he did? When? *(Change of tone)*

Insomnia: He did? When?

Aisha: Quite silly, really. I returned home from New Jersey. My Air India flight was cancelled. I had no money. You remember Suryavanshi Janakidas? He was on the same flight.

Insomnia: The computer software fellow?

Aisha: Yes. Yes. He helped me. We reached Mumbai, together. Some neighbours saw us – together. They began to gossip. Eventually the stories reached my husband. The whole community was talking about what might have happened between the two of us.

Insomnia: And ...

Aisha: Humiliation. What else? Kicked out for Zinah.

Insomnia: Any alimony?

Aisha: Arrey, nothing. A broken jaw, whipped on my back, a kick on my tummy.

Insomnia: Hmm.

Aisha: It's ok. Life plods on. Aisha plods on.

Insomnia: How's your cousin, Hamna?

Aisha: Ha. She is the one who spread slanderous lies about me. She and Zainab!

Insomnia: What now?

Aisha: I'm an incharge in a hospital. I take care of patients. Farmers, labourers and women. I practice my two thousand *hadiths* on the *kafirs*. Ha Ha.

Insomnia: That's good. Aisha finally has an audience!

Aisha: We have a hospital joke. Ha ha. You will like it ... When you have unsafe sex, you get AIDS! Right? But when you have unprotected phone sex, you get ... what?

Insomnia: No idea.

Aisha: Hearing AIDS!

Insomnia: Ha-ha. It's actually funny.

Aisha: It's an original joke. These days, jokes help me take arms against a sea of troubles.

Insomnia: I'm sure. Ten years ago it was the Koran. Do you still recite the Koran?

Aisha: Oh yes. All the *aiyaats*. Or at least some of them. But I don't wear a *hijab* any more.

Insomnia: Hai rabba. Then you must be looking beautiful?

Aisha: Not as gorgeous as you, my *jaan*. You're a Jinn.

Insomnia: A good Jinn? Or an evil one?

Aisha: All women are evil! Haven't you heard?

Insomnia: Hush Aisha. Hush

Aisha: Chalo. *Khuda hafeez va eltemas-e dua!* I have hospital duty.

Insomnia: Shabba khaer!

Aisha: Whataboutyou?

Insomnia: I've a morning flight to Hong Kong.

Aisha: Mashallah! Bahut khoob ji! Take care. *Jyaada badmashi mat karna*.

Insomnia: Muah! Hong Kong … here I come.

Aisha: **Beware:** Hong Kong. Woah Woah Woah. Here she comes.

Insomnia (Alter Ego) continues humming.

SCENE 4

Insomnia (Alter Ego) begins humming and playing the harp and then begins to sing. Insomnia hums and then she sings a song.

I'm on a project in Hong Kong.

I'm a graffiti artist.

Street-signist and tech stylist –

It's my dream to be Miyazaki!

Insomnia: Aah! Miyazaki san! ... Hai!

Insomnia (Alter Ego) sings

Redo the setting of the sun on the sea;
I'm here for the money.
I hear bells
This city's in the well
Ding ding dong
Wing Wong
Ching Chong
King Kong.

Insomnia talks the Talk.

Insomnia: So, I was in Hong Kong for twelve months and when I returned home, I tried to tell them about my favorite things ... No one gave a bloody damn!

Insomnia (Alter Ego) plays the harp and sings along with Insomnia

American
Publisher
Wants me to hippify
Shakespeare's plays.
First project: Romeo and Juliet;
Recreate the Montagues and Capulets
To be rival families in Tokyo;
Yakuza families in Tokyo!

Insomnia talks the Talk.

Insomnia: It was no use. At any rate, those twelve months of my life were just gone. Obliterated. People only listen to what they want to listen to. People want to reduce others' lives to mundaneness. I often wonder what will remain fifty years from now. Will my existence be completely decimated? Like it was for those twelve months of my life? Fifty years from now – what will be some of my favorite things?

Counsellor: Kleenex and nosedrops and needles for knitting.

And walkers and handrails and new dental fittings.

Insomnia begins to sing. Counsellor joins her. Insomnia (Alter Ego) hums/plays the harp. Aisha joins in the chorus.

Kleenex and nosedrops and needles for knitting –

Walkers and handrails and new dental fittings –

Bundles of magazines tied up with strings –

These are a few of my favourite things!

Counsellor: Aah! Cockroach! I luuuuuve roaches! Come here sweetie pie!

The song continues

Cadillacs and cataracts and hearing aids and glasses

Counsellor: What?! What did you just say? Speak up young woman! Can't hear you!

Insomnia (shouts): Polydent and Fixodent and false teeth and glasses!

The song continues

Pacemakers, diapers and porches with swings

These are a few of my favourite things!

When the pipes leak;

When the bones creak;

When the knees go bad;

I simply remember my favourite things,

And then I don't feel so bad.

Counsellor: I hate you! I hate you! And I hate your mother!

The song continues

Hot tea and Maggi and corn caps for bunions;

No spicy hot food or food cooked with onions!

Dry scabs and rashes and the stench which they bring

These are a few of my favourite things!

Back pains, confused brains and no need for sinnin'!
Thin bones and fractures and hair that is thinnin'!
And we won't mention our short shrunken frames,
When we remember our favourite things.
When the joints ache
When the hips break
When the eyes grow dim
Then I remember the great life I've had
And then I don't feel so bad!

SCENE 5

Silence. The screen lights up with an email chat between Insomnia and unknown person.

Message: Beep! Beep! Beep!

Insomnia: Who's there?

Message: Me.

Insomnia: Me? Who?

Message: Me.

Insomnia: Come on, answer me: stand, and unfold yourself. Who are you?

Message: Shakespeare!

Insomnia: William Shakespeare?

Message: Yes.

Insomnia: You come most carefully upon your hour?

Message: I do.

Insomnia: 'Tis now struck twelve; and I must get me to bed.

Message: Hamlet.

Insomnia: So you're Shakespeare?

Message: Yes.

Insomnia: You must be very old, considering you were born in the sixteenth century!

Message: Yes.

Insomnia: Where are you? London?

Message: Kovalam.

Insomnia: Ha-ha. Good one.

Message: ☺

Insomnia: Hmm. Listen. I've an appointment.

Message: OK.

Insomnia: BRB!

Message: OK.

Insomnia: Shakespeare, huh?

Message: William Shakespeare.

Insomnia: Ya right?

Message: Adieu.

Insomnia: Adieu ... to you too.

Cross fade

SCENE 6

Counsellor asks a series of questions in a staccato, emotionless tone.

Counsellor: So? Shakespeare chats with you?

Insomnia: Yes.

Counsellor: Daily?

Insomnia: Pretty frequently.

Counsellor: And he is in Kovalam?!?!

Insomnia: He was in Kovalam. Now he is in Mumbai.

Counsellor: I see.

Insomnia: Are you mocking me?

Counsellor: No. Not at all. Tell me about your dream.

Insomnia: The Shakespeare dream?

Counsellor: Yes.

Insomnia (Alter Ego) begins to hum.

Insomnia: I am racing through the streets. I have my handbag in one hand and a colour photograph in the other. This is the only thing in colour. Everything else is in black and white. It is a photograph of Shakespeare. I show it to people who are passing by. I ask them, 'Have you seen this man?' The people reply, 'Yes, we have seen him'. I ask them, 'Can you tell me where I can find this man?' The people look at me and say, 'He's not far.' That's all there is to it. I continue running.

Counsellor: How long do you run?

Insomnia: Till I'm tired. Then I put my laptop on the ground and sit on it ... like a cushion.

Counsellor: Hmm.

Insomnia: What does it all mean?

Counsellor: You're seeking something that you know does not exist. Have you, er ... heard of Franco Magnani ...?

Insomnia: The artist?

Counsellor: Exactly! Franco Magnani was obsessed with his home village of Pontito in Tuscany. Although Magnani had not seen his village in many years, he had constructed a detailed, highly accurate, three-dimensional model of Pontito in his head! Amazing!

Insomnia: I see.

Counsellor: Medically speaking, the eidetic quality of both your recollections and your work is leading to an interplay of memory and of the relation between the brain's physiology and artistic inspiration.

Insomnia: Bleh? Bleh? Bleh? What?

Counsellor: Your dreams are a kind of minute and accurate detail of memories. They are characteristically represented through photographs or diagrams, not conscious recollection. Thereafter, such memories reappear through your waking state. Like your online chat with William Shakespeare.

Insomnia: But the online chat is real. He told me so, last week. He is a student in the University. He flunked in one paper: Shakespeare Studies. The teacher told him he knows nothing about Shakespeare.

Counsellor: I see. So William Shakespeare knows nothing about William Shakespeare?

Insomnia: Imagine that? These academics and their pedagogy. Pah!

Counsellor: What was his project about?

Insomnia: Oh. He told his project guide that the play should **not** have been called *The Two Gentlemen of Verona*. It should have been Milan, since he meant Milan. And *Measure for Measure* can't be set in Vienna.

Counsellor: And why is that?

Insomnia: Because all the characters have Italian names!

Counsellor: And...

Insomnia: Hamlet is a student when the play begins and is 30 years old when the play ends; although there is no indication of time passing in the play. He told the guide, he wanted to rewrite the play.

Counsellor: I see. This... William Shakespeare wants to rewrite Hamlet?

Insomnia: Yes.

Counsellor: He can do it.

Insomnia: I do it all the time. I rewrite – all the time.

Counsellor: You do?

Insomnia: How do you explain this, then?

Counsellor: Well ...

Insomnia: You can't deny William Shakespeare's existence, can you?

Counsellor: Hmm. What is striking about William Shakespeare is his tangible reality, as if entire moments consisting of sounds, sights, smells, and even touch are superimposed on the present.

Insomnia: So all this … is not real … ?

Counsellor: It is.

Insomnia: Then?

Counsellor: It could be a kind of temporal lobe epilepsy as a possible explanation for the qualitatively distinct power of such memories. And yet, let me be cautious enough – because to over-apply diagnoses would be potentially reductive.

Insomnia: I see.

Counsellor: Let's move on to … Pongas! What is a Ponga?

Insomnia: Ponga is everything, and everyone! But Ponga can also be nothing, and no one.

Counsellor: Is this the Ponga mantra?

A beat

Insomnia: Nope. It's my mantra. Will you have a pomfret fillet?

Counsellor: Now?

Insomnia: I can get it for my next session. It's very simple! I love to cook it.

Counsellor: Really?

Insomnia: You see, one just has to scrub lime juice (since pomfret has a fishy smell). Sprinkle herbs. I prefer bouquet garni or even parsley. Let it marinate for 30–45 minutes. Dribble water, or white wine. Sprinkle salt. Cover. Bung into a microwave for about 15 minutes. During which time, I read a bit. These days, that's the only time, I read.

Counsellor: Is this a clause from the … Ponga charter?

Insomnia: Ponga Charter? Ha ha. There is no such Charter or Constitution. We live in the era of dead manifestoes. The Ponga philosophy is: all things humans have been dehumanised and vulgarised. Everything. If someone came down from Mars, that someone would NOT read our charters and manifestoes, that thing would observe us!

Counsellor: This is an ultra pessimistic view of planet earth!

Insomnia: Perhaps.

Counsellor: Perhaps?

A beat

Insomnia: I believe that ... there are only two things that can save the human race. The first is, Chocolate fudge. Ummmmm. Take one teaspoon of vanilla essence. Mix it in a heavy bottomed saucepan. Slow fire. Stir. Stir. Stir. Or else the chocolate will burn. And then ...

Counsellor: What's the other thing?

Insomnia: The other thing?

Counsellor: The other thing that can save the human race?

Insomnia: I would have said – a sweet smile. But there's daggers in a man's smile. Hmm. So I would say what Aisha said.

Counsellor: And what is that?

Insomnia: Sheikh Saab.

Counsellor: Sheikh Saab! Who is that?

Insomnia: Shakespeare!

Counsellor: Shakespeare?

Insomnia: In our university days in our English Drama course, we had to submit a project. Aisha being Aisha had a point of view. She said sixteenth century London is equal to twenty-first century Mumbai.

Counsellor: That's interesting. Sixteenth century London is equal to twenty-first century Mumbai!

Insomnia: The clamour, the clutter. The endless jostling. Busy bustis and makeshift tradeshops. The stench and the shit. No open spaces. Immigrants and traders and their labourers, arriving, every day. Infectious maladies. Mosquito bites, TB, pneumonia, encephalitis, maladies, infections, exhaustion.

Counsellor: And so?

Insomnia: Aisha adorned a burka. She borrowed a digital camera from Bijju. Then she roamed through the streets of Mumbai. In search of Shakespeare's characters. She discovered amazing characters: Shylock at Masjid Bunder station. Romeo and Juliet at a shopping mall. Cleopatra at Vasai Koli Village. Wait! Let me show you!

Counsellor: Fascinating.

Insomnia: Yes, isn't it? Except if I would have done it, you would have called it ... what ... medically speaking, the eidetic quality of ... blah blah blah blah blah ... and of the relation between the brain's physiology and artistic inspiration.

Counsellor (laughs): Ha ha. Aisha's photographs of Shakespeare characters in Mumbai. Please.

Insomnia: Oh yes.

Counsellor: Thank you.

Insomnia snaps her fingers. The screen lights up!

Insomnia: Sheikh Saab In Mumbai. Presented by Aisha.

Insomnia (Alter Ego) plays the harp and hums.

SCENE 7

Insomnia (Alter Ego) plays the harp and hums.

'SHEIKH SAAB in MUMBAI

By

Aisha'

...

And the pictures shot by Aisha on a cheap camera — start to scroll! A four-minute photograph tableau scene

SCENE 8

Insomnia (Alter Ego) begins to hum. Insomnia joins her. They begin to sing.

Aisha's father uttered an 'ism'

Mumbai meri jaan – Mumbai mera jism!

He travelled with family to this city

Left his bungalow, such a pity!

Aisha, she lived in a nameless town
On her tenth birthday, she wore a silk gown
A really old man – tried to woo!
Aisha, she cried boo hoo hoo!

Insomnia talks the Talk. Insomnia (Alter Ego) continues to hum.

The man chased Aisha
She dropped her dolls
She ran quite fast past the chawls
Past the chawls. The chawls were past.
Aisha was hungry – very, very angry
Angry! Hungry! Angry! Hungry! –

Aisha: Who are you?

Insomnia continues to talk the Talk.

She asked the outlandish old man.
Ha ha ha! I am your husband in this world and the next!
Aisha screamed her loudest scream
Till she vomited her *thandai* and yesterday's ice cream!

Insomnia (Alter Ego) hums and Insomnia joins her. The song continues.

Aisha's father heard of the incident
Banished the man and forfeited the rent
Aisha stopped playing with the frogs and snails
Climbed the mango tree in her brand new veil
Since that day, Aisha slept with her mother
From head to toe covered with *chaaddar*
Scared of scorpions falling on her head
Stinging and stunning until she was deader than dead!

Insomnia talks the Talk.

Aisha's father was very sad.
He said this is awfully bad
The girl is losing her mind!

Her memory is wedged.
What will happen to her tons of knowledge?
Aisha said:
Aisha: The laws of nature are approximate
Human ways are inaccurate
Philosophically, we are completely warped
Scientifically, we have been dwarfed
Is the moon a big rock?
Is everything an atom, after all?
Does gravity have an effect on the brains?
Can Maths be flushed down the drain?
Insomnia talks the Talk.
O Dajjal
O Iblis,
O Shaitan
O Dushman
Aisha's grandmother hissed
Ban her education!
Make her hear the *Khutbah*
Instead of multiplication tables!
Make her memorise the *Sunnah*
Plus the *Surah*!
Aisha: Wa alaikum assalam!
Insomnia talks the Talk.
Said Aisha.
And she recited the *Zaboors*
Her grandmother would have swallowed her dentures
If Aisha's father hadn't stopped the little girl
Insomnia (Alter Ego) hums and Insomnia joins her. The song continues.
That's how Aisha came to our school

Wore a *hijab*; and followed all the rules
Never back-answered, never played the fool
Slaved like a mule, *lekin sab ne diya hool, hool*!
Mid-term exams, results are announced
Teacher's stupefied – Aisha's name is pronounced
She said – Aisha? Aisha who?
How can the first-rank be scored by you you **you**!

Insomnia (Alter Ego) hums and Insomnia joins her. The song continues.

She swallowed insults, she stopped attending
No one ever knew what the hell was happening
I caught a bus – and visited Aisha's room
And all I saw was a second-hand hand loom!
I saw Aisha lying on a mat
The room had no current, the ceiling had a bat
There were scab marks on her body
Her entire house was sooooo dowdy, sooooo ploddy, shoddy!

Insomnia talks the Talk.

Over there: A gunny bag of rice and wheat
Some stale, leftover food which she tried to eat
Tobacco leaves in the corner of the room
And tanned leather which provided the aura of a tomb
Aisha was genuinely delighted to see me

Aisha: Oh ho ho! *Zehenaseeb*!

Insomnia talks the Talk.

She told me, her father had organised the school fee
In my hand she saw my book
She grabbed it – just for a quick look

Aisha: Like my father, this writer is a Sheikh
My father is a Sunni
But this fellow is a Speare Sheikh.

Insomnia talks the Talk.
I laughed aloud. She started to quake.
Aisha: I want to read this?
Should I consult my parents?
Insomnia talks the Talk.
I was perplexified, stupefied, mystified.
I told her I read what I want!
Full stop.
Khatam.
Shoodh.
Zero.
Shunya. Shunya. Shunya.
She thought it was a taunt.
She asked me:
Aisha: Are you from Medina?
Insomnia talks the Talk.
I said, Eh? Na!
She whispered:
Aisha: In Mecca the men tend to dominate the women.
But in Medina the women tend to dominate the men.
Insomnia talks the Talk.
So she said.
And cackled at her own gag.
Which to be honest, I didn't sort of bag.
Ineluctably
Quite delectably
Aisha borrowed my copy of
The Complete Works of Shakespeare
Each and every play, she read from *Tempest* to *Lear*
Thirty-eight plays in all.

Aisha: Arrey Baba.

He created the Universe in Seven Days.

Surely I can complete Sheikh Saab's plays in less time than that!

The song continues

That's how my friendship started with Aisha

Who said, I've worked it out and hai Allah!

Discounting all the thous and thees and thys

Sheikh Saab coined words – 2035!

Aisha: Arrey baba! Don't you realise, you and me are superior to him!

The song continues

Aisha also said:

Drop the pentameters and screw the plot!

He's a plagiariser; his narrative is rot!

Waah waah! I told her – *kya baat kahi!*

Peace be upon you till eternity!

Peace be upon you till eternity

Na na – Peace be upon you till eternity

Na na! Peace be upon *you* till eternity!

Upon you!

Upon him!

Upon us!

Upon them!

But Peace Was Never Upon Us!

Aisha nor me!

Cross fade

SCENE 9

Counsellor continues. She asks a series of questions in a staccato, emotionless tone.

Counsellor: So peace was never upon you ... Or Aisha. You know, her life is pretty impressive.

Insomnia: Aisha flunked. The teacher knew as much about Shakespeare as she knew about her backside. We called her – Atilla the Hen!

Counsellor: What did Aisha say?

Insomnia: Well, she being ... un-hackneyed and all that ... had a positive disposition to the matter. For her Sheikh Saab was peerless. Her greatest hero of antiquity.

Counsellor: And you?

Insomnia: Me? I said education is the inoculation of the incomprehensible into the ignoramus by the incompetent.

A beat

Counsellor: When did you have your first attack of insomnia?

Insomnia: Around that time. My GP said I'm a victim of impaired psychomotor performance. When I heard that diagnosis I felt like an automobile at the garage. My academics came to a grinding halt.

Counsellor: Why?

Insomnia: Firstly, I was allergic to my teacher. And then the insomnia made me feel like I was perennially jet-lagged. Totally boooshed. I tried everything. Lavender oil, jasmine oil, hot Horlicks, homeopathy, herbology, mirtazapine, trazodone, doxepin, acupuncture, love.

Counsellor: You loved?

Insomnia: Yes.

Counsellor: How?

Insomnia: He was a skating instructor in Shimla with Buddhist affiliations. Talked about metta stuff. That much metta would cure me. He wooed me. Cheap roadside meals, paans, a course in Mahayana Buddhism. He spoilt me with low-brow tackiness. You want a drink?

Counsellor: No?

Insomnia: Not even a teeny-weeny sip?

Counsellor: And none for you, as well. What happened to the skating instructor?

Insomnia: Every night, I would stay awake, making notes in my head. Who is going to change the sheets? I did. Who is going to fill the water? I did. Who will water the plants? I did. Who was going to think? He was, he said. As far as he was concerned, I was just an impoverished screwing machine which hadn't reached its puberty.

Counsellor: Impoverished screwing machine...

Insomnia (hums): He used to joke; Insomnia – you have all the questions, but I have all the answers.

Counsellor: Did he?

Insomnia: He said he was born for greater things. He told me to stop smoking. So I started hiding my cigarettes and ashtray in my bedroom closet. It was a decent house. Rental. A living room with landscapes. My version of Claude Monet's impressions, which I painted, during my insomnia attacks. The room, with its two-tone shag rug, and a couple of Irani Café chairs and lap dogs, and one aubergine sofa. Life was a time capsule.

Counsellor: A time capsule.

Insomnia: One day the relationship was over. Kaboom!

Counsellor: How come?

Insomnia: He had a wife. He hadn't told me about her. I met her, once. The bitch had incomparable bosoms. Breasts, breasts, breasts: every man's ultimate destination.

Counsellor (mischievously): Er ... that's three breasts.

Insomnia: Yes. Two for the hands and one for the mouth. Old jungle saying: Woman needs memories. Man needs mammaries.

Counsellor: Oh ... Returning to the skating instructor ... You were... er... er...

Insomnia: Dumped. You can say it. I couldn't proceed through life without tears in my eyes. I tried to forget him. Memories stalked me. Once, he tried to call me. I snubbed him. He tried to maim me with some sort of acidic petroxide. It made me rethink my life.

Counsellor: In what way?

Insomnia: I discarded my capri pants, and comfy sweaters, worn shoes. I said to myself, a man wants a woman who is intellectually desirable or is it desirably intelligent. I opted for a sexier version of myself. I mean, a girl can wait for the right man to come along, but in the meantime that still doesn't mean she can't have a wonderful time with all the wrong ones. No?

Counsellor: What about your father?

Insomnia: Oh. That is a scream. Did I tell you that I started colour co-ordinating out of necessity?

Counsellor: No you didn't, actually.

Insomnia: It was a style perspective thing. One day, my clothes and my men began to tally. What colour will my man be, today? Ha ha. I became very independent. I don't like having to ask. My father called me a slut. A busybody. Men tend to do that. Classify women. Two basic categories. Slut and virgin. According to father, I was a slut and my mother was a virgin. I tried to explain to him the biological impossibility of mother being a virgin, if she gave birth to me. Ah well. Father glared at me. I think, he wanted all women to be virgins till their dying day. Are you a virgin?

Counsellor: Me? Well, I don't really think that I should –

Insomnia: Unraped. Unwrapped. Unaxed ... I am a woman who gets her living through an immortal sex life. You must try sex, too. It's really good for the central nervous system

Counsellor: I know.

Insomnia: I wrote an arty-farty proposal. Thanks to a chap in the Consulate, it was approved. Lousy lover. As a rule, men are disappointing in bed. But women! Aah, now that is another super story ... Anyway, I got a freebie. Some exchange programme thingie. I travelled to Italy. I realised, endless is the search for – romance!

Counsellor: Romance?

Insomnia: I was a hopeless romantic.

Counsellor: In what way? Explain.

Insomnia: Like all romantics, I boarded the Euro-Line and meandered my way to Verona. The City of Romeo and Juliet. The entire town is manufactured. There is a Juliet House, a Romeo House, but it is fabricated. Amazing, no? How the mythologies of our times are created? This is what I gleaned from my guide who accompanied me on a walking tour through the twisted alleyways, antiquated arches, little grassy squares, monasteries and medieval buildings. At Juliet's tomb, when I touched the stone sarcophagus, I get goose pimples. I dashed to a cafe, in close proximity to the river promenade. I'm offered a choice of two soups. Capulet and Montague. A tribute to the two premier families of the city. I select the latter. It turns out to be sumptuous portion of bean soup with pasta. My first spoon transports me. My mind wanders to the busy market in Piazza Erbe with a mansion inhabited by Romeo's family of Montagues. Nearby, there's Juliet's thirteenth-century house in Via Cappello.

Counsellor: Hmmm.

Insomnia: My insomnia is **almost** cured.

Counsellor: Really? In Verona?

Insomnia: Momentarily.

Counsellor: Nice. Your story is nice. Our remedies often in ourselves lie.

Insomnia: It is fiddle-faddle.

Counsellor: What?

Insomnia: The Endless Search for Truth! The similitude of my knowledge about Sheikh Saab, is not too spurious! If Verona is one way of seeing the man; there were others.

Counsellor: Meaning?

A beat

Insomnia: Long ago, I was the replica of a sperm. In my mummy's tummy, I heard my grandfather's bombastic baritone.

My grandfather used to train students for the administrative services. He said, you've got to study the Greek gods if you want to run a country. His mantra: if you want to join the IAS: read Shakespeare.

Counsellor: Interesting.

Insomnia: To what avail? He was reading the Sunday Edition of a newspaper on the pavement. He was shot dead by terrorists in Jallandhar.

Counsellor: I'm sorry ... Did the search for truth, continue?

Insomnia: My childhood was spent neither here nor there. I was part of a rum-and-whisky club The Pongas.

Counsellor: You said so. Earlier.

Insomnia: We met (informally) and discussed Sheikh Saab. We called him Sheikh Saab because he shook everybody. The club was the creation of our guru and mentor, Prospero the Colonialist who died of diabetes. He worked for the British Consulate and could procure oases for performances by international theatre groups. We saw 'A Tragedy' by the Royal Shakespeare Company. It was maha borrrrrrring! I vomited on Row B. Seat 17. The occupant of Row B, Seat 17 was furious. Her dishy skinny malinky gown had been ... vomited upon. Strange as it may seem, whenever I saw a Shakespeare play, I used to vomit. Prospero swore at me and called me and disowned me. You know ... it's curious, but every member of the Ponga Club is dead.

Counsellor: You said that, too. Earlier.

Insomnia: Ponga Two was Lady Hotspur, thus known, cause she was HOT. She drowned with her ship near Iceland (the ship was never found!). Four months after her death, I received a post card she had sent from a 10-day Gay Shakespeare Festival. Here it is. See it?

Counsellor: It's colourful.

Insomnia: Ponga Three was Sweet Juliet. She had a brain tumour and lapsed into coma for nine months. She was an understudy to Ophelia. I always found that touching. Pray, how can Juliet be Ophelia, I asked her? Instead of Ophelia, I imagine Juliet saying to Romeo, how should I of your love know?

Counsellor: That's Hamlet, isn't it? Act IV?

Insomnia: Speaking of Hamlet, Ponga Thirteen was Hamlet. His mother had remarried – and the poor boy used to watch his mother do it through a keyhole. He told us, mother knows, I'm watching. One day, he fell off the train and never got up. The play was over in Act II. The mother divorced after Hamlet died.

Counsellor: Were there other woes that tread upon the heel?

Insomnia: O yes. Ponga 687 was Brutus. He was a Manglore Christian who renounced the world, converted to Islam. These days, Brutus goes to the Hajj pilgrimage, every year. He does side business in cane furniture.

Counsellor: Any happy stories?

Insomnia: There were the Ponga twins, Antony and Cleopatra. Their dad was called the sexiest man on earth by Pamela Anderson. The dad was working for one of the huge international film companies in the world and had a Sunday film club for children. We saw film versions of the great Shakespeare plays. He used to play the children's game: Name, Place, Animal, Thing with us. The difference being, the names, places, animals and things had to be from the plays of Shakespeare. What seemed like a happy story was catastrophic. Antony and Cleopatra were electrocuted in a swimming pool. New Year's Eve.

Counsellor: Oh no.

Insomnia: Are my gracious words electrifying your drooping thoughts?

Counsellor: Oh of course they are! Please proceed.

Insomnia: Oh. We had a proper Ponga romance. Near the *chaiwallah's tapri* at college. Every morning, there was Helena, who was wooing Demetrius who was wooing Hermia who was wooing Lysander. This scenario was enacted, day after day. In the Diwali vacations, they went to Kaziranga. Lysander was a bird watcher. The others followed. Demetrius spotted an Oriental Honey Buzzard, Black-Shouldered Kite. When he spotted a Himala, he did **whooopie**. A one-horned Rhino woke up and roared when he heard the **whooopie.** Helena ran. Demetrius **also** ran. Hermia rolled down. Lysander broke his crown. Langoors and baboons and gibbons started howling. A herd of wild elephants chased the quartet, who ran and ran till they fell into the Brahmaputra and drowned.

Counsellor: Hmm.

Insomnia: Love is such madness, no?

Counsellor: Love is madness. What happened to Aisha?

Insomnia: The night I slept and my heart started to pound ... pound, pound, pound.

Cross fade. Insomnia (Alter Ego) begins to hum. Insomnia joins her.

SCENE 10

Focus on Insomnia and Aisha. A beat

Counsellor: You were saying about Aisha ...

Insomnia: I spoke to Aisha again!

Aisha: She sounded very despondent.

Insomnia: I wanted to thank her for caring about me. I told her I'm too mild to do anything drastic actually.

Counsellor: Like what?

Insomnia: Like last year when I genuinely wanted to kill myself I convinced myself that it was too silly. How middle class can I get?

Aisha: She needs ... something. What, I don't know! Just ... something.

Insomnia: That's when she told me the news.

Aisha: That's when I told her the news.

Insomnia: Damn.

Aisha. Damn. Damn.

Insomnia: Damn. Damn. **Damn.**

Aisha: That must be a really big dam.

Insomnia: I told her, don't joke Aisha!

Aisha: What to do? At times, ours seems like a life with no purpose?

Insomnia: Oh. And once, we were young and foolish! Remember, how we found that cane-basket of eggs at the bus stand. No one claimed it. So we dragged the cane-basket – and hurled each of the 123 eggs into the local pond.

Aisha: That old man shouted at us ... saying ... we've contaminated their vegetarian water. We ran away and hid behind a tree.

Cross fade to Counsellor

Counsellor: And then? What did you do?

Insomnia: Oh, I hid with her, naturally. I recall, the man with a dog. They were connected by a harness.

Counsellor: Really? What sort of man was he?

Insomnia: The man did not look around. He looked up and to the right, somewhere, at nothing. But that's the thing, he was staring precisely at nothing. And the dog looked at no one. Strange, because that's what dogs do in crowded spaces; they look at everyone. But this one just moved forward, as if going to work, but with fewer worries. Who was leading whom? The dog or the man?

Counsellor: The man or the dog?

Focus back on Aisha and Insomnia.

Aisha: She made a bizarre portrait of a dog and a man on a *chattai*! It was soooooo real and yet sooooo outlandish.

Insomnia: Life has no meaning.

Aisha: And meaning has no Life.

Insomnia: Yet we try to give Life a shape. No?

Aisha: That's when I asked her about that Eeeeeky fellow?

Counsellor: Eeeeeky?

Aisha: She was seeing him, I think. He was twice her age!

Insomnia: I told her Eeeeeeky was the portrait of a blinking idiot. He got married ... to a ... woman. She had incomparable bosoms.

38 inches. I didn't stand a chance with mammoth hooters like that!

Counsellor: You said so. Earlier.

Aisha: And she? She didn't marry? Never?

Insomnia: Marriage? For what? I've my cigarettes and ashtray, and liquids and fluids and two lap dogs for companionship. What more does a woman want?

Counsellor: What more does a woman want?

Insomnia: I think I'm going to have a drink! A stiff one. My throat is parched. She says, Ok.

Aisha (in changed tone): I say, Ok.

Insomnia: Then I say, my fair lady, there are better things in life than booze ... but booze makes up for not having them. Right?

Aisha: She asks me about Father!

Insomnia: How's Sheikh Saab?

Aisha: Father. Ha. Armed with a magnifying glass he reads all the newspapers for something about Bhaijaan.

Insomnia: God, if She exists, have mercy on him.

Aisha: He has stopped visiting the mosque. Occasionally, in spite of his rheumatism he climbs up the three flight of stairs to collect his pension. There is silence. Men stand up. I don't know what it is? Respect! Repentance! Repugnance!

Insomnia: No news about your brother?

Aisha: None whatsoever. I remember there was terror in the *mohalla*, fear in the *busti* ... Cops came and rounded up all the young men ... Since that day we haven't seen Bhaijaan.

Insomnia: Fie o fie!

Aisha: Father and me have been attending court hearings ever since then, but no good news about Bhaijaan ...

Insomnia: Such deception ...

Aisha: It's ok ... When beggars die there are no comets seen! Thus is the way of the world.

Insomnia: But ... The heavens themselves blaze forth the death of the princes.

Aisha: And fools? Don't forget the fools. They rule our world.

Insomnia: Three cheers to the idiots and morons of the world. May their reign end! Finally!

Aisha: Cheers.

Insomnia: Bottoms up.

SCENE 11

Aisha: Once upon a time, we travelled by BEST.

For Bhaijaan's court hearings

I love BEST buses.

They are the **best**!

Father is a BEST bus expert.

And two of my Chachus are BEST bus conductors.

A visit to Shivaji Nagar Aagar is sooo creepy.

Why should BEST operate a depot in such a remote corner of the world???

It's like Planet Pluto.

One day, we travelled in an A/C Bus.

I liked it.

Koooooooooool.

Father told me senior drivers don't want to drive star bus and AC buses.

They prefer *khatara* models, since you cannot race the new buses!

Arrey, the other day, we met Chachu in Majas.

It is a punishment depot.

It has the worst buses and a horrible set of unlimited routes.

Chachu told us to forget about Bhaijaan.

Chachu told us, Bhaijaan is history.

But how could we?

Father was silent.

I had *chutney* sandwich and *pakoras*.

The BEST trade union leader joined us.

He was Chachu's friend.

He fixed an appointment with the Deputy Chief Minister.

Our photograph was clicked.

Father and me.

But no progress in Bhaijaan's case.

Father never gave up.

Chachu tried to distract me.

He told me, the conductor's badge reveals a lot.

The first two letters tell which year the conductor was recruited into the BEST.

He told me innumerable things.

Father and me used to travel by 65.

It starts from the trucker's terminal in Wadala.

It goes to Regal Cinema via Kamathipura!

One thing I notice.

Men are not good bus travellers in the same way as women

I mean, why do men just **have** to sit with their knees wide apart

Sometimes, father and me boarded 6 Ltd.

From Trombay it goes via Bhendi Bazaar to Navy Nagar.

I have two memories.

The first memory is … this.

Father used to always shake the driver's hands before he disembarked.

I asked father why.

Father replied, it was in appreciation of their driving skills.

The drivers were baffled.

No one complimented them.

Ever.

'Tis true, you know.
The second memory is ... this.
My Copy of Sheikh Saab.
All the plays.
Father and me sat in the High Court
Awaiting the hearings
2,300 registered cases
800 pending
30 decided
1,375 cases, closed under 'A' summary category
In the midst of all that
I would read Sheikh Saab
One day, Father showed an interest
A random page
He would read a line or two
He said
Waah, kya baat hain
I would say, what?
Yeh tumhara Sheikh Saab kaafi achcha hain
Ees ko likhne aata hain
Then with a pencil which he kept in his kurta pocket
He would underline
Today
After hundreds of court hearings
This is what remains
Father's jottings
And markings
In the margins
Of Sheikh Saab's plays
No judgments.

No justice

Just this

Father's salaam to Sheikh Saab.

Wait.

Let me show you!

Father's markings and jottings along with my photographs.

Cross fade

SCENE 12

Insomnia (Alter Ego) hums and plays the harp.

'A TRUE STORY OF SORTS

By

Aisha and Aisha's Father'

And the pictures scroll with the phrases Aisha's father has underlined in court!

A four-minute scene of pictures shot by Aisha with Aisha's father's favourite Shakespeare phrases.

SCENE 13

Counsellor continues – one final time. She asks a series of questions in a staccato, emotionless tone.

Counsellor: Nice. Quite nice.

Insomnia: Is today's session over? Time to say, Ciao Meow?

Counsellor: No no no... We continue.

Insomnia: Damn! I was in the garden of my hotel in Venice, when I heard about Aisha's brother. He wanted to lead a monastic existence. Vanished from the face of the earth. No one knew where and how. You know what?

Counsellor: What?

Insomnia: Living is a dying art form. And it seems we can't do anything about it.

Counsellor: Hmm. See. You've to understand that civilisation moves on.

Insomnia: In what way?

Counsellor: Like ... where are all the fresco painters now? Where are the landscape artists? What are they doing now? The world is changing. You're fortunate to be able to do what you do.

Insomnia: Perhaps.

Counsellor: What's your next project about?

Insomnia: It is a children's story about pinballs. No fixed symbols of good and evil. Everyone will just bounce like pinballs. A story with no cuts, nor edits.

Counsellor: Ah! Sounds like an experimental film.

Insomnia: Experimental? Our planet is doomed, no?

Counsellor: That's one way of looking at things.

A beat

Insomnia: How's your baby?

Counsellor: Bonny!

Insomnia: See that's the point, no? Personally I am very pessimistic, but when, for instance, you have a baby I can't help but bless both of you – a good future. I can't be honest and tell that child, 'Oh, you shouldn't have come into this life.' You're chumped humped in this obstreperous world of ours.

Counsellor: Obstreperous? That's a very fancy word!

Insomnia: I'm learning one new word, daily. Concatenation, and vilipend, and ultracrepidarian ... and ...

Counsellor: You've chosen well.

Insomnia: I've no clue what these words mean. My organs have dulled.

Counsellor: You need to sleep.

Insomnia: Ah. The same rituals. The same routines. Everytime. Everyday. DAMN! Should I collect my prescription from the counter? On my way out?

Counsellor: Yes.

Insomnia: Thank you.

A beat

Counsellor: Er … Just one moment…

Insomnia: What?

Counsellor: You know, unlike you, I'm not an artiste. My love for the arts is that of an amateur. A few years ago, Friday night, I got into double decker. I like doing that. Like your friend – Aisha…

Insomnia: Aisha?

Counsellor: Yes … The bus was crowded, only one empty seat on the top deck, next to me. A man climbs up the stairs carrying a ventriloquist's monkey. He is humming to himself. I turn round and watch his progress towards me. The other bus passengers are grateful that he can't sit next to them. He sits next to me in silence. A few seconds pass. Then the monkey turns to me with a chirpy 'Hello!' Good lord, I think. The monkey starts chatting about the weather, the traffic service, rising prices. I try to ignore him. But the trouble is, he's a VERY interesting monkey. Before long, we're engaged in an animated conversation about the pros and cons of every subject under the sun. Throughout all this the man stares ahead, deadpan. After about 10 minutes – after all the other top deck passengers have fallen silent one by one to listen to our conversation, the monkey announces that the next stop is his and he'll have to get off. As if following orders, the man rises, still deadpan. I say thank you. No response. The monkey raises a paw in farewell.

Insomnia: It's ummmm poignant. You should write a short story out of it…

Counsellor: Will you?

Insomnia: What?

Counsellor: A sort of animation thing … you know… That's what you do and you're good at it …

Insomnia: I … er …

Counsellor: This is the monkey.

Insomnia: This!

Counsellor: Yes. The very same. I followed the man to his home.

Insomnia: What? You're a lunatic.

Counsellor: Not as much a lunatic as you, though.

Insomnia: Can I … keep this … monkey?

Counsellor: It's yours!

A beat

Insomnia: What a piece of work is man

How noble in reason

All the actors join in, one by one.

How infinite in faculties

In form and moving how express and admirable

In action how like an angel

In apprehension how like a god!

The beauty of the world

The paragon of animals —

And yet, to me, what is this quintessence of dust?

Man delights not me —

Nor woman neither

Though by your smiling you seem to say so.

A beat

Insomnia: Freeze tableau.

The session – more or less – came to an end!

And … a vague sort of conclusion

I could have said –

Finito

Adieu.

The end.

Ah.

But wait, wait, wait, there's one final epilogue of sorts.

SCENE 14

Silence. The screen lights up with an email chat alert

Message: Beep! Beep! Beep!

Insomnia: Who's there?

Message: Me.

Insomnia: William Shakespeare?

Message: Yes.

Insomnia: Whatsup?

Message: Happy birthday.

Insomnia: You remembered my happy birthday!

Message: Yes.

Insomnia: Thank you

Message: ☺

Insomnia: You have a birthday gift for me?!?!

Message: Yes.

Insomnia: You want me to shut my eyes?

Message: Oh yes.

Insomnia: Ok.

Message: ☺

SCENE 15

Insomnia (Alter Ego) enters. She sings.

A dot appears on the screen. Many dots appear. The dots finally become Insomnia!

Jazz

Dedicated to NARESH FERNANDES and DENZIL SMITH
(for the music and for re-introducing Bandra to me)

Actors: Bugs Bhargava Krishna, Rhys D'souza

Supporting cast (on video): Lionel Pereira, Ashley Nazareth, Neal Pires, Shaukat Baig, Clara Pereira, Yvette Braganza, Anisha Fernandes, Annabel Ferro Dsilva, Ella Atai, Marita Nazareth, Gopi Kukde, Ursula Da Costa

Playwright: Ramu Ramanathan

Based on research by Naresh Fernandes

Director: Etienne Coutinho

Producer: Denzil Smith

Music Composer: Merlin

Asst. Director/On Lights: Amogh Pant

Production and Light Design: Etienne Coutinho

Lighting Consultant: Viraf Pocha

Costumes: Asif Ali Beg

Production co-ordination: Akanksha Gupta

Backstage: Pooja Pant, Sudeep Modak, Sudeep Naik, Sameer Lukka

VIDEO

Director of Photography: Ramesh N

Camera: Pankaj Singh

Lights: Rajkumar

Sound: Dinkar

Production: Dezadd Dotiwalla, Rajesh Raoulo, Ashok Vishvakarma

Editor: Parag Dilip Sheth

The audience light is on. A dim spotlight on stage. There is a huge

white screen in the background. The Jazzer is seated. He does not notice the audience enter.

An overture of BOMBAIYYA JAZZ may play in the background. This continues for 10–15 minutes. Then the third bell rings.

Blackout. The Jazzer pulls out a cigarette and talks the talk with a bit of a bluesy feel ...

The screen depicts the blurred interiors of The Jazzer's house, which is a bit like the vintage homes in Bandra).

SCENE 1

The Jazzer belts out a snatch of blues

Hey Maan

It is a contemporary story that I've to tell thee

A shortish autobiography about me

A little bit of this, a little bit of that

Alternatively, you may brand it as the Epiphany of Jazzzzzzzzzzzzzzzzz

Today

I hate music, as much as I hate my mum

Instead of music I prefer cigarettes and rum

Today

Music is detestable, horrible, abominable

Disharmony, out of tune, just decibel

In 1959

Hamid Sayani's Amateur Hour was broadcast on Radio Ceylon

Now, my transistor is cast off, I'm ancient and forlorn

75 paise for an Espresso; plus ogle at cabaret chicks

Swing and bepop and the blues with Chocolate Chic

Here I pause.

For there are three elementary possibilities to let this saga unfold.

1. Tell it – like a story teller
2. Describe it – like a poet
3. Think about it – like a **Jazzin Jazzer**

So swingers and all ye buggers –
Just unlock thy minds, open 'em wide,
Forget thy sins; try to hear above the din;
My life has set; we can no longer bet
About my existence which is dumped in a bin
Dumped in a bin
In a bin
A bin
Bin
So,
I won't be cheered, my bank balance is cleared,
Merrily will I drop
From a womb to tomb,
Inside-outside.
Upside-downside
Dignified-gentrified
Chutnified and screwed

Boy saunters in. He plays some of that jazz.

SCENE 2

Me: Music. Marvellous music. What better way to die! That night, was the night, I almost died. Do you remember, boy!

The boy appears.

He: Yes.

Me: Speak up, boy!

He: Yes!

Me: Don't just stand there and gawp. Help me. My instrument has got stuck in the crevice of this chair. It's got wedged in the gap.

He: Duh!

Me: I'm going to prosecute the chair company. Take legal action.

He: Instrument???

Me: My organ.

He: Organ?

Me: Good lord. Are you some kind of half-wit? Must I spell everything, out?

He: Oh!

Me: My pee pee has got stuck.

He: Pee pee?

Me: Pee pee. Wee wee.

He: Wee wee?

Me: My Easter Eggs. Rescue me, maan. Get a cutter!

He: Oh!

Me: Yes maan. Hurry! And so he tried to free me

He asked me how I managed to get into such a situation.

I told him *(Me belts out a bit of Jazz, again):*

Boy, it's quite an art, disintegrating body parts
This bitch of a life doesn't begin at 60. That's a crazy lie.
The few teeth I have are beginning to rot.
My friends are dying, my arthritis is not
I smell of Tiger Balm, not Chanel # 5;
My new pacemaker's all that keeps me alive.
When asked of my past, every detail I know,
Except – what was I doing 10 minutes ago?
Well, you get the idea, what more can I say?
One day, you will read my obituary, like I do every day;
You will find my name is there, and I'll be dead

A two-bit musician, who died in his bed

A beat. A huge grandfather clock on the screen strikes time and then stops.

Ah.

Did you hear that?

My pee pee is stuck. And –

Time has stopped –

It's Tick Tick Tick.

Perhaps Time is Sick?

Of me?

Perhaps Time wishes to bid au revoir.

To me?

A beat

So let me stare at you with my cataract eye –

While all of you sit still,

And listen like a three-year-old child:

From the day I was born to my final will.

SCENE 3

The following scene is enacted on the giant audiovisual screen: Church music. Various people who played a part in the Jazzer's life come on the screen to offer their condolences.

Priest 1: We gather here to offer worship, praise and thanksgiving to God for the gift of a life which has now been returned to God.

Man 1: Ya. He was a nice bugger. We wanted to give him typical jazz funeral. A march by the family and friends; a brass band from the home to the cemetery. But no money, maan. And no family and friends, maan. He was a loser.

Priest 1: We gather here to commend the dead to God's merciful love and to plead for the forgiveness of their sins.

Man 2 (desperate): Arrey. Chedva Poder. Susagad. Sorpetol. You owed me for all the money you lost on the horses at the Derby! How could you die? I'm *kadkaa*! Totally kaput!

Priest 1: We gather to bring hope and consolation to the living.

Woman 1 (in Konkani): He passed away, did he? Oh! *(makes sign of cross)*

Woman 2: I hope you rot in hell for having left me with three girls and one in my tummy for that whore.

Woman 3: He was a boozard. I hope he has left me some money from his will. I need cash to run my beauty parlour. Big problems, ya.

Woman 4: Who died? I'm not feeling too good. In other words: nauseous. Ever since my chemotherapy. What was the name of the person who died?

Woman 5: You were so unhappy with that woman! She ruined you.

Woman 6: Hallelujah! I'm waiting for you, honey. In heaven! Praised be the lord.

Priest 1: We gather here to affirm the Church's belief in the sacredness of the human body and the resurrection of the dead.

Man 1: He and me had planned it. Throughout the march, the band should play sombre dirges. Perhaps a hymn like *Closer Walk With Thee* ...

Man 2 (desperate): Chedva Poder, what is this? I opened your safety vault at Goa Urban Co-operative Bank and what do I see! Hundreds of cheques, I'm delighted. But saala, all bounced cheques from those big-shot music directors in Bollywood! I'm petulant. I'm angry. You let those *haraami* parasites exploit you?

Man 1 (continuing): ... Then we can play the *Saints Go Marching In* belted out in a swinging fashion.

Old Man: Although he was not a Hindu, he was almost like one of us. *Ishwar uski atma ko shanti de.*

Priest 1: We gather to renew our awareness of God's mercy and judgment and to meet the human need to turn always to God in times of crisis.

Man 3: He hated violinists. He used to say why is lightning like a violinist's fingers?

Answer: Neither one strikes in the same place twice.

Old Woman (in clipped tones): The Managing Committee of our Housing Society express their sincerest condolences for this loss. Our thoughts are with the kith and kin of the deceased soul. The points he raised about tree grafting in our last Managing Committee Meeting were well worth considering. He was a pillar of strength; and a friend to all.

Man 3: He picked up that John Coltrane DVD in New York. Koooooool. He played for Shankar Jaikishan, Laxmikant Pyarelal, R D Burman, for the money.

Priest 1: Holy God, Holy Strong, Holy Immortal, have mercy on us

Man 3: He used to hate Bollywood music directors. His favourite joke was: A Bollywood music director and all the Bollywood villains are standing in the middle of the road. Which one do you run over first, and why? Answer: The music director. First the pricks – and then the kicks.

Priest 1: Blessed are you, O Lord; teach me your statutes. Blameless in the way. Alleluia.

Woman 1 (in Konkani): Blessed are the blameless in the way, who walk in the law of the Lord. Alleluia.

Woman 2: My soul has longed to desire your judgements at all times. Alleluia.

Woman 3: My soul slumbered from weariness; strengthen me by your words. Alleluia.

Woman 4: Incline my heart to your testimonies, and not to covetousness. Alleluia.

Woman 5: Dejection took hold of me because of sinners who abandon your law. Alleluia.

Woman 6: I am a companion of all who fear you, and who keep your commandments. Alleluia.

Priest 1: Again and again, in peace let us pray to the Lord.

Man 3: He used to say, why don't Jazz musicians play hide and seek. Answer: Coz if they hide, in this country, no one will ever look for them. Ha-ha. He had a corny sense of humour.

Priest 1: Lord, have mercy. Lord, have mercy. Lord, have mercy.

Everybody: Amen!

SCENE 4

As before, the boy appears

That was that.
Yooo hoo hoo.
Four three two –
One disadvantaged night.
In the not so distant past,
Out of the blue came he!
A shining knight, he gave me a fright
Oh boy
Could he hold a High C???

The boy appears and plays the saxophone

Higher and higher every day,
He riffed and raffed; without any lax
He wouldn't rest, I would beat my breast,
When I heard him serenade his sax.

Me: Do you remember our first meeting, boy?

He: Yes.

Me: You found the place easily?

He: Kind of.

Me: Forgive the house. It's a mess.

He: It's ... it's ... ok.

Me: What is your hammer?

He: What?

Me: What do you wield, boy? *(Jazzer mimes)*

He: Sax.

Me: What sax?

He: ? ? ? ? ? ? ? ? ?

Me: Alto? Tenor? Baritone? Soprano?

He: Well ...

Me: And you want to learn jazz?

He: Yes.

Me: Do you know what Jazz *is*?

He: Jazz is ...

Me: Hey! Speak up, boy. Cat got your tongue? ... Jazz is ... music invented by the devil for the torture of the saints.

He: Ok.

Me: You know who said that?

He: Who?

Me: Me!

He: Good.

Me: So boy, tell me something about you? Who the fuck are you? Are you religious? *Ad majoram dei gloriam.* Do you believe in the greater glory of a God who has forgotten all about us? Do you? Do you smoke? I used to. *(In a false baritone)* Go gay with Gaylord fine filter cigarettes. Smoking it – was good for my pitch, boy! You do pot? The stuff from Afghanistan is stupendous, no? How quickly can you roll a joint? 30 seconds? 20? Or you smoke that ready-mix stuff? How many girlfriends? None. Yaaba daaba doo. I had six. Now divorced. All gone ... with the wind. I'm a free homo sapiens. Women! Such vermin, I tell you. Hey boy. Why are you shivering?

He: I'm not ...

Me: Why are your fists, clenched?

He: My fists aren't ...

Me: No girlfriends, huh? Beware of women. The damnedest of our tribe. You want a whiskey?

He: No?

Me: You've a letter of recommendation. Ha. This obsession with order. With classification.

He: Yes.

Me: You play for a band?

He: Yes.

Me: Any good?

He: Well ...

Me: This letter is signed by your mother. I know your mother.

He: She sends her regards.

Me: How's she?

He: Fine.

Me: She was a little one. Your mother. She and me used to attend the Teatro. She sat on a pillow and watched it. With her basket of cakes, pattice, cucumber sandwiches, lime cordial. In Colvale. Open air. Cashew plantations. Full moon. Heaven maan!!! Ask her? Ask her?

He: I will.

Me: At the end of the show, your granddad was honoured. Shawl and coconut. He played *'Aye dil hai mushkil'* on his clarinet. From *CID*. If O P Nayyar would have heard it, he would have had a musical paralysis. Totally improvised, maan. He chucked out all the pre-meditated arrangements. Ha-ha. Crazy bugger.

He: Right.

Me: She did that studio deal?

He: Who?

Me: Your mother?

He: Negotiating.

Me: Negotiating?

He: 16 tracks.

Me: 16-tracks studio. That's good. Tell her to be tough. It's business out there. *Dhanda*. No one is bothered about the music. We were fools. All of us. We thought it's about the compositions, about the tunes. We were soooooooo stupid. Tell your mother to be a smart ass. Ok?

He: Yes.

Me: So, you want to practice on Tuesdays, Saturdays and Sundays?

He: Yes.

Me: Sunday is not possible.

He: Oh.

Me: Let me be straight. I don't work on Sundays. It's a holiday. Even your grandfather believed in that philosophy. Six days a week. Sunday holiday. Did you know that?

He: No.

Me: When did he die? Four years ago?

Me: Three and a half.

Me: 93, no?

He: 92.

Me: Not a poop when he died. He, Chic Chocolate, Chris Perry, Frank Fernandes, Anthony Gonsalves, Mickey Correa. Saala, the Badshahs of Bollywood. Jazzed their way through. All gone. Just like that. Whooosh. No one cares a damn.

He: Yes.

Me: We used to jam at C Ramchander's house. Your grandfather used to pencil the notations. Then that Keshavrao would go and make the score sheets for next day's recording. For a few annas. Tough times.

He: Yes.

Me: Braz Gonzales. He was super duper on the alto sax, maan. And Leslie Godhino, the dada of drums. You know him? Died recently. He's the silhouette in *Teesri Manzil*. That drum solo. '*Oh haseena zulfon waali.*' That's not Shammi Kapoor. That's apna Leslie, maan.

He: Yes.

Me: For the shoot, they gave him a rotten drum set to play. Leslie said, no. Then someone told him he gets thrice the amount he gets for recordings. So Leslie did it. He got paid for 10 minutes of shooting. Grabbed the cash and hit the bar. He used to joke. I get more money when I pretend to drum. Sad, no?

He: Yes.

Me: Drumming is more strenuous than any other instrument in the world. It kills you. Saala whored his talent. For whom? Those phillumy musicians always missing the first beat. Out of synch. So sloppy. Listen to those songs. Worthless. All stolen. And we had to play it like monkeys. Imitate and duplicate. What to do. *Paapi paet ke liye, biddu!*

He: I went for Leslie's funeral. Half expected him to get out of the coffin – and drag his handmade drum from studio to studio.

Me: Crazy bugger.

He: Yes.

Me: Leslie met Dave Brubeck in Delhi. You heard of Brubeck? Crazy bugger.

He: Yes.

Me: In those days there was prohibition. No booze. So they jammed in a hotel room at Claridges. There was: Leslie, Frankie (powerful saxist, maan), Brubeck, and that drummer – whatshisname ....

He: Joe Morello ...

Me: Good, you know. Morello and Leslie. Leslie demonstrated the phrases from Indian tabla. Gave them a flavour of rhythm patterns. *Ten matras*. Mathematical progressions. He played the bols on his drum set. The phirangs were *maha* impressed. Saala, he was good. Apna Leslie. He used to read books about music. He lent me. You know, Jim Cooper, Mac Bacon, Portgelli. I've them lying around. If you're interested.

He: I am.

Me: Then that Brubeck returned to his studio and created 'Take

Five'. It has a drum solo. Leslie used to play it for us. In 5/4 time. It a classic. I feel so proud when I used to listen to it. You know 'Take Five'?

He: Yes.

Me: Composed by Paul Desmond. He was a *baap* among alto sax players. Can you play it?

He: What?

Me: 'Take Five'.

He: I'll try.

Me: Boy, musicians don't try. Either they play. Or they can't.

He: Yes.

Me: 'Take Five'. It used to be our national anthem, maan.

He: Yes.

Me: Hit the notes, maan. ... Wait, wait, wait. Where's the ephing balance?

He: Balance?

Me: You're playing the sax. Not the *toor toori* at Chowpatty.

He: Yes.

Me: Remember: one thing. When you play music, you have to find the truth.

He: Yes.

Me: Finding the truth is not easy.

He: Yes.

Me: You know why? Cause truth in music is that whose contradictory is also true. You knew that? No? Good, now you do. You want a whiskey before you start?

He: No.

Me: Me, I'm going to have a peg. Hope that's ok with you?

He: Yes.

Me: Okey dokey. Now, don't gawp. Take it away, boy. Show me what you got.

The boy plays 'Take Five'.

SCENE 5

The Jazzer talks the talk, again. A bit like Jim Morrison doing his Lizard King monologues – with an occasional riff, here and there. On the screen, there are old black and white pictures; and a collage of songs as the Jazzer speaks.

Years ago.

I was born.

An inconsequential sort of occurrence.

Even then, I wasn't worth twopence.

Everyone was Busyyyyy.

A new country was being given birth to, you see.

Ha ha.

It would make no diff

My Grandma said – we will continue to be scrrrrrrrewed, happily, ever after

Time passed

Riots unabated.

From Karachi to Bombay, we crossed borders

From one disarray to a bigger disorder

Blood on our tracks

Blood everywhere

The army was escorting us.

Grandma said, What do you get when you drop a piano on an army boss.

A flat major.

Ha-ha.

Grandma was a riot!

When I had my first breath

My Mummy almost bled to death.

So, did **The New Country.**

It was the era of the quiet forgotten static, you see.

Lots of austerity.
Less of affluence.
A time when people like my Grandma – believed that happy days would be here again
Church choirs, Gregorian chants, symphony orchestras
The samba, the ramba, a little ditty
Above all – a bit of human dignity.
I was born in this city
And that is a real pity
My birth was a tedious process.
It took my Mummy ten and a half months of duress
To throw me ... 'from the frying pan into the high seas.'
The hospital recorded my birth
Onto this earth
It was strife.
There was a hopeless midwife
Then Dad played music on his sax
His half-tones lifted me out of the tummy
And unshackled me from my Mummy.
Grandma, who witnessed it all, said ... Dad's sax is better than his sex.
Two months after my birth, Dad was missed
Your Dad is a bigamist, my Mummy hissed
What bigamist meant I did not know.
There was talk Dad would be sentenced to six years imprisonment.
So Dad absconded from the bus station
Partition, everywhere. For me and the Nation!
They say, Dad ran away with the Manager's son
There was a scandal. But Dad was fun.
We never saw him, again.

Mummy endured the pain
Sigh
Grandma brought me up.
Grandma had alternative sources of income.
She was a seamstress and a tuition teacher
Not to mention the proceeds from two of the rooms which she rented out.
In Dhobhi Talao.
Under normal circumstances, this would have been more than sufficient for the three of us
But yabada yabada doo.
No one had not taken into account my musical streak.
I wanted to be a drummer.
A pianist.
Some kind of frrrrrrrrrrrrrreak.
Next door was an empty room
17 by 14 feet full of doom and gloom
Except for Augustus who played the bass
Oh, and his songs they were class
Every afternoon, Augustus rehearsed musical strands
He and Mac and the Teetotaller's Band.
I watched them practice, I saw them jam
Till, they vamoosed for their gigs in the local tram
Augustus constructed me a biscuit drum
Mac bought me a Five Rupee Piano and became my chum
One sunny day,
When I was a seven-year-fool
Mummy decided that I better be admitted into a school
The Princie told us they admit only the best
Saying so, she gave me a simple test
I stood up on my toes.

And on that day – began my woes.
Princie asked me to do the multiplication sets
She asked me to recite the alphabets
I said –
A for Armstrong
B for Billie Holliday
C for Chick Corea
D for Davies. You know, Miles Davies
E for Ellington
F for Fitzgerald
G for Goodman. You know Benny Goodman
H for Hubbard. You know Freddie Hubbard
The Princie was bamboozle-ified.
She was flabbergasted.
She said, the boy's kind of strange but otherwise OK!
I was admitted.
On the screen, the fuzzy dot has grown into Jazzer Junior.
Oh yeah –
That's me
I'm going to school
Oh boy –
I resemble someone
I wonder who?
I wonder who!
I wonder! I wonder?
Who Who?
Jazzer Junior plays a ditty on the screen.

SCENE 6

The following scene is enacted on the screen. The six wives appear;

resonances of The Order of Service. The wives or their caricatures come on the screen to offer their condolences.

All six women (chanting): O perfect Love, all human thought transcending,

Lowly we kneel in prayer before thy throne,

That ours may be the love which knows no ending,

Whom thou for evermore dost join in one.

Woman 1 (in Konkani): We are here in the presence of God to witness marriage with him.

Woman 2: After the Goa Carnival, he said let's go to Bombay. That's where there is work for musicians. So, we came to Bombay. At that time Bombay was beautiful. Not like this. *Bakvaas.* Bullshit.

Woman 3: I first saw him at Churchgate. In those days, Churchgate was **the** jazz jamboree. His band was jamming at Hotel Astoria's famous Venice restaurant. He was handsome. A hunk. Hot!!!! He used to crack these wonderful jokes in between songs. Why was Jesus Christ not born in Bombay? ... Because they could not find three wise men and a virgin. ... I told him I was a virgin. He said, prove it.

Woman 4: I'm sorry I've no memory of who you're talking about ... a Jazz musician you say at the Taj ... did you know The King of Jazz – Duke Ellington – stayed at the Taj Mahal Hotel in 1963? He was forced to eat rogan josh for four days because when he ordered fish and prawns, the waiter said ... *(shakes his head from side to side)* ... and the Duke thought he was saying, No. It's there in the Far East Suite.

Woman 5: He did a good Duke Ellington imitation at The Talk of the Town ... Whatdoyoucallit, Not Just Jazz By The Bay. Ah yeah. He said I was very good singer. Beyond that, I was nothing for him. I got a break. He made a contract. I couldn't sing without his permission. I had no brains, therefore I signed. And he? He went back to his wife. Indian men, I tell you? Wimps.

Woman 6: He travelled with his wife to New York for a show. He called me. I asked, why me? He said you're the only one I know who has a phone.

All Six Women (chanting): That ours may be the love which knows no ending,

Whom thou for evermore dost join in one.

Woman 1 (in Konkani): According to the teaching of Christ, marriage is a lifelong union between two persons who have been joined together as husband and wife.

Woman 2: He tried to join the film industry. No one gave him a break. So he joined a small orchestra, for entertaining private parties. Faltoo time pass. Sometimes, he would play for those Parsi weddings. They wanted all that high-and-mighty classical music. They gave a lot of money – and very nice food. He would bring the food home. And brandy too. They called that a Parsi peg, a large one, four fingers. He used to bring it for me. Then get me tight and then ... That's how we have four children; and three are *khallas*. Seven in all. It's too much, *mhanje,* too much.

Woman 3: It was too much. One day we were at the Taj, a Latin band came there, called Garimbas. He had a two-hour break. We strolled next to the Gateway. Along the sea. Those were wonderful moments. Then we slipped into the ladies cloakroom. He on the pot. Me on him. Super. Sublime. My first time. I was surrounded by toilet paper and a flush tank. His hands on my buttocks. He took me. Umm. Like he took his sax. He played me. Every note on my body. He was something.

Woman 4: You like jazz, don't you? Here, listen to something from the Far East Suite .... The Duke ... Splendid sound ...

Woman 5: The sound system at Berry's was splendid. Bombaywallahs call it Mocha, or Locha. The Tandoori Chicken was mast kalander. Oh yeah. After singing, I ate two. What to do? No lunch. He didn't let me perform with anyone else. He broke the bones of one Muslim chap who tried to sing with me.

Woman 6: He called from a Beatles bar in Liverpool. He was drunk. Said he was slurring because he had gobbled fish and chips. He asked me, if I knew what was John Lennon's last hit? I said, no. He started laughing and said, 'the pavement'.

All Six Women: O perfect Life, be thou their full assurance
Of tender charity and steadfast faith,
Of patient hope and quiet, brave endurance,
With childlike trust that fears no pain nor death.

Woman 1 (in Konkani): Marriage is part of God's good purpose in creation. It is therefore not to be thought of lightly but held in honour.

Woman 2: Film industry is sooo communal. It's too much, mhanje too much. They didn't want non-Hindus to play. It's a fact. Except Shanker Jaikishen who didn't want non-Catholics. They weren't communal. We were planning to return to Goa, the next day. Luckily, that evening, he got a small recording. They liked what he played. They told him, 'If you leave Bombay we will break your legs.' Ha-ha. They wanted him to play music for them. No auditions. He got regular work. He became a workaholic.

Woman 3: He was sooo lazy. *Kaam chor.* Used to trip with the other guys. No self control. One night during a show, he came backstage. He caught me with Richard ... or was it Jude? Can't remember. He didn't take it, well. *Bacha saala.* Men are such babies. He bought a bike. Thought it was a Harley Davidson, but it was a *khatara* Bullet. We had an accident. It was deliberate. He had *that* streak. So I left him. Started a beauty parlour in Kolkata.

Woman 4: We shifted to Kolkata from Burma. My husband met Sonny Rollins and Stan Getz in Bombay. You heard Getz's salaam to Bombay? Here it is ...

Woman 5: Dejection took hold of me. I popped pills like crazy, maan. But I can still hold a high octave. I cut a record. In Konkani. It's doing so-so. I'm the Bessie Smith of Konkani. Oh yeah.

Woman 6: He was the last person I spoke to. I told him to scatter my ashes in the Ganges – like Charles Mingus. Then, I slashed my wrists. By the time he reached me, I was dead.

All six women: Grant us joy which brightens earthly sorrow;
Grant us peace, which calms all earthly strife,

And to life's day the glorious unknown morrow
That dawns upon eternal love and life.

SCENE 7

Jazzer talks the talk again, a bit like a Frank Zappa song.
Me: Yeah,
Grandma spoke of evenings at the Rendezvous
When she went to The Apollo Room.
Sizzling as the steak on her plate
She sipped pink champagne; umm, how she ate!!!
Dial 21901 – you got that right?
Candle light, her gown is white
Chris Perry and Laura and Chic Chocolate
They made music that was grrrrrrrrrreat
Oh yeah.
To have a rendezvous with the trumpet
To venerate the trumpet, oh, to kick that ass
Not muted nor mutilated, like Sunday Mass
Trumpeter, what are you sounding now?
Asked a fat cat, top hat.
Cherry Pink Apple Blossom Time
Speaking of time.
Do you realise
The Physical Impossibility of Living – In the Mind of Someone Who Is
Actually Dead
The Ludicrousness of Talking About Music – With Someone Who Hates Music.
This takes me to one day in the distant past
Long ago

A pool of light. Jazzer adopts staccato speech. A ticking clock appears on the screen, keeping time.

The cock crows

The sun rises

I walk past Bandra village

The stink of fish manure

I'm at the Basilica of Our Lady of the Mount

The priest preaches

I whistle a bit of the West End Blues

I dream.

I am in Portugal

Invited, by a bony, hyper-ventilating woman

She likes improvisation; so-called free jazz; bits and pieces of stuff like that

She says, come

I go

Like everyone else I am happy

I think – like maan – I'll have a wife at home and a horny girlfriend in Lisbon

That's not to be

She hates sex

She is a nun

That leaves me 'none' too happy.

The school is down town

It's pretty … run down

The children have, like, learning disabilities

By Portuguese standards, they are from poor families

Ha ha.

They would be bloody bourgeoisie, here

Their pocket money would be greater than my DRM, I fear.

I cphing don't know what to do.

I speak English
They don't
Silence
I look into my *thella*
I have my pocket trumpet
A tenor saxophone
A conch
Bells and whistles
I plonk them in the middle of the floor
It is a broken down factory
Amazing acoustics, maan
The kids are shy, scared
I didn't look like any of them
The nun gestures
They pick up the instruments in the middle of the floor
They make noise
Screech
Squeal
My ears are sore
I have an ephing headache.
I pop a pill
I try to chill
Maan,
Then I clap my hand
The nun helps me out
She translates and shouts
I do a few rhythmic exercises
I pound the factory floor
I clap my hands
I get their attention

I make them disperse to far corners of that one-acre room

I get them to listen

They giggle, they snigger

They return

I asked if they figured

What did they hear?

They say, they heard the person next to them laughing or belching, shuffling or scratching, burping or farting

We break for lunch

My migraine is malignant, maan

I puke

I panic

I want to go home.

Amen,

My mind is organised

Next day, I do exercises at seven

Oh yeah

No manna from heaven

They – still – hear the people next to them

Then one of them

She hears trucks, and airplanes, a guy on a bicycle with his cycle bell

And then,

Birds, leaves rustling, wind, the sound of snow.

Next day, a miracle happens

A young boy, with scabs on his skin, Francis Almeida says something

He says he can hear the breathing of the person next to him

He hears his own heartbeat

He senses his own nervous system

I smile

This is it, children
This is Jazz
It is that simple.
Aaaah
But everyone laughs their loudest laugh
Francis Almeida is the class clown, you see
They think
I'm a crazy bugger
So
I ask them to try and play the instruments
In the centre of the factory floor
They don't want to
I order them to
Any instrument; any which way
A circle is formed
They try the pocket trumpet – they fail
They puff their cheeks and puff and stuff – they fail
Someone says, let Francis Almeida do it
And he does it, of course
He does play the trumpet – I mean – not play it,
But make music
A little boy raises his hand
Garcia da Orta
He plays the piano
In the lunch break, the others surround him
He is a hero
Garcia da Orta is a Jazzer, maan
He and Francis Almeida
Three days to go
Francis Almedia points me a cupboard

It's locked

I open it with my Swiss Knife

It's full of instruments

Francis Almeida mimes to me

I understand

In that school the teachers never let the children play with it – because they thought the kids would break them

I do dumb charades

Francis comprehends

Next thing,

He and me carry every instrument out of the closet and bring it to the factory floor

The next class is brilliant

Everyone runs into the room

They see me

They see the nun

They halt

They think they are at fault

On cue, I twist and scream

They join me

There is a charge of the light brigade to the huge pile of musical instruments

Chaos. Cacophony.

We repeat Day 1

We repeat Day 2

I get them to listen

I give them instruments

I create sections, music sections

They follow me

10 to 15 minutes I have an orchestra

By next day, we complete an unfinished ballad

The nun is seated
Her mouth, open
'How did you do that? They never listen to anything. These brats never do what we tell them to do.'
That's that, maan.
My moment of glory
I return to the Basilica of Our Lady of the Mount
Father Harry welcomes me
I boast
He beams and raises a toast
I wonder, why?
He tells me
In 1508 the first Portuguese ship, which sailed into Bombay harbour was captained by who?
Francis Almeida
I hear trumpets
Tra la la la la la.
And there was a Garcia da Orta, too
He built a manor house on the island in 1554
Crazy maan
I say to myself
How time passes
Look around
This was a village, with paddy fields
All of us – cultivators
Some cultivated fish
Others rice, cabbage, colewort, radish
And water-melons, and onions as sweet, and tasty as an apple
Some were potters, some tapped toddy
And some like me – they jazzed all day and all night!
Today,

Nothing remains
The land beneath me – reclaimed
The history behind me – rewritten
The music around me – remixed
And jazz?
A note or two – of razz ma tazz
A little bit of rock n roll
Bollywood, Hollywood, taking his toll
Most of us in penance!
Coz better than music is **silence!**
No more legends about this land
That's our disgrace
Our lives are grandiose
Everything else is paltry
RIP
RIP
RIP
Rest in peace
Jazzer walks away. Lights dim.

SCENE 8

A rapid-fire five minute scene with Boy on stage and Boy on screen. This scene is the Jazz In Bollywood Antakshri Competiton.

The bits between the songs will have Charlie Chapin type slides to aid the audience. These slides can contain information about the Film, the music director and arrangers!

It should be wild and wacky not nostalgic and humdrum!

SCENE 9

The Jazzer and the boy have a final talk.

Me: Somebody there? Fee fie fo fum. I kind of smell a … human bum!

He: Hello.

Me: Who?

He: It's … er … me …

Me: Of course I know who it is. I never forget a voice. Especially if it's off-key.

He: Yes.

Me: Do you remember our first meeting, boy?

He: Yes.

Me: Now my retina is detached. Mind is demented. But the hearing is good, so far …

Knock. Knock. The other day, there was a piece being played on the radio – and I thought it was me. Of course, it wasn't. It was Jean Luc Ponty *(cackles)*. Let's see how good your mind is? Tell me, you are participating in a race. You overtake the second person. What position are you in?

He: First.

Me: Oh. Shit of the Holy Ass. Concentrate, boy. If you overtake the second person and you take his place, you are second! Ready? Try not to screw up the next question. If you overtake the last person, then you are...?

He: Second last?

Me (cackles): Wrong, maan. How the eph can you overtake the last person? Think, man, think. You're on planet earth. There is no escaping that, is there? Get me a Brufen. Ah. My head!

He: Yes.

Me: So, you have a scholarship. For music. That's good. Your mother must be proud of you? Does she continue to be pushy? Overprotective?

He: Well …

Me: She, almost screwed you up! I had warned her. No soccer, no goal-keeping. You lied to me. Unfortunately, for you, I saw you at Cooperage before you broke your fingers. Remember?

He: Yes.

Me: You were an untutored Bandra boy. You needed equipoise. When do you exit?

He: Tonight.

Me: Tonight. Super. So you have come to bid your adieus and au reviors to the old bugger. Who knows if the old bugger is alive and kicking when you're back. Ha ha.

He: Er … It's not like that …

Me: So, boy you want some words of wisdom. Eh? Here goes, boy. Write it down. Jazz uses a human being … and not the other way around.

He: Hmm.

Me: How's that girl?

He: Girl?

Me: The girl you fell for? You and she were at it. The cops got you – in the car. They busted you. You had no money for the bribe. So they tonked you in the jail. You called me. At three in the morning. I came and got the two of you. Made hot chocolate, some salad. Played some Artie Shaw. You were virile and I was full of tenderness and affection. Right?

Me: Right!

Me: Next day, you were in form during the class. Your best. That's why I, always, say one good enough reason to fall in love is … you play better jazz.

He: Hmmm.

Me: So, where's the girl?

He: Eh?

Me: Abandoned, eh? A pity. We have become a world of overworked, over-exhausted buggers in this treadmill of life! Hmm. How long will you be away from home?

He: Three years.

Me: Three years. Waoh. That's something. Music for three years.

It's like intoxication. Enjoy yourself. If they ask you shovel their snow, do it! Make money. Go to the Jazz Café. Busk and jam. Ask people, what they played? Avoid discos and DJs. Rehearse. Practise. Smoke them, cigarettes. You smoke?

He: Yes.

Me: Super. Life would have been unpleasant, if it was not for smoking, no? Light me up!

He: Sure.

Me: Umm. Cigarettes is like good art. You die for it. Ha-ha. I'm so brilliant tonight. It must be my drugs. Taken a bigger dose than usual. Drug me two times, babe. Hence the lucidity. Hmm. Let's forget the sentimental phrases and goodbyes. Play something for me, boy?

He: Yes.

Me: A final finale, as it were. Jazz blues score. *(Snaps his fingers)* I'll sit this one out.

He: Yes.

Boy plays a chord.

He: Wait, a moment.

Once I met Bismillah Khan Saab.

A crazy bugger.

If he was black, he would have been Armstrong

You know what he said to me?

He said –

Musicians don't invent music

The music is somewhere behind

It's been there for a long long time

The musician merely discovers it

You got that, boy?

He: Yes.

Me: Now, play. Follow the music and it will take you home. Turn me on, boy!

Boy plays. Jazzer listens. Dozes off. Boy stops. He stands over the Jazzer. Stubs his cigarette. Freeze tableau.

SCENE 10

The following scene is enacted on the screen: The three men gather (as in Scene 3). They are The Surviving Male Members of the Malignant Migraine's Club. They come on the screen to offer their condolences.

All three men (chanting): We are The Surviving Male Members of the Malignant Migraine Club.

We are four of us.

One Down; and three to go!

Man 1: The last song we did together was at Famous Studios for RK Films. That dream sequence in *Awara*. You remember? Hundreds of musicians with chorus and all. '*Ghar aaya mera pardesi.*' He packed up after that. *Said khuda hafiz* to film songs.

Man 2: All four of us used to swim. We used to go to gym, fly kites. Some like Shanker of Jaikishen did boxing, kushti. All of us did it. Otherwise, we would have gone totally insane with the music. Non-stop headache. Film music paid us better than a gig at the Taj. Play a film song and get Rs 400–500.

Man 3: The 'informers' came every morning with a chit of paper – and informed us about the recordings. They decided who played. All hundred musicians. There was no telephone, cell phone in those days! One informer worked for 3–4 music directors. *Saale, jhugadoos.* The music director had no clue. Whatyousaying, you didn't know this?

All three men (chanting): We are The Surviving Male Members of the Malignant Migraine Club.

We are four of us.

One down; and three to go!

Man 1: After a recording we used to pop two aspirins and two strong pegs. It was our daily *dawai.*

Man 2: Chic Chocolate used to say Sohrab Modi is a baap. Even a blind man can see his film. Chic Chocolate was a trumpeter. He could also play the clarinet, sax, piano, combo, bongo, maracas, and chicolo. He created magic for Madan Mohan. That Donkey's Serenade in *Taxi Driver*. He died on 18th May. All four of us were there. In Colaba. We returned from the cemetery. O P Nayyar came. Asha Bhonsle said, salaam. Memories ...

Man 3: Let's get this straight. There was undue prestige attached to classical music. Once Anthony Gonsalves did some chords and rhythms. Anthony was good. Laxmikant's teacher. But the music director shouted, this is not Bhairavi. So we had to re-harmonise, everything. The music director thought he had God's gift! Saala, two-paisa idiot!

All three men (chanting): We are The Surviving Male Members of the Malignant Migraine Club.

We are four of us.

One Down; and three to go!

Man 1: Anil Da met him. You know, Anil Biswas. He wanted to know about fugues. He gave him a lec-dem. Micro-tones, shrutis, scales. He told me afterwards, it's tough. These chaps won't get it. Background nahin hain re.

Man 2: RD, or was it SD, sent me to Regal. Here, take money. Watch film. Listen to that score. Make notations. I did it with teeny-weeny pencil. They liked the sound. They adapted it. It was lazy fusion. I used the word for the first time: **fusion.** I was given Rs 10. Extra tip.

Man 3: We did background music. Entire reels. From start to finish. Huge orchestras. No breaks. The Hindu fellows had to by-heart it. We called them by-heartkars. Ha-ha. Saala, it was painful. Coz we could read the staff notations, they couldn't. Pure suffering, maan. Sometimes it was three days and three nights with bed roll and all. These days, it's better. *Aao, gao, jao*!

All three men (chanting): We are The Surviving Male Members of the Malignant Migraine Club.

We are four of us.

One Down; and three to go!

Man 1: He was a good man, but ...

Man 2: He was a good teacher, but ...

Man 3: Whatyousaying but ...? He was a good musician. Strong double bass. Very solid technician. Left hand was very light. No?

All three men (chanting): We are The Surviving Male Members of the Malignant Migraine Club.

We are four of us.

One Down; and three to go!

Amen!

SCENE 11

Boy comes on stage. He speaks for the final time.

He: Ma woke me up –

It was early morning in New York

He's gone, she said.

I knew – who.

There was silence.

His life flashed.

Our first meeting

He rescuing me and Wendy from the police station

The tongue lashing at Cooperage

The pee pee meeting

Our last meeting

So many moments

That sneering, leering tone

– Boy, hit me with your best

I did

He said, no good.

He knew what he was talking about
He was a servant of jazz!
A true-blue servant!
Boss, there was no one quite like you
When he was in the ICU
Ma went to look him up
There was silence
How's the boy, he had asked?
Not so good, Ma replied.
Why?
Racism and such, Ma said.
He roared –
In the stores there
In the hotels about the streets
Indians and street dogs are measured by the same yard stick
Niggers, pariahs
Is this the abuse they fling at him???
Yes, said Ma.
Ah
Deep down in my heart a thousand and one scorpions sting me
Hearing this I feel so damn good
Now that boy has a taste of what I suffered
In this country of ours
Hmm
This is what Ma reported to me.
I laughed.
She said what –
I said, nothing.
What else could I say.
He was a ... crazy bugger!

But

Stop it

No more sighs, no more tears

No more words to ruin the final finale

As he would say,

Boy, sometimes the best musician is he who knows how to hold his silence

So from one crazy bugger to another.

Farewell!

Till we meet in heaven or hell

Or in a café in Paris

Wherever we meet

We'll play that jazz

Boy plays his instrument – in silence. A beat

Lights dim.

Interview with Ramu Ramanathan

What were the challenges you faced when you did theatrical adaptations of fiction?

I adapted Vaikom Mohamed Basheer's *Me Grandad 'Ad An Elephant* and Margaret Duras' *L'Amante Anglaise*. Both are extraordinary writers. I used to sleep with a copy of Basheer under my pillow and dream about Beypore. Later I visited Duras' grave in Paris. She is in great company. There's Beckett, Ionesco, Sartre, Proudhon. I kept visiting that graveyard. There was graffiti above Proudhon's grave, 'Private property is theft?'. It was hilarious. I don't believe in ghosts but I imagined all these guys popping out of their grave, sipping unlabelled wine, and reading each other's work ... My point is, when you encounter such greatness, you learn to surrender, unconditionally. The more you resist, the more the work is contaminated. Basically actors in India try to impose their imprint on the words. You try to ensure they keep it pure. It's tough. I feel, actors in this country are taught to act. They are rarely taught to think.

Did Theatre Positive do anything for you? Did it do anything to you? Do live interactive sessions like workshops etc. feed into your work or outlook?

During the Theatre Positive years (1997–2003) we read more than 75 unperformed, unpublished playscripts in six different languages over five years. Sanjna Kapoor and Prithvi Theatre supported this activity on the first Monday of every month for five years. And so it had very little to do with me. It was the Prithvi aura. Playwrights got a kick in having their plays read out to an invited, enlightened audience at Prithvi.

For me, what was gratifying was the discovery of little gems like *Sangeet Debuchya Mooli* by Paresh Mokashi, *Master Fulmani* by Chandrakant Shah, *Tumbara* by Sayaji Shinde at Theatre Positive. All three went on to become important productions. Furthermore, there was Shafaat Khan's *Shobha Yatra* and Rajeev

Naik's *Sathechya Kay Karaychya* (*So what do we with Sathe?*). Rajeev's play was the second play which was read. I recall the poster had a mistake. It said: '*Thackerayche Kay Karaychya*' (instead of Sathe). Now the Thackerays besides being who they are happen to be Rajeev's neighbours in Kalanagar in Bandra. Some theatre friends said, it was all my evil scheme to get rid of a fellow playwright. It was scary.

To answer the second part of your question, I used to love work-shopping; especially when I worked with young people. I did it all the time. Tons of workshops. I did one with street children, all rag-pickers, in a shelter home in Wadala. It was an ephemeral moment. Within the first two minutes, when I turned my back to play some music, 17 of them jumped out of the second-floor window. I rate that as my best workshop. There were others which resulted into full-fledged productions for *Me Grandad 'Ad An Elephant*; or *Yaar, What's the Capital of Manipur*; *Medha and Zoombish II* and *Shakespeare and She*. Some of the work which we produced (and did not produce like *PM @ 3 AM*) was quite nice.

Could you try and describe your European experience? Since your plays are so strongly India/Mumbai based what did you imbibe through this experience. How did others (culturally alien) react to your plays?

My experience is confined to Germany and Belgium. In Berlin and Brussels, I met people who had a highly evolved sense of aesthetics. This reflected not only in the work they did on stage but also the beer they selected, or the flowers plucked from the garden, or the manner in which they made love to their work. So you learn that it's not always about the art, it's about the little things.

In 2007, I attended a residency course in Brussels. That was interesting. The game had changed. I was exposed to cutting-edge, postmodern stuff in which the text along with the actor was chucked out of the window. Some of it was complete crap which is usually the case with subsidised art. But I got to encounter the greatness of William Forsythe, Pina Bausch and masters like that. I realised how sub-standard Indian theatre is. We have a long way to go.

Research seems to be an important part of your writing process, hence the docu-dramas. How is your research done? Have you done plays that are non-docu-dramas?

I guess, it's bad habit. And now I'm addicted to it.

Yes, I have done many plays that are not docu-dramas: *The Boy Who Stopped Smiling*, *Curfew*, *Shanti, Shanti*, *It's a War*, *Collaborators*, *Tathasthu*, etc. In May 2011, a play called *Comrade Kumbhakarna* opened in Delhi. That is un-researched. Most of my one-act plays and radio plays are not researched.

Tell us a little about the range of music or the genres we experience in your plays. Why is music so important to you? What about speech vs silence vs music? How do you use these in your plays?

Oh, I like music. It accompanies me all the time. I used to play music on a radio in my school days. That's the only way I could go to sleep. The music could be anything. From Vividh Bharati to Classical Rock. My mother plays the sitar and I got accustomed to hearing Malkauns or Malhar around the house. If the tabla was out of tune someone in the house would point it out. It was part of growing up.

Recently, I've got myself a great pair of headphones on one of the auction sites. So I listen to BBC Radio which plays fabulous western classical music. BBC has a bit of commentary which is helpful. It provides context to the piece. And then, you hear something nice, it stays with you. And you conspire to plonk a bit of music into a play simply because it's one way to listen to the piece inside a darkened auditorium. We used protest rock for *Yaar, What's the Capital of Manipur*; rap and pop for *Medha and Zoombish II*; Mohammed Rafi for *The Sanjivani Super Show*. We did a play called *Angst Angst Coonth Coonth Boom Bam Dhandhal Dhamal Kaput*. The play didn't work. But Nagesh

Bhosale and Ahlam Khan created live music for it. They did tons of fabulous ditties; set Nagarjuna's poem '*Om Mantra*' into a cult song. We should have cut an album.

In *Shanti, Shanti, It's a War,* please comment on how the various characters are actually brought together in the play. Mentioned as four isolated instances they may not seem important to the reader. What drove you to put them together in a play?

India is a crazy country. And one tries to make sense of it in some way or the other. That's how *Shanti, Shanti* ... was born. It was a fun play which derived a lot of its inspiration from the work I had done in Mumbai's inter-collegiate competitive circuit. The play bagged a prize of Rs 25000/- from *The Hindu*. I could buy a computer (a 286) with the prize money. That 286 supported my writing work in those days.

The Madras Players produced one show of the play in Chennai which was directed by Yamuna. It was grand and they spent huge amounts of money on the production.

***The Boy Who Stopped Smiling* is a very powerful play. Could you please elaborate on issues of parenting, social pressures, expectations etc. that are raised in the play. Why was this play in particular so successful and why was it staged by PT itself so many times?**

The Boy ... was part of the Grips theatre movement. Thanks to Mohan Agashe I came across the Grips children's plays in India. I used to attend rehearsals being conducted by Wolfgang Kolnderer in Pune. I liked Wolfgang's uncluttered approach to theatre. As a quid pro to attend the rehearsals, I promised Mohan a play. I do that and then I vanish from the scene. But Mohan hounded me. He called me from all kinds of places (Frankfurt airport, Subhash Ghai's film set, Sassoon general ward) at all times of the day, asking about the play. I think I wrote *The Boy* ... to get him off my back.

Sanjna Kapoor and Little Prithvi Players produced the play. According to me, that was the reason the play was such a success.

Prithvi has tremendous goodwill; and Sanjna was able to cash in on it. It did 150 housefull shows. In a sense the whole thing was a fluke. The right talent came together. There were the actors who rehearsed four straight months for the play, which is a rarity in Mumbai. Plus there was Mihir Thakker's eclectic sets, Rajat Dholakia's live music, plus this lad who used to hang out at the Prithvi Cafe called Vineet who created *The Boy* ... icon for the posters and momentos. It was a good team.

Later I did another play (*Medha and Zoombish I*) for Sanjna and LPP – and it was quite bad. I suspect I destroyed most of LPP's reputation with that horror show. I don't think Sanjna produced another play after *Medha and Zoombish I*!

The play *Curfew* seems fairly loosely constructed compared to the other plays. What is the significance of the structure, the duplication of the characters and the stylistic devices used?

Curfew was penned sans the songs. Those got written when Manoj Aggarwal walked into the play with his guitar. So we improvised the song and made him a Peepal Tree in the play. The form is cabaret meets agit-prop theatre. This is a form that I'm very fond of. Whenever there's a screening of *Moulin Rouge* or *Bhavni Bhavai* (Ketan Mehta's first film), I watch it. I find the structure very engaging. The flexibility in narrative, a bit of burlesque and subversion. That's what I tried to do with Yama's story in *Curfew*.

In *Mahadevbhai* did you wish to juxtapose Gandhian politics with today's politics? The stylistic device of narration is particularly effective in this play. What made you choose this device rather than a more conventional multiple-character setup?

When we began *Mahadevbhai*, there was Jaimini Pathak, there was me and there was a huge terrace in Santacruz on which we rehearsed. So it was a question of writing a play which he could rehearse – and then perform.

In terms of the form, the thing is, I was exposed to Chakyar Koothu in my childhood. The original Chakyar Koothu is traditionally performed by the Chakyar community and there is a codified mode of gestures plus traditional costume. Somewhere those performances stayed with me. I tried to recreate that on stage with *Mahadevbhai*. The idea was to underplay and tell a story in a simple Gandhian way.

Tell us a little more about *Collaborators*: the plot, the characters, the juxtaposition of the ideal/imaginary with the actual etc.

This play had an intriguing journey. It was a stage play adapted for a radio play and re-adapted into a stage play.

My premise for penning *Collaborators* was twofold. One: In India, conversations do not have a final climax. Fire-crackers do not burst in the sky when someone utters a killer dialogue (in spite of what playwrights would like to believe). And our *gup-shup* is just that – *gup-shup*. It goes nowhere. It tends to have a beginning, a middle and then a beginning again.

The other thing, *Collaborators* was trying to probe is: a clash of two worlds. The certainty and smugness with which urban India lives is unreal. In *Collaborators*, the sophisticated veneer of Altamount Road tumbles down the hill into the rough-tough world of Faizabad. And then what?

This play is one of my favourites because of what it doesn't say. The main action is offstage. When we staged this play, it was a colossal fiasco. I don't think more than 25 people attended the premiere run of 15–16 shows. I poured tons of money and a lot of my energy. Kinnari had to pawn her things. Therefore the failure hurt a lot.

How did the Dutch react to *3, Sakina Manzil*? The play's characterisation is very strong. What made you choose this particular episode from history?

I wanted to tell a love story. I was challenged by friends that I couldn't. Hence the play.

Amrit Gangar told me about the dock explosion and its impact. We met a lot of surviors. I have over a hundred hours of interviews. The play was thanks to the inputs from Amrit Gangar. He played

Virgil to my Dante. I visited Dongri, Keshav Naik Marg, Chinch Bunder with Amritbhai. Later, in the middle of the night. I stood in front of a building which burnt on 14 April 1944. I tried to relive those moments. It taught me empathy.

Later, when the play was staged, I heard of audiences in Mumbai who saw the play and then went off in search of 3, Sakina Manzil. They never found it, because the building is in my head. But they returned and said, it's the still the same, it's still the same. That's true. The *jharokhas*, the balcony, the Gujarat–Rajasthan style of architecture, little details on the shop front, the Kutchi traders. And that makes you think that was so much more one could have done, if not for this ridiculous obsession with staging two-hour plays. As Vijay Tendulkar said, when he saw this play, some plays should run for 100 hours, at the very least! This is one of them.

The Dutch version was translated and directed by Rudy. He is Flemish and a lovely person. It was an austere production; played with contemplative silences and lots of finesse. I think they struggled to find the English equivalent of *sookha bhel* and *farsan* and *shrikand-puri*. I told them this is the Indian equivalent of rare French wine.

Jazz is an unusual play in many ways. What made you choose this particular topic?

Jazz owes it birth to Naresh Fernandes and Denzil Smith who helped and guided me into the world of music through the bylanes of Bandra.

With Naresh and Denzil, I met people whose fathers, uncles or grandparents. The food and booze I was served was awesome – and I suspect – it forms a big part of my so-called research process.

Through the black and white photographs and telling of tales, I was fed information about the large orchestras of the Bollywood music directors. Since not many musicians knew how to play saxophones or clarinets, the Goan musicians came to form the bulk of the orchestras.

The play and the central character is about this tribe who had the talent to note down these fragments which the composer would piece together into an entire song; drawing from their bicultural heritage to give Bollywood music its charm, slipping into Dixieland stomp, Portuguese fados, Ellingtonesque doodles, cha cha cha, Mozart and Bach themes. Long before fusion music became fashionable, it was being performed every day in Bombay's film studios.

Again a residue from our past. Unfortunately, the past is ugly and unpleasant. I created a character who was the sum total of the times. Thankfully, Naresh and Denzil and the people I had met, approved of what I did. To me that matters the most. It always has.

Glossary

Bhala teri kameez mere kameez se saphed kaise: How come your shirt is whiter than mine (a well-known tag-line from an ad)

Saala, ladka itna hi chaiye – toh ek ke jagah ek sau le: If a son is what you want, here, take a hundred (referring to the hundred sons of Dhritarashtra)

Aao, gao, jao: Come, sing, go

Aavya, Aavya, Baba Aavya: The Baba has come; the Baba has come

Ahara, Ahara: A yogic mantra

Anaaj ki dukaan: Grocery shop

Arre Miya, yeh toh patta ke jaga satta ho aaya: Instead of a card game, this has become gambling.

Arrey mishraji, aap pooch rahe they na ki Mahadevbhai kaun hain? Yeh dekhiye!!!: Mishra ji, you were enquiring, as to who Mahadevbhai was? Here, have a look.

Baap re baap, bade boozurgon ke liye ... kya kya karna padta hain: Gosh. The things we have to do for our elders

Baari barsi khatan gyaasi: A refrain from a Punjabi folk song

Baari: Turn

Bad-badofying: Tattle and talk

Bandobast for your chai-paan and tambakoo: Organise your tea, betel leaf and tobacco

Bardasht ki bhi hadh hoti hai: There's a limit to one's tolerance

Bas shor: Such cacophony

Batata powa, bhel puri and chiwda ... nashta: Indian snacks

Bayein Mud: Left turn

Bhago. Bhago: Run, run

Bhajan mandali: A group of devotional singers

Bhavnagar thi ganthiya lavya: He has got gathiya (a snack) from Bhavnagar

Bombaiyya Jazz: Bombay-styled Jazz

Brahmachari: Celibate

Buddhu: A moron, idiot

Chalo Mathura. Chalo Kashi: Let's go to Mathura. Let's go to Kashi

Chalo, Shashiji, ghar jaana hain. Ya hum latest film dekh sakte haih. Soona hain DEVDAS wapas ban rahi hai. Er ... Oh ... Eh ... Kya, itni raat ko taxi milegi ...: Come on, Shashiji, we've to go home. Or else we can watch the latest film. I've heard there's a re-make of DEVDAS ... Er ... Oh ... Eh ... Will we get a cab at this time of the night?

Chawls: Tenements which are typical of the working class areas in Mumbai

Chedva Poder. Susagad. Sorpetol: Terms addressing a lazy Goan

Chhachhunder: A shrew (mouse)

Chi Dikra: Dear son

Choomantar kalikalantar: Abracadabra

Dar lagta hain: It is frightening.

Dekho, oon logon ne apne Titanic ka kitna dhindora peetha. Aur ek hain hum ...: Look, they made such a hue and cry about their Titanic, and on the other hand, there's us ...

Devdas badi hit hai. Naach, gaana, pyaar, tragedy: The film *Devdas* was a big hit. It had song and dance, love and tragedy.

Dhanda: Business, trade

Dharma, Artha, Kama, Moksha: Dharma—Righteousness, Duty; Artha—Wealth; Kama—Desire; Moksha—Liberation

Dhobhiwallah: Washerman, laundry man

Doodhwallah bhaiyya: Milkman

Gadheda sambhle che ki nahin. Ter varas ni umar ma lagann thayi gaya ta, ane haveh taro olo suputra ane maro poutra ... trees varas noh ghodo thaiye gaya che ... pan lagann karto nathi. Tanne joiye toh ayan ek mast nih chokri che. Sundar ane viveki. ... ane gadheda pag upar kar: Are you listening, you twerp? He got married at the age of 13. And look at you. You've reached 30, and still a bachelor. I've seen a lovely girl. Nice and humble. ... And twerp, didn't I tell you to stand on one leg.

Gadheda tane aatlie pan khabar nathi ... ki Mahadevbhai kaun hatta? Too diwali maan aiyaan awish toh taro udhado lehi naakish! Haveh

– ek pag par ubha raheineh – waach!: Ass, don't you understand … as to who was Mahadevbhai … When you come here during Diwali, I'll give you a solid thrashing … Now stand on one leg and read

Ghisa-pita kahani.: Same old story.

Gunnies, chota-bada: Small and big, jute sacks

Haath-gaddi: Hand-cart

Hai Rabba: Oh god

Hai tauba: Oh god.

Hajjis: Those who travel to the Holy Hajj on a pilgrimage

Har baar woh hi drama-baazi: Every time it's the same theatrics

Hari tum haro jan ki bhir: A line from a bhajan

Hayan pailas ka? … Kase: Missing person

Husn ki mallika: A princess of beauty

Jab uparwallah deta hai, to chhappar phaad ke deta hai.: When the god lord who lives above bestows, he bestows aplenty

Kadkaa: Bankrupt

Kaka: Uncle

Khadoos: Stern

Kholi: A small room

Kidon ki tarah. Mujhe laga budmasshi kar rahein hain: They were crawling like insects. I thought they were playing the fool.

Kundan Lal Saigal songs … Do naina matware: A song about two eyes

Kutchi Ne Bachchi se shaadi kar liya: The Kutchi married a bachchi (girl)

Kya aap sukhe-grast illake se aye hain?: Have you come from a drought-prone area?

Kya karta, baccha hain: What could he do? He was a child, after all.

Kya patta wahan kya aafat aayi hogi: Who knows what kind of catastrophe must have transpired

Kyon? Kaise?: Why? How?

Ladka khaandani hai: The boy has noble lineage

Maidani khel, dashavatar, naman, tamasha, lezim competitions, bharood, the great shahirs, kushti, bullfights, jatras: Various forms of folk dance and people's theatre

Maike: The girl's parents place

Matka-Adda-Amar-Rahe: Long live the bookie's place

Mazdoor: Labourer

Mere bas main hota toh sab ko ek line main bitha kar main unko music suna thi. Zabardasti: I would make everyone stand in a line and make them listen to music. Compulsorily.

Munjo: Mine

Nakhras: Playful mannerisms

Nataka: The theatre

Nautanki: Folk drama

Nava Rasa, Nava Bhava, Nava Ratna: Nine tastes, nine emotions, nine gems

Ooos taraf par, purane Freye Road se, shor aur awaz: On the other side of the old Freye Road, was noise

Oos waqt sab kuch narak lag raha tha: Everything was hellish.

Paapi paet ke liye, biddu: It's all for the tummy, buddy.

Pagaar: Salary, wages

Pancha-patram: The vessel with five elements used during rituals

Parsi Topi and a chotta beard: A Parsee turban and a small beard

Phuta-phut: Pronto

Pir, babarchi, bhisti, hamaal: A wise person, cook, water-carrier and porter

Puja Thali: A plate filled with ritualistic objects for the worship of Hindu gods

Raakhee: A sacred thread which is tied by a sister on the brother's wrist

Ranga Puja: An invocation praying for smooth conduct of a play

Rasik: An aficionado of the arts

Sab kuch tabah ho gaya tha. Log idhar udhar bhaag rahe thay, apni bachi-khuchi cheezon ke saath: It was devastation. People were running helter-skelter, clutching their belongings

Sach kabhi bahar nahin aaya. Angrez toh theek hain. Unka agenda tha:

The truth wasn't disclosed. With the British one could understand. They had an agenda.

Sargam, mukhda, antara: Beginning, middle and end in classical Hindustani music raga

Shahenshah: An emperor

Shuddha ghee, shuddha teil, sab kuch shuddha aur sacha tha, bhaiyya. As the Kutchi business people used to say, ke pachhi e badhi pari katha to nahoti? Pari katha, pari katha aney shaher ni pari katha!: Pure ghee, pure oil, in fact everything was pure and tip top. As the Kutchi business people would say, it is a fairy tale. A fairy tale, a fairy tale, the city's fairy tale.

Shukar hain: Thank heavens

Tame pan magaj noh ladoo lo ne ... saras che ...: You have this home-made sweet. It is very tasty.

Thella: A cloth bag

Tirth: Holy place

Toor toori: A cheap street-side musical instrument

Usme ek bahut pyaara communal harmony-wallah gaana tha: In it, there was a sweet song about communal harmony.

Yeh tumhara Sheikh Saab kaafi achcha hain / Ees ko likhne aata hain: Your Sheikh Saab is pretty good. He actually knows how to write.

Yojanas: Plans